"I love this book. What seems like a light-hearted romp through a world of small creatures and fantastic settings, becomes a significant story about life, love, death and rebirth. An intoxicating journey, fun all the way through. I didn't want to stop reading."

—MARSHA MASON, ACTRESS

"Wildly imaginative, quite possibly crazy, and a delight to read. So hilarious and wise about love and death, that anyone who doesn't love it should be incarcerated at Gitmo and broken down by the torture which our nation performs so beautifully."

—RICHARD DRESSER, PLAYWRIGHT

"If you're a fan of *The Hobbit* and *The Wizard of Oz,* you'll love *The Wheel of Nuldoid!* Woody takes the reader on a whirlwind trip to a hundred magical places that are both wildly funny and awe-inspiring. If you think funerals are fun and weddings are depressing… you might be a Nuldoidian."

—JEFF FOXWORTHY, AUTHOR OF
NEW YORK TIMES BESTSELLER,
DIRT ON MY SHIRT

"Russ Woody is a masterful storyteller. He writes with insight, warmth and a great sense of humor about a lot of surprising things like death, life and short, quarrelsome creatures. There is so much to keep readers turning the page. Get on board for a wild ride."

—DAVID KESSLER, CO-AUTHOR
WITH ELISABETH KÜBLER ROSS
OF *ON GRIEF AND GRIEVING*

"Without a doubt, the funniest, finest, most comprehensive book ever written about the creatures of Nuldoid."

—TED DANSON, ACTOR

"Vivid imagery, unforgettable characters and wisdom for the ages are just a few of the delights that await all who travel into the magical, mystical world of Nuldoid. Settle into a comfortable chair, you won't want to move for hours. A brilliant read for adventurers young and old."

—BJ NATHAN HEGEDUS; *PORTRAIT
OF A BOOKSTORE,* STUDIO CITY

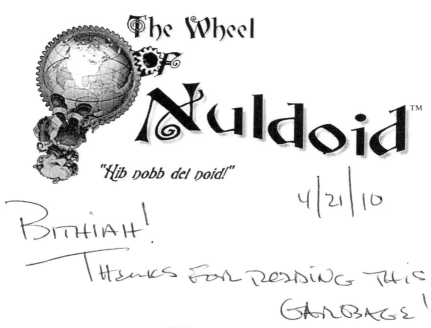

The Wheel OF Nuldoid™

"Kib nobb del noid!"

4/21/10

BITHIAH!

THANKS FOR READING THIS GARBAGE!

WRITTEN BY
RUSS WOODY

ILLUSTRATIONS BY
NORMAN FELCHLE

A POINTLESS INK BOOK ■ THE POINTLESS COMPANY, INC.
Los Angeles

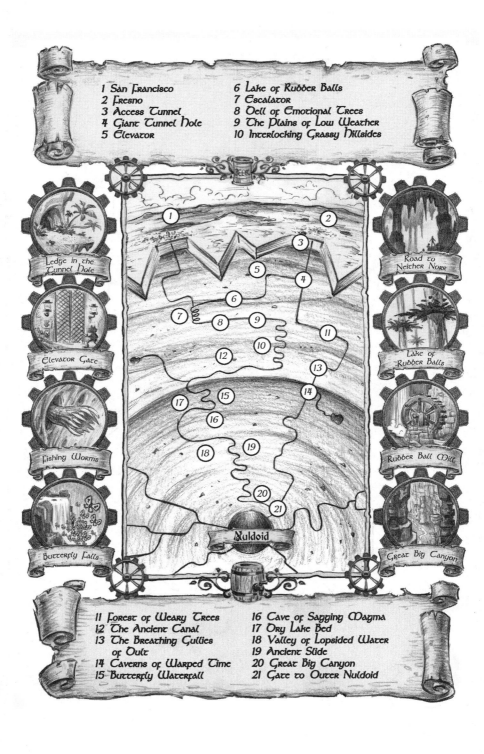

1 San Francisco
2 Fresno
3 Access Tunnel
4 Giant Tunnel Hole
5 Elevator
6 Lake of Rubber Balls
7 Escalator
8 Dell of Emotional Trees
9 The Plains of Low Weather
10 Interlocking Grassy Hillsides

11 Forest of Weary Trees
12 The Ancient Canal
13 The Breathing Gullies of Oult
14 Caverns of Warped Time
15 Butterfly Waterfall
16 Cave of Sagging Magma
17 Dry Lake Bed
18 Valley of Lopsided Water
19 Ancient Slide
20 Great Big Canyon
21 Gate to Outer Nuldoid

Ledge in the Tunnel Hole

Elevator Gate

Fishing Worms

Butterfly Falls

Road to Neither Norr

Lake of Rubber Balls

Rubber Ball Mill

Great Big Canyon

Nuldoid

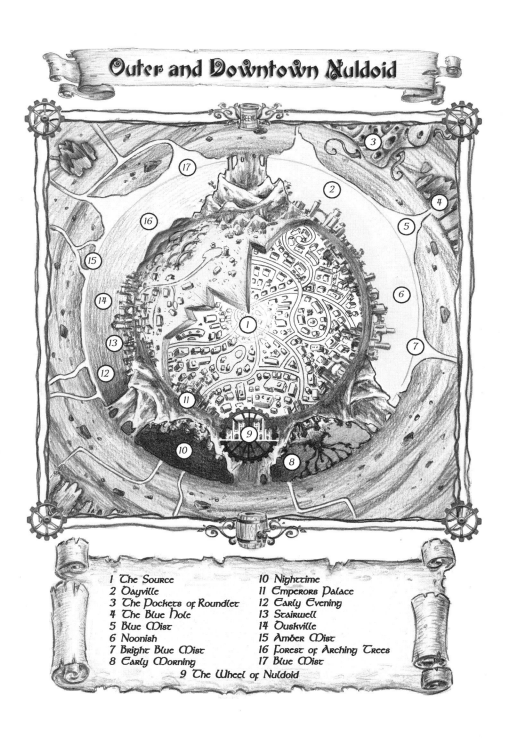

Outer and Downtown Nuldoid

PUBLISHERS
LOS ANGELES

www.Nuldoid.com

The Library of Congress has cataloged this edition as follows:
Woody, Russell, 1955-
The Wheel of Nuldoid by Russ Woody
LCCN: 2008940223
Fantasy. I. Title
First Edition

ISBN 978-1-4276-3480-1

Text set in Palantino
Illustrations by Norman Felchle
Cover designed by Design Just 4 Me

Printed in the United States of America
Delta Printing Solutions

DIONLEDBBONBIH

For
Stephanie Miller
(and Jim and Chris)
Thom Hartmann
&
Randi Rhodes

*Who gave us not only hope, but strength,
in our long dark journey past the Oidenoids of Neither Norr.*

Contents

The Wheel of Nuldoid ™

"Kib nobb del noid!"

A Warning

*This story, dear reader, is not a happy one, nor a
particularly pleasant one, but it is a peculiar one and,
while there seems to be many smart and publicly
educated people who are quite certain that these
events took place, there are just as many who scoff at
the notion that anything like it ever happened.
So… as with any story, you'll simply have to consider
all that is presented and decide for yourself.*

The Wheel of Nuldoid™

"Hib nobb del noid!"

Grampa's Story

GRAMPA WORST WAS old and dying of something old people die of, which was just fine with everyone and, surprisingly, even fine with him. What was not fine with everyone was that he had something he wanted to tell his grandchildren, and he was determined to tell them if it was the last thing he ever did… which it probably would be.

He had been very successful in his long life and made a great deal of money. Scads of money. In fact, by the 2060s he was considered one of the richest men in Northern California. He lived in an enormous house with a long, sweeping driveway, tons of rooms and bathrooms, even a wine cellar that he had converted to a beer cellar. But few people knew anything about him—anything important that is—least of all, the people closest to him, like his wife, who wasn't around anymore because she was dead. Or his daughter, who wasn't dead but didn't care to be around because he had always been such a sour and disagreeable old man. That one could always have been an old man might seem odd, but in Grampa Worst's case, even when he was young, he was old.

"Oh my," said his daughter, when he insisted she bring her three children to his bedside so that he could tell them about the Wheel of Nuldoid. "The wheel of what?" his daughter asked with grave concern because she was beginning to suspect that her father was not as in touch with reality as perhaps he once was.

"The Wheel of Nuldoid!" he said a little louder than he needed to, and then started coughing and hacking and, well, flatulating, all at the same time. It was a rather unpleasant sight. And sound. And smell.

"The wheel of what?" the daughter's husband asked in the car on the way home from Grampa's house.

"Nuldoid," she said. "He says he wants to tell the children the story of Nuldoid."

"What's a Nuldoid?"

"I don't know. But he wants to tell them about it before he dies."

"So, he's lost his mind?"

"Well, he's getting near the end. It's possible he's not thinking as clearly as he once did."

"Right."

Neither the old man's daughter nor her husband knew for sure if Grampa had truly slipped off the tether that binds us to what's real, but an argument was made that he was indeed the children's grandfather, and therefore deserved an audience with his grandchildren before, well, before the end.

() () ()

The next day, the three children stood like frozen chickens beside their grandfather's enormous bed, where they looked down with dread at his shriveled and creaky frame, at the lonely strands of thin white hair that swept aimlessly over the crest of his naked dome, the dark veins that wiggled along his forehead, the loose turkey skin beneath his chin. Their biggest fear, of course, was that he would, at any moment, draw his last breath, that his mouth would flop open like its hinge was busted, that his eyes would roll back in his head and that he would make some ghastly ghostly noise that would sound like someone opening a rusted door. And then he would be dead. Right there in front of them. Dead.

"Sit down," he said abruptly before they stiffly obliged. "What's your name, son?"

"You know my name, Grampa. It's Joe," Joe said, pushing his blond hair away from the ridge of his eyebrow.

"I thought you were Henry."

"I'm Henry, Grampa," said Henry, who was sitting next to Joe and was the oldest of the three children. He had a full mop of dull red hair that curled in bunches and shot out in any direction it pleased. And though he was not quite twelve, his face was losing its boyish roundness and his voice cracked on occasion.

"Well, I'm not going to argue with you," the grumpy old man said. "Francie? You're still Francie, right?"

"Yes, Grampa," Francie said, and smiled, displaying a gap where her front tooth had been a few days earlier.

Grampa drew back at the sight of the empty space between her teeth. "What the hell happened to you?"

"Nothing, Grampa," Francie said, and probably would have laughed if she'd not been so scared of him. "My baby tooth fell out."

3

"Ah. Well, I suppose that's good." He moved a scraggy finger to his eye, scrunched his face and scraped a hunk of something out of its corner, briefly examined the hunk and then flicked it out into the room. Then he turned back to the children. "Anyways, I'm gonna tell you kids a story about a place that's far, far away. It's a story I've never told any—"

"How far?" Joe asked.

"What?"

"How far away is this place?"

"I don't know. Far, far. It happened back in—"

"What, like a million miles?"

"I said I don't know."

"Well, it would help to know," Joe said.

"Fine. Four thousand miles! Is that what you want?"

"Which way?" Joe asked, mostly just to prove to his brother and little sister that he was not afraid of the old man. "North, east, west, south?"

"Doesn't matter."

"Of course it matters," Henry said, deciding to jump into the fray.

"Fine then. None of them."

"How can it be none of them?" This was Joe again.

"Can I tell this story or not?" their grandfather barked.

The children all nodded and sat quietly like a row of condemned convicts, their fresh faces full and wide-eyed at the shock of their grandfather's blunt outburst. Francie moved her chair a little closer to Henry's.

"Now then… it started right here in San Francisco, 1989—the year before I was born. There was a huge earthquake. Go ahead, look it up if you think I'm lying. Huge earthquake, 1989. Look it up!" he said, challenging them to actually look it up, not because he thought they didn't believe him, but because he was just that disagreeable.

The children, though, had no way of looking up anything: no computer, no *e-Zapp*, and certainly no books or encyclopedias, those having all but disappeared in the mid-21st century. Henry finally ventured, "We can't look it up, Grampa."

"Well then, you're just gonna have to believe me, aren't you? There was an earthquake in 1989—whether you think there was or not—and it was huge and a lotta people died. And that's a bona fide fact! Bridges collapsed, buildings crumbled, tragic, horrible, everybody got very upset and wah, wah, wahk, wahk, wahak, kack, kack..." He was suddenly coughing and hacking like hairless old cat trying to rid itself of a hairball. Finally, up came a large wad of greenish-black something or other, and it plopped down on the bed beside him like a blob of wet cookie dough. The children stared at it in horror, while Grampa squinted curiously at it and then poked it with his index finger. "Humph," he said after a moment and then put his head back on the pillow, closed his eyes and stopped breathing.

When the children realized he'd stopped breathing, they too stopped breathing, but for a completely different reason. They were afraid to move. It appeared that Grampa had died right there in front of them. Just like that. Just like they'd feared. And there they sat. Waiting. While Grampa continued to be dead. And still they did not know what to do.

Except sit there.

Then Grampa made a noise. But not a mouth noise. Apparently, when someone dies, the body often releases pent-up gas. And that's what Grampa's body was doing. And while the situation for the children was certainly awful and awkward, it was also funny. Francie couldn't help it; she started to laugh. When she did, Henry and Joe started laughing too.

Then Grampa started laughing.

When Francie realized Grampa was laughing and not dead, she started screaming. When she started screaming, Grampa started screaming because her screaming startled him. Then his screaming startled Joe, who started screaming too, and it all became very noisy and disconcerting and it took a few moments for Henry to calm everyone down.

"I thought you were dead, Grampa," Francie finally said to him.

"Well, you were wrong, weren't you? I can't be dead. Not until I tell you about the Wheel of Nuldoid."

"What's Nuldoid?" Joe asked.

"The place that's far, far away. The place that my father had to go to right after the earthquake here in San Francisco, whether you believe me or not."

"Why did he have to go there?" Henry asked.

"Because, if he didn't, millions of people would die," Grampa said, as if it were obvious. "He was trying to stop a boy named Leo, who was just about Joe's age," he said, pointing at Henry.

"I'm Henry," Henry said, starting to get a little exasperated.

"That's what I said," the old man insisted.

"No, you called him Joe," Joe said.

"You," he said to Joe, "you're a smart aleck! Now, if my father hadn't gone after this kid, Leo, the earth would have kack, kack, hahkack, haaahkack..." and again Grampa was coughing and wheezing and hacking. When he was through, he leaned back on the bed, closed his eyes and said to Henry, "Go lock the door."

Henry looked over at the bedroom door, then back at his grandfather. "How come?"

"Because no one else can see what I'm about to show you."

Henry considered this for a moment and then moved to the door and locked it. Grampa had Joe help him sit up and move his thin, bony legs over the side of the bed so that he could sit on the edge of it. The children watched then with growing concern as the old man leaned over and addressed the nightstand beside his bed. He moved close to the top of it and whispered something very curious. He whispered, "Hib nobb del noid."

But nothing happened.

He whispered the strange expression again, but still nothing happened. Then he said it in his regular voice. "Hib nobb del noid." But still there was no reaction whatsoever from the nightstand. The children exchanged concerned looks as their grandfather grew angry and started yelling, "Hib nobb del noid! Hib nobb del noid, ya stinkin' nightstand!" It was yet another very disturbing and uncomfortable thing for them to have to watch.

Finally, out of frustration, Grampa whacked the top of the nightstand with his scrawny fist and said, "Hib nobb del noid!" The bottom drawer popped open, and Grampa smiled. But, when the children looked into the drawer, they did not see anything spectacular. Certainly there wasn't anything worth making into a big secret. The drawer was full of marbles.

Grampa smiled as though he'd accomplished something significant and then reached down into the marbles and dug out a large tattered notebook that he held with great reverence. There were perhaps a hundred worn and dog-eared pages within its cracked and peeling black leather cover. It was, he explained, his father's. In it, his father had made many notes about Nuldoid, about the young boy named Leo, and about the trip to Nuldoid in the fall of 1989. Grampa's father had written dates and times and many explanations of things, though much of his writing was sloppy to the point of being indecipherable. He had even made some drawings, though he was not at all a very good artist.

Henry exchanged another concerned look with Joe. The book was not small and would no doubt take Grampa a considerable amount of time to read and explain, having, of course, to stop periodically to wheeze and hack and cough things up.

So, as Grampa leaned back with his father's old notebook and began to tell the story of Nuldoid, the children prepared themselves for what they were sure would be a long and excruciating experience.

This is the gist of the story Grampa told them.

The Crust

Part One

To dat Crust ye noids does scurry,
Where up der comes dat big Crystal
In blusts o' wind and mighty flurry.

Den grabs it good an' off ye cops it.
'Cause moves it does we Hoidenall.
So makes be sure ya doesn't drops it.
                    The Book of Nuldoid
                    Contentions 13:3

The Noodge

WARREN WORST WAS sitting at his kitchen table grading papers in the late afternoon of October 17, 1989. His orange cat, Howard, was dozing peacefully on a dirty blue pillow in the corner, his body twisted as though mangled in a car accident, head upside down, left paw outstretched to the kitchen floor. A light breeze lifted the plaid curtain that hung over the sink, and then gently floated it back down. This was pretty much the scenario that played out every afternoon in Warren's kitchen, although, on this particular day, the radio was on and bleating baseball stats in the moments before the third game of the World Series over at Candlestick Park. Other than that, it was a normal typical ordinary Tuesday afternoon and Warren had no reason whatsoever to suspect that everything in his world—everything in *the* world—was about to change.

Warren Worst, as you've probably already guessed, was Grampa's father—which would make him the children's great-grandfather. At six feet and change, he was fairly tall, thin, some would say lanky. His hair was straight black and fell loosely to either side of his head. His nose was sharp, pointed, and, for some reason, reminded people of Abe Lincoln. Having rounded thirty a couple of years earlier, his face was decidedly a man's—square, firm, serious—yet here and there, remnants of the boy he once was peeked through.

He'd been teaching sixth grade social studies for ten years, which he was no longer excited about. When he was younger, he had wanted to be a teacher because he wanted to teach young people new things—unlike the bored and boring teachers who'd taught him. He wanted to show kids how to look at the world in different ways. He wanted them to question the system that was in place. He thought that if kids did that, they could find the best answers, the best solutions to the problems they would face. What he found, was that there were a great many regulations and rules, rigid guidelines and dull textbooks—all very irksome, very tedious—that had to be strictly and specifically followed. It seemed that everything taught in the past had to be taught in the future, the same way it had always been taught in the past.

Despite the rules, he brought in magazine articles about ridiculous goings-on in society, commented on TV shows that his students had never seen, and made fun of Presidents Nixon and then Carter and even made fun of Alexander Hamilton—for which he was reprimanded by the school. He persisted for a time, but he didn't like being reprimanded and eventually decided to just teach what he was supposed to teach. Though he didn't know it yet, he'd become exactly the kind of bored and boring teacher he'd set out not to be. What he also didn't know, couldn't know, was that at the very moment he was grading school papers at his kitchen table, two very small, very unusual creatures were emerging from a crevice on a hillside nearby.

They would change everything for Warren Worst.

They were each not quite two feet tall, and while they both wore faded and scuffed denim overalls, one of them, the older one, seemed to fill his at the belly much more snugly than did his companion. They wore solid work boots for their oversized feet, and stood, the both of them, like stalwart fireplugs. The pudgy one had a significant beard, generously speckled with gray and white. He had white caterpillar eyebrows that ended abruptly and pointed at the stark lines that creased his forehead. The younger creature was clean-shaven, though he would have benefited greatly from a beard, not having much of a chin to speak of, which, with his large nose and generous ears, made him look somewhat like a mosquito.

But what was perhaps most significant about these creatures was their attitude. It was sour. Very sour. They didn't seem to like much of anything, seemed mostly to enjoy complaining about everything, including each other, and they especially liked complaining about the weather. Which might seem kind of pointless—as Mark Twain once brought up—unless you intend to do something about it. But these two did not seem to appreciate weather of *any* sort: not wind or rain certainly, not snow or hail, not fog, not cold, but neither did they care much for sunshine. All of it annoyed them tremendously.

They had traveled a great distance to be where they were, but neither seemed to care since they were, at the moment, busy quarreling over something that apparently happened hundreds of years earlier. There were several other small creatures traveling with them, but they had not yet emerged from the opening in the ground. These other creatures were male and female and, well, one was neither male *nor* female.

13

But these other creatures never emerged from the opening. They almost did, but just as they climbed to the lip of the crevice and were about to hoist themselves up and out, the earth itself began to shift and move and then, most unfortunately, the sides of the crevice collapsed and slammed together with a deafening roar, crushing all the creatures inside like so many pancakes. Or crepes, which are very thin pancakes. At any rate, it was horrific.

Amidst the thunderous collision of the tunnel's walls and the violence of the earth's tectonic plates in motion, the two surviving creatures were knocked to the ground like wobbly bowling pins. When they managed to get to their feet again—no small task for the chubbier of the two—they looked down at the opening and saw that it was no longer an opening at all. It was instead just a thin jagged crack where only a small, pitiful, peculiar-looking hand protruded as it reached up to the sky like some pathetic twig that a child might have jabbed into the dirt.

The two creatures stood on the hillside looking at the crack in the ground where their companions had been killed. The younger of the two survivors suddenly grew angry. "Well, murk fuddle!" he grumbled. Which you'd have to assume was, if you'd been there to actually hear it, a swear word.

"Yup for dat," said the older one. Both of them nodded in agreement, possibly for the first time ever. Then they shouted that peculiar phrase, "Hib nobb del noid," into the crack where the crevice once was. They did this several times. And each time, they seemed disappointed that their words did not cause the crevice to reopen. They stood on either side of it, looking defeated and drawn, like waifs over a sidewalk grate where their only nickel had fallen.

Finally, the creature with the beard turned to the mosquito-looking one. "It doesn't gonna open, Kyle. Is all busted fromma noodge."

The younger one especially had reason to be upset since, of those below who were now smashed and dead, one was his brother, another his aunt. But that wasn't what was mostly bothering him as he looked down at the tomb of their companions and friends and family. He shook his head sadly. "Ach," he said, "they had alls we beer."

Warren Meets Lily

IT WAS AT that very same moment that the electricity sputtered and blinked and disappeared altogether, abandoning the broken city, and leaving Warren in the dark. He was shaken and very concerned about Howard, his cat, who, when the house started to move, bolted straight up from his comfy snooze and flew like a fiery streak out the kitchen door into the living room and off to parts unknown.

But Warren quickly forgot about his cat when he looked out the window and saw his car—an aging Chrysler LeBaron with a rusted fender and a missing side mirror—teeter on its jack, fall off and begin to roll down the steep street in front of his house. The driverless car was not rolling fast at first, certainly not as fast as Warren was running after he blasted out the front door of his house, and sprinted down the street after it like a cheetah or a gazelle or an ostrich. Granted, ostriches look funny when they run, but they're plenty fast.

All of it was pointless because, once he caught up with the car, he didn't have his car keys, so he couldn't open the door to get inside and stop it. Nor was he strong enough to stop the car's growing momentum as it continued to roll down the street. All he really managed to do was look silly as he pushed and pulled, grunted and strained, like he was giving birth to a fatheaded baby. The car ignored him and rolled smack into the side of a warehouse at the bottom of the hill.

That's how he met Lily. She lived in the warehouse.

The warehouse's large steel door slid open with a metallic screech as Lily stepped out to see what had smashed into her warehouse. Warren noticed right away how pretty she was, and not just because her cheeks were flushed red with anger. She looked about 30, had a small upturned nose and piercing steel blue eyes that he guessed could be very bright and kind, when she wasn't so angry. Her reddish brown hair was swept back into a tight ponytail that made her look a little like a schoolgirl. Of course, she sure didn't sound like a schoolgirl when she looked at Warren's Chrysler and saw the dent it had made in the side of her warehouse. She turned back to him and accused him of a number of things, but mostly of driving like a lunatic.

"Well?" she finally asked.

He realized then that he'd only been *watching* her talk, and now she was expecting him to answer. "Uh, I wasn't actually *driving* the car. It fell off a jack and rolled here."

"Then why didn't you make sure it wouldn't fall off the jack?"

She was starting to sound unreasonable—despite how pretty she was—and Warren was himself beginning to get angry. "Gee,

I'm sorry," he said, "but I didn't know there'd be an earthquake today." The last was said with a good dose of sarcasm.

"Uh-huh. So, I guess an earthquake in San Francis-*co* is a great big *surprise* to you." She too, apparently, was plenty capable of sarcasm.

"Look, I'll take care of it," he told her.

"You'd better."

"I will!"

She stood with her hands on her hips, sizing him up. "Fine," she said finally. "But I don't like you."

"You don't know me," he answered. "If you knew me, you'd like me."

She looked him over another moment. "No, I don't think so."

When they went inside to exchange phone numbers and insurance information, Warren saw that she was an artist and that she'd been working on a great many paintings and sculptures. Everything, however, was very much in disarray because of the earthquake. Many of the paintings had fallen off their easels, and a number of sculptures had toppled over. Some were broken. Though it was very much a mess, he could see that she was very talented.

One of the oil paintings lying on the floor was beautiful in its sweeping blend of cheerful yellows and deep blues, yet it seemed to tell of sadness in the dirt-smudged face of a little girl standing beside a military tank. Another painting showed a man and a woman holding each other while a giant wood screw passed into the woman's back and jutted out of the man's back. Near a sidewall there was a sculpture of a limousine parked on top of some farm workers.

Judging from her work, she was not happy about war or hungry children or poverty or greed. When he asked her about a couple of the paintings, it was pretty clear that she felt strongly about them and that her paintings and sculptures brought her great satisfaction and pride. Which left Warren feeling envious and a little sad because he no longer felt that way about his own work.

"What do you teach?" Lily asked him after they had exchanged information and she'd finally stopped being so angry and, of course, after he complimented her artwork.

"Social studies. Sixth grade."

"Oh. That's interesting," she said, trying to sound polite, because she remembered how very uninteresting it was when she was in school.

"But I really don't know how much longer I'll be a teacher," Warren found himself saying, despite his never having said so before. He said it, he realized later, because he was trying to impress her, because he didn't want her to think he was just another ordinary typical boring schoolteacher—which is what he was beginning to suspect he was.

He also realized that he liked her.

A Kid Named Leo

THAT NIGHT AND the following day, the city was alive with misfortune and confusion and worried people trying to find other people who were sometimes hard to find, or completely missing, or not where they were supposed to be. Sirens wailed all over the place, fires broke out here and there, news people from everywhere around the world showed up to take pictures of the devastation and havoc. A bridge collapsed and killed many people. Buildings slid sideways, were nudged off foundations, were splintered and ruined. Nobody had any electricity for days.

It was the largest earthquake to hit the San Francisco Bay Area since the great quake of 1906. In all, 67 people died and over 3,700 were injured. The damage was catastrophic. But not as catastrophic as it could have been—if not for the efforts of a young boy named Leo Fickett.

Leo was a student in Warren's social studies class, a scruffy-looking kid of eleven, his hair the color of dirty sand, never combed, dominated by stubborn cowlicks. He wore baggy clothes that looked like they were seldom washed; his pant legs had holes at the knees, and were frayed at the bottom where they scraped along the ground. His sneakers were worn and held together by shoestrings knotted in several places. A splash of stark brown freckles bridged his nose and sprawled across rosy cheeks. And, once in a while—away from the classroom—he smiled, pushing the freckles up and causing his deep brown eyes to sparkle. In the classroom, however, he never did anything of the sort.

Like a lot of kids who don't like school, he wasn't a very good student. Even though—as you'll find out—he was really smart.

A few days after the earthquake, when school started again, Warren walked up and down the aisles of the classroom returning test papers, his footsteps echoing like a prison guard's at lockdown. Leo had not done well, and when Warren handed him his paper, he told the boy he was very disappointed, that he wanted Leo to stay after class.

"Leo, what are you doing?" he asked when class was over and Leo had stayed behind.

"You told me to stay after class, remember?"

"No. I mean, what're you doing with your life?"

The boy shrugged and looked down at his tattered green backpack that was slumped between his knees. He hated it when adults asked questions that had no real answers. *What was he doing with his life? He was eleven. He was being eleven. What else could he be doing with his life?*

"You answered three of twenty questions on the test. Why?" Warren was looking at him as if he was looking over the top of invisible bifocals.

21

That was another thing adults did that Leo hated. He shrugged again. "Because I knew the answers to those ones."

"That's not what I meant. Why didn't you answer the other questions?"

Leo shifted in his seat and moved the broken zipper at the top of his backpack. "Dunno."

"How are you going to get anywhere in life if you don't apply yourself at school?"

Another shrug.

"Look, you don't pay attention in class. You stare out the window when I'm explaining things. Or else you doodle in that sketchpad of yours. No wonder you don't know any of the answers."

"I knew three of them."

"Give me the sketchpad."

"What? Why?"

"Because I want to see it."

"But why?"

"Just give it to me."

Leo realized there was no way out of this. He sighed to let his teacher know he was not happy about giving up his sketchpad, and then jammed a hand into his backpack, found it and handed it over.

"Thank you," Warren said. "I'll just keep this until the end of the semester."

"But—"

"No buts." Warren put up a hand to show Leo that he was indeed the person in charge. "And I'm going to call your parents."

"Good luck. My dad's in jail."

"Oh." Warren didn't know that. "Well, what about your mom?"

Leo laughed. "My mom split when I was like six."

Warren was shocked. "So… who do you live with?"

The boy knew, at that very moment, that he had given away exactly too much information. He did not want his teacher, or any other adult, getting the idea that he was living alone because, well, kids his age weren't supposed to live alone. Even though that's precisely what he was doing. "Uh," he said, thinking, thinking, "my aunt. Oleta."

Warren eyeballed him. "You don't have an Aunt Oleta."

"Yes, I do."

"Fine. Then let's go to the office and call her."[*] Warren stood to emphasize his conviction.

"Wull…" the wheels in Leo's brain were spinning, "she's at work… and she can't take personal calls. At her work."

Warren narrowed his gaze. "Uh-huh. Where's she work?"

"She works… at a high-security prison."

"You're lying, aren't you?"

"Absolutely not."

"You're living by yourself, aren't you?"

"No."

His teacher continued to stare at him until he felt like an ant on the sidewalk beneath a magnifying glass. It was all entirely uncomfortable and he wished he could slink down in his seat and squirm away, disappear. But he couldn't. And, finally, it was too much. "Okay, yeah. So what?" His tone was defiant to be sure, but his eyes brimmed with tears that verged on rolling down his cheeks.

To the *So what?* Warren didn't answer right away. He saw that Leo was about to cry, and suddenly his heart broke. He knew that if someone didn't help this kid, he'd grow up to be a

---

[*] This was, of course, in the days before cell phones, and obviously way before the electronic ear chips of the late 21st century.

pitiful adult. He'd follow in his father's rotten footsteps, and there he'd be, one more misguided miserable soul taking up space in the universe and, probably, the nation's penal system.

So Warren decided to offer him an alternative: He could stay at Warren's house—until they figured out something better. But he knew full well that Leo would say no, and that he, Warren, would then have to call Social Services to have him placed in a foster home. It was not something he was looking forward to.

Still, he gave it a shot. He asked.

"Sure," Leo said.

"Then you leave me no choice but to call—" Warren stopped. "Wait, what?"

"I said sure. I'll stay with you."

"Oh."

There it was.

So Warren took Leo home, where, that night, the boy sat down to his first home-cooked meal in a long time. A long time because, even before his loser of a father went to jail, the man seldom cooked meals. At first, Warren was just going to heat up some take-out food because that was one thing he had plenty of. But when he saw how hungry the kid was, he decided to cook up some hamburgers and make macaroni and cheese. Then after dinner, they made brownies. And, yes, it may sound like an ordinary meal to you—it was hardly chateaubriand or duck l'orange—but Leo loved it, savored every bite of the juicy burger, smothered in mustard and catsup, and, believe it or not, he very nearly came close to actually smiling when he bit into the first of the fresh brownies they'd baked.

He, of course, would never *say* how much he appreciated everything, but he did. Even though plenty of kids fantasize about living in a house without parents or adults telling them to do all the useless stuff they tell them to do—like brush their teeth and take out the trash and mow the lawn and pull the weeds—those who really do live on their own don't seem to like it at all. *At all.* And Leo was altogether sick and tired of the whole thing. It was a lot of trouble, a lot of work, trying to keep food in the cupboards and the fridge. And he hated having to search through the clothes hamper for shirts and pants and socks that looked less dirty than what he was wearing. He was sick of avoiding phone calls from people who wanted to be paid for things that his father hadn't paid for and he, Leo, had no idea how to pay for them. The electric company had just shut off the electricity and the water company was threatening to shut off the water and the phone quit working. But, most of all, he'd really had it with trying to keep everything a secret from everyone.

() () ()

Beneath a large cozy red comforter, Leo drifted off to sleep on Warren's couch. Warren smiled when he saw the boy sleeping so soundly, and then turned off the living room lights.

Then he took Leo's sketchpad to bed with him. He wanted to find out what Leo was so busy doing when he should have been paying attention to what was being said in class.

After he brushed his teeth and put on his pajamas, Warren turned on his bedside lamp, pulled back the sheets to his bed, climbed in and began to leaf through the book. But, where he expected to see silly drawings and doodles and the senseless scribbles of an eleven-year-old boy, he saw something quite different. Something astounding in fact.

He was amazed and captivated, and he became even more amazed as he turned from one page to the next. What he saw were intricate sketches of gadgets and gizmos and incredible machines that didn't actually exist—at least not in 1989. The boy had drawn them as though they were patents or blueprints for some kind of official government project. And though there were far too many sketches and ideas to describe here, a few of the more spectacular ones included a stationary bicycle that generated more energy than was exerted. The bike was attached to a massive series of interlocking cogwheels and counterweights that created their own "internal tension." So, according to Leo's notes, someone could pedal the bike for, say, half an hour, and the internal tension would build exponentially, creating enough electricity to power a home for *several months*.

On the following page, Leo had drawn a train that never had to stop to let passengers on or off because of a detachable sidecar that caught up with it, exchanged passengers and then returned to the train station.[*]

There was a telescope that saw into the past. If you pointed it down your street, for instance, you'd see your street the way it looked a hundred years earlier. It worked, as the drawing showed, by a series of concave and convex pieces of glass that "filtered out the faster moleckular [sic] vibrations of newer stuff" until the only images left were those of objects that had been in place for more than a century.

There were other pages where Leo had written down one incredible idea after the next—with, okay, an awful lot of misspelled words, but incredible nonetheless. One such entry was something he called "Circular Energy." Warren had to read it twice to figure out if it was just nonsense or too complicated for him to grasp. According to Leo's writing, time and… well, here's what Leo wrote:

---

[*] These nonstop trains, Streamlines, would of course become commonplace in the United States and most industrialized nations, but not until nearly a hundred years after Leo drew the sketches.

26

TiMe and ENERGY excist together Inside and Outside of
EVERYthING..
But— Energy and Time they **NEVER** *move in a* **Strate Line!** **Can't!**
They can't— because their Together and Their Different!
So— they **MUST** *move in a Circle!* **HAVE TO** *move in a*
CIRCLE!!!

Which is why—as Leo went on to explain—things change, but seem to stay the same. So that… throughout time, for instance, different people exist in different shapes, different sizes, different bodies… but they're not really any different than they were.

Whether nonsense or not, it was all very heady stuff. Brilliant stuff. But here's the thing that Warren couldn't shake, the thing that kept gnawing at him: *This* is the kid who's failing my social studies class?

() () ()

He did not wait until the end of the semester to give the sketchpad back to Leo. He gave it to him the next morning, and asked him how he came up with all of the contraptions and machines and theories. The boy shrugged and stuffed it into his backpack. "Eh," he said, "my dad thinks it's stupid."

"Well, your dad's wrong."

Strange Strangers in the Basement

WARREN'S RUNNING SHOES were starting to fall apart. The "experts" said to buy new ones every six to eight months, but Warren was pretty sure that was just a marketing ploy to sell more shoes. There was, after all, still air in the see-through air cushions. And he wore double-thick socks for extra cushioning. Nope, the shoes were good for another thousand miles, at least.

"See, this whole idea of runnin' in circles so you end up where you started," Leo said, watching Warren pull the laces taut and then tie them, "it makes no sense." Warren was about to defend the idea of exercise when Leo said something very peculiar. Startling even. He said, "I'd rather just stay here and do some homework."

That certainly caught Warren by surprise. And, while Leo settled in on the couch and opened a textbook, Warren felt a bit of satisfaction and even smiled a little, careful that Leo didn't see him do so, and then he headed out for his run.

As soon as the front door clicked shut and his teacher was gone, Leo tossed the book aside, pushed himself up off the couch and padded into the bedroom, where he found Warren's brown leather wallet on the dresser beside a splay of loose change and a ring of keys. No high security here. Inside the wallet, there were several tens, a few twenties, enough that a ten spot wouldn't be missed. He plucked a bill out, shoved it in his pocket and replaced the wallet. Then, on the off chance his teacher might keep a larger stash of money hidden away, he slid open a dresser drawer. Then...

Thud!

He froze.

A noise. Somewhere in the house. He cocked his head like a dog listening to a siren.

Thud!

Down. Under the house.

Then... someone's voice. But not Warren's. No, it definitely wasn't Warren's. Quickly, he slid the dresser drawer closed and tiptoed out of the bedroom to the living room, where he stopped, looking this way and that. Listening, listening. Then...

Crash!

From beneath the house! Definitely!

He moved cautiously down the hall, into the kitchen, where a door opened to a dark shaft of wooden stairs that led down to a darker basement. Leo stood at the door, considering, still listening. It was quiet. Whoever it was had heard him. He stepped back, grabbed the toaster from beside the sink and yanked its cord from the wall. It would do for a weapon.

He took a deep breath and flipped the switch at the top of the stairs as light shot up from the basement. He raised the toaster over his head—cocked, ready to hurl it at any moment—and slowly he edged down the stairway, his jaw tightening with each step, anticipating the mousy squeak of the wooden stairs. When he stepped onto the cold concrete of the basement floor, he looked around and found, well... nothing. The toaster, still suspended over his head, dropped annoying crumbs of toast onto his hair. He moved to a stack of file folder boxes and peered around them. Nothing. Dust bunnies. He looked behind a dust-covered stereo, behind a battered old barbeque grill, tilted to one side due to a missing wheel. Still nothing.

He lowered the toaster. Listened for another moment. Waited. Silence. Finally, he turned and started back up the steps—

"Ach-fooof!"

He froze, stock-still.

Was that a sneeze?

Then a small angry whisper: "Ya doesn't never covers your mouth, ya drobbs horkel!"

Another voice: "Drobbs horkel? Why doesn't we covers yer stinkin' head!"

Then an "Ooooff!"

Then: "Shoves we, will ya?"

Then another "Ooooff!"

Leo raised the toaster again and moved to the edge of an old filing cabinet where he hadn't looked. Cautiously, he leaned around the side of it. When he did, he saw two small... what? People? Creatures? They were clutching each other's throats and trying to kick each other. They did not, however, notice Leo—peering at them from around the filing cabinet with a toaster over his head. Leo stood there, stupidly, waiting for them to notice him, until finally he cleared his throat. The little men then froze like short statues, their hands still clutching at each other's throats, their heads rigid, their eyes darting back and forth.

"Who are you?" Leo asked.

At the sound of his voice, the creatures screamed and began to scramble for a place to hide—their screams, by the way, sounding vaguely little girlish, yet horrifically more high-pitched. Leo dropped the toaster and grabbed his ears. "Stop it! Stop it!" he howled. And, when finally they stopped, he cautiously removed his hands from his ears and asked again, "Who are you?"

The little men exchanged looks and then straightened themselves as though about to make a formal presentation. That's when Leo first noticed their hands, that each had only three digits: two fingers and a thumb. The younger of the two spoke stiffly, as if Leo were mentally impaired. "I... is Kyle," he said, and then nodded toward the older one. "Him der... is Morton."

Leo looked down again at their hands. "So... what exactly are you?"

The two little men exchanged another look before the younger one, Kyle, turned back to the boy and spoke even more slowly and more loudly. "I... is Kyyyle. Dat is Mooooorton."

"No, I mean—"

"An' if your plans is to kill and eats we..." Kyle continued, jabbing a thumb in his partner's direction, "ya starts with him der, eh?"

"I'm not gonna eat you," Leo assured them.

The younger creature leaned toward the other and whispered, "Is lying him."

Leo, of course, heard him. "I'm not lying. Why would I eat you?"

"Why wouldn'ts ya?"

"I've never eaten anybody in my life."

"Maybe you is true..." ventured Kyle. "Or maybe ya just hasn't been 'nuff hungry."

"You're not friends of Warren's, are you?" Leo asked, though he was pretty sure they weren't.

"Warren?" the older one said.

"Warren Worst. Mr. Worst. This is his house. He's a schoolteacher."

"Uch to dat!" Kyle said, scrunching his nose like someone had just passed gas.

"Dat Warren, he gots food, huh?" Morton asked hopefully.

"Food? Sure."

"Good. We needs food. We hasn't done no eatin' since dat noodge."

"Noodge?"

"Yeah sure, dat big noodge. Coupla days back ago."

"You mean the earthquake?"

"Sure yeah, dat *ert-quack*, sure."

"Look, you want food, right?"

"Food, yeah sure. An' beer. Ya gots beer, right?"

"I don't know."

"An' doesn't yas forget dat chips. Yas got chips, eh?"

"I'll check. Anything else you guys want?" Leo was getting a little irritated at the demanding nature of these two.

"Nah to dat." Then, "Ach, we needs a car."

"A car?"

"A car…" the one with the beard said slowly, "… is ta moves we along inna—"

"I know what a car is," Leo interrupted. "But I can't get you one."

"How not?"

"'Cause I'm a kid."

"Don't matter to we," said Kyle.

"No, you don't understand. I'm eleven." They stared blankly at him. "I can't do that."

"Nah, dat understandin' yas isn't does too good. We gives ya not a choice."

Leo almost laughed. "So, wait… you're threatening me?"

"Sure yeah to dat," Morton said, pushing out his tiny chest.

Quickly the younger one interjected. "Nope, we doesn't."

"Whah?" Morton said, turning to his partner. "Sure we does."

"Nah we doesn't," Kyle insisted, giving his partner something of a shut-up-you-idiot look before he turned back to the boy. "See, we knows where is buried dat what's worth mucha plenty. An' we needs dat car for yas to be gettin' we der."

"Worth much?" Leo was cautiously interested. "What is it?"

"More a much than yas ever spent eyes on."

"What do you mean? Like a treasure or something?"

The two small creatures exchanged another look before the older one turned back to Leo. "Yup yeah, a treasure."

"Uh-huh. What type of treasure?" Leo narrowed his gaze skeptically.

"Diamonds," said Kyle quickly, before Morton could speak. "We knows where der's diamonds. Big giant diamonds. Buried inna ground, inna big park ya gots is near here."

"Right. So… Golden Gate Park? And you two know about these diamonds, how?"

"We puts dem der. Long time back from now," Kyle offered.

"You stole them?"

Both creatures drew back as though shocked and offended— or they were pretending to be shocked and offended. "Nah, nah to dat. We doesn't steal," the older one said, while his partner shook his head vehemently in agreement.

Leo could not tell if they were lying, but he was a kid who was, as you know, open to possibilities. He figured, even if what the creatures were saying wasn't entirely true, maybe some of it was. If, for instance, the part about diamonds being in the park was true, even a small amount of diamonds, well, it might be worth his time just to, you know, check it out. Stolen or not. "Okay, look…" he said, "if I help you, I get a cut."

Kyle rubbed his chin, a little confused. "We can does it, sure. We has weapons. But how is yas wantin' ta be cut?"

"No, no. I don't want to *be* cut. I want *a* cut. We split the take. Say… twenty-eighty?" Leo watched their faces as the two of them mulled it over. "More than fair," he added.

The younger creature scratched his ear and then he shook his head. "Nah. Is doesn't sound no good to we. Twenty-eighty. Nah to dat."

"Then I'm not helping you."

"Oh, yas'll be helping we. Otherwise we has ta do hurtin' on yas." Kyle planted his feet firmly on the floor as though readying himself for a fight.

"*You're* gonna hurt me?" Leo stifled a laugh. "You barely come up to my knees." As soon as he said it though, he winced in pain, and grabbed his forehead. "Ow!"

"See der," Kyle said with puffy pride.

"My head hurts," the boy said, rubbing above his eyebrows.

"We makes dat pain."

"No, I just got a headache."

"Ah, but we was givin' it to yas."

"Yeah," said the other one, "an' ders plenty more a what's dat from."

"Like what?" The pain in his head lessened slightly.

"Like… okay, see, der's dis," the little man with the beard said, and then appeared to be concentrating very hard. After a moment, he jumped into the air, but only about an inch or so. Clearly he was not able to do whatever it was he was trying to do. "Ach, murk fuddle!"

"I can does it," Kyle said.

This seemed to irritate the older creature. "Is can does it here!" he shot back. And then concentrated even harder than he had before.

Leo's headache was all but gone as he watched the little man. "So, what exactly are you trying to do?"

Morton suddenly let out a burst of air, and shot Leo an icy stare, as though the boy had screamed in church. Morton turned to Kyle. "We doesn't can works with 'im crackin' the rackets as such!"

"I didn't know I was supposed to be quiet," Leo said.

"Ya thinks it does easy?"

"Wull, what exactly were you trying to do?"

"Yas'll see," Morton snipped.

"An' nots ta forget, we makes ya dat pretty good headache too, eh!" Kyle added.

"Okay, look," Leo said, feeling now like he was getting an upper hand, "if I help you out, I want a fair cut. And that's final."

"Nah to dat! Ya doesn't gonna takes eighty percent!" the older one said defiantly. "We gives ya seventy! An' if ya doesn't like dat, yas can go eat a stump!"

Well, Leo certainly didn't expect that. *Seventy percent?* Not wanting to belie his astonishment, however, he frowned momentarily as though a little disappointed with the deal, all the while realizing, and delighted to realize, that these two weren't the brightest of bulbs and that this could be an altogether excellent partnership. Finally he extended his hand to the one without the beard. The little creature looked dubiously at the giant appendage with so many digits and then reached out to grasp it.

The deal was sealed.

() () ()

Grampa closed the notebook, closed his eyes and put his head back on the pillow to take a little rest, expecting, apparently, that the children would simply get up and quietly leave. But they did not. They only sat there. Waiting. And, when, a few minutes later, he opened his eyes, there they were. Sitting.

"Are you rested now, Grampa?" This was Francie, sitting very properly, her hands folded neatly in her lap.

It was clear that Henry, Joe and Francie now had different feelings about the story. Joe was anxious to learn more about the diamonds, figuring it might explain how Grampa ended up with so much money. Henry had decided he liked Leo, related to him, and, frankly, kind of wished he himself could live in a house without any adults. And Francie—well, she loved the little creatures. She wanted to hug them, to take them for a walk, to keep them in her room and dress them up.

Grampa grunted, mumbled something about how he should be able to do whatever he wanted, like sleep, since he was on his own deathbed. But then started, nonetheless, to tell the children about how Warren met the creatures.

Making a Break for It

THE REFRIGERATOR'S MOTOR whirred to life as Leo stood hunched in front of its open door, piling one thing after the next into his cradled arm—peanut butter, bologna, a chicken leg, yogurt, an old piece of pizza—where he had already stacked Doritos, crackers, bread and Cheez Puffs from the cupboards.

"What're you doing?"

He whirled around as the Doritos bag flew from his arm and slid on the kitchen floor. Warren was standing in the doorway, having just gotten back from his run, his T-shirt, the neck and chest of it, dark from sweat. "Nothing. Just gettin' a snack."

"That's a heck of a snack." Warren said as he picked up the bag of Doritos and put it beside the sink. He reached around Leo then to lift the milk carton from the fridge.

"Yeah, well, hungry." Leo was trying to appear casual. "You got beer, right?"

"Beer? Yeah, lots of it."

"Great."

"But you can't have any."

"Why not?"

"You're eleven." Warren leaned back on the counter and lifted the milk carton to his lips.

"My dad used to let me have beer."

"Well, that's certainly my goal—to be just like your dad."

"Okay then, if I can't have any beer, can I borrow your car?"

"Leo, are you listening to the words that are coming out of your mouth? They're not making sense."

"It's for something important."

"Is that right?" Warren waited for Leo to explain.

The boy shifted. "But... I can't really tell you what it is. Just... it's important."

Warren took another swig of milk, wiped his mouth and then pushed the top of the carton closed. "Well, I hope this doesn't come as an enormous shock, but the answer's still no." He put the milk back in the fridge. "And what are you doing with all that food?"

"Oh. It's, uh... for the homeless." Which, as far as Leo knew, wasn't untrue. But he could tell Warren wasn't buying it, and he, Leo, was smart enough to know that, sometimes, on occasion, now and then, it was more effective to tell adults the truth than it was to lie to them. So he decided to give the truth a whirl. "Okay. See, I met a couple of guys..." That was true enough. "And... it's possible they know where something valuable is buried." True—that's exactly what the creatures told him. "In Golden Gate Park." True *and* specific. But Leo could still see the skepticism in his teacher's face. "Just hear me out, okay." It was time to appeal to Warren's sense of logic. "Now, maybe they're lying, maybe not. But, if they aren't lying—and if I help them out—I stand to make a lot of money. Ten percent." Okay, partially true. "And if you help me out, I'd be willing to kick a percentage of that right back to you. Seriously." That part, entirely true!

Warren, of course, did not believe a single word Leo was saying. But he bunched his lips in his fingertips and furrowed his brow as though he were seriously thinking it over. "Hmmm," he said, "and where exactly are these 'couple of guys' right now?"

Leo weighed for a moment just how much further to go with this whole truth business. He wasn't sure how much more of it this particular adult could handle. But he couldn't really see a way around it—it was, after all, Warren's basement. "In the basement."

As you can probably guess, this last was not joyous news to Warren. "Boy," he said, nodding his head like it was perfectly normal to have a "couple of guys" in his basement, "I'd sure like to meet these guys."

Leo wasn't sure now who had the upper hand in this game of cat and mouse. "'Kay," he said, hoping to get more of a read on what his teacher was thinking. He moved toward the basement door, his mind playing out various scenarios—then he thought to mention, "Oh yeah. Don't bring up that ten percent thing. They're super touchy 'bout money stuff." Bases covered, he opened the door. "Oh, and get some beer, will ya. They like beer."

Warren was about to say fat chance, but realized if there really *were* two guys in his basement, something as easy to throw as a full beer can would come in handy. "Two beers, comin' right up."

As they made their way down the steps into the basement, Leo was sure the little men would have to be coaxed out of hiding. But, as it turned out, they were not hiding at all. They were quarreling. Again. And shoving each other's chests and calling each other unpleasant names like "frump dobbler" and "skag hasper."

"Ya does this always, ya dirty droib!"

"Hah! The lies ya is!"

"How 'bout dat Big War a Wobble Drobb? Ya takes dat compass den too, ya stinkin' dreen mubble!"

"Big War a Wobble Drobb? Again to dat Big War a Wobble Drobb! Ya doesn't never gonna drops it! Was fifty an' three hun'erd years gone now, an' still ya brings it up to we, dat Wobble Drobb War!"

"Fifty-*four* an' three hun'erd, ya stoop nubble!"

They were on the verge again of coming to blows. In fact, so angry were they with each other now that they did not see Leo and Warren standing there watching them.

Warren was, yes, a little surprised there were actually a "couple of guys" in his basement, but he was absolutely bewildered by how unusual these particular "couple of guys" appeared to be. He certainly was not expecting to find "little people"—which, of course, is what he thought they were, though they were smaller than any he'd ever seen or met. At the same time, he was relieved that they were as small as they were because strangers in the basement almost always needed to be thrown out on their ears, and these two miscreants looked pretty easy to throw just about anywhere.

Only when Leo finally interrupted them to show them the armful of food did they notice the boy. They were famished and grabbed at the offering like they had not eaten in days—which they hadn't—never bothering once to say thank you for any of it. They were eating so hungrily, in fact, that they didn't notice Warren, who was standing a few feet behind Leo. Not until they started to complain about the selection of food did the older one see him. Morton, his cheeks ballooning with Cheez Puffs, suddenly stopped shoving them into his mouth and squinted up at the larger human.

When Kyle saw him, his eyes grew wide with terror—until he saw the beer cans. He looked at them intently. "Yas got what der inna cans?"

"Uh…" Warren, a little flummoxed by all of this, looked down at the beer in his hands. "Beer."

"Beer is come from inna cans, huh?"

Though neither of the creatures had shown any great agility before this, the two cans disappeared from Warren's hands as though by magic. But, as delighted as the creatures were to have the beer in hand, they were altogether stumped by the ring-tops. "How's ya ta gets 'em open, eh?"

"You pull up on that ring there," Leo said.

And, as the creatures began to pry the ring-tops up, Warren noticed their hands for the first time. Suddenly, he was not at all sure who, or what, he was dealing with. He had certainly seen plenty of unusual individuals—he did live in San Francisco—but these two… "So, where exactly are you guys from?" he asked cautiously.

The creatures answered off-handedly, as they were so focused on opening the beer cans. "Nuldoid."

"Nuldoid? Haven't heard of it. Where's Nuldoid?"

By this time though the beer had been opened and the creatures were much too busy quaffing it down to answer any questions. When they had finally guzzled the last of it, they wiped their mouths and belched ferociously.

"Is plenty good in cans," Kyle said, admiring the empty container.

"Okay then," Warren said, having seen enough, "I think it's time you guys left."

The little men looked as though they were both highly offended, the younger of them whispering to the other, "Toids is doesn't got no honor ta beer." The other agreed, looked at Warren and shook his head in pity.

Both then closed their eyes and, together, they recited, well... a prayer.

> *Thanks we heaps at Lloyd below,*
> > *For beer we drinks*
> *To fills dat belly.*
> > *An' belch we does*
> *Dat's good an' smelly,*
> > *Where taste is yum*
> *An' makes we fatter.*
> > *Then wee we goes*
> *To empties bladder.*
> > *So thanks we heaps at Lloyd below.*

When they had finished their "prayer," they routinely touched their lips, their stomach and the fly of their trousers to indicate—as they explained—"All dat's good at dat beer."

"Ahhhh," said the older one, who nodded at Warren. "Ya gets we anudda, heh? An' pronto."

Warren practically laughed. In no uncertain terms then he made it clear that there would be no more beer for these two connivers and that he wanted them to leave his house immediately. *"An' pronto!"* he added, mimicking them.

The creatures accused him of being a very bad host and, worse, they said he was a "stinky droib." Warren was quite irritated by then and pointed out that he was not their host, that he wanted them out and that he wanted them out now! *Now, now, now!*

Leo, though, did not see the point of kicking them out. So, while Warren was telling them off, the boy moved up the stairs to get them some more beer. When Warren realized what Leo was up to, he yelled for him to come back, but the boy, like a great many eleven-year-olds, was pretty good at not hearing certain things that he didn't particularly want to hear.

Meanwhile, the creatures were wholly unimpressed with Warren's threats to throw them out. They were, however, very impressed with how much larger he was than Leo, and, quietly, they mentioned that they would be happy to cut the boy out, if Warren agreed to take the deal himself.

"What deal?" he asked, goading them to repeat what he knew they'd already told Leo.

"We has ta be movin' some things," Kyle said.

"Really? What things?" Lots of fake sincerity.

Kyle moved closer to him. "Big horkin' diamonds. Is waitin' ta be plucked up froma ground."

Warren studied the two scoundrels another moment, more certain now than ever that they were up to no good. "Well…" he said in a whisper, "I'm gonna have to say no. And if you two don't leave, I'm calling the police."

"Ach!" said the older one to his companion. "Now we has to tells 'im dat other story 'bout death."

"Death?" Warren's curiosity was piqued. "What about death?"

Kyle heaved a beleaguered sigh. "Big lotta death comin' to yer Crust."

"Crust? Crust of what?"

"Ach, dat Crust! Is where ya lives, ya droib!"

"The crust of Earth?"

"*Ert*, sure yeah." Morton shrugged apologetically. "Big lotta death."

"Uh-huh. And let me guess… the diamonds have something to do with this death on the crust?"

Morton shrugged again. "Sorry."

The younger creature took a deep breath and explained, "Ya see… diamonds is fulla power. To Hoidenall."

"Hoidenall?"

"Hoidenall. Ya doesn't know Hoidenall?" Kyle looked fully exasperated. "Holy Lloyd an' Floyd! Hoidenall! Ya calls it dat winky name! *Ert* ya calls it. Ert!"

"Earth?"

"Sure yeah," said Kyle. "Hoidenall. It doesn't gonna be rollin' no more 'cause der is its power, see? Is diamonds dat's havin' its juice, see? Is diamonds der dat makes yer Hoidenall ta move 'round an' 'round."

"Oh, I see. So, the earth is going to stop rotating and *that's* why all the death. Got it."

"Sure yeah, is gonna slow big. Lotta death for Crustoids."

"Right. Well, listen—thanks for the heads-up. Really." His patience was stretched like a rubber band on the verge of snapping. "But I think it's time you two really left now. *Really.*"

"Nah. See, we doesn't can go nowheres least we got help."

The rubber band was stretched a little further.

"An' so ya gives we dat car, huh?"

Snap!

"Okay, that's it! Get out of my house! Now!" But, as soon as he said the words, he winced and grabbed his forehead. "Ow!"

Kyle watched him a moment, and then seemed pleased with himself. "An' more is where dat's comin' from!"

"My head hurts." Warren rubbed his left temple.

"See der ya is wit dat pain. So ya doesn't wanna mess with we," Kyle said and then jumped into the air again, landing an inch or two from where he was. "Ach! Dobble fik!" he said, now angry with himself.

"I got beer here!" Leo said as he reappeared at the bottom of the steps.

"Holds ya der!" Kyle said, unwilling to be diverted now even by beer, as he jumped again into the air and, this time, stayed. In the air. Inches off the floor.

Warren was stunned. He studied the creature a moment. Saw no strings, no support. "How are you doing that?"

The instant he spoke, however, Kyle lost his concentration and dropped, falling backward onto his butt, hitting his head on the metal file cabinet. "Aw, croib! Doesn't ya toids* never shuts up?" He lightly touched the back of his head and looked at his hand. "Hmmm, is blood der." He rubbed his fingers together and then his eyes rolled up into his head and he fell back in a dead faint.

"Hah!" Morton yelled at his partner's unconscious body. "Ya couldn't never not stands yer sight a blood! Ya pulled this two hun'erd years an' forty back from now! Dat Stinky War a Smells! Ya gets all smooky then too! Mr. Biiiiig Noid! Bah! Ya studies with dat ballerinas!"

Though he was enormously irritated by the intruders, Warren was nonetheless concerned about the injury. He moved closer and bent down so that he could reach behind Kyle's head and check the wound. He withdrew his hand a moment later and saw there was indeed blood, but... it was green. The creature's blood was green! He looked again now at the little man's hand. *Three digits! Green blood! What were they? Martians? Monsters? What* were *these creatures?*

---

* The creature here was using the diminutive form of "Crustoid"—its use obviously derogatory.

He stepped back. Whatever was going on here, he knew it was not a situation that he—or Leo—should be handling alone. Suddenly he grabbed Leo's arm and bolted up the basement steps like a fireman rushing into a burning building. They burst into the kitchen—he slammed the door shut and locked it. "Stay here!" he shouted at Leo. "Stay here! Don't let them out! Whatever you do, don't open that door!"

Warren rushed to the living room, grabbed the phone and quickly punched 9-1-1. His heart was pounding like a jackhammer as he waited for the operator to pick up.

"Nine-one-one. Can I help you?"

"Yeah! Yes! I need someone here right away! Police! Right away!"

"Tell me what's going on."

"Okay, okay... the little men! In my basement! Not human!"

"Not human, sir?" The dispatcher's voice was calm. She was not easily ruffled and obviously received plenty of calls like this.

"Yes! Yes! They're not human! Their blood is green! And they can fly! Please send someone right away!"

"Uh-huh. And when did you first notice these little green men?"

"No, no! They're not green men! Their *blood* is green!"

"Uh-huh. And are you currently on any medications, sir?"

As you're no doubt realizing, Warren's efforts to summon help did not go well, and, in fact, the discussion became more about his mental state, his medical history, that sort of thing, than about the little men in his basement.

As Warren's voice grew louder and his frustration greater, Leo was not about to simply stand in front of the basement door and wait for his teacher to convince someone to come and arrest the creatures. Not when the creatures could possibly be a link to great and enormous wealth. (Leo had not heard the creatures talk

46

about death on the Crust, or the diamonds' effect on the earth's rotation.)

Leo was smart enough to know that he should not entirely trust the creatures, but he was intrigued—as you would be too, frankly—by their story. If it was true, if there were actual diamonds in the park, he'd become rich. And, if he were rich, he wouldn't need anybody or anything. He wouldn't need his deadbeat jailed father and he wouldn't have to live in a house with his teacher. He wouldn't have to go to school anymore. He could buy a twenty-five-speed bike, have an underground mansion built with his own bowling alley where he could have all the electricity he needed and he could hire people to fill the fridge and cupboards with anything he wanted. Better yet, he could order out every single night: cheeseburgers, chilidogs, burritos! It would be the perfect life!

So, by the time Warren was yelling at the top of his voice that he was not taking any medication—nor was he *not* taking any medication he *should* be taking—Leo had quietly slipped into Warren's bedroom, grabbed the bundle of keys off the dresser, helped himself to the rest of the cash in Warren's wallet and hightailed out of there. As Warren screamed to the 9-1-1 operator that he paid her salary, that she worked for him, and demanded that she let him speak to her supervisor, Leo quietly summoned the creatures, motioning that they follow him outside to Warren's car, where he quickly climbed in behind the wheel and opened the passenger door. And when the two little men began to squabble over which of them would ride "gun-shot," he hissed at them to knock it off and just get in the car!

While Warren explained to the operator's supervisor that he had never been institutionalized, Leo put the key in the car's ignition—the car having been repaired since it rolled down the hill during the earthquake. After Warren shouted something very unkind at the 9-1-1 supervisor, slammed the phone down and returned to the kitchen, he saw that Leo was gone, and that the basement door was wide open! Then he heard a car start up out front. He pulled back the curtain over the kitchen window and felt a curious sense of déjà vu when he saw his Chrysler LeBaron rolling down the hill again.

Once again, he was flying out the front door, sprinting down the hill after his car. But that's where the déjà vu ended because, this time, his car was not rolling slowly, nor did it go crashing into the side of anybody's warehouse. Warren realized Leo knew how to drive as he watched his car squeal around the corner at the bottom of the hill, and disappear like a getaway sedan in a black-and-white movie.

When Warren finally stopped in the middle of the street, he felt as if his lungs would explode. He bent over, put his hands on his knees and greedily sucked in air. A moment later, he stood up and, for lack of anything better to do, violently pumped his fist into the air and howled, "You! You kid! You rotten kid! Those guys aren't normal!" Well, aside from the volume of his voice, which was very loud, the words themselves weren't all that satisfying. And the only one who even heard him was an old lady on the opposite sidewalk who was out walking her dachshund—a hotdog dog. Understandably, she stopped when she heard him yelling those things and pumping his fist in the air like he was an emotionally troubled person. Abruptly, she turned the dog around and hightailed back the direction she'd come.

By now, Warren was so angry and outraged and frustrated that he felt like he needed to kick a fire hydrant or a mailbox or… something. He decided finally on a light pole, and let his foot fly—realizing a moment later that he had only added excruciating pain to his situation. At almost the same instant, something else occurred to him: He was standing next to Lily's warehouse. She would help him. She had to.

When the huge steel door at the side of the warehouse slid open, Lily did not look happy to see him. "Well, isn't this a pleasant surprise," she said, which was her way of saying the opposite.

"I need to borrow your car!" he blurted.

"Great, no problem." She smiled. "Let me just get the keys. Oh, and I'll see if I can dig up some gas money too." She smiled again and slid the door closed, dead-bolting it from the other side. Warren stood there, weighing her peculiarly thoughtful response and the sound of the deadbolt. She had just blown him off.

He banged on the door again.

This time, the door flew open and she was visibly angry. "Are you out of your mind?! Why would I loan you my car?! You can't even take care of your own car! You drive it into other people's houses! And you're annoying! Now go away!" She grabbed the handle to close the door again.

"Look, my car was stolen! By a kid!" He spoke quickly before she could close the door. "And I can't call the police 'cause I know this kid! Please, I need your help! Please!"

She stopped.

"It's a kid I teach," he continued, seeing he'd gotten her interest. "He's a good kid, see, but he's gotten in with the wrong crowd is all. And these guys he's with, they might be dangerous. And I want to find him, stop him, before he messes up his life. That's why I don't want to call the police. That's why I need to borrow your car. So I can stop this kid. Please."

She stood beside the steel door, sizing Warren up. Finally she sighed and said, "Fine. But I'm driving."

Hibb Hoiden Hill

LEO COULD BARELY see over the steering wheel of Warren's car while he worked the gas and brake pedals. He knew how to drive because his father had often sent him out to buy cigarettes or beef jerky or Hostess Cupcakes. His father was frequently too drunk or too hungover or just too lazy to get up and go get those things himself.

The two creatures were beside him, hunched over a strange-looking map that they'd spread out across the passenger seat. It was a worn leather skin that Morton had kept rolled up and stuffed in his overalls pocket. Kyle took out an ornate brass compass and held it a few inches over the map. As he did, the features of the map appeared to bulge in three-dimensional hillsides and moving bodies of blue water, all beneath small tufts of white clouds. It was quite astounding really. Although every time Leo turned a sharp corner, some of the water spilled out of the map and onto the seat where it vanished altogether.

The creatures, of course, were quarreling again. Apparently, Kyle was not directing the compass at the particular places on the map that Morton wanted to see.

"Ya gives we dat compass!"

"Nah to dat, ya mubb stuttle. We does dat compass."

"Dat compass ya gives to we afore I has to poppin' yas inna fat head!"

"Why you an' some army is a flabby chance, ya lousy dreen mubble!"

"Dreen mubble? We shows ya, ya frump dobbler!"

Well, naturally, they lunged at each other and clutched each at other's throats again and were about to come to blows when Leo, having grown tired of their bickering, pulled the car over and took the map and the compass away from them, spilling a little ocean water as he did. *It was like dealing with children. Honestly.*

Once he got the hang of moving the compass over the surface of the map he wondered where such a thing had come from. It was peculiar in that it was three-dimensional, but beyond that he could hardly tell what it depicted, even though he knew it was supposed to be San Francisco. Everything was labeled upside down, and when he turned the map around so that the words were right side up, the *land* was upside down. And nowhere did it say San Francisco or Golden Gate Park, and there was no Golden Gate or Bay bridges. Instead, all of the landmarks— landmarks that he was quite familiar with—were labeled in peculiar and unfamiliar names. For instance, Telegraph Hill was called Fribb Sibbler Mound. And Nob Hill was labeled Drubb Hoydle Bump. "This is stupid," he finally said. "You can't tell nothin' from this."

"Says yas to we."

"It says we're facing north when we're facing south."

"Ach, ya has a wad a baloney," Kyle said, and then pointed at the street ahead of them. "Dat way der is south."

"No, it's not," Leo protested.

"No, it's yeah. Sure as hot butter!"

"Well, I'm sorry, but *that* is north," the boy said pointing the opposite direction. "And *that* is south," he said, pointing the other way.

"Ach to yas! Now ya is bringing we to mad anger."

"Hey, a fact's a fact, buddy! And that is—" He was suddenly stopped by a sharp pain in his forehead. "Ow!" Leo looked at Kyle. "Did you do that?"

Kyle nodded. "Hah! Is no match for a noid!"

Morton finally interjected. "Why doesn't dat toid looks it over on his upside down, an' *you*," he said to Kyle, "ya does the other side-right up, eh?"

Both Kyle and Leo considered the older creature's suggestion for a moment before they did exactly that—Leo looking at the map from one side, Kyle from the other. The boy soon located Golden Gate Park, labeled upside down as Durben Fribble Park. Kyle pointed then to a red X at the top of a hill—Hibb Hoiden Hill. "Der's where is dat diamonds."

Leo looked more closely at the map and realized that Kyle was pointing to Strawberry Hill. He'd been there many times. "Strawberry Hill. No sweat," he said, and moved back behind the steering wheel. "We just head south on 25th. We'll run right into it."

"Sure yeah to dat," Morton said, and began rolling up the map.

As the car pulled out, Kyle muttered quietly, "Is *north* on 25th."

The Crystal

A FEW MOMENTS later, Warren's car was lumbering up a narrow road of Golden Gate Park toward Strawberry Hill with Leo behind the wheel and the two little creatures standing on the opened door of the glove box, leaning on the dashboard and peering gleefully out the front window. Leo pulled off the road near the old stone bridge that crossed Stow Lake and backed the car into the shadows of a huge live oak.

They got out and walked across the bridge—the creatures taking many hurried steps to each of Leo's. When they reached the other side, Kyle took the brass compass from his pocket and studied it intently. After a moment, he shoved it back into his pocket and led the other two up a small dirt path that wound along the hillside beneath the thick drooping arms of a Monterey cypress and through a tangle of sagging willow tree vines. Farther up the hill, Leo pushed aside a dense thicket of shrubbery that his companions had only to walk beneath. The path was nearly covered by tall grass that reached over it from either side. In short order they came upon a large circular clearing where the ground was blanketed by a layer of moist fallen leaves. It was perhaps ten yards from one side to the other, and almost perfectly round, the circle being defined by fifteen or twenty towering blue gum eucalyptuses.

Kyle walked to the center of the clearing and raised the compass over his head with both hands, while Leo watched from beside a gum tree. Kyle closed his eyes tightly and moved about the clearing. A moment later the compass began to vibrate, its copper shell glowing in a rich amber hue. After another moment, it became still again. Kyle's eyes popped open. "Is here dat, uh, diamond!" He took a small worn book from his back pocket, its pages bent and torn from use and travel, and opened it to a marked page. At the same time, Morton began to straighten himself as though preening for an appearance before royalty. Then he moved next to his partner and, together, they read from the book:

> 'Round an' 'round is Hoidenall,
> Where up from down it comes ta get.
> Where shines is power to dat ball.
> And makes we haste away wit it
> From weathered Crust of blustery fright,
> Ta where we was whenst we slept tight.

() () ()

Unbeknownst to Leo and the creatures, Warren and Lily had arrived at the park in Lily's battered red pickup, a '64 Chevy. Slowly they wound their way through the narrow roadways of Golden Gate Park, searching for Warren's car. Lily was starting to think they would not find it and suggested that perhaps the boy had changed his mind and was sitting back at Warren's house, waiting to apologize.

Warren shook his head. "Not this kid. Besides, the two, uh, guys he's with…" He paused, unsure if he should tell her about the creatures. "It's just that, they're not…" He was going to say they weren't good or they weren't honorable, but suddenly he found himself saying, "…human."

Lily was quiet for a moment as she steered the truck up another hill. "Okay," she said finally.

"You don't believe me, do you?"

"I didn't say that."

"Well, it's true. They're short and they're not human. They only have three fingers on each hand, and their blood is green."

"Fine."

"So… you *do* believe me?" he asked, suspecting that she most certainly did not believe him.

"Didn't say that either," she said.

"Then you think I'm crazy, don't you?"

"Possibly. It's also possible that there's life on other planets, and, possibly, those that live on other planets have traveled to this planet. I believe these things because, unlike many of the people who teach in our public institutions, I haven't shut myself off to new and different ideas. I'm still open to possibilities."

"Okay, first off," Warren said, "I'm as open as the next guy. But you honestly believe in UFOs? 'Cause that's insane."

"I said I believe in possibilities."

"Yuh…"

"Is that your car?" Lily nodded towards the front end of the Chrysler that was protruding from beneath the low-hanging branches of the oak beside the stone bridge.

She parked the truck down the road a ways, and they walked back to Warren's car, where they decided to cross the stone bridge and check out Strawberry Hill. At the foot of the hill, Warren stopped and stood quietly for a moment, listening. Thinking. He turned then to tell Lily something, but she was ducking under the branches of the Monterey cypress—the ones that hung over the path that Leo and the two creatures had taken. He quickly caught up with her and was about to ask what she thought she was doing when she stopped and shushed him to be quiet. They both stood listening for a moment before they heard the small voices of Morton and Kyle. They followed the sound up the hill to the edge of the clearing and then crouched in the grass beneath the branches of an old elm.

Warren and Lily saw that the boy was sitting at the base of a huge eucalyptus tree while the two small men stood in the middle of the clearing, reading aloud from a small book. When they had finished, the younger creature put the book in his back pocket, then they reached up to lock hands over their heads like children playing London Bridge.

"Those are the 'aliens' you were all upset about?" Lily whispered to Warren.

"I wasn't 'all upset,'" he whispered back. "And don't let their size fool you!"

"So, what are they doing?"

"I don't know."

"Well, why don't you just go out there and beat 'em up?"

"Shhh..." he said, studying the two figures in the center of the clearing.

After a moment, the creatures, in unison, said, "Hib nobb del noid!"

"What?" Warren whispered to Lily.

"They said, 'Hip hop' something."

56

They watched as Kyle and Morton shut their eyes and appeared to be concentrating very hard. "Hib nobb del noid!" they repeated more loudly.

"It's 'Hib nobb Detroit,'" Warren whispered to Lily.

"No," she said, "they said 'del noid.' 'Hib nobb del noid.' What does that mean?"

"No idea..." he said, and saw that the creatures had opened their eyes.

"Circle of round is round of the circle where der's all dat is," the younger creature said, and then repeated, "Hib nobb del noid!"

Suddenly the creatures began to lift off of the ground—their hands still arched over their heads—while they began to turn in mid-air as though standing on a turntable or a lazy Susan.

Lily's eyes grew wide, and Warren gave her something of a told-you-so smirk. The two creatures began to spin, slowly at first, then faster and faster, 'round and 'round, until they were moving so fast they were no longer distinguishable as the odd little beings they were. And just as it seemed they could spin no faster, their hands came away from each other's and they were sent hurtling through the air in opposite directions, landing with a thud as they tumbled through the leaves, end-over-end to the opposite sides of the clearing. After a moment, they struggled to their feet, wobbled for a few steps in random directions and then bent over and threw up. Both of them. And both of them looked oddly pleased at having done so.

Leo—like Warren and Lily—looked perplexed by this whole strange ritual. "So..." he said to Kyle, after Kyle plopped onto the ground beside him, "where exactly are these diamonds?"

"Diamonds? What diamonds?" Lily whispered to Warren, still hidden beneath the branches of the elm tree. Warren was about to explain the creatures' claim that there were diamonds buried in the park—a claim he found nearly laughable—when Lily said, "Oh, my." He looked out at the clearing and saw that the two patches of vomit—or whatever it was—were glowing brilliant red. Each patch began to slither over the leaves toward the other like two snakes. On meeting at the center of the clearing, they began to twist around each other until they were spinning into a red tornado funnel, blowing leaves and dirt and rocks in all directions as they swirled faster and faster. The bottom tip of the funnel began to burrow into the bare earth like a drill bit until, a second later, the funnel itself was suddenly sucked into the ground, where it disappeared altogether.

And then, just as suddenly, everything was still. Silent. Warren peered through the hanging branches, and saw that now there was not even a hole where the snakes of red vomit had disappeared.

Then, without warning, the earth beneath them jolted with a thundering crack, and the ground at the center of the clearing bulged, wrinkling and popping, until it erupted like a small volcano, spewing dirt and rocks high into the air.

As Leo and the creatures scrambled for cover, Warren and Lily quickly moved closer to the trunk of the elm so that they would not be hit by the falling debris. When it appeared safe again to look, they saw that the volcano was spitting sparks into the air like a Roman candle. At the same time, the bark on the eucalyptus trees surrounding the clearing began to crumble and fall away, revealing brilliant phosphorescent colors. Then, as though in concert with each other, the trees' glowing trunks began to change hues, each in synchronicity with the next, slowly at first and then more rapidly until they began to strobe in colors that Warren and Lily had never seen before. Yellows and blues like a flashing Van Gogh sky; radiant laser reds; greens that clutched the base of the heart like the boom of a bass drum; all of it in a stunning display.

At the center of the clearing, a glass pyramid began to emerge from the ground as though it had been summoned by the vibrant light from the trunks of the trees. As it rose, it turned slowly, taking in the flashing light, absorbing it, refracting it and throwing it back out into the sky like a fountain of electric paint. When the pyramid was fully exposed, Warren and Lily could see that it was the top of something much larger- -it was, they realized, an obelisk! A crystal obelisk! And when it had completely emerged from the ground, they saw it was perhaps three feet tall—enormous, certainly, by crystal obelisk standards. As it hovered in the air, it began to spin more rapidly, while the earth and leaves beneath it closed up like a healed wound. Soon the crystal was hurling a dizzying array of brilliant colors in all directions—even as the tree trunks began to fade back to their natural colors.

It was magnificent. Spectacular!

It was... well, not of this world! *Except it was!*

And then, just as suddenly—and certainly a lot less spectacularly—the crystal stopped spinning and fell over with a very ordinary *thunk.*

Again, everything became still. Quiet. Everything looked normal. Except, of course, for the large crystal obelisk that was now lying on the ground in the middle of the clearing, residual steam rising up off of it like a floating ghost.

Leo and the creatures stepped out from behind the trees where they had been hiding. The boy approached the crystal cautiously, and slowly ran his finger along the edge of it. "Holy smokes," he said, his eyes wide with visions of wealth. "This is like the hugest diamond in the whole world. How many more are there?"

"Much of many more," Kyle said, sharing a look with Morton. "Everywhere dey is, sure as spit an' beer."

Lily moved close to Warren and whispered. "That can't be a diamond."

Warren shook his head. "It's not. A diamond doesn't refract light that way," he said, calling up what he knew about diamonds from the geology course he had taught for two semesters at the junior college. "It's a crystal of some sort. But they want him to think it's a diamond."

Leo was excited. "So, you're gonna do that spin-and-barf thing again, huh? That 'hip hop dear knob' thing, huh? Sooo cool."

"'Hib nobb del noid,'" Kyle corrected him, and then turned to Morton. "Toids."

Morton shrugged. "Eh, expects yas what—dey lives in weather."

"So, okay," Leo was still staring at the crystal, "let's start bringin' up those other diamonds? Get that compass thing out, huh?"

"Nah, we hasta first gotta puts it in dat car's butt-end trunk. We comes back den, we gets more."

The creatures obviously could not carry, or even lift, the crystal, so Leo bent and, with some difficulty and a grunt, hoisted it onto his shoulder.

"Okay, here's what we're gonna do," Warren whispered to Lily, pleased at last to have come up with a plan. "After they put that thing in the trunk, and come back here to get the other ones, we're going to steal the car and drive to the police station. They get a look at that crystal, they'll help us out." He looked at her smugly.

"Or..." Lily said, "you could run out there, chase those little guys off and rescue the kid right now."

"No, no…" he shook his head. "Those 'little guys' do things that aren't normal. They have powers. They could seriously hurt me."

"Uh-huh," she said skeptically.

"Seriously. They gave me a headache!" As soon as he said it, he knew it sounded stupid and, even if he hadn't known it, Lily's look would have told him as much. "And they can hover!"

"Hover? Oh my!" she said, putting an open hand on her cheek, clearly mocking him.

"The point is, I don't know what they can do. So, we'll go with *my* plan." Warren turned and watched the small creatures trudge down the dirt path behind Leo and the crystal. "Come on," he whispered as he got up and moved quietly through the brush behind the trio, careful to keep a safe distance so that he and Lily would not be seen or heard by them.

As they neared the car, the creatures rushed ahead of the boy to open the trunk, and then Morton hoisted Kyle into it, where he helped Leo carefully place the crystal.

Then—once they were sure the crystal was safe and secure and would not shift or roll around when the car was moved—something very disturbing took place. Kyle, who was already up in the trunk, reached over and cupped his hands over Leo's ears. Warren and Lily watched as, in the next instant, the boy slumped and fell, face-first, into the trunk like a limp dishtowel, his legs still hanging out. Morton quickly grabbed hold of his legs and pushed him the rest of the way into the trunk, while Kyle pulled the boy's torso from above. Once the unconscious body was completely in, Kyle took hold of the trunk lid and pulled it down as he jumped out and onto the ground. Morton moved up swiftly to the driver's door where he turned and stood with his fingers interlaced in front of him, so that he could boost his partner up and in through the window. Once Kyle was inside, the door swung open and Morton climbed in. A moment later, the car's engine roared to life.

"Remembers ya, dat wheel goes 'round way wrong," Morton said as he positioned himself on the floorboard next to the gas and brake pedals.

"Ach! We knows! Ya doesn't has to tells we!" Kyle shook his head as he studied the steering wheel. "Crazy."

Meanwhile, Warren, stunned by this ominous turn of events, knew he had to act quickly if he was going to stop these creatures. "Hey, hey!" he yelled and bolted up from behind the thicket that he and Lily had been hiding behind.

Kyle turned, his eyes suddenly wide at the sight of a colossal human coming at them. He yelled frantically to his partner, "Holy Lloyd an' Floyd, gas it, Morton, gas it!" Suddenly the car's back wheels were spinning in the dirt and pushing the car into the street, where its tires gripped the pavement and threw the vehicle screaming down the road, zigzagging this way and that as the little driver struggled to get the feel of the steering wheel.

"Stop! Stop!" Warren yelled as he ran out after them, and then stood there and watched helplessly as his car careened down the street away from him. Again. "Stop! You… aliens!" It was pitiful and pointless, but it was all he could think to yell in his frustration.

Lily was suddenly at his side, tugging his arm, pulling him down the road toward her truck. "Come on, come on! Get in the truck!"

A moment later she was clutching the steering wheel and turning the ignition as Warren climbed in and slammed the door shut. Lily threw the truck into reverse, shooting it out onto the road where she jammed the gearshift into drive and jammed her foot down on the gas pedal. As the truck blasted past the Boathouse and swerved out onto Presidio Boulevard, Warren started looking for a seatbelt and realized there was none. "Where's the seatbelt?" he hollered.

"No seatbelts!" she yelled. "Where are they going?"

"No seatbelts? Are you kidding me?"

"It's an old truck! Get over it!" She squinted out at the cars in front of them. "I think they're headed for the bridge!"

The creatures were indeed headed for the Golden Gate Bridge, and Lily pressed the old truck to keep up with them.

What did the creatures want with Leo? Did they plan to hurt him? Or worse, kill him? Were they driving to some hidden spaceship somewhere where they would take off for who knows where? And what was the crystal all about? That it might power the rotation of the earth was absurd, but did it possess magical powers? Why was it so important to these creatures?

As they sped north on U.S. 101, Warren squinted ahead at the taillights of his car and then felt the truck suddenly snort and sputter and lose power.

"Uh-oh," Lily said, as she whacked the dashboard.

"What?"

"I think we're out of gas."

Warren looked over at the gas gauge. "But it says full."

"Gauge is broken." She banged the dashboard again.

"Well, great," Warren said as the truck lost power and began to coast onto the gravel and dirt patches beside the freeway. He sat angrily as he watched the taillights of his car quietly shrink into the distance and disappear altogether over the curve of the next hill.

"I'm sorry," Lily said, not sounding all that sorry. "I meant to put gas in the truck today, but I was just too busy."

Warren jerked the door handle, swung the door open and stepped out. He wanted to ask her how any sane person could drive around, day in and day out, without a gas gauge. Instead, he turned and squinted at the hillside next to the freeway ahead of them and saw the top of a Chevron sign. "Hey! A gas station! There's a gas station up there!" And suddenly he was striding in its direction. "I'll call the police!" he yelled over his shoulder.

The door to the truck banged open and Lily jumped out to catch up with him. "Listen, I'm sorry," she said as the gravel crunched beneath her feet. "So if you're mad at me, why don't you just say it?"

"Not mad."

"You're mad."

"I told you, I'm not mad," he said in a very abrupt tone that, frankly, sounded mad.

It didn't take them long to get to the filling station, where Warren called the police straightaway, and Lily paid the attendant to fill a canister with gasoline.

While the police still had plenty of problems dealing with the aftermath of the earthquake—lost people, hurt people, vandals—they were nonetheless very interested to hear of a kidnapping. Kidnappings were the sort of thing that police like to jump on with all sorts of enthusiasm and purpose. They sent out fleets of patrol cars with eager cops and loaded guns, both to talk to Warren and to start looking for his car and the "alleged kidnappers." Warren had decided it best, this particular go-round, not to include any of the stuff about green blood or the creatures not being human, having learned from experience that those sort of details only muddied the process.

After he and Lily got back to the truck and poured the canister of gas into the tank, they drove back to the gas station and filled it.

It's Just Not Right

OKAY, THIS PART of the story really threw the kids for a loop—especially Francie. Not only did the cute little Nuldoid creatures lie to Leo and trick him, which was plenty bad, but they knocked him out, locked him in the trunk of Warren's car and kidnapped him. In fact, this particular section of the story took a little longer to tell because Francie kept stopping Grampa, backing him up, demanding clarification—which Grampa, of course, was none too pleased about. But Francie found it difficult to accept that Morton and Kyle turned out to be so diabolical. She'd decided early on that they were cute as could be, so—in her mind anyway—they were supposed to be good guys. And now, clearly, they weren't.

Every time she interrupted her grandfather, he would look exasperated, lay the notebook on his chest and shoot a look to

Henry or Joe, so that they would ask their sister to be quiet and let him tell the story. "Now, where was I?"

"They put Leo in the trunk and kidnapped him," Joe offered.

"Thank you, Henry."

KYLE GRIPPED THE steering wheel tightly and pulled himself up so that he could see into the rearview mirror. When he was certain that Lily's truck was no longer behind them, he yelled down to Morton, "Lets up onna pedal der!" The car rolled to a stop beside the freeway, and the two creatures climbed out to open the trunk.

Leo was still unconscious lying next to the Crystal, his face meshed firmly against the treads of the spare tire, creating snakelike squiggles up and down his cheek and forehead. One creature boosted the other up into the trunk, and the other pulled the first into it. Kyle took out a large roll of duct tape that he'd stolen from Warren's basement, and, with Morton's help, wound yard after yard of it around the boy's feet and hands. When they were confident that he could not break free, the younger creature put his hand on Leo's forehead and said, "Hibble dobs dropp stobble!" Both of the little men watched the boy's face intently, but he did not wake up. "Ah, fik dibble!" Kyle blurted, and whacked Leo on the side of the head as though trying to get a television set to work properly.

"Ow!" Leo blinked his eyes a couple of times and saw that he was lying in the trunk of a car, bound by duct tape. "What the heck!" He struggled to free himself, but Morton and Kyle had been generous in their use of the tape, so it was pretty much no use even trying.

"We gotta needs ya-hoo's ta help we," the bearded creature said.

"Yeah, well fat chance of that, you little freaks. And why am I all taped up like this? And where's my seventy percent?" Leo insisted.

The creatures laughed. "Eh, they doesn't gonna happens. See, we winkhoods ya," Kyle said with a fair bit of pride.

"So, you're keeping all the diamonds for yourself?"

They laughed again. "Ah, diamonds, they doesn't much happen neither. See, we winkhoods yas more!" Kyle could hardly contain himself from giggling as he said this. "Is not no never diamonds."

"What do you mean no diamonds?" Leo asked. "What about that big one? The one in the park that I—" He realized then that he was lying next to it. "This one! What about this diamond?'

"Nah, it doesn't not no diamond. Is dat Crystal! See, we fibs to yas! Ha-haa!" Now they again were both howling, Morton even slapping his partner on the back as though they liked each other, while Leo made a couple more futile attempts to squirm out of the duct tape. When the creatures had again composed themselves, Kyle took a more serious tone. "'Kay. See, we gots dat Crystal der 'cause a it soaks up from dat big hot one. Is from der dat's fulla power."

68

"Big hot one?"

"Sure yeah, dat big hot one. Dat round one 'at's all hot up der." He pointed toward the sun. "Way up inna air der!"

"The sun?"

"Sure yeah, dat hot one up der."

"So this diamond gets power from the sun?"

The creatures were growing frustrated. "Is not no diamond," Kyle said, enunciating the words clearly, before he turned to Morton. "Ach, toids is playin' der wit half a sturkle, eh?"

"Hey!" Leo recognized an insult when he heard one.

"Now, here's what we's havin' dat troubles of..." Kyle said, "Drobbs Mubble. We doesn't finds it nowhere. An' we needs ta. We needs ta lotta much."

"Well, tough beans. I ain't helpin' ya," Leo grunted.

Morton turned to Kyle. "So ya *has* to tells 'im. Has ta."

Kyle nodded and pulled himself up onto the boy's chest, where he folded his stubby legs and sat down, so that he could talk earnestly and closely. "'Kay. Here's why yas gonna be helpin' we. In times not long from now, Hoidenall's ta be stoppin' from its movin'."

Leo looked blankly at the creature.

"Hoidenall! *Ert!* Ert's ta be stoppin'!"

"You mean Earth?" Leo said.

"Is what I said. Ert!"

"But... if the earth stops rotating... lots of people will die. Lots of things."

"Sure yeah. Is a stinky basket a horkk for alla dem toids."

"But... why is the earth going to stop moving?"

"Ah, see, dat Crystal is how power is der. An' we gots it here, see. Now we has ta gets to Drobbs Mubble afore all goes to kaplooey. Hoo-hooey, ya doesn't gonna wanna be 'round for dat, sur-no-ree"

69

"Drobbs Mubble? What's that?"

Morton took out a small black book and leafed quickly through its tiny pages to find the translation. When he did, he held his finger on the page and pronounced, "Fresh-noo."

"Fresno?"

"Sure yeah. Drobbs Mubble. We has directions says ta be goin' north."

"North? Fresno's not north. It's south."

"Ach," Kyle exclaimed. "Here again we goes. Ya doesn't know piddle from paddle!"

"What's that supposed to mean?"

And, as Leo and Kyle began again to squabble about what was north and what was south, Morton took out the compass and flipped the lid to study it. He looked up then at the green posted sign at the side of the freeway, and back at the compass. "Kyle?" he said finally. "Kyle? We is heads south by this. An' dat sign der says we heads north."

Kyle took the compass and looked at it a moment. "Well, spit on Lloyd. We is heads south." Both creatures scratched their heads, puzzled that the posted signs would say the exact opposite of their compass. They concluded, of course, that the humans who posted the signs were simply shorb scoids.[*]

It was, however, more a matter of perspective. You see, many years earlier—well, thousands of years earlier—when creatures of their ilk first charted the earth's surface, they assumed they were looking north when they were looking south. After all, there is no real basis for believing that north is "up" or "down" since the earth floats in space where there is no such thing as either.

When the two little men had finally figured out what was what—with Leo's help—they agreed that they should be

---

[*] Incompetent nincompoops.

following the signs that said "south," misleading as they were, if they were going to reach Fresno.

"So, what are you gonna do with me?" Leo asked. "Kill me?"

"Ya has questions all over," Morton said as he and Kyle began the difficult task of pushing and pulling the duct-taped boy out of the car's trunk.

"We doesn't has ta—uhhg!—kills you," Kyle said as he strained to push him over the lip of the trunk, while Morton got out and tugged at the boy's legs from the ground.

"But yas *is* gonna die, sure as Sloid's a slob," Morton added, just before Leo fell out of the trunk and slammed onto the ground with a disturbing *thud*.

"Ahhhh!" Pain shot through his shoulder.

The two little men winced sympathetically. "Holy Lloyd an' Floyd, that's gotta lotta hurts much, huh?" the older one said and shook his head.

"So… you *are* gonna kill me?" Leo asked again as the two creatures began dragging him around the side of the car like a gunnysack of rocks.

"Nah to dat," Kyle said.

"But I'm going to die, you said."

"Doesn't see how ya isn't." Morton grunted as he pulled Leo along the popping gravel.

"So you're gonna leave me here, taped up—ow!—until the earth stops rotating? You're going to let me die here with everyone else?"

"Nah to dat. Ya has ta be goin' where we is," Kyle said as he pulled open the passenger door. "Otherwise we doesn't gonna get dat Crystal nowheres ta sum day. Is too big a clunk for we."

Leo was now more certain than ever that these two creatures—wherever they were from, whatever they wanted— did not care whether he lived or died. In fact, they didn't seem to care if *anyone* lived or died. But—at least for now—they needed him.

After they managed to hoist and tug and shove the boy into the passenger seat of the car, they climbed in behind him, closed the door and crawled across his lap to take their places behind the steering wheel and next to the gas and brake pedals.

Kyle started the engine and quietly muttered to himself that the steering wheel turned *left* to go *right,* and *right* to go *left.* A moment later, the car was bouncing across the median that divided the northbound from the southbound freeway, and soon they were speeding off towards Drobbs Mubble.

At the same time, scads of police cars were wailing toward a section of the freeway several miles north of them (our north). They were looking for Warren's car, where, of course, they wouldn't find it. Still other police cars sped this way and that over the connecting freeways, roadways and streets, all looking for a Chrysler LeBaron that was supposed to be "traveling north" (ours).

"You know," Leo said a few minutes later, "I'm not gonna be able to carry your precious Crystal anywhere unless you guys cut this tape off me."

Both creatures chuckled at the very idea, Kyle holding his mosquito cheek, Morton's belly bouncing against his overalls. Finally, the older one explained that they could not free him until his mind had been "fixed." Though neither explained what exactly "fixed" meant, Leo was pretty sure he didn't like the sound of it.

○ ○ ○

At the gas station, Lily filled the truck's tank and then paid the attendant. But, as she pulled back onto the freeway and headed north toward the police roadblocks, Warren looked at the other side of the road and saw his car traveling the opposite direction. "That's them!" he shouted. "That's my car! That's them! That's them!"

Lily saw the car too and cranked the steering wheel hard as the truck careened onto the lonely strip of weeds that divided the two sides of the freeway and whipped onto the southbound lanes. If they stayed far enough behind the creatures, they figured, they would stay undetected. Then, whenever the creatures got to where they were going, Lily could pull over and they could call for help. That was the plan anyway.

Little did they know they would be driving for nearly 200 miles.

Several times during those 200 miles, they tried to figure out where the creatures were taking the boy but they did not once think it would be Fresno. Fresno, after all, was not the sort of place where you'd expect anything of significance to happen. Well, except raisins. There were a lot of raisins in Fresno. And certainly there were plenty of nice communities in Fresno. But, as a stage for exciting, world-shattering events? Not really.

Warren was trying not to let his imagination get the best of him, but he had seen so many unusual things in the last few hours that he could hardly be blamed for concluding that these strange beings were extraterrestrials of some sort, here to collect human specimens. Like Leo. Painful medical experiments, torture, dismemberment, the extraction of brains to be kept alive in jars—all of it went rushing through his head.

And the Crystal? What was the Crystal all about, he wondered. Why was it so important to them? He remembered they had said something about its power. In fact, they had said it powered Earth. As absurd as it first sounded to him, now he found himself wondering if perhaps it were possible.

When he told Lily about all of these things, the things he'd seen and heard and thought might be true, he feared that he was starting to sound as crazy as the people he thought were crazy. In fact, when he heard himself saying the words out loud, he realized they couldn't be true. It was impossible. Imagine thinking that a Crystal could actually power the rotation of Earth. That was lunacy. And he was not a lunatic.

Of course, his concluding that the whole idea was preposterous made Lily believe all the more that it *was* possible. She wondered out loud if these two creatures had indeed come here to steal the Crystal that powered Earth? And what if they really *were* evil? Naturally, the more she hypothesized, the more Warren pooh-poohed her ideas and began to think *she* was a possible lunatic, until Lily accused him of being more afraid of sounding crazy than of actually getting to the truth. "What's worse?" she asked. "To believe something is possible, and be wrong? Or to be so afraid of sounding crazy that you let the worst happen?"

He could tell that she was looking to start another fight, and, frankly, he didn't want to fight. He was also beginning to suspect that she rather enjoyed fighting—which added even further to his lunacy theory. He reached over and turned the radio on, hoping to avoid any further discussion. That, of course, made Lily angrier, so she reached over and turned the radio off. When she did, Warren turned it back on, which made Lily boiling mad. She was not a woman to be ignored. But, as she reached to turn it back off, Warren grabbed her hand to stop her. Oh boy, you can only imagine how mad that made her. Mad mad—verging on hopping mad. And she was about to yell some very unkind things, the sort of things that can't be included here, when Warren said, "Sssshhh," and nodded at the radio.

An announcer was reporting a story that had started in Australia. It was not a big story, certainly not one that the announcer seemed to treat with great import. It seemed that some members of the "scientific community" were concerned that the sunset in Perth that evening was nearly two seconds later than it should have been. Yes, it was late October—Spring in Australia—where the days are expected to get a little longer, but this was highly unusual. What was most disturbing, however—especially to Warren and now Lily—was that scientists were reporting the same phenomenon in the Northern Hemisphere: San Francisco, Anchorage, New York, London, Madrid. And none of the scientists had an explanation for why it might be, nor did any seem to have knowledge of such a phenomenon having happened in the past. All agreed, though, that it was probably just a temporary lull and nothing to be terribly concerned about. The announcer concluded the story with a dumb joke about how the days always seem longer to him when his mother-in-law was in town, and then he moved on to a story about how President Bush (the first of three) signed a $3.45 billion earthquake relief package for California.

Warren turned the radio off.

Neither he nor Lily said anything for another mile or so as the truck rattled down Highway 99 behind the creatures and Leo. He was weighing everything—all of it.

The earth was slowing down.

And just *after* the creatures took the Crystal from the park. Was it cause and effect? It had to be. The earth had never slowed down before. The Crystal *must* power its rotation. And these creatures stole it. But why? Why would they want to stop the earth's rotation? Were they trying to destroy life on this planet?

Finally, Warren turned to Lily. "We have to stop them. We're the only ones who know about this. It's up to us. We have to get that Crystal!"

Lily stared at the oncoming road, and nodded—she'd been thinking a lot of the same things. She pressed the gas pedal to the floorboard as the truck sputtered a little, then picked up speed. Soon they were barreling up to Warren's car, inches from the back bumper.

Lily hollered to Warren, "Okay, I'm going to pull up beside them, and you're going to leap into their window!"

"What? No!"

"You have to!"

"No, I don't!"

"Yes, you do!"

"No, I don't!"

She was about to accuse Warren of being afraid—"chicken" is the word she was going to use—when the car ahead of them, Warren's car, suddenly jutted left across two lanes of traffic going the opposite direction, miraculously clipping only the fender of a Peugeot before hurtling like a skipping rock out across the lettuce fields between Highway 99 and Avenue 7 on the outskirts of Fresno.

In an instant, Lily jerked the wheel of the truck, Warren's right shoulder crashing into the passenger door, and then they too were flying over the opposing lanes of the freeway and out onto the unforgiving rows of growing lettuce. *Thuda, thuda, thuda, thuda, thuda, thuda...* And while Warren was practically overcome by adrenaline and fear, there was still a tiny part of him that was duly impressed with Lily, with her ability to so skillfully handle an old pickup truck at such speeds, a truck that seemed at any moment on the verge of flying into a hundred battered, skittering pieces.

Several times he thought he might die as she followed the bumping, careening car up an embankment to Road 35 and then made a sharp right turn onto Avenue 9. Both vehicles were again picking up speed, heading east—the creatures, of course, thought they were heading west—until the road jutted left and Warren's Chrysler did not, and so it went flying down another hillside and then sailed between rows and rows of stout green walnut trees.

Lily and Warren were not far behind them, barreling through the branches and ripening walnuts that spattered hard against the truck's dirty windshield.

Leo sat wide-eyed, bouncing in the passenger seat—still bound by duct tape—as the terrifying scenario unfolded. He could do no more than watch and scream, which he did every time Kyle spun the car in a new direction, and the boy realized they were plunging down another embankment or racing toward a tree or headed for a cliff or crashing down a ravine with a river at the bottom of it—which is what they were doing at that very moment! Kyle too was screaming because he couldn't tell if the river they were about to drive into was *inches* deep or *miles* deep.

"Oh no!" Warren yelled from the passenger seat of Lily's truck as he saw his Chrysler plunge into the river and send out two thick layers of water on either side of it. Fortunately, the water was not deep, and the car bobbled its way to the other side and then spun its wheels up another embankment and onto a small dirt road that ran along the edge of the ravine.

Lily didn't let her foot off the gas as, a moment later, the truck too went bobbing through the same water and then chugging slowly up the other side of the ravine, spitting out chunks of gravel and dirt from beneath its balding tires. When they reached the small road at the top, she spun the truck to the left in the direction of the car and its flying trail of dust.

As they sped closer, Warren could see that the creatures and Leo were traveling much too fast to make the sharp turn in the road just ahead of them, where there loomed a huge rock. In fact, it looked to him like the creatures were driving full speed *toward* the rock. He was frantic as both he and Lily watched the car rush closer and closer toward it where, surely, the creatures and Leo would perish.

It took a mere second or two. Inside the car, Leo was screaming because Kyle was screaming, and now Morton, down below, was screaming along with them. While the rock may have looked small from a distance, it suddenly towered in front of them like the side of an aircraft carrier. And yet Morton was still pushing the gas pedal to the floorboard. "Is der! Is der! You doesn't turn!" Morton screamed from beneath the steering wheel. "Ya does steady! Ya does steady!" he yelled as he held the gas pedal with one pudgy hand and studied the peculiar compass in his other.

And as the car sped even closer, Kyle stuck his head out the window and shouted, "Hib nobb del noid! Hib nobb del noid!"

"Four, three, two—dat's der, Kyle, dat's der!" Morton hollered from below.

"Hib nobb del noid!" Kyle screamed one last time, as suddenly a streak of radiant lightning shot across the face of the giant rock's surface and highlighted a screeching fissure that suddenly cracked and split open like the jaws of a shark, swallowing the car and all it contained, instantly slamming shut behind them in a thundering clash of solid rock colliding with solid rock. Chips of stone burst from the crashing walls as dust engulfed the falling debris and mushroomed out across the dirt road, where Lily slammed on the brakes, and the truck slid sideways to a weaving stop in the cloud of dust that swallowed them.

There they sat, Warren and Lily—the brown dust slowly settling in around the truck—both of them certain, but not so certain, of what it was they had just seen.

After a moment, Warren climbed out and stood dumbfounded in front of the towering wall of stone. They were gone. Just gone. He banged on the rock and heard no echo—it wasn't hollow—it was nothing but thick, solid rock. He examined the fissure and found not even a small gap. It was as though the rock itself had simply fused together.

He could think of nothing else to do except kick the rock as hard as he could.

The Region of
Neither Norr

Part Two

Down in dat Circle what all exists,
An' 'round it moves to come 'round
Where finish starts,
An' up is down.
Where bad is strong to holds all good.
Where good comes 'round with bad beside,
Where 'round goes it
In all exists.

The Book of Nuldoid
Revulsions 11:4

Still Not Dead

GRAMPA WORST DID not die when he was supposed to, and everyone was disappointed except for Henry, Joe and Francie, who wanted very much to learn what had happened to Leo and Warren and Lily.

The following day, after everyone realized that Grampa was still not dead—he was, in fact, *very much* not dead; barking orders at the help, complaining about whatever caught his attention, grumpy, grumpy—the children insisted that they be allowed to go back and see him. Their mother and father were fairly impressed that they wanted to spend this time with their grandfather, a man they barely knew. So, their mother drove them back to the enormous house, where the children returned to Grampa's expansive room and sat beside his sprawling bed to visit with him "one last time."

Francie pushed her chair closer to the side of his bed and jumped to the heart of the matter—skipping right past any "Hello, Grampa"s, "How are you, Grampa?"s, niceties like that—and whispered, "Okay, Grampa, what happened to Leo?"

Grampa didn't seem to mind her directness, never having been one much himself for pleasantries—of any sort. "Leo?" he said, delighted that the subject had been brought up. "Leo was one of my father's students back in 1989, the year of the big earthquake! Go ahead, look it up, if you don't believe me! There was a big earthquake!"

"We know all that, Grampa," Henry said, after his younger brother and sister looked to him. "You told us that part yesterday, remember?"

"Of course I remember," he said, testily. "You were here yesterday."

"You told us how Leo and the creatures drove your dad's car into the rock wall and disappeared," Joe prompted.

"Of course I did 'cause that's exactly what happened," he said to Joe. "If you think I'm lying, you can ask your brother Joe."

"I'm Joe," Joe said.

"Aw, don't start this again!" Grampa moaned and then struggled to move his frail, spindly legs over the side of the bed where he could address the nightstand again with "Hib nobb del noid," where, again, the drawer did not open until he repeated it twice more and angrily whacked it with his frail, spindly fist. After the drawer slid open, he again took his father's notebook from beneath the marbles, opened it and began to cough and fart and spit up another something. Though, this time, the children were unfazed, taking the terrifying glob in stride, grabbing paper towels and cleaning it up, so that Grampa could get on with the story.

When they finally sat down, the old man leaned back on his stack of pillows, opened the notebook, and closed his eyes, appearing again to have stopped breathing. This time, though, the children calmly waited a moment, and then Henry reached over and jostled Grampa's bony shoulder. Grampa startled upon waking and began *again* to tell them about the earthquake in 1989. They reminded him *again* where he had left off in the story—how Leo and the creatures had disappeared into the giant rock wall near Fresno—and, after Grampa leafed through the notebook to find that part of the story, he looked up and began to tell them about the journey to Nuldoid.

The Tunnel-hole

AFTER THE ROCK'S wall slammed shut behind Warren's Chrysler, Leo and the creatures were suddenly enveloped in darkness. The car shot down a sandy slope that slowed it somewhat, but not enough to keep it from flying out and into a massive round hole, where it bashed into the other side, and then plunged down, down, down, scraping and knocking its way farther into the earth as it fell and fell and fell, all three of its passengers screaming as it hurtled and banged its way into the dark abyss.

It fell for miles.

Leo knew they were going to die when they hit the bottom of whatever it was they were plummeting into and splattered or crashed or shattered into a zillion pieces. In the darkness, he could hear Morton and Kyle screaming wildly, but as his eyes adjusted to the lack of light, he saw that they were not screaming in terror. Like two dogs in an open car window, the creatures' eyes were wide with excitement, their nostrils flared in the wind. He realized that their screams were screams of, well… joy.

Curiously then, Leo saw that the layered wall of the giant tunnel-hole was no longer speeding by them as quickly as it had been. Their fall was slowing. And there was now light. Not much at first, but some. As the car's fall slowed even more, the boy wormed his way up to the passenger's window to look out… and down. He could see that the light was coming from beneath them—a bright spot in the distance, getting closer. He heard wind coming up from the belly of the tunnel-hole, far, far below them as the car slowed even more.

And then they stopped falling altogether.

They had not hit anything. Had not landed on anything. The car appeared to be floating on air, suspended above the endless darkness, apparently held aloft by a fierce wind coming up from the depths below.

Just across from where the car was floating, Leo saw what looked like another sandy beach, though this one jutted out from the wall of the tunnel-hole on a huge precipice. At the top of the beach was an enormous opening where a few odd-looking palm trees bunched to one side.

Morton and Kyle squealed with delight and suddenly flung themselves out the window of the car into the open air, where they began to swim in raucous circles, somersaulting end-over-end, bellowing with laughter and yelping merrily as they bopped about on the howling wind.

Leo was still duct-taped and growing irritated that they seemed to have forgotten all about him as they frolicked girlishly outside of the floating car. He tried yelling to them, *at* them, but could not be heard over the wind. Finally, he leaned to the driver's side of the car and held his head against the car's horn.

Its blare floated out over the roaring wind, and the creatures realized, they could clearly see, that Leo was very annoyed with them.

Though Morton and Kyle were small, and the car was—relative to them—gigantic, they could move it with a simple push of a finger. And, while they had no trouble guiding it to the sandy hill, they had forgotten that the engine was still running. As you might expect, when the car reached the sandy bank of the precipice, it quickly started to climb toward the opening at the top, where it hit the wall and spun a hole in the sand. Kyle and Morton climbed the hill to the car. Morton boosted Kyle through the window so that he could crawl in and turn off the engine.

Leo wiggled to sit up so that he could look at Kyle. "Thanks a lot." This was sarcastic.

"Ach, we wasn't forgettin' ya."

"Fine. Look, you said you'd cut this tape off when we got here."

"Sure yeah to dat." Kyle turned and opened the car door where Morton was waiting. "Ya has dat blade?"

The older creature pulled a folding knife from his pocket and handed it to Kyle. "Yas fixed dat brain der, eh?" Morton asked Kyle, nodding to Leo.

"Sure yeah," said Kyle, taking the knife. "Dat kid believes what we says is true. He don't give we no pains." He unfolded the knife. "We doesn't besides us has no choice. He's hoistin' for we dat Crystal."

Kyle moved across the seat to Leo, and sliced the tape that bound the boy's wrists and arms. As Leo worked his hands free, the creature sliced the tape around his ankles and legs, and soon he was tearing at it himself. Kyle folded the knife as both creatures watched him intently. They were looking for some sign that he might not, after all, be on their side—that his brain might not be "fixed."

"Man, that's a big hole there. So cool." The boy rubbed his wrists where the tape had been and then looked over and saw that the creatures were staring at him. "What?"

"Where is ya?"

"Huh?"

"Is yas for we? Or dat other?"

"Ah, gimme a break, will ya. We gotta get the Crystal to Nuldoid. I know that."

The creatures watched him for another moment before they felt reasonably confident that their efforts to alter his thoughts had been successful.

"This place is wild," Leo said as he grabbed the door handle, flung it open and climbed out of the car. He walked up to the large opening as the creatures quickly hopped from the driver's side and scuttled along the sand behind him. "So, how much farther?" he asked, looking through the opening and down the path that led away from the tunnel-hole.

"Ah, we doesn't has much far now."

"Sure yeah to dat. A hop, jump and a skip we does."

The creatures were lying, of course. After all, the tunnel-hole they had just fallen through had not taken them all that far, that is, in the big scheme of things. Nor did the creatures mention the many perils, possible and probable, that they'd face along the way. Not that it would have mattered to Leo as he seemed quite enthusiastic about—seemed to see great purpose in—making this journey with the Crystal. Whether he felt this way because they had used their peculiar powers to change something in his brain, or because he was convinced that they were doing a "good thing," is hard to say. But it was not difficult to see that he was more than willing to help them in their quest.

() () ()

This part of the story did not sit well with Francie. In fact, Joe and Henry had to shush her several times when she mumbled her increasing displeasure with Morton and Kyle. She was fit to be tied that these two creatures would do something so devious to Leo—whatever it was they did—not to mention carting off the Crystal that fueled the rotation of the earth!

Oh, she was mad.

And it didn't help matters when Henry told her that it was just a story, that it wasn't real, because that got Grampa's goat, who angrily reminded Henry—whom he called Joe—that the story was as real as any story ever told!

The Oidenoids

HE OPENING AT the top of the sandy precipice was large enough for the Chrysler to be driven through. So, after they pushed it back from the wall of the tunnel-hole and climbed in, Leo drove the car through it. On the other side, a narrow dirt road sloped down and away amidst thick vegetation which scraped along the side of the car. The boy drove slowly since he was so unsure of where he was going, and he was not so experienced a driver. In fact, twice along the way, the creatures complained that he was driving like "a Delnoid," which Leo did not understand, but took to mean that he was not driving fast enough. "Ach, put somma dat pedal inna metal." But there was hardly any room on either side of the car between the bushes and trees and the occasional jutting rocks. So, he did his best to ignore their badgering and rude comments.

There was enough light so that he did not have to turn on the headlights, but there seemed to be no source to the light. They were underground with no open sky above them, yet it felt to Leo as though they were beneath a sunny sky.

The road grew rougher, bumpier, as the car passed into a dell surrounded by brush and odd-looking trees with fruit that Leo had never seen before. The fruit glowed amber as they approached, then faded as they passed. When Leo asked about the fruit, he was told that it was not "fruit" at all, but what the creatures called "froote," which was pronounced "fruit." It was their source of food—and most everything else—beneath the Crust.

They had not been driving long when they came upon a rusted sign beside the path that had very nearly been overtaken by the vines of a plant.

HALT!
TO YA is DANGER!

ENTERIN'
Region a Neither Norr!

YAS Maybe MIGHT EMERGE
AGAIN dat OTHER SIDE!
YAS Maybe MIGHT NOT!

When Leo asked what the sign meant, Kyle explained that it was an old one from the "Doiden Frobble Dynasty," and the danger it referred to had long since been eliminated. He told the boy that the Region of Neither Norr was completely safe, that it was a short distance from one side to the other, and that there was nothing whatsoever to worry about.

Which was, as you've probably guessed, not true.

When they had passed the sign, the road suddenly narrowed between large rock formations of granite. The Chrysler clearly would not be able to pass. They would have to leave the car behind and, from hereon, carry the Crystal themselves—which meant that Leo would have to carry it, since the two creatures together could barely lift it. And, though he wasn't really the type of kid that jumped in and helped out, he seemed only too happy now to do exactly that.

Leo opened the car's trunk to get the Crystal, while Kyle took out the brass compass and studied it. "Says a mile afore dat elevator."

"Nah, it doesn't take no mile."

"Yas is with rotted brains. Says der a mile!"

"Ach, ya doesn't know how it reads! Gimme here!"

"Nah to dat, ya drobbs horkel!" Kyle said, holding the compass away from his partner.

"Ya doesn't calls me a drobbs horkel! Gimme dat compass."

"Ya gets dat compass when it's dat cold day in Oyden Dibble."

"Why, ya dirty droib!"

And, once again, they grabbed each other's throats and furiously tried to kick each other. But just as the younger of the two managed to connect with the older one's shin, a voice boomed out from above them.

"Ahoy ders to yas!" Morton and Kyle froze, still with each other's throat in their hands. When they looked up, they saw several small creatures—the same type as themselves—peering at them from the ledge above. The two quickly released their grips and saw now that there were perhaps five or six of the other creatures. They were neatly dressed—compared to Morton and Kyle anyway. One wore a cowboy hat, another a leather flying cap with goggles. "Holds der," the leader shouted down to them. "Down to yas we climbs our ways."

The creatures then disappeared to scale down the backside of the rocks. Kyle turned to his partner. "Could be is we trouble, huh?"

In a moment, the creatures emerged from some shrubbery at the side of the rocks. Morton and Kyle could see now there were seven of them, including two women. The men were clean-shaven, except for the leader, who had long brown hair pulled back into a ponytail, and a bushy beard beneath thick black-framed glasses. A couple wore hardhats, and one a football helmet. "You is here for why, friend?" the leader of the group asked.

"Ah, we has official business on our ways through Neither Norr."

"Official business says yas, eh?" one of the smaller creatures in a hardhat said. "So, ya has beer, does ya?"

"Nah to dat," Kyle said. "Was smashed up in days gone 'way."

"Ach!" said the leader. "There doesn't no problem. We has beer, so yas helps yourself for dat journey."

The female added, "We has dem cheesey chips, too, heh."

Kyle and Morton would have loved to drink beer and eat cheesey chips—it was something they were good at—but it did not come to pass. The other creatures heard a grunt, and watched as Leo appeared from behind the car with a huge blanket-wrapped object slung over his shoulder. There was absolute pandemonium amongst the other creatures as they screamed, bumped into each other, clung to each other, some scampering and scrambling for the cover of the nearby shrubbery.

When Morton and Kyle realized they were reacting to Leo, they chortled knowingly. "Ach," Kyle said, "is a toid dat doesn't hurts nobody!"

After a moment, the other creatures began to cautiously reemerge. "Is a toid, eh?" the leader of the others asked, keeping a wary eye on the towering youth.

"Sure yeah. A fida-boned Crustoid," Morton said with an air of authority as the other creatures gasped, a few from within the bushes. "Ya doesn't never seen one, huh?"

"Nah to dat," one of them said. "But how dids ya—" He was about to ask how it was they came to have in their company a Crustoid, when the blanket that was covering the Crystal slipped down and a glint of light bounced off its protruding point.

"Holy Lloyd an' Floyd," one of the other creatures muttered as she drew back in astonishment. "Is dat Crystal der."

Suddenly the others dropped to their knees and spit on the ground.

"Sure yeah to dat," Morton said as he puffed out his chest importantly, for amongst these creatures it was a great honor to be in the presence of the Crystal. "We takes dat Crystal to Nuldoid," Morton said, not noticing that Kyle was glaring savagely at him, trying quietly to convey that his partner stop offering information. "An' we takes it not in no slow boat to pronto neither."

The leader of the others suddenly looked much more serious. "Ya takes it from dat Crust, did ya?"

"Nah!" Kyle suddenly blurted. "Nah to dat, nah!" He had positioned himself between Morton and the others. "Isn't not dat genuine real Crystal! Nah-hah, we fools ya! Here's one only for looks. We brings here dat phony fake one to dat Museum a Nuldoid, is all. Yup, is hogus bogus, as fake as a three-grumplett wad."

Though Leo did not understand all that was being said, he knew that something was wrong, could tell that Kyle's voice was strained, that the little Nuldoid was nervous about revealing what they were up to.

The leader of the others narrowed his gaze and stepped closer to Kyle. "We thinks ya doesn't takes dat Crystal no more any further." There was an ominous tone in his voice. "We thinks it be takes back to dat Crust. Dat's as is supposed to be."

Morton leaned slightly to his partner and whispered, "Oidenoids." Kyle nodded but held his stare with the leader.

"Sure yeah to dat, Oidenoids we is!" the leader declared, having heard Morton's whisper. He pushed his thick glasses back up the ridge of his nose. "An' as Lloyd is our wish list, we stops ya from your evil! We takes ya from dat Crystal! 'Cause dat Crystal we takes!" And, from a sheath at his side, he withdrew a sword and pointed the tip at Kyle's chest. "So ya hands it over to we, so as we doesn't has to cut yas inna pieces!"

Kyle, though, stood firmly, his voice surprisingly steady, his gaze fixed, his eyes aware of everything. "Ya doesn't takes dat Crystal from we," he said, knowing his words might push the blade into his heart. "Ya tries..." he added, focused now only on the eyes of their leader, "...an' ya dies where ya is."

The leader smirked and looked away to the others only momentarily, but in that instant, night became day, up became down, as Kyle drew a wire from his side that produced at its end a weighted blade. Suddenly it was airborne and swinging wildly over his head, its razor edge flashing, as Morton did the same. The others, brandishing more weapons now, rushed at them, metal meeting metal, metal meeting flesh, the deadly wire blades spinning too fast to be seen.

Leo stumbled and fell back with the Crystal, surprised, stunned by the violence around him that became vicious—and then bloody. Though the blood being spilled was green—making it look more like a food fight with spinach smoothies than a life-and-death battle—it was still unnerving.

"**W**ELL, I HOPE those two got it, but good!" Francie said to her grandfather, referring to Morton and Kyle. "I hope they got sliced up in little pieces and put right in the garbage!"

"So, what happened, Grampa?" This was Joe. "Did these new guys stop the Nuldoids?"

Henry now. "Yeah, did those other creatures get the Crystal and bring it back to San Francisco? They must have, right?"

But Grampa did not answer because he had fallen asleep and was snoring peacefully.

"Go ahead, Henry. Wake him up," Francie said as she moved to get a better look at Grampa's face, and then grimaced when she found herself inches from the bold gray tufts of hair protruding from his nose. Henry turned to his younger brother, who nodded that he agreed with Francie, that Grampa needed to be awakened. So, Henry reached out and gently pushed his grandfather's shoulder. Nothing. No effect whatsoever. He waited a moment and then shook the old man, but still Grampa would not rouse and, in fact, began to snore even more loudly. Henry jostled Grampa's shoulders now, so much that he was afraid he might loosen the old man's teeth or his hearing aid or his new hip or his artificial heart or something they didn't even know about.

That didn't work either.

Francie, angry that he would fall asleep at such a crucial point, stepped over and shouted, "Grampa! Wake up!"

His eyes fluttered a moment and then popped open, the sound of his granddaughter's shrill voice having cut into his sleeping brain like a steak knife. When he'd regained his senses, he demanded to know how the children got into his room and what they were doing there.

"Grampa," Joe said, "you were telling us the story, remember? The story of the little people."

"Huh? Oh, right, right. The story." He paused momentarily to dig something disgusting out of his nose, for which Henry handed him a tissue. "Ah, good, Joe."

Henry nodded. "Yeah."

"Well, see, there was an earthquake in San Francisco, the very year before I was born, and if you don't believe me, you can look it up! Go ahead!"

"Grampa," Henry interrupted, "we know all that. Leo and the creatures were inside the earth, and they were fighting with those other creatures over the Crystal. Remember?"

"Yeah, Grampa." This was Francie. "What happened? Did the other creatures get the Crystal and take it back to San Francisco?"

"Ach," Grampa said, leaning back, thinking. "The creatures…" He noticed then his father's notebook that had dropped down between the pillows. He picked it up and found his place, but not before leaning to one side and grimacing fiercely, only to become disappointed when he realized he could not produce any gas. "Bah!" he said, and then began again to tell the story. But he didn't say right away what had happened to Morton and Kyle and Leo. Instead, he skipped to another entry in the notebook and told the children about Warren and Lily, who were still up near Fresno, outside the rock that had slammed shut in front of them.

The Big Rock Wall

WARREN WAS ANGRY after he saw his car disappear into the rock wall. He even kicked it with the very same foot he had used when he kicked the light pole outside of Lily's warehouse. Of course, as soon as he did, he remembered that his toe was still sore, possibly broken, and he regretted it terribly.

He and Lily knew that they had few options except to get help from someone else. But who? The police? The fire department? The FBI? They dreaded having to explain what they knew about the Crystal, about the creatures—and, besides, they were sure no one would believe them. Even still, they had to get help, *had to*, and quickly, because the consequences to all of Earth's inhabitants would be disastrous.

They climbed back into Lily's rickety pickup and sat gloomily for a moment, weighing their dismal options. Dust had settled on the dashboard and the steering wheel. Then, suddenly, Lily brightened and looked at Warren. "What's that word?"

"What word?"

"That word. Those words. The ones they used? At the park. Remember? 'Hip hop deltoid'?"

"Hib nobb del noid," he said and then his eyes lit up. "Yes! Hib nobb del noid!"

They ran back to the wall, and Lily yelled, "Hib nobb del noid!"

Nothing.

She yelled it again.

Still nothing.

Warren yelled it.

Nothing.

"Okay, I've got an idea," she said, grabbing his arm and pulling him back towards the truck. "We have to be moving toward it. They were moving toward it."

"Oh, I don't know about that."

"Come on, come on! We have to try!" she said when they were perhaps thirty feet from the wall. "Okay, here, take my hand..." He did. "Now, run! Run!"

And as they ran toward the wall, Lily shouted, "Hib nobb del noid!" just before they both smacked into the wall. *Wham!*

"Oooof!"

The rock did not budge. Lily hit her head. Warren had the wind knocked out of him. He held his stomach and bent over. His voice was a squeaky mouse. "Great... idea."

"Shut up."

"Look, it's not gonna... not gonna open," he said as he straightened up and regained his composure. "They're gone. We won't catch 'em. We'll never catch 'em... all because of this stupid rock!" And even though his foot—his big toe specifically—still hurt like the dickens, he used it to kick the "stupid rock," and, of course, felt excruciating pain fly up his leg. "Ahhhh!"

But here's the thing: After he kicked it, there was a blast of lightning across the face of the giant wall, where it cracked and split open with a deafening roar and a *wooosh!* And there they stood. In front of a gaping black void between two halves of a massive solid rock wall. The wall did not slam shut either, as they'd seen it do when Warren's car shot through it. It stayed open.

They were breathless at the sight of the enormous cavity that somehow looked as though it were waiting for something, like it was breathing, its breath falling down from above in the form of steam and dust. Cautiously, Warren leaned forward to have a closer look. "Don't!" Lily whispered. "It'll close."

They didn't know what exactly to do next.

"Do you trust me?" she finally whispered without looking at him.

"No."

"Fine," she said, and shoved him into the opening, leaping in behind him, as the walls squawked and slammed shut with blazing speed and a thundering crash. In the darkness beyond, they tumbled down the hill, rolling end-over-end, before falling out into the open air of the tunnel-hole and down into the endless, bottomless chasm. Down, down they dropped, certain, like Leo before them, that they were falling to their deaths.

And—like Leo and the creatures—after a while, after they fell and fell, they began to see light. It was a pinhole at first, many miles away, but, as they continued down, it grew larger. Soon they realized they were no longer falling at the same rate of speed, that they were slowing down because of an opposing wind, the force of it coming up from beneath them with tremendous force, until finally, like Warren's car, they stopped falling altogether and were floating on air. And as they bobbed about, they saw that they were across from a sandy precipice that jutted from the wall of the tunnel-hole.

Lily put her arms out and ducked her head to roll in the air, laughing as she did. Warren, though, was not so sure they were yet safe, fearing the wind might stop at any moment. When he realized that he could "swim," he grabbed her arm and towed her to the sand, where they crawled up the slope and lay down, exhausted. Warren, looked up at the dark hole above them, and, after a moment, quietly said, "I still don't trust you."

Lily began again to laugh.

Joining Forces

WHEN THEY CLIMBED the rest of the way up the sandy hill and ventured into the opening at the top, they found the small dirt road where Leo and the creatures had driven the car. As they followed it, they saw the Chrysler's tire tracks and then the trees with strange froote that glowed amber.

Lily knew they were in a hurry, but her curiosity got the better of her and she stopped at a tree to pick one of the glowing frootes. Its amber hue quickly faded to a dull brown as soon as she did. The froote was about the size of an orange, its skin fuzzy like a peach, and a small curled tail protruded from its bottom. Warren watched as Lily dug her fingernails into the rind and tore it open. A light steam rolled out and curled in front of her. She brought the opened froote to her nose, sniffed it, and looked puzzled.

"What?"

"It smells like…" She thought another moment and then bit into it.

"What are you doing? It could be poison!"

She chewed it, chewed it, thought about it, then shook her head. "Ham."

"Ham?"

She took another bite and nodded. "Ham."

Warren saw a smaller froote on the tree next to them and plucked it from its branch. It too lost its amber glow, but this one faded to a dull white. He tore it in half and saw a plume of steam curl out. He looked curiously at what was inside, smelled it, looked up and smiled at Lily. "Scrambled egg."

They stepped back onto the road and continued on for another mile or so, when, finally, they came upon Warren's Chrysler, its trunk still open. Cautiously, Warren walked around it to look at the narrow passage between the rocks. He turned back to Lily. "So, I guess they went this way."

But Lily put her finger to her lips to quiet him. She was listening for something.

"What is it?"

"Shhh…" She tilted her head, looked to her left.

Then they both heard it.

A moan.

It was coming from behind the bushes beside the path. Lily brushed past the shrubs and moved aside some low bracken to find one of the creatures that had confronted Morton and Kyle. He was lying on the ground, holding the side of his head, his shirt sliced near his left shoulder, where a splotch of dark green blood had soaked through and had started to dry. Warren quickly moved to his side.

"Ya doesn't gonna eat us, is ya?" the creature asked.

"What? No." Warren pulled his torn shirt back and pinched the skin around the wound to stop the new bleeding.

"What's for dat others?"

"Others?" Warren asked.

"Others is here. Others is kaput?"

At the side of a large tree, Lily found a female who had been hiding. Her name was Beatrice. She told Lily that there had been seven creatures in all. Four had been killed. On the other side of the path, Lily bent back a thicket of underwood and found the third survivor. He was smaller than the others, though his nose was the largest.

Beatrice explained to Lily and Warren that the creature's name was Roggo. The one with the torn shirt was Hammet—he had been their leader.

Hammet rubbed his arm, cautiously sizing up the humans. "You also is from dat Crust?"

Warren nodded as he helped the little man to his feet. "We're from San Francisco."

"Doesn't never heards of it," Hammet said. "But we bets it lovely."

"I'm really sorry to have to tell you this," Warren said, "but the others, your friends… they didn't make it."

"Didn't dey makes what?" Hammet asked.

"Well, uh… they're gone. I'm sorry."

"Where is they gone to?"

"No, see… they're dead. There's just you and the woman. And the little one. I'm really sorry."

Hammet scratched his head, looking on the ground for something. "Ach, dat's fooey for dat. Where's we glasses? Can't we gonna lose dem glasses. Whew-hew, is blind as a hat."

"Okay, you heard me, right? I said your friends are dead."

107

"Sure yeah, isn't nuthin' wrong with Hammet's ear bones," he said as he spotted his glasses beneath a splay of fronds. "Ah-hah! Der dey!" He picked them up and put them on as Beatrice approached.

"Them Nuldoids, they takes we beer, for sure," she said.

"Well, furk dobble." Hammet immediately caught himself—embarrassed at having let slip a profanity—and added, "Uh, but, dat Lloyd works in mechanical ways."

"Ya was right as weather, Hammet. Shoulda we hided dat beer from dem."

He put his hand on her shoulder. "Ya doesn't blames yourself, Bea. We wasn't knowin' how evil dem was. Whew-hew, dem was evil, like a river a spit."

"Who was it? Who did this to you?" Warren asked.

"Two a dem an' dat big Crustoid is like you is."

"Two of them? Morton and Kyle?"

Hammet shrugged. "They doesn't say whose names is what."

"Right, but they were, uh, little guys like you, with three fingers?"

Hammet nodded. "Was Nuldoids, sure as yeah."

"Nuldoids? So, what *are* Nuldoids?"

Hammet hesitated before he answered, unsure if Warren was very bright. *"We…* is Nuldoids."

"Yes, right, but… what are *you?*"

Hammet looked even more confused. "Nuldoids."

"No! Okay… where do you, where do Nuldoids come from?"

Hammet exchanged a look with Beatrice, then turned back to Warren and very carefully said, "Nuuuldoid." He was trying in earnest be polite, given the human's obvious limitations.

"Okay. How 'bout this: *Where* is Nuldoid?"

"Oh. Is center-middle a Hoidenall. Other side a Neither Norr."

"Hoidenall?" Warren was flabbergasted. "Earth? It's at the center of the earth?"

The two little creatures looked at each other—confused by Warren's strange name for their planet—and turned back to him. "Center-middle a *Hoiden-all!*"

"Right, yes, I get it." Warren stopped to think, deciding to try another tack. "Okay… why did those other Nuldoids do this to you? Why did they hurt you like this… I mean, if you're all Nuldoids?"

"Oh, they isn't *good* Nuldoids. We tries to stop 'em wit dat Crystal. Takes it dey way far from dat Crust. Isn't not no good for nobody. Even so says Lloyd dat."

Warren was at least heartened to learn that not all Nuldoids—however many there were—wanted to take the Crystal away from where it belonged. He was heartened as well to realize that these creatures were allies.

Lily was busy helping the other smaller creature, Roggo, while Warren was learning all of this from Hammet and Beatrice. The community of Nuldoid, they explained, was once a place where kind and decent creatures lived in harmony and peace. It was, however, taken over, many years earlier, by a group of Nuldoids who were not so pleasant, not at all pure of heart, who were, in fact, evil. These loathsome creatures argued and bickered and drove out all of those who were good and kind and who truly believed in the word of Lloyd (the founder of Nuldoid, author of *The Book of Nuldoid).* Since then, these banished creatures, called "Oidenoids"—like Hammet, Beatrice and Roggo—have roamed the Region of Neither Norr in small bands looking for food and beer, while reading to each other passages from *The Book of Nuldoid.*

Warren and Lily were warmed and encouraged by the way the Oidenoids treated them. And by the way they treated each other. They showed great respect for one another—in stark contrast to the Nuldoids, Morton and Kyle, with their constant arguing and nitpicking and squabbling.

The humans, of course, wanted to hear much more, and the Oidenoids were quite agreeable to telling them more, but time was of the essence if they hoped to catch up with the Crystal. As they learned from Hammet, if they did not do so *before* the Nuldoids and the boy reached Nuldoid, all would be lost—since the Oidenoids were forbidden from entering Nuldoid. Once the Crystal was inside the gates of Nuldoid, Warren and Lily would probably never see the boy again, as Hammet ominously pointed out, since they, the Nuldoids, would no longer "has a need for dat kid." Adding, "Dey chucks 'im inna hooey for kaput!"

Warren vowed, then and there—perhaps a little too dramatically with the jabbing of his finger in the air—that he and Lily would find Leo and the Crystal *before* they reached the outskirts of Nuldoid, "come hell or high water!" They were going to stop the evil Nuldoids, or die trying!

Right after he made this bold declaration, however, he had to admit that he and Lily could not do it alone, and that they needed the Oidenoids' help. The Oidenoids, of course, were only too happy to help foil the Nuldoids.

It was agreed they would take the humans into the Region of Neither Norr to capture the Crystal and thwart the Nuldoids. And the Oidenoids even offered to help the humans return the Crystal to San Francisco (which, if one were the suspicious type, might seem a little above and beyond the call).

At least now there was a plan. Now there was hope.

The Sloidelobb in the Elevator

THE OIDENOIDS WERE fortunate enough to find a discarded beer froote, with a puddle of beer still in it—left behind by the Nuldoids. They sprinkled some of it over their dead companions, which was an important ritual. After doing so, they touched their lips, their bellies and the fly of their trousers, the same way Morton and Kyle did in the basement of Warren's house.* When the bodies were buried, Hammet stood on a flat-topped boulder and addressed the others with a prayer:

> To Lloyd dey veers
> 'Cause dead dey is.
> 'Cause dead dey is,
> We gives 'em beer.

---

* The true meaning of this ritual was to acknowledge the Drinking of the Beer, the Filling of the Belly and the Peeing of it Out.

An' goes dey off
In sprinkled stout,
Where Elders pick
dat Roundabout.

An' see dey we,
When dead is done.
When dead is done
Here dey be.

He then listed the many grievances against the dead, as well as their outstanding debts—detailing extensively each—adding afterward that he would not collect or complain again about either. It was a very odd way to pay tribute to a dead colleague or loved one, but not surprising, given how peculiar these creatures were about death.

As they picked up what few belongings they had and set out on the path toward Neither Norr, Beatrice—the chubbiest of the three and clearly the chattiest—explained to Warren and Lily that it was customary down in Nuldoid to only *complain* about the dead, especially during the funeral. But, she said, Oidenoids saw the death of a friend or loved one differently. Oidenoids, she explained, used the opportunity to complain and then *forgive* the dead for their faults and offenses, their infractions, their annoying habits, their mistakes, their wrongheaded viewpoints, their foibles and their debts. And they did so by listing all of them in great and specific detail.

For the next few hours they made good time, despite that Roggo was still a little shaky from being hit on the head, and that he was shorter than the other two, having to practically run to keep up. Lily, in fact, stopped twice to pick him up and carry him on her back.

As they walked, the humans craned their necks like owls at every peculiar sight. The rock ceiling of the cavernous passage domed high above them as they passed along the dirt road. There were pockets in the walls that cradled small cityscapes of stalagmites, each collecting wind from beneath it and whistling a different pitch, all of them together sounding like a herd of whales.

Later, they crossed a small arched footbridge that traversed a creek bed, where the sound of trickling water babbled up as though from a Japanese garden. But there was no water—only hundreds of small beetle-like creatures, each silver-blue. They were called Wett Woggs and, though the Oidenoids had no idea why they did it, the little bugs spent their days and nights imitating the sound of water. They filled the creek bed, standing on their oversized hind feet, each wobbling "downstream," falling, rolling, bumping into each other, tumbling along, getting up, tumbling again, like hundreds of tiny Charlie Chaplins. They were making a lot of noise until Beatrice mentioned that they were quite tasty once "ya gets dat shell off an' fries 'em up some." The Wett Woggs suddenly became mute, and stood stock-still until the group had passed.

When they came upon a cluster of trees that bore a great deal of froote—all of it glowing amber as they approached—Hammet shouted, "Who's wantin' eats?"

"Nah for we," Roggo said from Lily's back. "We doesn't has dat belly growl."

"Is foods sound good to we," said Beatrice. "But if ders no hungry on ya, we doesn't needs ta eats."

"Nah to dat," said Hammet to Beatrice. "If ders dat hungry for eats, we can stoppin' easy."

"We doesn't has to stops for we," Beatrice countered. "Only we stops if Hammet finds ya hunger."

"Nah," Hammet replied. "Is hungry only some, but we doesn't has needs to stop."

"Stop is good wit we if others has dat belly growl," Roggo chimed in.

The discussion went on like this even after they'd passed the trees and the froote had begun to fade. Finally, Warren suggested that he and Lily could help them pick some of it, if they wanted. At that, the Oidenoids turned back and scampered up the side of the path to the trees, thrilled to have someone as tall as the humans to help pick the froote.

The humans were amazed to find that some of the froote bore chocolate muffins, while some opened up to a variety of yogurts. Froote, they were learning, provided many things for these creatures including, of course—and most importantly—beer. There was, however, no beer froote on the trees in the cluster, and the Oidenoids were quite disappointed. They had to settle instead for plucking a few cola frootes, which were hardly the same.

They decided to eat while they walked, in order to save time. As they did, Beatrice jabbered on about other froote in Neither Norr that was full of clam chowder, chili, beef and chicken meat, (the chicken froote distinguishable by a small beak on the side of the rind. But the froote that grew in the outer regions of Neither Norr (near the Crust), she explained, was richer-tasting, fuller and fresher than the froote that grew close to Nuldoid. That was because Nuldoid was evil now, and the closer the trees were to Nuldoid's evil, the less flavor they provided. She said that this would change when good was brought back to Nuldoid, when the Oidenoids returned to their home, as Lloyd said would happen.

Unfortunately, the rich froote of Neither Norr—this was still Beatrice prattling—drew many undesirable elements from

Nuldoid, the worst of which were Harvesters. Harvesters were Nuldoids who roamed the untamed areas of Neither Norr, collecting exotic froote to bring back to Nuldoid at a sizable profit. They were greatly feared, and for good reason: They were bloodthirsty marauders who—when they were not collecting froote in their battered shopping carts—enjoyed, for sport, slaughtering Oidenoids, skinning them and then trading and collecting their skins.

Before long, the group came across a deep opening in a jagged wall of dark granite. The Oidenoids led Warren and Lily into the opening, where there were two closed steel doors behind a rusted metal scissor gate. On either side of the gate, bleak-looking pier lamps spilled dim light along the rough edges of the rock and down onto a rusted push-button beneath a sign that said "DOWN TA GO."

When Lily asked what it was, both Beatrice and Hammet started to explain at the same time. They stopped when they realized they were talking over each other, each then waiting for the other to begin again, and then both starting to talk when the other had not. Again they stopped to let the other speak.

"Ya goes on," Hammet said.

"Nah to dat." This was Beatrice. "Ya does the spoken."

"Nah, ya goes with talking."

"Ach, you can does it."

Finally Roggo stepped past them and jumped up to punch the button on the wall beneath the light. A distant bell rang somewhere behind the steel doors and, a moment later, a very disagreeable voice grumbled to life from within. "Whah, kah, hah! Scats, ya does! Scat is to ya, ya stinkin' droibs!"

Hammet leaned over and yelled into the slight crack between the doors. "We doesn't goes 'way. No how, buster! Needs we to be in dat elevator der!"

"Ach to dat," said the voice. "Ya goes 'way! Is sleepin' here!"

Roggo looked to the other creatures and rolled his eyes. "Sloidelobbs," he said, while Beatrice and Hammet shook their heads knowingly.

Lily leaned to Beatrice and asked quietly, "What's a Sloidelobb?"

"Eh, Sloidelobbs," she said. "Hibernators is they. An' eats they does. Eats an' sleeps. Dey is ta works all dat naggy machines."

Throughout Neither Norr, these creatures, Sloidelobbs, held the most menial of jobs, operated the most mundane of machinery, in the most boring of conditions, because the work—or lack of work—afforded them extended periods of peace and inactivity so that they could sleep. And sleep and sleep. Which might lead one to assume they were fairly mellow or even somewhat pleasant in nature, but that was not at all the case. Not at all. They were very *un*pleasant, always grumpy (when they weren't asleep—though some would argue, even then), the type of creature you really wouldn't want to spend much time with.

The steel doors behind the metal scissor gate squawked open with the sound of ancient metal being drawn against itself. When the doors had fully opened, a foul odor wafted out from the inner chamber like thick, rancid soup. Warren and Lily were, at first, taken aback, and then cautiously leaned in to peer through the diamond-shaped holes of the scissor gate so they could have a look at the Sloidelobb. He was most peculiar-looking. Like the Oidenoids, he was not quite two feet tall, but here's the thing: He was *enormously* overweight—enormously meaning, in this case, he weighed perhaps 300 pounds. *Two feet tall, 300 pounds!* Rolls of blubber flowed out and over an invisible beltline onto the floor of the elevator, or what *would have been* the floor of the elevator if it had not been covered with discarded froote rinds and all sorts of other trash. In fact, he was so wide, so blubberous, that it seemed doubtful he could even fit between the elevator's opened doors. He was sweating profusely—which is what Sloidelobbs did a lot of, besides sleeping—as he stood next to the controls, his pudgy three fingers anxiously gripping the rusted crank that opened and closed the elevator door.

"Ach!" the little man said through gelatinous cheeks. "Two times two is too many for Hoyt. An' toids ta boot! Too many of ya is today. Hoyt has sleep to does. Now skedaddle yas!"

"We're very sorry to bother you," Lily said, leaning on the scissor gate, "but we're trying to find some people—well, not 'people' exactly… okay, *one* person and two little, uh… creatures like yourself… sort of. And we have to stop them from taking the—"

"Hoyt!" Hammet blurted when he realized Lily might be saying too much. "Hoyt! We has needs as to reach Nuldoid afore dat ceremony at dat Wheel. Great big hurry we is!"

"Under orders we is of Emperor Ed," added little Roggo just as quickly.

"Orders of Ed, says yas to Hoyt? Orders of Ed, ya says?" The huge creature narrowed his gaze on Beatrice. "An' yas to Hoyt says what ya does for Emperor Ed, eh?"

Beatrice was suddenly paralyzed with fear. "For Ed?" She glanced at Hammet. He nodded gently for her to continue. She hated lying, but knew it had to be done, swallowed and looked back at the Sloidelobb. "For dat Emperor, we has the tailorin' of clothes as for dat ceremony."

"Sure yeah to dat," Hammet added. "Tailors of Ed! Tailors we does for Ed, our lowest citizen!"

"*Tailors* says ya to Hoyt? Tailors indeed, Hoyt says back. So, yas tells Hoyt why is yas bring dem toids along? Hmmm?" At this, Hoyt raised an eyebrow and pursed his lips to one side, as

117

though his line of questioning would be too much for them to bear.

"Toids..." Hammet said, using the derogatory term for Crustoids, "toids is goin' so as to...uh... uh..."

"Toids," Roggo blurted, "is for to lift up dat Emperor! So as dat Ed can be measured up afore dat ceremony at dat Wheel! Sure as a dirty noid* stinks, his lowness, Ed, needs a hoist, eh?"

As lies go, it wasn't a great one, but Hoyt was considering it very seriously, rubbing the underside of his enormous chin before deciding that it was a reasonable explanation. "Sure yeah to dat," he said. "Now, ya shows Hoyt dat paperwork, an' goes yas to Neither Norr."

"Paperwork?" Hammet asked. "We doesn't never needs paperwork afore."

"Paperwork ya has to has," Hoyt said. "Season a dat Crystal, an' ya doesn't has paperwork?"

"We's lost it," Roggo offered. "Stolen was it."

"Hah!" shouted the Sloidelobb, his demeanor suddenly resolute and defiant. "Oidenoids ya is! Oidenoids! After dat Crystal ta stops it ya is! And hah to ya! Ya rides dat elevator on a cold day in Oyden Dibble, ya dirty drobbs horkels! Ya stinkin' mubb stubbles! Ya rotten droibs!—"

Warren, though, had noticed something about the elevator's scissor gate. Something rather important. And as the Sloidelobb was spitting out this litany of obscenities, Warren stepped closer. Then, just as the disagreeable creature called them all "rotten droibs"—and just before he was about to call them "bick stibbles"

---

* It was unusual to hear an Oidenoid use the word "noid," the derogatory term for a Nuldoid, but he was clearly trying to present himself as one of those disagreeable Nuldoids—who frequently use derogatory terms, even about themselves.

(an extreme obscenity amongst these creatures)—Warren put his hand on the metal scissor gate and jerked it open!

Everyone was shocked, of course, but none more so than the poor Sloidelobb, who was, it's safe to say, downright dumbstruck, stupefied and in shock, terror-stricken, beside himself with rage. "Locked was dat lock! Locked was it!"

"Apparently it wasn't," Warren said, now leaning into the elevator and towering over the blubbering creature who had shrunk back into the corner—as best he could—his eyes bulging and one plump hand covering his open mouth.

"Morton!" the creature yelled. "Dat drobbs horkel, Morton! We tells Morton he's ta locks it! But dat one is a shorb scod for sure! Ach!"

"So, they were here? Morton and Kyle? And Leo? And the Crystal?" Lily asked.

The Sloidelobb folded his huge flabby arms with great effort, refusing to say anything further.

"Well," said Warren, "you're taking us where you took them!"

"Nah to dat! Is a flat day in Hoidles! Hoyt knows what dem Oidenoids is up to. Stinkin' Oidenoids, to dat Crystal dey wants to stop on account—oweeee!" Hoyt suddenly clutched his massive side in pain, and then looked at Hammet, who was starring intently at him. "Hoyt's innards ya pains! Ya pains dem innards!" The rotund creature was concentrating now very hard while he glared at Hammet.

"Ow!" Hammet said, grabbing his ear. "Ach! Ya pains dat ear, ya bick stibble!"

"Okay, all right, stop it!" Lily demanded. "We're taking the elevator." She bent down and stepped through the doors into the chamber with the Sloidelobb. "Just get out of the elevator, Hoyt."

At that, all of the creatures, even Hoyt, laughed—it was a naïve thing to say on Lily's part. Sloidelobbs, Beatrice explained, can only walk when they are young, *before* they have perfected their eating and hibernating skills. Some, such as Hoyt, are given elevator jobs in their adolescence, while they can still be moved into and out of doorways.

As it was, Hoyt said he would not be moved and he would not operate the elevator for them. And they—the Oidenoids and humans—would never be able to run it themselves because they were not licensed to operate an elevator in the Region of Neither Norr and, more importantly, they had no formal technical training in the official operation of Neither Norr elevators. Lily looked over at the control panel and saw two buttons beside the crank: one that said "UP" and another that said "DOWN."

"That's okay," she offered, "I think we can figure it out."

"No, no, no, you doesn't do it!" Hoyt was furious. "Ya gets out! Out! Out yas pronto from Hoyt's elevator!" He was so frustrated that he even stomped his feet, or rather *tried* to stomp his feet, and he started to scream because the whole situation had become much too much for him. The scream of a Sloidelobb, by the way, is even more high-pitched than that of a regular Nuldoid and can be extremely painful to the human ear, so Lily and Warren had to cover theirs.

What happened next is difficult to describe, and it's certainly not for the faint of heart. Because Sloidelobbs lead such sedentary lives, they are not at all accustomed to the sort of intense emotion that Hoyt was experiencing. In fact, he had reached his absolute limit, and so his head suddenly, and most grotesquely, exploded.

Oh, it was horrifically hideous. Stinky, sloppy, gooey pieces of brain and an eyeball, an ear, fragments of his big skull spewed in all directions and all over Warren and Lily and even the little Oidenoids, who were still standing outside of the elevator. Again, you'd think it wouldn't be so revolting and disgusting since everything was such a cheerful and vibrant shade of green, but it was revolting and disgusting to an extreme!

A moment later, after everyone had recovered from the shock and began picking pieces of Hoyt off themselves, Roggo mentioned to Beatrice that he'd heard of Sloidelobbs doing this sort of thing, but he'd never seen it happen.

After they'd rolled and squeezed and pulled and pushed Hoyt's headless body out of the elevator, and after they tossed a good deal of the trash out that Hoyt had accumulated, everyone piled in and Lily pushed the button marked "DOWN."

The Crust

THOUGH THERE WASN'T any way for Warren or Lily to know it, things back on the Crust were becoming very peculiar indeed.

When government officials in the United States first learned of the earth's slowing rotation, they became quite concerned about the public's reaction, fearing that a general panic would break out and that the Dow Jones Average might be affected. Scientists and researchers were therefore quietly told, but in no uncertain terms, that they were to keep their findings to themselves until an "official" explanation could be trumped up.

The explanation, however, was never necessary—at least not in the United States—because, as luck would have it, officials stumbled upon a way to divert the public's attention from significant news stories.

It happened when an actress in Hollywood stepped out of her limousine just as a photographer snapped her picture, revealing that she was wearing striped underwear. The story dominated the national news for several days and completely drew everyone's attention away from any leaked information about the earth's slowing rotation. Officials in the U.S. soon realized that they'd stumbled across a valuable tool for keeping the masses "unengaged." They would use this "mind candy" technique many times in the years to follow.

Though the earth's rotation had slowed by only a few seconds—in the couple of days since the Crystal was taken from Golden Gate Park—gravity was becoming more pronounced because there was less centrifugal force being exerted. The effects were subtle, of course, but nonetheless disturbing in small and, as you'll see, larger ways.

The extra weight made people feel sluggish, dull, lazy. Television viewing went up significantly. As a result, national ratings for a number of questionable television shows rose significantly. Shows like *Night Court, Who's The Boss?, Mama's Family, Perfect Strangers,* and *Murphy Brown* drew some of their biggest audiences ever.

Sporting events were slower. Shot put and javelin scores were considerably lower. Football quarterbacks were frustrated with their passing abilities. High school wrestling events got started later because wrestlers were not weighing in at their weight classes.

People felt tired. Grumpy. Irritable.

State and city police throughout the country and the world reported nearly three times more incidents of road rage. ("Road rage" was a phenomenon prevalent before transportation was controlled by computerized synchronization—CompuSynk—in the late 2040s.)

Riots broke out in Hong Kong after the government there decided to kick out its Vietnamese refugees. In London, demonstrators took to the streets to protest the government's decision to tax the voting process (called a poll tax). Four hundred seventy-one people were injured, and 341 were arrested in Trafalgar Square.

Though 1989 was more than three years after the horrific Chernobyl nuclear power plant meltdown in the Ukraine (an explosion that sent radioactive contaminants into the air over a number of European communities), protesters only took to the streets in outrage after the earth's rotation began to slow. More than 30,000 gathered in the streets of Minsk to express their anger with the government. In Romania, after a week of bloody protests, communist dictator Nicolae Ceausescu had to flee his palace by helicopter to avoid being executed by the citizens of his country.

Demonstrations and protests began to spring up all over Europe. The irritation people felt—due to the slowing rotation—ultimately led to significant changes. The unrest began in Poland and spread throughout East Germany, Czechoslovakia, Hungary, Bulgaria and Lithuania in what was called The Velvet Revolution of 1989.

These small, unpleasant uprisings eventually led to the collapse of The Soviet Union in 1991 and the end of the Cold War.

() () ()

As you can imagine, Grampa's explanation of world events just about put the children to sleep. Still, they sat quietly, all three of them, their eyes open, but heavily glazed.

Grampa studied them a moment and grew suspicious. He barked, "What'd I just say?"

"Whah?" This was Joe, who didn't mean to say anything, but was so startled by Grampa's outburst that he blurted it out.

Henry cleared his throat. "You said that everybody felt tired and got in fights, and then Bulgaria ended."

"Grampa," Francie interrupted, "We really don't care about all that. We want to know what happened to Warren and Lily?"

Grampa shot his granddaughter a look, but saw, from her broad smile, that she was no longer so intimidated by him. He held her gaze for another moment, then reopened the journal and told them about Warren and Lily.

Into Neither Norr

THE ELEVATOR RIDE took much longer than either Lily or Warren expected—much longer than any elevator ride on the Crust—and probably seemed longer still because the humans were very uncomfortable having to stay hunched and bent for the duration of the ride. Warren guessed they were confined in the elevator for nearly two hours as it descended farther into the earth.

The tiny Oidenoids, of course, did not mind so much the elevator ride, but they were very uneasy about the mess left behind by the miserable Sloidelobb. Oidenoids, unlike regular Nuldoids, are very neat and tidy—fastidious by some standards—though they would never actually complain about it. In the elevator, there was, of course, nowhere to throw out all the garbage accumulated by the Sloidelobb, and Beatrice wished out loud that they had taken the time to clean *everything out* before they closed the doors to begin the trip down. Their decision not to do so, however, turned out to be a stroke of good fortune.

Roggo and Beatrice, in the time it took the elevator to descend, came across what, at first, looked like a useless flier announcing some pointless provision to be enacted in Neither Norr. But it turned out to be a very significant map, as you'll see. Though it was greatly worn and very old—printed during the Droiden Frobble Dynasty hundreds of years earlier—it detailed many passages and shortcuts that were no longer in use, passages that would certainly be missed by any casual or contemporary travelers... *like Morton and Kyle, for instance.*

By the time the elevator came to an abrupt and jarring stop and its rusted doors screeched open, they were deep within the Region of Neither Norr. The Oidenoids gathered their knapsacks and various belongings, while Warren and Lily emerged wearily from the cramped chamber and gazed around in wonder.

They were standing once again on the warm sand of a beach, though now they were beside a lagoon that opened to a large lake beyond. Light glowed from the ceiling high above them through streaks of what appeared to be bluish dolomite deposits—that is, translucent quartz formations. The lagoon was nearly surrounded by trees that were not like any trees the humans had seen before—each extending from the ground below up to the ceiling overhead, apparently growing from both directions to the middle, where palm fronds splayed out as though smashed between opposing trunks.

As Warren wandered out toward what he thought was the water of the lagoon, he realized it was not water at all, but small rubber balls. Hundreds of them. Millions. Some were blue, some greenish blue, each the size of a marble or a golf ball. He stepped into the "water" and picked up a couple of them to squeeze between his fingers. He turned then and yelled to the others. "Hey! They're rubber! It's all rubber balls!"

Hammet shouted to Warren not to go out too far, then turned and explained to Lily that the lake had no lifeguard, that swimming was considered very dangerous. To allay her fears, he flatly denied the rumors of a snarling and vicious, several-eyed, many-fanged monster, *supposedly* living in the lake. His denial, of course, did not allay anything, and Lily, a moment later, signaled Warren to get out.

They decided to follow the edge of the lake to the falls at the other side where, according to the old Droiden Frobble map, there was an ancient slide that wound its way far into Neither Norr. The enormous slide had been built during the last years of the Big War of Froote so that Droiden Frobble troops could move quickly through Neither Norr to the ledge of the Great Big Canyon (near Nuldoid)—a strategic stronghold for the empire. Cartographic depictions of the ancient slide virtually disappeared from maps drawn thirty or more years after the war.

If they could find the ancient slide—if it was still there and had not fallen into disrepair—it could very well put them in the Great Big Canyon well ahead of the others and the Crystal. There were alternative routes, certainly, by which one could reach Nuldoid—other than the Great Big Canyon—but more often than not, they were extremely dangerous, if not downright terminal. Many were the stories of travelers who decided to enter Nuldoid through the Sliding Plates at Ambit and ended up in the Breathing Gullies of Dult, and were never heard from again. Still others had perished in the Pockets of Roundlet, trapped in one of its deadly *doidell voids*—a looping wind tunnel that continued indefinitely.

As they emerged from behind the double-rooted trees of the lagoon, Warren and Lily could see that the lake itself was much larger than they had at first assumed. Much larger. In fact, it stretched for several miles beneath an expansive limestone ceiling, from which huge cones hung down with holes at their bottom tips that dripped hot blue and blue-green rubber. The rubber cooled as it fell, forming perfectly round rubber balls that plunked into the lake.

The path along the edge of the lake had been used frequently enough that it was easy to follow, but the Oidenoids soon found tracks in the dirt made by shopping carts and became quite concerned. The dreaded Harvesters always traveled with shopping carts, and there was nothing the Oidenoids feared more than Harvesters, so they quickened their pace—Roggo having to be carried on Warren's back, since he was so small.

As they made their way around a small cove, perhaps a few miles from the elevator, everyone was beginning to feel hungry. They had not passed any froote-bearing trees in quite some time. When they came upon the opening to a small cave, Roggo suggested that Warren put him down so he could check the cave for wild Blobalobbs. Blobalobbs, Lily and Warren learned, were furry creatures, flat and round like throw pillows—adults were usually about a foot or so in diameter—with no appendages whatsoever. They were quite harmless, yet entirely miserable creatures that growled at anything larger than themselves, and ate anything smaller than themselves. But, Roggo explained, they were as easy as pie to catch, and downright scrumptious when lightly cooked.

"Holds up!" Hammet said, who had been examining more shopping cart tracks. "Ya doesn't goes in der yet, huh." He picked up a rock and tossed it into the cave. When he did, the edges of the cave's opening, both above and below, suddenly slammed together with a thunderous crash, and then moved from side to side, before they pursed and blew the rock back out into the dirt. "Baaach!" came a sound from within the cave. Then the "lips" widened again and blended into the edges of the cave's opening.

"Fishing Worm," Hammet said, and smiled at Roggo, who was holding his beating chest. "Yas woulda been eated, sure as rot stinks."

"Ya gots we thanks," Roggo said.

"Is welcome."

"How did you know?" Lily asked.

Hammet shrugged modestly, while his head wobbled a bit with bubbling pride. "Hammet does plenty a travel in Neither Norr. Many danger stuffs we eyes is wide to," he said. "Plus, we was seein' dat big tongue in der."

As they moved past and over the next gully, Hammet explained that many of the mountains and walls of Neither Norr were infested with giant Fishing Worms that lived in the confines of intricate tunnel systems. These worms were named after the way they captured their prey, since they were capable of waiting in silence for months before something, or someone, wandered into their massive jaws.

Fortunately, farther along the trail, they came across some froote trees. Unfortunately, they bore only fruitcake froote, which the Oidenoids were radically fond of, and which Lily and Warren weren't so enthused about. The humans did, however, manage to have a few bites to tide them over until they could find something better.

Before long, they reached the falls, where the lake drained its rubber balls down a steep series of steps. The balls bounced and flew everywhere, as the group cautiously made their way along the side of the incline toward a large wooden mill wheel. The mill wheel's buckets were filling with rubber balls and slowly moving down with the wheel until they emptied at the bottom, where the balls continued on to bounce and roll their way still farther down the hillside. Finally, at the bottom of the slope, they flew out over a ledge.

As the humans and the Oidenoids made their way down the hill, they saw a wire cage near the base of the wheel. A Sloidelobb sat inside, sleeping soundly next to a control panel, the folds of his massive stomach pressing out against the lattice of the cage, creating tiny square pillows of flesh.

They moved toward the ledge where the rubber balls bounced out into open air and then fell into a small blue river at the bottom of the gorge. The river fed a molten pit, Beatrice explained, where the rubber balls melted into liquid form and then bubbled up through tiny air holes, until the rubber filled the ceiling's cones again, and then dripped back down into the lake as rubber balls.

Warren stepped to the ledge and looked down, as the balls flew out over his head. When he saw that the drop was perhaps two hundred feet, he was suddenly gripped by fear, and nearly teetered over. "Oh my..." he said, and slowly, cautiously, sat down on the rocks, where he, very un-heroically, scooted his way back up the hill, away from the ledge.

The old map had shown that the ancient slide was just beside the falls, but clearly there was no sign of it anywhere. They had reached a dead end and would certainly have to backtrack, have to rethink their route.

Hammet sat on a rock and rubbed his chin. "We is missed somethin'," he said, deep in thought, as Lily sat down beside him, and Warren, having recovered from his vertigo, joined them. "Somethin' we was missed."

Warren looked up the hill to where the old mill was still collecting rubber balls and dumping them farther down the hill. He nodded at it. "What's that mill for?"

"Ach, der is for electric," Hammet said, craning his neck to give it a momentary glance... which, apparently sparked a realization. "Electric!" The little man was on his feet again. "Electric!" he said, clambering back up the hill toward the mill. Lily and Warren got up to follow him, yelling for the other creatures to grab their belongings and fall in behind them.

When Hammet reached the mill, he scanned the hillside, looking for something, but did not appear to see it. He climbed down below the mill's wheel and made his way to the other side. Again he stood and looked out over the landscape as the others caught up with him. "Ah-hah!" he yelled a moment later and began climbing along the rocks, away from the mill house toward a cluster of bushes that was perhaps forty or fifty yards out. The bushes stood in front of several large stones that surrounded an opening. When the others arrived, they pushed the bushes aside and looked down it.

Warren was stunned. "An escalator?"

"Nah," said Roggo. "Is 'movin' steps.'"

"We call them escalators," Lily told him peering down into the entrance.

"Hmmph, ya has names for funny, huh," Roggo said as Hammet took the map from Beatrice to look it over.

"Dat slide," he said, studying the map, "goes below der, sure as butter." He folded the map and handed it back to Beatrice.

The escalator was like none Lily or Warren had ever seen, spiraling down in a corkscrew tube for nearly half a mile, its rock walls dimly lit by industrial lighting, all of it powered of course by the electrical mill at the lake. It had been overlooked because it appeared on the map only as a small faded circle.

At the bottom of the winding escalator, they stepped out onto a worn wooden platform beside a rock wall. The platform rested on the edge of a small field of willowy grass that billowed up to a towering escarpment of dark stone, pockmarked by hundreds of cracks and crevices, many of them stuffed with dried grass.

They couldn't tell any longer which direction they were facing in relation to where they had been before they entered the escalator—it had turned them around many times on the way down—so they figured they might as well make their way across the field and start looking wherever they could for an entrance to the ancient slide.

But, when Hammet and Roggo jumped down off the platform, a large net suddenly dropped down over the top of Lily and Warren! The looping of the net was quite wide, however—the holes of it large, too large—so the net itself quickly dropped past Lily and Warren's heads and fell to the platform, where it landed on Beatrice. "Ach!" came a voice from behind them, as several small creatures suddenly appeared on the ledge above the escalator's exit. In a flash, they jumped down and ran at them, screaming a sort of battle cry that—because their voices were small and high-pitched—did not sound terribly fierce and not much like a battle cry at all.

"Nuldoids!" Roggo yelled as he pulled up a fistful of tall grass, a clump of dirt hanging off the end of it, and hurled it at their assailants. Tiny fists were flying everywhere as Warren and Lily stood there somewhat awkwardly, unsure whether or not to join in the fray, and if so, how, since the creatures were all so small. Then Warren suddenly felt a sharp pain in his calf and looked down to see a tiny creature—smaller than the others—wrapped around his leg, biting him. "Ow!" He shook his leg vigorously and saw the small creature fly out and disappear in the tall grass.

Hammet grabbed one of the attackers by the throat and wrestled her to the ground, where she quickly turned him over, her hands now at his throat. "Where ya gots dat Crystal, ya frobbs drobble!?"

"Ach! We doesn't has no Crystal, ya hoydle obb!"

"Ya has Crustoids! So ya has dat Crystal! An' we stops ya! Hah!"

"Ach! We doesn't has no Crystal! Oidenoids we is!" Hammet managed to say.

"Hah, *you* is? *We* is!"

Suddenly she stopped choking him. Both spoke at once. "Oidenoids?"

They were all Oidenoids, it turned out.

The strangers were on the lookout for Nuldoids traveling through Neither Norr with a human. Word had apparently spread throughout the region that the Crystal had come from the Drobbs Mubble (Fresno) entrance. It was an honest mistake the other Oidenoids made and they apologized profusely, even to Lily and Warren—though the little creatures were still leery of the humans and felt especially uncomfortable about all of the fingers on their enormous hands.

Then, just as introductions were about to be made, the smallest of the other creatures—the one that Warren had earlier thrown off his leg out into the grass—returned to the wooden platform, where he struggled onto it and then leapt back onto Warren's leg and bit into it again.

"Ow! What're you doing?"

"Elo!" one of the others yelled at him. "Oidenoids these is! Ya stops yerself! Is Oidenoids!"

The little creature stopped and looked up. "Ach," he said and let go of Warren's leg.

He was the youngest and appeared to be the son of the others: Mully and Obbman. The two adults looked to be middle-aged, were neatly groomed and conservatively dressed. Obbman was quite serious, had large pendulous ears that swayed when he walked and eyebrows that bunched like cowering rodents. Mully's eyes were sharp, brown; she had stark brown hair that swept back into a tight bun behind her head, giving her a severe look. The fourth of them was an older creature named Newt, who had long white hair and a full beard, and might've been mistaken for Santa Claus if he were not two feet tall and did not have only three digits on each hand. They were all, of course, quite pudgy, as so many of these creatures tended to be.

Once the misunderstanding had been sorted out, Obbman explained that Oidenoids throughout Neither Norr were very concerned about the Crystal, but that there was also a great deal of misinformation going around—like the rumor that the human traveling with the Nuldoids was ten feet tall with shoulders as wide as four or five Oidenoids, which is why the net they used to capture Warren and Lily was so big.

"What we hears 'bout Ed," Mully was saying, "is beside hisself he is, a'cause dat Crystal's late. All a everybody's way horked up 'bout dat rotationing—"

"Yeah, yeah, sure for Ed!" Hammet said, practically interrupting her as he suddenly bolted to his feet and added, "Best we get movin' if we's to catch dat Crystal and save we Hoidenall!"

Lily thought Hammet's behavior odd, especially when she considered how the Oidenoids were, in all other instances, so polite to each other. They seemed never to bicker or quibble, so Hammet's interruption was very peculiar.

The Oidenoids agreed, however, that there was no time to be wasted. Beatrice told them about the ancient Droiden Frobble map they'd found in the elevator, and then laid it out on the wooden platform. She explained that there was an old military slide nearby that would take them to the inner side of Neither

Norr and empty them out near the Great Big Canyon. They would then, hopefully, be ahead of the Nuldoids and the Crystal. The other Oidenoids studied the old map with great interest, but none seemed to have any inkling where such a slide might exist. They were, in fact, greatly confused by the map.

Obbman sat back after a moment and rubbed the smooth skin of his chubby face. "Elo," he said to his son, "gets we dat map we has, hah?"

"Sure yeah, we lovesome dad (a common term of affection used by Oidenoid children for their fathers)." The tiny Oidenoid stood quickly. "Is it where?"

"Dat knapsacks," his father said.

The boy rushed off and returned a moment later with another map, a newer one, that Obbman took and unfolded next to the ancient one.

With both maps opened side by side, Hammet and Beatrice saw that there were great discrepancies between the two. As Obbman pointed out on the newer one, the Great Big Canyon was far from directly below them. In fact, he reckoned it was perhaps two entire sectors away from where they were. Warren and Lily, looking over the small shoulders of the Oidenoids, could figure out none of it. Apparently the older map had been triangulated differently, and somewhat inaccurately. But, after carefully lining up common landmarks between the two maps, the Oidenoids were able to pinpoint the location of the ancient slide, between the Valley of Lopsided Water and the Weary Forest. They were relieved that they would only have to cross the Valley of Lopsided Water and not the Weary Forest. The forest was quite dangerous when its trees grew tired and simply fell over.

As they prepared to set out across the grass field and into the dell that opened at the far end of the large granite wall, Lily heard Hammet tell Beatrice and Roggo to move ahead with the humans while he had a word with the other Oidenoids. He assured them that they would catch up shortly.

Lily squatted to let Roggo climb onto her back, which he did with a small grunt and a "Thanks der to yas," and, as she and Warren and Beatrice began to cross the field, she glanced back and saw Hammet pull the others in close to speak quietly with them. What, she wondered, would he be telling them that he did not want her or Warren to hear?

It was a short moment later that Hammet and the others were yelling for Warren and Lily to wait up, which they did, as Lily watched the little creatures make their way through the open field toward them, their small heads bobbing up and down just over the top of the tall grass. Beside them, a trail magically formed where tiny Elo trudged along unseen. When they were all together, Warren suggested—and all agreed—that they would be able to move more quickly if he carried the youngster on his back.

As they neared the towering granite wall, Warren asked why there were tufts of dried grass sticking out of the crevices in the rock formations. Newt, the old Oidenoid, explained that Gloibs (pronounced Gloy-ibs) made their nests up there.

"What's a Gloib?" Lily asked.

"Gloib's a nitwit bird," Newt explained. "Was so much stupid, dey doesn't exist no more." He was about to explain further when, because of his advanced age, he found himself too winded from both walking *and* talking, so Obbman finished the story.

"Gloibs has wings 'at flaps above so as ta hovers. But is birds 'at's got way lotta problems inna head."

The males became competitive with each other, and used their offspring to establish their superiority. Male Gloibs pushed

137

their young out of the nests to prove to the other males that their chicks were superior and could fly earlier than any of the others. Unfortunately, competition became so intense that the Gloibs began pushing their offspring out of their nests before any were mature enough to fly. The young birds fell to their deaths and the Gloibs ended up dying out. "But," as Obbman added cheerfully, "bones a dem is makin' good teeth pickers."

The dell they entered into at the far end of the granite wall was dark at first, but grew lighter by the glow of pinecone-looking froote that hung from the trees beside the path. Elo whispered to Warren that trees in this part of Neither Norr were very sensitive, very emotional. The trees were, he said, happy to provide light, but, if someone picked their froote, they would become upset and let out a high-pitched sound that could shatter one's taste buds—a loss among the creatures considered tragic.

After they had been walking for a while, Lily's back was beginning to ache from carrying Roggo, so they stopped momentarily, and Warren exchanged the smaller Elo for Roggo. When the little Oidenoids had been comfortably transplanted and the group again picked up and continued down the path of the dell, Hammet and Mully suddenly realized that they'd known each other from "The Rotten Spooch of 765."

"What's a spooch?" Warren asked.

"Ach," said Hammet, "dat spooch is too much overload with dat electric."

"You mean a surge?"

"'Surge'? Ach, yas Crustoids wit yas names. We doesn't has no light in Nuldoid for days long gone."

"Nuldoid?" Lily said. "So you lived in Nuldoid?"

"*All* we lived in Nuldoid," Beatrice said.

"When?"

"Is gotta be a couple hun'erd years gone 'way now."

138

Warren stopped. "You're kidding. So how long do you—" he wasn't sure if the term "people" applied "—guys live?"

"Ach," said old Newt, who had stopped to lean against a rock and catch his breath, "too long."

Mully took several beer frootes from her knapsack and passed them around. "Is time for song we sings." The others took the froote and opened it while they walked.

"So, wait. You live for hundreds of years?" Warren persisted, catching up with them.

"Hah!" Hammet laughed. "Nah to dat."

"But she said you lived in Nuldoid hundreds of years ago. She said that."

"Sure yeah. An' we is missin' it big too, dat Nuldoid, dat NoideLloyd," he said dreamily, using the literary reference.

"So you *do* live for hundreds of years!" Warren persisted as though he'd caught them in a lie.

"Sure yeah," Obbman added. "But ya has ta adds it up right."

"Add it up right? What's that mean? What does that mean?" But Warren's question went unanswered as Mully started to sing and the others joined in, and their voices echoed melodically through the dell.

Way Down Below we all is for,
For all we from,
Dat Middle Core.
But lives we must so far 'way
'Cause choose we Lloyd
An' doesn't stray.
So says we us, we do abhor
This land we roams
Called Neither Norr.
But feels we not no never void
'Cause holds we in our Livers dear,
Dat land we loves called NoideLloyd.

But we is One
An' One we is,
An' we is well annoyed.
　　Oh, hoideloy an' oideloy
　　Is loidelee to hoidelee!
To takes we back
Dat land we loves
Dat blessed NoideLloyd!

The song was an old one, so everyone, except Warren and Lily, knew the words. The humans were a little confused by the reference to holding NoideLloyd "in our *Livers* dear." Later, they learned that the creatures believed the liver, not the heart, was the center of emotion. Beatrice even went so far as to claim that this had been clinically proven years earlier.

Elo was very excited about singing the song and climbed down from Lily's back to race ahead and join the others. He seemed most comfortable with all the words and its verses, more so even than Newt, who had not sung it in many years. Both Lily and Warren were impressed with the quality of their voices and their seemingly natural ability to harmonize. It was a lovely sound that flowed like silk through the close confines of the dell, and, by the second verse, the froote on the trees glowed even brighter.

So lives we now nowhere but here
　　With backsacks, shoes
　　An' not much Beer.
'Cause many years we doesn't wake
　　An' lives we did without no sight,
　　'Til up came evil to fortake.
An' wander we to avoid
　　Dat land we loves,
　　Called NoideLloyd.

140

For now it does dem frightful sights
Where streets is full
Of brawls and fights!

But we is One
An' One we is,
An' we is well Annoyed.
Oh, hoideloy an' oideloy
Is loidelee to hoidelee!
To takes we back
Dat land we loves
Dat blessed NoideLloyd!

Though we is feeling oh so sore,
On we goes,
To Middle Core.
Where many words by Lloyd was said,
Dat got wrote down
Insides we head.
So sings we does ta honor Lloyd,
With words we takes
From NoideLloyd.
Dat Book it says dat we belong
'Cause we is right,
An' dey is wrong!

But we is One
An' One we is,
An' we is well Annoyed.
Oh, hoideloy an' oideloy
Is loidelee to hoidelee!
To takes we back
Dat land we loves
Dat blessed NoideLloyd!

After many miles, and after Warren and Lily again shouldered the smaller creatures, they reached the edge of the

141

dell where it narrowed to a gulch and then opened to a wide plain blanketed by bright orange flowers. But these were not poppies, were not even bright in color, but only seemed so because they were lit from the horizon by what looked like a setting sun. The sun was, as well, nothing of the sort. Rather, it was a sizable deposit of crystalline dolomite that diffused light from a source somewhere far behind it.

From there they crossed into the Plains of Low Weather, where thick and forbidding clouds gathered a few feet off the ground and enveloped the little Oidenoids—except for Roggo and Elo, who sat comfortably above the elements on the shoulders of Lily and Warren. Several times, the humans lost track of the other Oidenoids, who were making their way, as best they could, beneath the cloud cover. Since the clouds came and went every nine or ten minutes—in a very tight and peculiar weather cycle—it was not long before the Oidenoids caught up with the humans, but only to complain vehemently about the weather, until they were enveloped again by more incoming clouds. As a third cycle of clouds rolled in, the Oidenoids were in such a hurry to get past it all, they were practically running out ahead of the humans.

When they neared Durwin's Splatt Bluffs, Roggo explained that the bluffs were named after Durwin Pogg, who jumped to his death after learning that the Oidenoids had been forever banished from Nuldoid.

He pointed to several large animals grazing languidly at the base of the bluffs. "Globb Trobbers," he said. The animals were difficult to see at such a distance—their silhouettes darkened by the amber hue of the bluffs' layered sandstone—but they were magnificent wooly beasts that stood on two bent hind legs and a single front leg that extended to a grasping claw. They had furry ears like koalas and eyes perched on two stems at the top of their huge heads. Despite their menacing appearance, "Globbers" were entirely approachable and somewhat social. In fact, as Roggo explained, doctors often advised patients suffering from nasty head colds or painful cases of the gout to approach these beasts, since a sneeze in the face by one would instantly cure either.

When they were well past Durwin's Splatt Bluffs, near the far end of the Plains of Low Weather, Warren looked back to admire the Globb Trobbers and saw that they had grouped in fours and fives, to form huge wheels, each group of beasts having interlocked, end-to-end, so that they looked something like enormous clumsy Ferris Wheels that began to roll through the newly forming clouds of the plains and then off into the distance.

"Oh my," Lily said. "What are they doing?"

Roggo turned to look over his shoulder at the rolling Globbers. "Eh, is how dey gets ta other places."

"That's how they travel?" Warren said. "Incredible."

"Eh," Roggo said, "isn't not so great. Is always dey runnin' into things."

The group left the Plains of Low Weather through an opening that led to a grassy field. It sloped down away from them beneath a ceiling of more green grass. To the side of the sloping meadow, froote trees grew in abundance, and the Oidenoids took the opportunity to stop and refill their knapsacks with bread froote, turkey froote, and mashed potato and gravy froote.

As they walked down the grassy slope beneath the canopy of grass, Warren saw that the ceiling and floor ahead of them looked as though they converged in a dead-end.

"Nah, ya doesn't worry," Hammet assured him. "Under it tucks."

And indeed, when they reached the bottom of the grassy slope, the ceiling of grass scooped down around it and continued on again in the opposite direction, so that the ceiling became the floor and the floor the ceiling. They jumped down onto the curve of the grass ceiling—Warren and Lily first, so they could help the Oidenoids—and then walked down the next slope until it did the same again. There they hopped down from the floor to the ceiling and continued along the slope in the opposite direction until it curved under again, where they jumped down to the curve of the ceiling and followed it as it did so again and again and again. The interlacing pieces of land jutted in and out like the teeth of an enormous zipper that never touched. It went on for many miles until finally the last grassy meadow rolled down to a gravel clearing at the bend of a small arroyo. They decided to stop there momentarily to double-check their maps and see where they were in relation to the ancient slide.

Unseen by any of them, several other creatures appeared at the top of a small bluff that ran up the other side of the arroyo. They stood side by side, seven or eight of them, looking as menacing as they could—that is, for creatures not quite two feet tall. Several held large sticks, while others held knives and rocks. A few wore helmets that looked as though they had been issued in World War I. One wore a battered Norseman's helmet that was missing a horn and was too big for his head. And one, a female, wore a bonnet.

Warren was the first to see the other creatures. "Uh, guys?" he said without taking his eyes off them. "We've got company."

The others looked over at the bluff just as one of the other creatures—the one with a helmet and a red bow tie—lifted into the air, a couple of inches off the ground and hovered. He shouted, "Ya holds right der, ya drobbs horkel! An' pronto ya hands over dat Crystal!" Then he apparently lost his concentration, dropped and tumbled down the embankment into the arroyo itself.

Hammet stepped toward him so that he could look more closely at the stranger's face. "Borden?"

The creature looked up. "Hammet?"

The others were of course Oidenoids, all on the lookout for Nuldoids traveling with a human. Hammet knew Borden, it turned out, from The Unjust Purge of Nuldoid nearly 200 years earlier. They were "cousins back den," he explained without going into detail. He introduced Borden to the others, who greatly complimented the Oidenoid on his ability to stay aloft for as long as he did. In fact, his feat was so impressive that Obbman compared him to a Delnoid, which—Lily and Warren later learned from Beatrice—was a Nuldoid that was neither male nor female, and therefore very good at feats like hovering.

Several of the other creatures knew Hammet from encounters long since past, and another, Fitz, was quite pleased to see young Elo, claiming to remember him from The War of Decaying Values, which, as Beatrice explained, took place in Nuldoid just before The Unjust Purge.

It was all still very puzzling to the humans, this talk of time and past relationships. Elo, for instance, was barely an adolescent—so how could he have known the others from events that took place so long ago? They must live for hundreds of years, Warren concluded. *But if that's true, he found himself wondering, why weren't they any smarter?*

Borden and his companions were thrilled to hear about the ancient slide on the other side of the Valley of Lopsided Water. They were most enthusiastic about joining forces and were quite happy to learn that the slide would take them all the way to the Great Big Canyon in a matter of hours instead of days. They, like all the Oidenoids, were anxious to reach the Crystal before the Nuldoids got to Outer Nuldoid.

() () ()

Now they were a force of sixteen—fourteen Oidenoids and two humans. As they gathered their things and prepared to set out for the Valley of Lopsided Water and the slide beyond, a creature named Owen wandered over to Warren. He wore coke-bottle glasses that were held firmly in place by a heavy leather strap that wrapped around the back of his head. His nose was flat and off center, his ears were of unequal size and his eyes kept darting to Warren's hands whenever Warren looked away. "So, ya likes dat Crust, does ya?"

"Well, uh, yeah," Warren said, not knowing really how to answer a question like that.

"But den, ya gots all dat weather, eh?" The little Oidenoid shook his head sympathetically. "Ach, is gots ta be miserable. 'Rain', eh... gotta be like wee in yer eye, eh?"

Warren shrugged. "Actually, I enjoy weather. The rain. The change of seasons. The snow up in Tahoe. The fall, when the leaves change colors. The summer sunshine..."

The little creature thought about it for a moment. "Supposed ya gots to believe dat, huh?" He shuddered and then moved off to the others.

Meanwhile, Borden struggled to hoist himself onto one of the larger rocks so that he could address all of them. "Hey, hey! Ya listen ups!" His voice was gruff and authoritative, and Lily could imagine him inspiring a great many followers, except that his left eye constantly drifted to one side before bouncing back. The others quieted, and Lily—who had made a point to watch Hammet—noticed that Hammet looked worried when Borden started talking.

"We has dat big destiny we's headed inna!" Borden lightly whacked the side of his head when his eye did not move quickly enough back into place. "We is gonna stops dat Nuldoids! An' we takes dat Crystal is what we does! An' when we does—"

"Sure yeah to dat!" Hammet yelled as he quickly made his way through the others toward Borden, while a few of them gasped in shock. "But we hasn't all the times in Hoidenall! Hasn't not no times for dat speeches! So, we's good to be off an' gone!"

"Yup, yup for dat!" chimed in Obbman. "Off we goes! Off we goes to Blessed NoideLloyd, huh!" he said, trying to lighten the moment.

But it was again very peculiar behavior, Lily noted.

Borden had a surprised look on his face. "Hammet, ya doesn't lets we finish!" The words were perhaps the harshest that any of the others had heard Oidenoids exchange, and there was another collective gasp.

Though Hammet was contrite, he was determined that Borden not finish his speech. "We most certainly begs your forgivin', Borden. But we has haste ta makes if we is ta does what we gotta does." His words were met with cool acceptance until he thought to add, "An' as Lloyd was written, 'Time is a clickin', so oogly stuff we doesn't pickin'.'"

The others seemed impressed that Hammet could so easily reference Lloyd and, since no one could argue with anything someone said that had been said by Lloyd, they all agreed it was best to skip Borden's speech and get going.

They hoisted their knapsacks onto their backs, while Elo and Roggo climbed onto Lily and Warren's backs. As they set out following the arroyo downstream, Lily watched Hammet closely and saw him move first to Borden, then to each of the unfamiliar Oidenoids to speak privately, making sure, as he did, that he was not being heard—it seemed to Lily—by Warren or herself.

The journey itself was not unpleasant, though they had farther to go than either Warren or Lily expected.

Eventually, the arroyo crossed a dry canal that they decided to use because—according to the maps—it would take them to the empty lake, where it was a mere "hop, jump and yer skip" to the Valley of Lopsided Water. As they climbed down into the canal, Beatrice explained to the humans that the canal was built before the Droiden Frobble Dynasty, back in the Time of Workin'. Though the Oidenoids knew plenty about the Droiden Frobble Dynasty—dating back nearly a thousand years before Lloyd— they knew little about the Time of Workin'. All anyone could confirm about these ancient Nuldoids was that they built a lot of stuff, that they had not yet discovered beer and that the two things were possibly related.

Determined tufts of weeds pushed their way up between the stones of the canal, where there had not been any water for hundreds of years. It was used frequently by travelers making their way through Neither Norr, which presented a problem of sorts, since it was well known that Harvesters could be found moving along the twists and turns of its long passage. Since there was nothing the Oidenoids feared more than Harvesters, they'd have to be diligent about not making unnecessary noise—a task only a few believed Beatrice could pull off.

The canal climbed away from the arroyo and then sloped sharply downward, winding its way through deep gorges and gullies, over gaping chasms, and down, down farther into the earth. The group passed many more unusual plants and trees, the froote of which bore some unexpected things, including detergent and vodka. The Oidenoids had not known that vodka froote existed, and immediately began plucking all of it so that it could be destroyed. They explained to Lily and Warren that *The Book of Nuldoid* was very specific about the evil of all alcohol, besides beer:

An' Lloyd said unto 'em dat's der:
"Takes of ye dat beer,
For as we has gotta live without no vice
Is pure fooey."

The Book of Nuldoid
Conflictions 5:16

Neither Warren nor Lily were sure how the passage could be considered "specific"—and, in fact, it sounded to them more like an *endorsement* of vice than an admonishment—but they did not press the issue, opting instead to keep the group moving.

In places, the canal seemed to nearly tie itself into a knot, twisting up and over itself before shooting down again in another direction. Other sections were difficult for the Oidenoids to get through because the stonework had been so badly forced askew by the infrequent movement of the earth over the centuries. The upturned and jutting stones were especially difficult for the smaller Oidenoids to get past, and those who were not helped by Warren or Lily had to rely on a boost from another Oidenoid.

All things considered, however, they moved along at a pretty good pace, and were pleased with themselves for doing so. In fact, they were moving so quickly that they began to grow rather cocky, leading some to sing songs, quietly at first, but gradually more boldly. When an Oidenoid named Hazel, however, ran across the discarded wheel of a Harvester's shopping cart, they were reminded of the danger they faced, and quickly stifled themselves. They decided then it might be prudent to send a "scout" out ahead to look for possible dangers.

A creature named Ebnetter immediately stepped forward to volunteer for the job. He was wearing not only an army helmet, but shoulder pads of carved wood that looked like roof shingles, giving him an overall military look. A bow was slung across his back, the string of it crossing his chest, a bundle of quivers popping up from behind his wooden shoulder pads. He looked young to Lily and Warren—though the two humans were, by then, so thoroughly confused about the ages of these creatures that "young" could have meant just about anything.

It was clear that the other Oidenoids in their group did not think much of Ebnetter, as a couple of them exchanged looks and rolled their eyes when he so quickly volunteered for the job. The disrespectful exchange did not go unnoticed by their leader, Borden, and it was met by his stern gaze and an admonishing shake of the head. These creatures did not tolerate insults or bickering amongst themselves, and the two guilty Oidenoids were immediately contrite.

Feeling slightly more relaxed with Ebnetter out ahead, they rounded the next bend and came upon a waterfall that spilled not water, but thousands of small white beads, pearl-like in appearance. The beads flowed out over their heads toward a pond of real water on the other side of the canal, bursting open in midair like popcorn, to become brilliant butterflies that looked neon in their vibrancy—each of them an enchanting azure or a brilliant red. The butterflies fluttered about for a moment and then flew off over the limpid pond, where they were swept into a swirling funnel of air that drew them down into an opening at the center of the water. The sight of it left Lily breathless. She reached over and held Warren's arm. He looked at her hand as she did and smiled.

From there, the canal twisted into a dark tunnel with a high ceiling, where magma had cooled thousands of years earlier as it slithered down the tunnel's walls, forming huge bulbous gobs that hung now like thousands of sagging bellies.

As they emerged from the tunnel, they nearly stumbled over Ebnetter, crouched behind a small rusted barrel, holding a pair of binoculars to his eyes. He was intently studying something that lay in the path ahead of them.

"What's it?" Hammet whispered as he crouched down beside Ebnetter and signaled the others to stay back in the tunnel.

"We has almost certain a Blobalobb der."

Hammet took the binoculars from him to look for himself. "Sure yeah ta dat. Is a Blobalobb der is."

Ebnetter nocked an arrow and drew it across the belly of his bow. "Ya stays here," he said in a sharp whisper, and then moved quickly along the edge of the canal like a S.W.A.T. sniper, until he was standing over a flat creature that looked to Warren and Lily like a throw pillow. The little animal did not run, of course—had no legs to do so—but it did growl most audibly just before Ebnetter let fly his arrow into its center (though "fly" is perhaps not the right word here, since he was merely inches away). He stepped back from it, nocked another arrow, and moved in again to send it into the animal's middle, just to be sure it was completely dead. When he was certain it was, he turned and gallantly signaled to the rest that it was safe to approach.

The other Oidenoids stepped over to look at the dead creature. Warren and Lily peered over their little shoulders. Ebnetter took out a small bowie knife, flipped the animal over like a pancake and sliced it open so he could remove the skin.

While this was going on, Warren saw that Hammet was looking over the map again, and stepped over to ask him some questions. "So that's a Blobalobb, huh?" he said, nodding to Ebnetter and the creature.

"Sure yeah ta dat," Hammet said without looking up.

"Well… it doesn't have any legs… so it couldn't really move, could it?"

"Nah. But dem is wigglers dem."

"Right," Warren said, still confused. "But... that guy just hunted an animal that couldn't move."

Hammet looked up from the map then, rubbed his chin a moment and said finally, "Hmmph. Didn't never thinks much of it like dat. But, growlers dem, an' *gad* is dey wigglers."

"Right," Warren said, realizing the conversation had come full circle.

() () ()

With the wet skin of the Blobalobb hanging off his back, Ebnetter scurried out to his scouting position in the canal ahead of them. He took his new job seriously, and it was not more than a few moments before he came scurrying back, looking wide-eyed and pale and shushing everyone. "Harvesters!" he whispered as a hush swept over the others. "Ahead is dey! This way dey comes!"

Hammet quickly took charge. "Obbman! Borden! Ya gets your Oids over der in a pronto!" He pointed to a rocky area beside the canal where a ditch ran parallel. Then he nodded toward the other side of the canal. "We takes dat bushes!"

And with amazing speed, the Oidenoids clamored up the sides of the canal and hid themselves. Warren and Lily followed Hammet and Beatrice to a cluster of bushes where they ducked down behind them. A moment later, Roggo scrambled to join them.

And there they waited.

And waited.

Finally, they heard the squawk of wobbly shopping cart wheels rounding the corner, rolling and thumping along the uneven stone floor of the canal. Warren pushed a branch aside and peered out from the underside of the bushes. He saw that there were two Harvesters, each pushing a rickety cart, stuffed to

152

capacity with froote, sleeping bags, a broken lamp, plastic jugs, sticks, cans—all amounting to what looked like an assortment of junk. The Harvesters were brusque and unkempt. One of them wore a plastic shower cap on his head. Each had a full beard, though one's was tangled and matted, while the other's flowed into an odd braid, wrapping at the bottom around what looked like a small birdcage. Within the cage, Warren could see a tiny creature of some sort, clinging to the bars with its tiny fists. The Harvesters' heavy coats were dark and ragged, with perhaps fifty or so pockets that hung off the sides. The larger of the two creatures walked with a limp, his lame foot pointing out away from the other. And most distinct and peculiar were the spotlights, mounted a few inches above each of their shoulders, each pointing forward like a headlight. They were foul, vile-looking creatures, and though they, like the Oidenoids, were not more than two feet tall, they were frightening, even to Warren and Lily.

The Harvester with the limp spoke in raspy, staccato bursts that the humans could barely make out—despite that they'd become used to the strange language. He was complaining to his companion about his wife back in Nuldoid, whom he mistakenly married several hundred years earlier, divorced and then mistakenly married again. His companion plodded along, paying him no particular attention, singing a fairly unpleasant song, *in quite an unpleasant voice:*

> *Dem worms is fish*
> *We slews 'em dead.*
> *We chops 'em up*
> *An' serves 'em red.*
>
> *An' eats we eats,*
> *An' thinks we's fed.*

When up der comes
Dat howdy fred. *

The Oidenoids and humans—barely breathing—waited a good long while after the Harvesters had passed before they rose from their hiding places and rejoined each other in the canal. They still did not speak for fear they would be overheard, as Harvesters have extraordinary hearing.

Warren quietly hoisted Roggo onto his back, as Lily did Elo, and then all of them hiked briskly in the opposite direction, up over the crest of the next hill and down the slope on the other side, moving as quickly as they could away from the Harvesters. The canal wound its way around another hillside and then opened up to a large empty lakebed that had not held water in a thousand years. Gaping cracks crisscrossed the floor, creating a checkerboard effect. Skeletons of burnt trees lined the vast perimeter of the lakebed and stood like dark sentinels, reaching up toward an expansive ceiling of travertine, streaked by deposits of blue crystal formations, diffusing light from a source far above them.

This, Beatrice proclaimed, was the end of the canal.

As she and the other creatures sat down on the lakebed to again review the details of the two maps, Warren heard a noise overhead and looked up to see several winged creatures cross the "sky" just beneath the vast ceiling. It was difficult to gauge their size, but they looked to be a couple of feet long. He noticed their

---

* "Howdy fred" is the Nuldoid expression for throwing up into a toilet. Throughout Neither Norr and Nuldoid, toilets were referred to as "freds" (similar to humans' term "johns"). And, as many a traveler in Neither Norr discovered, the meat of the Fishing Worm tasted horrible and was, in fact, barely digestible. Those creatures who made the mistake of eating the meat of a Fishing Worm usually ended up getting very sick and throwing up in the toilet—that is, "howdy fred."

wings were webbed like bats, their bodies more like lizards than birds.

"What are those?" he asked, leaning to Obbman.

"Ach," Obbman said looking up, "Draggirds! Annoysome dey. Is big nuisance. Pesky pests is dey!"

"Well," Warren said as he watched them disappear over the tops of the dead trees, "they look like little dragons. Don't suppose they breathe fire?"

"Ach! If wishin' were a fangle." Obbman shook his head. "Is fire dat comes outta dey butts. Mad dey gets an' out farts fire!" He nodded to the horizon. "Is why dem trees is all burnt up like dat. Ach! Annoysome dey!"

The others concluded from the maps that they were not far from the Valley of Lopsided Water and the ancient slide. They had only to find a "hatch" that would take them to it. Several of the Oidenoids clambered up the sides of the lakebed and poked around between the dead trees. It was not long before one of them shouted from the top of the slope that they'd found it.

After they gathered their knapsacks, their hats and helmets, and climbed the side of the lakebed to regroup beside the hatch, old Newt suddenly felt weak from a pain in his chest and leaned against the trunk of a dead tree. "Ach," he said, "is 'bout time."

"Is ya what, Newt?" Obbman stepped over to the older Oidenoid and put a hand on his shoulder.

"Is dat heart goes sputter," the old Oidenoid said, looking up at Obbman. "Finally, dat nap!" Then he fell to the ground.

Dead.

Mully rushed to his side and quickly put her finger in his ear. She felt no pulse, withdrew her finger, and looked fondly at the old man as she brushed a wisp of silver hair from his forehead and then stood. "Old Newt is gone kaput," she said.

Newt's body was sprinkled with beer, and laid to rest at the foot of a dead tree where Obbman carved into the wood, "Newt Flerkk—Debt to Obbman Klepp is 21 Grumpletts!" After a few unkind words were said about the old Oidenoid, the others moved away. Warren and Lily stood looking at the grave, grappling with the way these creatures dealt with death; their casualness about it and their obsession with debts owed by the deceased. Obbman and Mully were certainly closest to the old man, but they showed little sorrow over his passing and, what mournful sentiment they did show, they now seemed to be done with. Not even little Elo—who was quite fond of the avuncular Newt—showed any great sadness. They did not appear to be cold or uncaring creatures, but when death took one of them, they seemed altogether ready to move past it with little emotion.

A Bathroom Break

"WHO'S GOTTA PEE?" Grampa asked.

The children exchanged looks and turned back to their grandfather. "Nobody, Grampa," Henry said.

"Well, Joe, you're wrong. I do!" He closed his father's journal and laid it aside, then threw back the sheet and dropped his toothpick legs over the side of the bed. "Help me up! Help me up!"

Henry and Joe quickly moved to either side of the old man and took hold of his elbows to help him stand. When he was on his feet, the boys held on to his arms.

"Ach, what're you doin'? What?" the old man barked.

"We're helping you."

"Well, I don't need help *now!* I gotta pee! So leggo me and get outta my way!"

The boys backed away, as Grampa mumbled something and shook his head. Then he teetered and fell like a redwood tree, face-first, onto the floor. And there he lay. The children stood on either side of him, looking down. Finally a muffled voice emerged. "Well, helf me up! Helf me up!"

They quickly did so. And, when Grampa was standing again, Joe and Henry were hesitant to let go of him until he barked at them again. This time he made it.

The children sat back down then to wait, while Henry reached over and picked up his great-grandfather's journal.

And they waited.

And waited.

Finally, Francie leaned to her brother and whispered, "You think he's okay?"

"Huh?" Henry said, looking up. "What?"

"You think Grampa's okay? In the bathroom?"

Henry looked over at the closed bathroom door and shrugged. "Guess so." He turned back to the pages of the journal. "You know, there's not much in here about Leo. And there's nothing about him at the end. It's weird."

Then the first of several agonizing, no, make that *blood-curdling*, screams emanated from within the bathroom. The children stood up, and Francie rushed to the door. "Grampa? Are you okay?"

"Huh?" came the reply. "Who is that?"

"It's Francie."

"Well, mind your own business, Francie!"

And, as she walked back to sit down again, the disturbing screams continued. When it was quiet again, they thought that, perhaps, the old man had actually died. But they didn't dare venture over to ask.

When finally Grampa returned to his bed, Francie asked him what happened to Leo.

"Leo?"

"Yeah. Where was he? Did he die? What happened to the Crystal?"

"Of course he died. He *had* to."

"Wait a minute," said Joe. "Why did he *have* to die?"

"We all do. What'da ya think? We live forever?"

"That's not what he meant," Henry said, growing impatient with the old man. "We want to know what happened to Leo."

"Who's telling this story?" Grampa demanded, his tone so combative that none of the children answered. "Now then," he said, satisfied that he'd stifled their irritating questions, "here's what happened to Leo and the Crystal."

The Ukg Coin

THOUGH THEY WERE still well ahead of Warren and Lily and the Oidenoids, Morton and Kyle, along with Leo, had made a couple of unfortunate turns after crossing through the Forest of Weary Trees. One particularly bad turn landed them smack in the middle of the Breathing Gullies of Dult, where they had been nearly crushed to death when one of the gullies sneezed. What was also unfortunate was that their mistaken direction had led them to the Fork of Warped Time. From there it was only a short distance to the Great Big Canyon that bordered Outer Nuldoid. But their dilemma was this: They had to pass through one of two passages leading away from the Fork, where one sign pointed to the right and said, "Tunnel of Squished Hours," and the other pointed to the left and said, "Cavern of Twisted Days."

Morton had been through the area once before, but long ago—several hundred years earlier—and he could not remember which was the correct passage. He knew there was a trick to the wording of the signs, but what that trick was, he couldn't recall.

It was a crucial decision they were about to make because, in one direction, they would experience time that stretched out for days and weeks, but they would arrive at the other end of the passage only a few minutes later. The other direction warped time in the opposite way; that is, ten minutes would pass for the travelers, but they would emerge several days or weeks later.

Morton stood in front of the two signs and scratched his head.

"Ya stinkin' drobbs hobble," Kyle said to him. "How we never gets nowhere is a dunno! Yas doesn't know yer grass from a mole inna ground!"

"Ach, is givin' we dat ache inna head yas!" Morton replied.

If they chose the wrong passage, they would emerge weeks later, and by then the earth would have stopped rotating altogether. And even if Warren and Lily and the Oidenoids *were* to find them within the passage, they themselves would be subject to the same elements. There still would be no chance of returning the Crystal to the earth's surface before its rotation stopped.

To make matters worse, or better, it didn't matter which sign they chose, because there was a real possibility that the signs had been switched by practical jokers—of which there were plenty in Neither Norr. And if the signs had been switched once, they'd probably been switched twice, thrice, ad infinitum, by other practical jokers. So, with a fifty percent chance of choosing the right passage, and a fifty percent chance of choosing the wrong one, they turned left into the one marked "Cavern of Twisted Days." And after walking "several hours," they realized they had made the right choice.

It was nearly a full day of hiking through sand, up and down the hills within the caverns, before they decided to stop and rest.

Leo insisted on it, having grown tired from carrying the Crystal. As Morton and Kyle began to argue about where best to sit, the boy plopped himself down where he was, and laid the Crystal in the sand. He rested his head against the cavern's wall and was about to doze off, when he felt something at his fingertips.

It was an old coin, darkened by age and smooth from wear. One side of it showed a creature in a guillotine and said, "Kingg Hal's Beann Choppin'." Apparently, King Hal was one of the last Droiden Frobble rulers, and made the mistake of believing that the "peeeple serves at dat pleeesure a Kingg Hal." The subjects of Droiden Frobble, as Kyle pointed out, disagreed and took pleasure "at dat choppin' offa Hal's head."

When Leo turned the coin over, he saw a depiction of an odd-looking animal called a Gorkken Stobble. It had a long, pointed snout, bulbous eyes and a bloated oversized body with stubby legs that looked barely able to lift its torso. The Gorkken Stobble was a utilitarian creature used by the Droiden Frobbles to suck up kitchen messes and spilled substances. Unfortunately, after a youngster named Budd Ferk discovered that stomping on the Gorkken Stobble produced a prolonged and humorous farting sound, the practice became common and ultimately led to the extinction of the Gorkken Stobble.

But what was most peculiar about the coin was that, when Leo turned it over again, he saw yet *another* side. Though some of the lettering had been rubbed off, there were three letters remaining: "uky."

Kyle looked the coin over and handed it to Morton, who explained that it was an "Uky coin" from the Droiden Frobble Dynasty, worth seven-and-a-half Drumpletts (the unit of currency within the dynasty).

"Wow," Leo said, taking the coin back. "A lucky coin. That's so cool. Now I'm gonna have good luck."

Kyle shrugged. "Depends," he said. "Does ya finds it right sides up, or wrong sides down?"

"Don't remember," the boy said, looking again at the coin. "Does it matter?"

"Sure yeah, der matters. One is fer good luck, one is dat bad."

"Nah, isn't dat," Morton interjected. "Ya sends 'im down a wrong road to fooey. 'At coin's luck is dependin' on who gots it last."

"Ach, yas got bags in yer bell jar!"

Morton turned to Leo. "Is best ta flops it inna trash, so as nothin' goes ta bad."

But Leo did not throw the coin away. He looked at it for a while longer and then stuffed it in his pocket and fell asleep.

After they argued for a bit about the Droiden Frobble Dynasty, the Nuldoids curled up at Leo's feet and went to sleep as well. Leo was, at first, uncomfortable with the little creatures sleeping so close to him, but each time he kicked them away, or got up himself and moved away, he'd find Morton and Kyle curled up beside him again. What he didn't realize at the time was that Nuldoids slept in klumpanoids—small groups of three, four or five.

Unfortunately, both of the Nuldoids were dead wrong about the coin's luck. This was because most Nuldoids spent as little time as possible in Neither Norr—where much of the Droiden Frobble Dynasty extended. Obviously, Oidenoids and Harvesters knew much more about the true nature of the coin, but Morton and Kyle were neither Oidenoids nor Harvesters.

While the Nuldoids were right about the coins bringing both good luck and bad, they were wrong about how it occurred. It didn't matter who'd had the coin before Leo, as Morton asserted. Nor did it matter if the coin was found "right sides up, or wrong sides down," as Kyle said. The unfortunate truth was this: An

Uky coin from the Droiden Frobble Dynasty brought good luck *and* bad luck, alternately. So, if one experienced good luck from the coin, he or she or sheesh[*] was sure to experience bad. As travelers in Neither Norr often said, there were "three sides to dat coin." But only *two* sides to its luck.

The two Nuldoids and Leo slept for nearly a full night and awoke refreshed and ready to move on. As they made their way through the passage, they chatted and bickered, stopped and ate, rested and slept again. Because there was no reason to hurry in the caverns, the creatures told Leo much about their home, about their lives, and about the Oidenoids. The boy learned about Good Riddance Day, when the Oidenoids where kicked out of Nuldoid after fifty years of trying to impose their peculiar values on Nuldoid. And he was told that Oidenoids believed in the word of Lloyd, but that they had come to many strange conclusions. Especially when it came to the Wheel of Nuldoid and the Crystal. The Oidenoids would, Leo learned, do anything to stop the Crystal from being where it was supposed to be. And it was supposed to be at the Wheel of Nuldoid.

After several days of hiking through the passage, the three of them emerged a few minutes after they'd entered it.

---

[*] The term "sheesh" was in reference to a Delnoid—Nuldoid's third sex.

The Valley of Lopsided Water

FAR ABOVE LEO and the Nuldoids, Lily and Warren were climbing into the opening beside the lakebed, and descending a ladder within a vertical tube that was dimly lit by a series of aging light bulbs, each protruding from the wall of the tube opposite the rungs of the ladder. At the end of the tube, the Oidenoids and the humans dropped down onto a ledge that looked out over the Valley of Lopsided Water, which was really more of a gulch than a valley. When they emerged and stepped onto the ledge, Lily and Warren hopped down off it onto the sandy floor of the gulch and then helped each of the Oidenoids down. It was narrow, perhaps twenty feet at its widest point. The wall to their left was no more than a span of jutting rocks, splashed with green patches of weeds and some peculiar-looking vines. The wall to their right, however, was covered by a river, its water moving idly along its contours, completely indifferent to the gravity that Warren and Lily and the creatures were subject to.

It was quite odd. Warren moved to get a closer look, while the Oidenoids seemed to pay it no particular attention, except for Mully, who cupped some water for Elo to drink. Warren was transfixed by the moving water. "Why does it do this?" he asked Mully as he too cupped some water for himself.

"What's it does?"

"It's going along the wall here, but it's not flowing downhill. Why does it do this?"

Mully thought about it a moment and shrugged. "Why not?"

"Ach," said a bald Oidenoid named Chuck, who had overheard them in passing, "it doesn't always does dis. Sometimes dem sides it switches."

"Switches?" Warren asked as Lily moved up beside him. "The water switches sides? So what happens if it does that while we're here?"

The Oidenoid thought about it, and scratched his round head. "S'pose we's drowned dead."

Fortunately the river did not switch sides as they made their way through the gorge, though the very thought of it doing so drove Warren to move more quickly. The truth was, however, that Chuck was mistaken about the river switching sides—it had never done so. He merely thought it had because he passed through the gorge a year earlier going the opposite direction.

When they reached the end of the gorge, the river just as mysteriously swerved away and then dipped severely down into a small opening that appeared to be entirely too small to accommodate the amount of water that was rushing into it. Again the Oidenoids paid the phenomenon no special attention, while Warren and Lily were astonished.

After they had passed the disappearing water, they assessed the towering walls of the gorge as it ballooned out to a wider space and then weaved in another direction. There was a dark opening to their right that Chuck stepped over to, proudly declaring that it, no doubt, led to the ancient slide. And, before anyone could stop him, he walked into the opening and yelled back out from the darkness, that all he could see inside was a "huge big tongue." In the next instant, the rim of the opening slammed shut and moved from side to side in a chewing motion as the others gasped.

As the giant Fishing Worm calmly ground the little Oidenoid into mulch, Warren saw into one of its cold eyes, and quickly took Lily's arm to move her back. A moment later, it swallowed Chuck and belched with great satisfaction, releasing an enormous gust of foul wind. As you can imagine, it was perhaps the worst smell—if one could even call it a smell—the humans had ever encountered. (Warren noticed later that the hair of his eyebrows had actually been singed by the worm's searing exhaust.) After another moment, the worm opened its mouth and filled the opening with its lips again to wait patiently for another victim.

Borden turned then to Obbman. "Dat Chuck—wasn't never too good of directions."

"Is a good bet, eh, dat slide is on 'at other side der," Beatrice suggested to Hammet, as though tribute enough had been paid to Chuck.

Hammet nodded. "Sure yeah to dat."

When they found another opening on the opposite side of the gorge, Roggo tossed a rock into it. When nothing happened, they entered. It was dimly lit inside by a few dusty light bulbs. Perhaps forty feet into it, they came upon several large wooden planks that had been nailed across the back wall of the cave. The wood was old, some of it rotting from age, the square nails that held the boards in place were rusted, many to the point of crumbling. A couple of bent and rusted signs, attached to the wood eons ago, said, "YA DOESN'T GOES HERE!" and "OUT YA STAYS! By Official Order of Department of Serious Official Orders & Genuine Don'tyas!"

The Oidenoids all stood silently in front of the wall for a moment, looking at the wooden planks and the two deteriorating signs. Finally, Hammet drew a woeful breath and said, "Well, 'at's dat."

Mully shook her head sadly. "An' comes we all this ways. Ach!"

Borden kicked the sand at his feet. "Drats to dat!" he said and turned to the others. "But we sure does gives it a horky bork of a try, eh?"

"Sure yeah," Hammet said with another sigh. "Welp, let's we head back, eh."

Borden shoved his stubby hands into his pockets, as several of the Oidenoids glumly began to file back out of the cave. Lily and Warren were befuddled. "Wait a minute!" Warren finally said. "Where are you going?"

Beatrice, who had not left yet, looked up and shrugged. "Is closed der."

"Is all dat wood der," Obbman added, "all boarded up, tight an' good. An' dat sign der says no to we. Fida-boned sign says rules is 'Official.'"

Lily turned to him, floored that they would give up so easily. "You're kidding, right?" Warren then stepped over to the wooden planks, grabbed hold of the top one and pulled on it vigorously. It tore away easily, its rusted nails snapping in half like brittle twigs. He tossed the wood on the floor of the cave, while the creatures stood where they were, stunned that the human had so blatantly defied the admonitions of an officially posted sign. Warren reached for the next board and pulled at it until it broke at its rotted middle. He tossed the fragmented wood on top of the first plank.

The Oidenoids who had nearly left the cave returned to watch as Warren and Lily pulled off one piece of wood after the next until the entrance to the ancient Droiden Frobble slide was yawning wide open in front of them.

Hammet let out a whistle. "Holy Lloyd an' Floyd. Looks ya der at dat."

It was a smooth, glistening tube—perhaps four or five feet in diameter, made of alabaster or porcelain or abalone shell. It dipped down and twisted away from them into utter darkness and, presumably, into the bowels of the earth like some bizarre theme park adventure.

A few, including Lily, ventured into its gaping mouth, careful not to slip as they looked down its cavernous throat, while the others stood outside with Warren to discuss what next to do. The question they faced of course was the condition of the slide and what possible dangers and perils might lie beyond the opening. Was it blocked somewhere? Had it collapsed or been pulled in two by the earth's movement? Or, worse, did it feed into the mouth of another Fishing Worm?

"Welp," Ebnetter announced, puffing his tiny chest out as he boldly stepped closer to the mouth of the slide. "If Ol' Ebby doesn't not comes back, ya doesn't wants ta takes dat slide, eh," he said, and dove into the dark void of the slide's opening, disappearing with a tiny *whooosh!*

The others stood for a moment, trying to figure out what it was exactly that was not quite right about Ebnetter's "heroic" gesture. The logic of it was askew somehow, and they all sensed it. Finally, Warren asked, "But… how will he get back here to tell us anything?" That was it, that was the problem with Ebnetter's logic: Even if he wasn't killed, even if he arrived safely in the Great Big Canyon, he would still have no way of returning to tell them of his safe arrival. And certainly not in any reasonable amount of time, the whole idea of the slide being that it was a shortcut. On the other hand, if he *was* killed—if he was swallowed by a worm, for instance—well, he would not be returning at all to tell them anything.

After some thoughtful and courteous deliberation, the general consensus amongst the Oidenoids was that they would all simply have to jump into the slide together, and, come what may, hope for the best. Warren certainly did not like the prospect of such an uncertain venture but, if they were going to use the tunnel, there was no other way.

But first, Obbman announced, they were going to take a nap!

"A nap? Now?" Warren was perplexed. "Aren't we in a hurry?" While he and Lily were perhaps more tired than any of them—they had traveled the farthest and had not slept in what must have been nearly two days—he felt they should keep going, nonetheless. There was too much at stake. But he was fighting a losing battle because, once the issue was raised, the Oidenoids were all fully behind the idea. Oidenoids were, after all, still Nuldoids—and Nuldoids were zealous nappers. In fact, a number of them were already getting sleepy just from Obbman's having mentioned it.

"Ach," said Hammet. "Dem noids an' dat kid with dat Crystal, they doesn't used no slide. Is a slow hobb to hoe for dey. An' dat slide takes we der in a zippity lick, an' der we is—way out afronta dem."

Warren considered it and then looked at Lily. She nodded to say that maybe a short nap was not such a bad idea.

"Asides," Hammet added, "dat slide might be makes we dead. Isn't not no hurry fur dat, huh?"

Luckily, there were some small pockets within the walls of the gulch near the cave's entrance—caused by air bubbles, formed within cooling magma a few million years ago—where the Oidenoids could squeeze in and curl up to doze off in klumpanoids. Lily and Warren looked on, somewhat stymied, as the creatures rushed to and fro, claiming all of the remaining cubbyholes at their level before nestling in. Warren stepped back and surveyed the wall for a moment. He saw a larger pocket, maybe ten feet or so above them, and pointed it out to Lily, suggesting that she go ahead and take it.

"Why? Because I'm a woman?"

"Uhh..." Warren knew she was kidding, but knew, as well, that he was still treading on thin ice, that a correct and diplomatic answer was a necessity (it was, after all, 1989, when such things were important). "No... I just thought I'd try being polite, you know, as a novelty," he said with a smile that was every bit as vague as he could make it.

She couldn't help but laugh. It was a good answer that easily put the next volley in her lap. "You're sweet," she said. "You take that one. I'll find another." She kissed his cheek and moved off.

He watched her walk away, surprised at how much his face flushed from her kiss.

There was plenty of room to stretch out, he realized, after he climbed the wall up to the opening. He laid back and closed his eyes and then found Lily in his thoughts. A moment later, sleep was enveloping him like a warm wave.

"Hey..." It was a soft whisper from nearby.

He started, not remembering where he was, then looked over at the ledge of the pocket and saw Lily's face.

"I couldn't find anything," she said.

"Oh." He moved his elbows beneath him, a little annoyed that she would expect him now to give up his sleeping space.

"Move over," she said as she climbed in and lay down beside him.

He moved as close as he could to the wall at the back of the pocket while she stretched out and made herself comfortable. But when he closed his eyes to return to slumber, his mind was racing again with thoughts of her. He shifted and opened one eye to look over. She was lying on her back, her hands locked behind her head, her eyes closed. He studied the contours of her upturned nose and the sharp angle of her jaw. He watched her eyelashes flutter slightly. He gazed at the lines of her lips, and found himself wanting very much to kiss her. When she shifted, and he thought she might see him, he closed his eyes like he was asleep. After a moment he couldn't help but venture another look at her. "Okay, I know this is crazy," the words were spilling out, "but I, uh... like you."

There. He'd said it. He had exposed his heart to her.

He waited for her to answer.

She said nothing.

Then he heard her quietly snoring.

He turned onto his other side to face the back wall of the pocket and waited to doze off.

A moment later, as he gently drifted again toward sleep, he felt her hand touch his shoulder. He tried to wake himself so that he could be sure he was not dreaming. But he wasn't sure if he was waking, or just dreaming that he was waking. He struggled to pull himself out of it, feeling vaguely like he was being drowned by sleep. And then he felt her snuggle against his backside, felt her hand slip from his shoulder to his chest.

She was spooning him.

He opened his eyes, or thought he was opening his eyes, when he heard her quietly whisper, "I like being with you."

And, when he turned onto his back to see if she was awake, he felt her lips touch his.

() () ()

"Hey, Crustoids! Up ya gets! Naps is done an' over!"

Warren heard the tiny voice shouting up at them from the floor of the gorge, but he did not want to get up. He felt as though he had hardly slept, while at the same time, he was not sure he hadn't actually slept well.

Lily opened her eyes and stretched. She looked at him and smiled. "Hi."

"Hi." He smiled and wondered if it had all been real.

He held her arm as she climbed out of the pocket. She didn't object to the help. He climbed down after her, and they joined the others as they regrouped and made their way to the ancient slide.

·

The End of the Oidenoids

WHEN THEY APPROACHED the opening of the slide, Hammet gathered the other creatures and instructed Beatrice and Roggo to hand out the last of the beer froote from their knapsacks. He took off his helmet then and knelt on one knee to recite a poem he had written while everyone was napping (as you've probably already surmised, these creatures were very fond of songs and poems):

> *Off for dat Crystal goes we...*
> *Inna dat hole we jumps!*
> *An' flies we down its gullet!*
> *'Til dat other end we dumps,*
> *An' hopes we isn't pellet!*

It was not much of a poem, as poems go, though it seemed to rhyme well enough. The "pellet" thing was peculiar though, since it seemed to be a fuzzy reference to their becoming waste. And, if that was the case, the whole of the poem vaguely compared the Oidenoids to food down a "gullet," to be dumped out like so much, well, pooh. But still, the others complimented Hammet, while some made mental notes to discourage him from coming up with any more poetry.

Beer froote was passed among them, and, as they partook and passed it on, they wiped their lips, touched their bellies and their crotches, some reciting the beer prayer as they did. When the last creature, Fitz, had done so, Hammet repeated "Hib nobb del noid," and then moved to the opening of the ancient slide where, quite unceremoniously, he leapt into the void.

Warren and Lily watched as one Oidenoid after the next did the same, until all of the creatures had vanished down the dark hole before them. He turned to her then and tried to sound casual. "Ladies first?" She certainly would have laughed if she had not been so scared, but she smiled and took his arm and together they jumped into the slide.

It was both exhilarating and terrifying as they flew down the tube, neither knowing if at any moment they would be crushed by the jaws of a ravenous Fishing Worm, or sizzled by a waiting pool of hot lava. The Oidenoids, on the other hand, screamed with glee and whooped at every violent twist and turn. The tube shot them left and right, up and down, through one sinewy breathtaking curve to the next, at times even looping up and completely around before whipping them off in another direction altogether. All of it at dizzying speeds that became apparent when they careened past the occasional light bulb from ancient times, still dimly glowing. There too were sections of utter darkness that made them feel motionless.

In another, especially long section of the slide, the ancients—anticipating the boredom of the journey—had drawn lines that seemed to move as they were passed, wiggling back and forth, then from side to side, becoming wide and then narrow, until the lines began to twist and swirl and gradually form vague images. It was an antiquated movie of sorts, created by the movement of the viewer. The images soon became characters, creatures like the Oideniods, that evolved from rudimentary figures to detailed warriors who marched toward their enemy in battle. But, as the troops moved closer, one of the warriors dropped a ring, and the others stopped to help him search for it, as did the enemy. And when the ring was recovered, there was no battle. Instead, handshakes and smiles were exchanged all around, then both sides returned home and executed their leaders.

Warren tried to lift his head, but could barely do so as they were moving so rapidly. Fifty, sixty, maybe seventy miles an hour! Down, down, down they went, zipping along the slide's smooth inner surface. The entire ride took more than a couple of hours, so Warren had plenty of time to notice that the inside surface of the tube was not greasy or wet, yet it didn't burn the skin from friction. Though he never found out what the material was, he knew it was not something that existed on the surface of the earth.*

It was an exhilarating ride that everyone but Warren enjoyed. Lily got a kick out of it, but only after the first hour, when she began to trust that she would not be killed in the process.

Finally, they were spat out into a pile of squirming bodies on a landing some thirty feet away from an opening to the Great Big Canyon. In total, eleven Oidenoids shot out of the ancient slide. First, Hammet, Beatrice and Roggo. Then there was Obbman,

---

* Not yet anyway. It was amazingly similar to a material called Silk Rock, developed by Grampa Worst in San Francisco later in the next century. Though he was already wealthy from several other inventions, Silk Rock made Grampa Worst a very wealthy man.

Mully and little Elo. Hazel, Borden, Merle, Fitz, and Owen. Lily and Warren came flying out last, landing on the stack of little creatures, causing a number of "uhhhg!"s and "oooof!"s and "ach!"s and "Is sorry!"s and "Aw, croib!"s.

As they began to untangle themselves, they realized that Ebnetter was standing beside them. He had apparently been waiting there for some time. He said he'd realized there was a flaw in his original plan the second he came flying out of the slide. But, he was also a little peeved at the other Oidenoids because he had been expecting them to have arrived sooner. He'd begun to think they'd changed their minds. None of this was expressed, however. Only, "Is glad to see yas finally makes it."

Hammet picked his helmet up from the ground and dusted it off as he sensed Ebnetter's irritation and apologized for taking so long, explaining that they decided to take a nap before jumping into the slide. Warren, sitting on the ground and listening to the exchange, could see that Ebnetter was unhappy with them, but the Oidenoid merely forced a smile and changed the subject, saying he'd been checking out some things… *since he had so much spare time.*

The others straightened their clothing and collected their hats and helmets and those few items that had skittered out of their knapsacks. Ebnetter explained that he'd seen no sign yet of the noids, the Crystal or—forgetting that Warren and Lily were there—the "toid" they were traveling with. He immediately realized his faux pas ("toid" was generally considered a derogatory term, though regular Nuldoids used it frequently), as some of the others' eyes—especially Mully and Obbman's—grew wide at the gaffe, and Hazel even gasped out loud. Ebnetter immediately offered an apology—though the humans had no idea the term *was* derogatory—and then continued with his assessment of the canyon.

As he explained what he'd seen, Warren and Lily ventured toward the opening at the edge of the landing. Ebnetter said that he had twice seen Harvesters passing through, on their way to Nuldoid, once on a ledge above him and once on a path that was farther down the canyon, closer to The Red River. And, as if that wasn't terrifying enough, he said he'd heard rumbling within the walls of the canyon, meaning Fishing Worms had infested it. It was news to many of the Oidenoids, since the Great Big Canyon had always been free of worm infestations. The danger was not only that the worms might "chomp" some unsuspecting prey, but that they—since they slept in large but snug tunnels—might suddenly awaken or be startled, and shift or jolt, causing the rock around them, and subsequently the canyon's wall, to crack or even fall away.

Though it was ominous information Ebnetter was relaying, for Lily and Warren it faded like background noise when they looked out onto the canyon itself. Its enormity was overwhelming, reducing them to teeny ants as they stood there in a virtual pinhole near the middle of the canyon's massive wall. It was every bit as deep and high and huge as the Crust's Grand Canyon. Overhead, they saw soaring vistas, and, when they looked far, far below, they saw the sweeping curves of the glowing Red River that ran along its floor. But, while Lily and Warren were awed, the Oidenoids were not impressed. The Great Big Canyon, to them, was no more than an obstacle they would have to contend with—Nuldoids disliked heights almost as much as they disliked weather—if they were going to capture the Crystal.

Across from them—perhaps a couple of hundred feet away— they could see a panoply of rich colors that graduated in layers of shale, siltstone, mudstone and fine-grained sandstone. Chocolate, vermilion, blue, pink, gray, green, each traversed the length of the canyon for several hundred miles, each blending into the layers of rock above and below, chronicling the millions of years it took to form. Varying shades of amber from sandstone rich in iron swirled around the curves of the opposite wall, where layers of green-colored shale blended into dark granite and bordered thicker layers of brilliant redwall limestone.

Warren squinted up towards the opposite ridge of the canyon several hundred feet above them and saw amber light sifting over its ledge like some expansive natural sconce beneath a vast ceiling of calcite, the source of the light unknown.

Holding Warren's arm, Lily ventured to the edge of the precipice to look down at the bottom of the canyon, where dark-colored metamorphic rock formed a narrow bed that cradled a bright red river of lava as it ran the length of the canyon floor. There she could see jutting rock formations and plateaus atop towering layered buttes that stood like abandoned Corinthian columns.

It was breathtaking in its splendor and terrifying all at once, for they knew they would have to venture out along the side of this titanic rift. They would have to climb the narrow path that hugged the wall and led up away from them toward a section of the canyon where the two walls came within a few feet of each other. On the other side of this narrowing, the walls separated again, and the footpath descended for another mile or so to the canyon's floor, where they would find the iron-gated entrance to Outer Nuldoid.

If indeed they were ahead of the Nuldoids and the boy with the Crystal, it was near this entrance that the Oidenoids planned to hide, to lie in wait, and then overtake the Nuldoids and rescue the Crystal.

As the Oidenoids and the humans ventured out, single file, onto the pathway—none of them speaking in more than a whisper for fear of disturbing a sleeping worm—they found that it was no more than a couple feet wide and looked unsteady at best. Deep cracks had formed in the rock and threatened to send the outer half of the footway hurtling into the abyss below, worm or no worm. It was not at all a comforting thing to see, and even though Warren wanted desperately to seem brave and fearless to Lily, he had to stop twice and breathe slowly to regain his equilibrium.

It was very slow going toward the narrowing of the canyon. The humans walked behind the Oidenoids, who had decided to put Ebnetter out ahead since he was most eager to lead the group. All in all, they made steady progress with only one minor mishap, when Borden stopped to pick out a rock from the bottom of his shoe, and Hazel bumped into him.

Then Warren heard a voice echoing from somewhere. He stopped in his tracks and held the wall so that he could slowly turn his head and look back to where it might have come from. Fragments of sound bounced around the canyon again, and now Lily heard it too. She stopped to look back at Warren. He was searching the path on the other side of the canyon that was, more or less, a mirror image of the walkway they were on. The Oidenoids stopped as well when they heard it.

It was a human's voice.

A young human's voice.

Beatrice was the first to spot them. A human and two Nuldoids. They were trudging up the path on the opposite wall, headed in the same direction, toward the same narrowing. She nudged Owen and pointed. Owen turned and tugged Lily's pant leg to point out where the voice was coming from.

Then Warren spotted them—Leo and the two Nuldoids, Morton and Kyle. The boy had been talking as he climbed the incline, still with the Crystal slung over his shoulder, behind the two Nuldoids. None of the three had yet noticed Warren and the others, in part because the boy and the Nuldoids were arguing about how long it would take a falling body to hit the bottom of the canyon.

Word quickly passed from one Oidenoid to the next, until Ebnetter, in front, looked across and saw the other party. Unfortunately there was nowhere to hide, so all that Warren and the others could do was crouch down, stay quiet and hope the Nuldoids and Leo did not notice them.

The echoing voices were becoming clearer now as Warren heard one of the creatures call Leo and the other Nuldoid "a couple a drobbs horkels" because neither was "knowin' squat 'bout dat big droppin's down!" The despicable creatures from his basement were still bickering, and when Warren heard Leo call one of the creatures a "clueless droib," he realized that the loathsome Nuldoids had transformed the boy. Not only did he seem to be just as disagreeable and argumentative as they, but now he was using their language!

Warren and Lily and the others hoped to remain unnoticed, at least until they reached the narrow part of the canyon. Some of the Oidenoids would then cross to the other side—putting them behind the Nuldoids, while Warren and Lily and the rest would continue along the footway they were on. Thus, they would trap the Nuldoids and the boy at the bottom of the canyon, near the entrance to Nuldoid.

It was not a bad plan, but it was never to come about.

As Obbman turned to pass the information on to Mully, he accidentally knocked a rock off the side that rattled down the canyon and flew out into the open air. It wasn't a lot of noise, but it was enough to draw the Nuldoids' attention. They looked from the falling rock up to the path where the Oidenoids and the humans were crouching.

"Ach! They is others!" shouted one of the Nuldoids.

"Is dat toid!" screamed the other Nuldoid, pointing across at Warren.

Ebnetter suddenly stood and yelled down to the other Oidenoids, "We cuts 'em off! We cuts 'em off!" Then he was hurrying up the path toward the narrowing.

Leo and the Nuldoids started to move quickly in the same direction, obviously realizing what the Oidenoids were up to, hoping to pass the narrowing first.

Ebnetter reached the narrow section well ahead of the others. And while it would have been reasonable for him to wait for help before he attempted to breach the chasm—perhaps three or four feet wide—he did not, because, as you already know, he was quite impulsive.

The problem was, when he leapt across the gap, his legs were not quite powerful enough to propel him safely onto the path of the opposing wall. Instead he hurtled, chest-first, into the edge of the path with a "boooff!" his arms shooting out in front of him, desperately clinging to whatever there was to cling to—which wasn't really anything—while he screamed for help, his legs dangling over open air, kicking at the wall beneath him. Pieces of rock crumbled away and fell out toward the Red River below, disappearing altogether in the infinite open drop.

All of the horrific things that happened next, happened very quickly, as these sort of things usually do—much more quickly, in fact, than the time it takes to describe them here. No one had any time to react to what was going on, not that they could have done anything about it anyway.

The Nuldoids and Leo were fast approaching on their pathway, obviously intent on getting past poor Ebnetter, possibly intending to kick him off in the process, while Borden—who had been only a few steps behind Ebnetter—stood now, fretting about how he might save Ebnetter.

It didn't really matter though, because Ebnetter's kicking and screaming had already put in motion a disastrous chain of events. Unfortunately, a giant worm had been asleep inside the canyon's wall next to the narrowing. And, as you've probably already surmised, Ebnetter's frantic commotion woke the creature, startled it, and caused it to jolt within the confines of the tunnel it was laying in. The entire wall of the canyon shook in reverberation, loosening a huge chunk of jutting rock that was perhaps twenty feet above where Ebnetter was clinging for his life. The rock cracked, broke free and dropped straight down, tearing out large sections from both pathways as it did, killing Ebnetter and Borden instantly and taking them with it as it broke through to open air and gradually shrunk to a tiny pebble before *plinking* down in the twisting Red River at the bottom of the canyon.

At the same moment, another section of the path—where three of the Oidenoids were standing—broke free from the canyon's wall and dropped suddenly into the void behind the giant rock. With it fell Fitz, Merle and Hazel, though they did not go quietly—their high-pitched screams could be heard almost until they created three tiny splashes in the Red River.

The Oidenoids in front of Warren and Lily—Owen, Beatrice, Roggo, Mully, Obbman, Hammet and Elo—suddenly found themselves standing on a path that was now a dead end. They scrambled back towards Warren and Lily, pushing frantically over the humans' feet to get past them. Warren knew there was nothing left to do but turn back and follow the Oidenoids.

But, as the creatures scurried toward the safety of the opening where they had earlier emerged, another section of the pathway broke from the wall and dropped into the void, taking with it

Roggo, Beatrice, Owen and Mully. And, as the four little Oidenoids dwindled into oblivion, Warren saw there was no longer any path behind them. Or ahead.

They were trapped. Warren, Lily and the three remaining Oidenoids. They were utterly, entirely, hopelessly trapped.

Something besides panic gripped Warren's heart at that moment. It was, after all, too late for panic, too late for anything but resigned, absolute and quiet despair.

He looked across the canyon and saw that Leo and the Nuldoids had turned back. They were moving down the other path in the direction they had come. A moment later, they ducked into an opening in the canyon's opposite wall and disappeared, along with the Crystal.

() () ()

Henry, Joe and Francie sat slack-jawed beside Grampa's bed. They had not wanted to take a break to get a snack or a drink or get up and stretch since all of this canyon stuff began. They couldn't believe that so many of the Oidenoids had died. Just like that. And now, what hope did Warren and Lily and the three Oidenoids have?

Grampa then asked, somewhat facetiously, if the children wanted to switch stories again and hear about Leo and the Nuldoids, who were on their way to the Pockets of Roundlet, just outside Outer Nuldoid. The children were emphatic that Grampa tell them what happened to Warren and Lily and the Oidenoids.

The Harvesters

THEY WERE DOOMED—Lily and Warren, Obbman, Hammet and Elo—as they stood on what was left of the path, a thousand feet above the canyon's floor. What could they do but stand there? The only way out, it became clear to Warren, was by slow and miserable starvation, or a terrifying and final leap.

Lily put her head sadly against Warren's shoulder and then wrapped her arms around him. He leaned back against the wall, and peered up at the light that crept over the top of the canyon's distant ridge. He rubbed her arm, closed his eyes and thought about God. But he didn't ask to be rescued—that was impossible—didn't ask for a miracle, didn't expect God to change the situation. He only thought... *So, this is it?* He knew that he and Lily would perish now in the bowels of the earth, where not a soul knew they had gone. He wished he and the others could have returned the Crystal to the Crust, but it was not to be. And soon there would be suffering and death on the earth's surface as it stopped rotating altogether.

It was all very bleak.
Very bleak.

Hammet and Obbman begin to blame each other for their troubles—their polite and kind demeanors now long gone—when, finally, little Elo told them both to "Shuts it up, ya stinky croibs!"

Then it was quiet.

The Oidenoids sulked about and, though these creatures were generally untroubled by death, they did not at all like the idea of dying miserably by starvation or terrifyingly by jumping from a great height.

Warren, his eyes still closed, his face still upturned toward the light from above, could hear no sound except the grim thoughts in his head.

And then he realized the light overhead was being blocked by something.

"Psssst!" It was a voice coming from above. He opened his eyes and saw a peculiar man's head sticking out of an opening in the rock wall above him. "Pssssst!" the voice said again. "Some pickle der ya gots yoo-hoos inna, heh?"

Lily and the Oidenoids turned and looked up.

"Uh, yeah," Warren said.

"Holy Lloyd an' Floyd," the creature said, looking Warren and Lily over more closely. "You is a coupla big uns, heh." Suddenly small spotlights on either side of his head lit up. "Ya looks like dat Crust yas from."

And then another head popped out beside the first. It was another strange-looking creature with spotlights on either side of his head, though this one had a silver eyeball with a keyhole in it. "Fiske here. Dat's Orskin," he said, nodding toward the other. "Have yas up in a pronto, eh." And then he disappeared.

The one called Orskin looked down at Obbman, Hammet and Elo. "An' what's dat story der yas has fer yoo-hoo?"

"Ach," said Hammet, who had suddenly taken on a gruff and combative tone, "Nuldoids is we, huh! An' what slows dat pronto, eh? We doesn't standin' here for we looks."

"Hah! Ya got a Nully's 'tude, we gives ya dat awrighty. Holds on," Orskin said and disappeared. A moment later, a rope rolled out of the opening and dropped down beside Warren.

() () ()

When they had all reached the landing above, they saw there was a third creature, smaller than the other two. Warren noticed shopping carts along the wall of the cave, three of them—one smaller than the other two. Now he was certain that these were Harvesters. The Oidenoids knew it right away, of course, which was why Hammet was talking like a Nuldoid.

Their names were Orskin, Fiske and Mishkin Hobble, the last of which—the smallest of the three—insisted that others use only his full name when addressing or referring to him. Mishkin Hobble was so much smaller than the other two that Warren and Lily assumed at first he was a child. But he was not, as he indignantly pointed out to anyone who made that mistake. He was a dwarfy Nuldoid and was perfectly capable, as he also pointed out, of tearing the liver from any "toid or noid 'at decides ta has hisself a laugh at ol' Mishkin Hobble's account."

The other two, Orskin and Fiske, were pretty strange-looking themselves. Orskin Wobb had a braided beard that held at its bottom a small bone. He had a bulbous nose, and his dark hair was parted starkly down the middle, where it shot straight out to either side and flipped up just above two wing-like ears that looked much too large for his head.

Harlo Fiske chomped vigorously on an unlit cigar butt that he neither lit nor threw away. His beard was thin and speckled with gray, while, in one eye socket, there was no eye, but a shiny metal ball that occasionally rolled up or down to reveal its keyhole. And, while his manner of speaking was decidedly rugged, the features of his face were round and soft. In fact, without the beard, one would be hard-pressed to determine if he was male *or* female.

All three of them looked as though they had not bathed in weeks. They wore large dark coats, pieced together like patchwork quilts, that trailed on the ground behind them. They were a motley crew of miscreants that belched and passed gas without shame, and Warren was very uncomfortable in their presence. He and Lily had certainly heard enough about Harvesters from the Oidenoids to know that they were in grave danger.

"You is here havin' business, is ya?" Mishkin Hobble asked as he leaned against a rock and unwrapped a large wad of old chewing gum. "'Cause we doesn't so much never see dem toids through here..." He jammed the gum, with some difficulty, into his tiny mouth and started chewing vigorously.

Obbman shifted uncomfortably and stepped up to address the Harvesters. "Sure yeah to dat," he said, trying to appear casual. "We is gettin' dem toids..." he jerked his thumb in Warren and Lily's direction... "inna Nuldoid for dat ceremony."

"Sure yeah," Elo said, trying to help with the story. "We takes dat toids der for as Ed to see."

While the other Harvester, Orskin, pulled the beak off the end of a chicken froote and began to peel the rind away, the one called Fiske ambled over to the Oidenoids, looked them over, rubbed his chin. Finally he turned to Hammet. "An' ya say a fact is dat?"

Hammet nodded. "Sure yeah, to Nuldoid we takes dem toids, 'cause dey is experts at timeclock adjustin'..."

The Harvester squinted his one eye to look more intently at Hammet's, then took the soggy cigar from his mouth and examined it as he spoke. "Timeclock adjustin', ya say? An' would yas say dey is good or middlin' adjustors a timeclocks?"

"Good! Is Good! Good, yeah!" they all said at once.

Fiske nodded. "Uh-huh, uh-huh." He jammed the cigar back into his mouth. "So yoo-hoo's all in agreement 'bout dat der, huh?"

"Sure yeah to—" Hammet said, stopping, sensing a trap. "'Cept fer dat biggerest one der. Is lousy, dat one."

Fiske turned to Obbman. "An' yas gonna 'gree with dat?"

Obbman too understood the snare they were being led into. "Nah to dat. Hammet der don't know a rock from dat hole inna plug. We doesn't nots 'gree 'bout nuthin'."

"Hmmm," the Harvester said as he continued to look them over. "So… yoo-hoo's in agreement… dat ya disagrees?"

"Sure yeah, we disagrees," Hammet said, becoming confused. "But we doesn't agrees 'at we disagrees."

"Ah. So ya agrees den, eh?"

Lily could see that the Oidenoids were now in dangerous territory. "No sirree…" she said. "They argue all the time. *All* the time."

"They sure do," Warren added.

But the Harvesters seemed not to hear Lily and Warren, as Fiske turned to Orskin and told him to "gets dat ball." The other Harvester, however, was in the midst of enjoying the chicken froote he'd just peeled and could not be bothered. "Ya gots broken arms?"

"Ach!" Fiske said, as he tossed his cigar aside and stomped over to a shopping cart where he rifled through the junk and froote, and pulled out a red rubber ball that he held up for the Oidenoids to see. "Color der is what?"

190

There was fear in the eyes of the Oidenoids as they studied the rubber ball intently, Obbman squinting and moving closer to it. Finally they spoke at the same time, Hammet firmly declaring it "Blue!" while, at the same time, Obbman tentatively offered, "Yellow?"

For a moment, none of the creatures moved, each weighing carefully what next to do, as suddenly a small knife flashed in Obbman's hand—he having drawn it from a sheath on his belt—and he rushed toward Fiske. The Harvester did nothing for a moment, and then his right hand shot out from his side, where from it burst a ball of blue flames that leapt into the air, distracting Obbman enough to miss Fiske's other hand as it withdrew a wire with a small blade at the end of it that whipped through the air, and neatly slid across Obbman's throat, dropping the Oidenoid to the floor of the cave. Dead.

The other Harvesters had by now drawn weapons of their own as they looked toward Hammet and Elo. Warren knew he had to do something, or they might all be killed. He reached for a rock, hoping he'd not be noticed. But the Harvester, Fiske, turned sharply, pointed his thumb at Warren, and instantly Warren could neither stand nor move his hand. "We doesn't has no beefs der, toid," Fiske said, and turned back to the other Oidenoids, as Lily knelt beside Warren to see that he was all right.

Hammet and Elo were backing toward one of the openings at the rear of the cave as the Harvesters were slowly advancing on them. Finally, Elo, little Elo, planted his tiny feet defiantly in the dirt, his hands held firmly at his hips, and declared, "Ya doesn't stop we Oidenoids! We stands here now, an' we doesn't not never run! Never!"

The Harvesters took another step toward them and Hammet suddenly shouted, "Phooey ya hooey at dat!" He turned abruptly then and ran as fast as his short legs would carry him toward the

191

opening at the back of the cave and out, leaving Elo to fend for himself.

Elo turned back to the Harvesters and faced them, still unafraid, still defiant. "Ya doesn't stops we Oidenoids!" he shouted. "Ya never stops us! Never! Oidenoids is we, an' lives we again inna Downtown Nuldoid!"

What Elo said next, though, changed the dynamic of everything.

His words shocked Lily and Warren—though Lily had long suspected there was more to the Oidenoids than she and Warren were being told. As the little Oidenoid stood so boldly in front of the Harvesters, he declared, "We Oidenoids is gonna destroy dat Crystal! We Oidenoids is gonna stops dat Wheel! We Oidenoids is gonna stops all dat Hoidenall! As Lloyd is our wetness (an Oidenoid idiom referring to beer), we is gonna stops dat Wheel all and for once!" And, as if that wasn't enough, he repeated, "All an' for once, we tells ya!"

He turned suddenly and moved away with great haste—to the apparent amusement and derisive laughter of the three Harvesters.

At that instant, Warren's frozen body loosened, and he dropped to the ground like a dishrag. Lily helped him sit up and then sat next to him. They were stunned by what Elo had said. *The Oidenoids wanted to destroy the Crystal? They wanted to stop Hoidenall, Earth, they wanted to stop it from rotating? That's what they were trying to do?*

A moment later, the humans watched as the Harvesters gathered around Obbman's lifeless body beside a small pool of green blood. Warren was sure they were going to skin the dead Oidenoid, and it was not something he wanted to see.

But, it turned out, the Harvesters did nothing of the sort. Instead, they sprinkled the Oidenoid's body with beer from some beer froote before they touched their mouths, their bellies and their crotches. Then they gently lifted the body and tossed it out into the canyon. As they watched the body turn and float toward the Red River below, Orskin mumbled, "Is gone he goes, a pain is he now for Lloyd," which, Warren guessed, was another sort of prayer.

Orskin Wobb
Harvester

It all seemed rather thoughtful, kind even. The Harvesters had no interest in skinning the Oidenoid, as Lily and Warren had been led to believe. But, as they were just beginning to find out, they'd been told a great many things by the Oidenoids that simply weren't true.

Fiske stepped over to the humans and offered them some brisket froote, apologizing for having to freeze Warren the way he did. But, he said, he sensed that Warren and Lily were not a part of the Oidenoids' fanatical plans, and he didn't want to harm them.

While they ate the brisket and tore open some baked bread froote and then gulped down fresh cola froote, Lily and Warren learned a great deal from the Harvesters, who seemed most talkative and not at all the savage brutes they'd been made out to be. They were rough and rugged, doughty and fearless to be sure—they didn't smell so great either—but they were not brutish.

The most important thing the humans learned from the Harvesters was this: While the Crystal did indeed power the rotation of Earth, it did not do so from the *park* in San Francisco, as Lily and Warren thought. It did so from the *center* of the earth. From Nuldoid. It was there that it fueled the machinery of the Wheel that was responsible for Earth's rotation. The Harvesters explained that Crystals were strategically placed throughout the Crust by Nuldoids to absorb energy and light. After 100 years, each was then retrieved and brought back to Nuldoid in order to fuel the Wheel.

Warren realized that the earth's rotation had begun to slow, not because the Crystal had been taken from the park, but because the Crystal was late getting back to Nuldoid—since the earthquake had prevented the Nuldoids from returning directly.

As for the Crystal's current whereabouts, the Harvesters shrugged and said if the two Nuldoids knew what they were doing—always something in question, Mishkin Hobble pointed out—it was probably in Outer Nuldoid, on its way to Downtown. Hopefully, the Nuldoids went *around* the Pockets of Roundlet, instead of *through* it, since it was full of dangerous doidell voids (looping tunnels of circling wind) where victims could become trapped, and circle indefinitely in the wind.

Orskin tried to assure the humans that the Crystal might already be in Downtown Nuldoid.

Lily—still reeling over, and preoccupied with, the Oidenoids and their devious plans—would not let the subject go. "So the Oidenoids *want* to stop the earth's rotation? Why?"

Orskin explained that the Oidenoids were kicked out of Nuldoid in 813 of the Cylindrical Calendar, almost 200 years earlier. Oidenoids refer to the event as The Unjust Purge of Nuldoid, while Nuldoids refer to it as Good Riddance Day. Good Riddance Day came about after nearly fifty years of the Oidenoids' vehement and annoying insistence that *only they* knew what Lloyd meant in *The Book of Nuldoid*. (This fifty-year period is referred to by Oidenoids as "The War of Decaying Values." Most Nuldoids at the time, however, were unaware that such a "war" was in progress, and went about their lives arguing as they normally did.)

Nuldoids did not agree with the Oidenoids' interpretation of Lloyd's writing. After all, the Oidenoids put a pretty odd spin on things. For instance, when Lloyd wrote, "Dat Wheel is ta be *still* of grease an' spit afore nobody goes 'way on vacation" (Maintenance 14:3), the Oidenoids insisted that Lloyd meant *the Wheel should be still,* since that is what the first half of the sentence "implied." Most Nuldoids—at least those who studied Lloyd's writings—believed, however, that Lloyd was merely saying the Wheel should be *well maintained,* even when, or especially when, going on vacation. And, when Lloyd wrote, "Ya doesn't bicker without conflict so as ders grease for dat Wheel," the Oidenoids took it to mean that disagreement and dissent, the cornerstones of Nuldoid culture, should *not* be allowed. This interpretation greatly puzzled scholars of *The Book of Nuldoid*, as most believed Lloyd was saying that Conflict was vital to movement, especially within a circle. (The passage, by the way, was known amongst most Nuldoids as, "Bicker Greases dat Wheel." Although, as Fiske explained, most older Nuldoids referred to it as, "Bicker On, Noid.")

The reason the Oidenoids justified all of this was a bit difficult to understand, but Orskin explained it as best he could—with some interruptions and corrections from Mishkin Hobble. Basically, their thinking shook out something like this: Lloyd said *Everything* exists in a circle (Hib nobb del noid), and *Everything* in a circle is valid. Therefore, the Oidenoids deduced, since *their way of thinking* was in the circle and part of Everything, it was valid. And, since they believed that no *other way of thinking* was valid, they concluded that *only* their way of thinking was valid. Which, by inference, meant that no one else's way of thinking had any validity whatsoever.

Lily scratched her head and whistled at the circuitous logic. "Boy, no wonder they didn't want to explain things to us."

That the Oidenoids believed this—twisted as many Nuldoids felt it was—wasn't really a problem in Nuldoid, until the Oidenoids began to lobby the Emperor and Congress to pass laws forbidding Nuldoids from "argumentin' an'/or bickerin' wit we dat's correct." They also wanted the Emperor to stop the rotation of the Wheel, as per their interpretation of Lloyd's writing.

The Emperor at the time, Boggmer Lutt, as well as most other Nuldoids, were perfectly happy debating the point with the Oidenoids—okay, they *relished* the ongoing arguments—but, at a certain point, the Oidenoids simply refused to discuss the matter(s) any further. Try as they might, the Nuldoids could not get another argument out of the Oidenoids—and that was the beginning of the end. That was when the Nuldoids decided to boot the Oidenoids out of Nuldoid (Good Riddance Day, or The Unjust Purge, depending on your perspective). Since then, the

Oidenoids have aimlessly roamed the Region of Neither Norr in small bands of what Nuldoids call "wandering conformists."

() () ()

With the pressure off them—the race for the Crystal no longer a factor—Warren and Lily began to relax as they sat on the floor of the cave and talked with the Harvesters. Warren rubbed his leg—it was sore from having been frozen by Fiske—for which Fiske apologized again. When Warren said he didn't need to apologize, Orskin pointed out that Fiske was neither a "he" nor a "she." "Heesh" was a "heesh" because "sheesh" was a Delnoid (Nuldoid's third sex).[*]

Delnoids, Lily and Warren learned, were much envied in Nuldoid for their special powers *and* because they had no "opposite sex." As a result, they were free most often to live out their lives unencumbered by any of the usual tension, stress, responsibility or heartache that the other two sexes were constantly subject to. Nor were they ever burdened by offspring and all that offspring entail. So, Delnoids were most often found in better spirits than regular Nuldoids. And they were free to pursue hobbies like chess, kite flying, goffle-off (a game of leisure, similar to golf on the Crust), or, in Fiske's case, collecting froote in the Region of Neither Norr.

Warren ripped open a baked bread froote and asked Fiske, "So, is that how you knew the others were Oidenoids? Because you have special powers?"

Fiske cackled as sheesh dug out another cigar butt from hish grocery cart. "Ach! Nah to dat. Oids, they doesn't able ta tell

---

[*] Nuldoids often interchange the personal pronouns "sheesh" and "heesh" when referring to Delnoids. "Hersh" and "hish" are intermixed as well.

what color's what. They doesn't know what color is dat rubber ball. They doesn't see nothin' but white an' black."

"Addin' to…" this was Mishkin Hobble, "dey is sorta just stupid."

"Ach!" said Orskin. "Don't they stupid! Some just doesn't seein' stuff."

"But whole lotta stupid is dey too," Mishkin Hobble insisted.

"*You* is stupid if yas think all is dey stupid!"

"Oh, we gives ya stupid, ya dirty hobbs drobble!"

Afraid the creatures might hurt each other, Warren quickly changed the subject: He wondered if they would take him and Lily into Nuldoid, explaining that he had to find the boy, Leo, who was carrying the Crystal. He said it was important that he return the boy to the Crust. As it turned out, the Harvesters were most agreeable to taking them, since they were headed there anyway to deliver their froote.

Orskin, Fiske and Mishkin Hobble

When they finished eating, Mishkin Hobble offered everyone gum from his cache of used wads. Lily and Warren politely declined, and Fiske harshly rebuked Mishkin Hobble for doing so. No one, Fiske pointed out, liked chewing somebody else's old gum.

Gum, like most everything else in Nuldoid and Neither Norr, grew within the froote of trees.[*] The Harvesters however found no gum froote on this particular trip, hence Mishkin Hobble's offer of only used gum. Mishkin Hobble himself though preferred old gum to new, once claiming, "No good's dat gum 'til somebody's broked it in."

"Set we is!" announced Orskin as he and Fiske finished attaching pulley systems to the tops of the shopping carts, while Mishkin Hobble struggled to extricate a harpoon gun from beneath one of the larger carts. The gun, with its ominous hook, looked enormous in the tiny Harvester's hands. He gave it to Lily and told her to follow him as he pushed the smallest of the carts into one of the openings that led back out to the canyon's wall.

Warren finished off the last of the cola froote and asked Fiske what the little Nuldoid was going to do with the harpoon. Fiske explained, as heesh and Orskin started rolling their shopping carts toward the same opening, that they would have to cross the canyon to get to the path that would take them down to Nuldoid's entrance. To do that, they'd have to shoot a hook with a cable into the wall above the opposite pathway, then relay themselves, via the cable, to the other side of the canyon.

When Warren realized exactly what it was Fiske was saying, he jumped to his feet and followed the Harvesters into the opening. "A cable? A cable? Other side of the canyon?" He emerged behind the two Harvesters at the ledge overlooking the

---

[*] Spearmint chewing gum grew in the buds of flowers, but only in Nuldoid.

canyon just in time to hear the boom of the harpoon gun echo off the stone walls and send its metal hook soaring through the air, the cable wiggling behind it, across the canyon's huge divide. The hook hit the opposite wall with a "clink" and dug into the rock just above the other path. The Harvesters and Lily seemed pleased with the hook's point of impact, while Warren grew pale and had to lean against a rock so that he wouldn't pass out. "You're not actually planning to—" was all he managed to say before Mishkin Hobble shoved his shopping cart over the ledge where it dropped down, its pulley system snagging the cable and swinging it wildly to and fro until it came to rest out in front of them. "Oh, dear God," Warren said while Mishkin Hobble happily climbed onto the top of the cart and began to pull his way across the breadth of the canyon. When he had safely reached the other side, another shopping cart was sent across with Orskin on top of it. The third cart was then attached to the cable by Fiske and made ready to relay the remainder of the party.

Lily moved to Warren so that she could gently rub his back and assure him they would be okay. But, here was the fundamental difference in the way they each saw the situation: Lily fully expected to reach the other side of the canyon, intact, still alive. Warren expected to plummet to his death.

There were terrifying moments for Warren—when the shopping cart jiggled or swayed a little one way and the other— but the cable didn't break, the carts didn't slip. Neither he nor Lily was hurled into the river of lava below. Yes, Warren was shaking like a thin leaf, but he reached the other side entirely alive.

() () ()

When finally Fiske crossed the canyon, and the grocery cart was hauled up onto the narrow trail—the harpoon gun collected and stowed on the underside of the same cart—they headed down the sloping path toward the canyon's floor, Warren and Lily following behind the Harvesters.

At the bottom of the path, near the far end of the canyon, they came upon the source of the Red River: an open geyser of lava that streamed into the air and splattered down in brilliant reds and pinks and bits of black, scalding steam rising up and dancing lightly into nothingness over all of it as it flowed down away from them, zigzagging along the winding canyon bed. The humans found themselves, once again, dumbfounded, open-mouthed, gaping at the spectacle before them, while the Harvesters were busy struggling fiercely with their shopping carts, swearing at them, kicking them, complaining bitterly that the sand was mucking up their wheels. Mishkin Hobble, of course, complained the loudest and used the foulest of (Nuldoidian) language.

Just past the geyser, along the narrowing walls, they finally came upon the entrance to Nuldoid. Well, technically, *one* of the entrances to Nuldoid. When they approached it—the Harvesters angrily pulling their carts behind them—Warren and Lily stopped dead in their tracks and looked up at the massive wrought iron gate that filled the opening in the wall. It towered over them, perhaps sixty feet, and must have weighed many tons. Hundreds of iron bars rose from the floor and crossed other iron bars in perpendicular support of each other before swirling into an elaborate design above a locked gate.

Behind the gate, in an overstuffed recliner, a massive Sloidelobb was sleeping soundly. Mishkin Hobble grabbed a metal cup from his cart and ran it back and forth across the iron bars of the gate like a prisoner in a jail cell until, finally, the

Sloidelobb woke with a grunt, his thick, doughy arms turning like walruses in the sun. "Ach! Khack! Sleep is we here, ya lousy murk fuddle!"

"Ach to you, ya lazy Slobber! Wakes yoo-hoos an' does dat job!"

The Sloidelobb squinted out at the two humans standing behind Mishkin Hobble. "Is what der ya got? Couple a toids?"

"Sure yeah, toids. Now opens dat gate, eh!"

The Sloidelobb sighed like oozing molasses, took out from beside his chair a large tattered book, and opened it. "Who is yer names? An' gives we dat last three mother's maiden names, eh."

Fiske, now entirely fed up with the Sloidelobb, stepped forward. "We doesn't has to answer yer askin'. We is dat Harvesters of Orskin, Fiske and Mishkin Hobble! Now ya opens up dat gate!"

The Sloidelobb did not take kindly to the Harvester's demand. He eyeballed Fiske suspiciously and then began to look up the names in the pages of the book, while he muttered loudly enough to be heard, "Season a dat Crystal, so as der's security concerns... case in yas doesn't not knows it." He flipped the page and ran his finger down it, mumbling as he did, "Hobble, Hobble, Hobble..."

But Fiske, clearly, was in no mood for such shenanigans and, suddenly, the pages of the book burst into leaping flames, flashing light on the Sloidelobb's round face and singeing his hand. He quickly threw the book down. Holding his burnt hand, he looked up at Fiske. "Ach! Is a Delnoid, ya is! A Delnoid *and* a Harvester! Holy Lloyd an' Floyd! We doesn't see none a yas afore!" He quickly pushed a button and the gate cranked open with the deafening yowl of grinding iron.

The Sloidelobb's surprise that Fiske was both a Delnoid and a Harvester was understandable, as Delnoids seldom undertook the ardors of Harvesting, and generally opted for a life devoid of stress. Fiske, however, had been a Delnoid since the Stinky War of Rotten Smells (250 years earlier) and had grown tired of the leisurely lifestyle.

Inside the gate, the Harvesters and the humans were given tokens for the turnstile to the Blue Hole and then instructed by the annoyed Sloidelobb to, in the future, feel free to use any of the many *other* entrances to Nuldoid.

() () ()

Just a quick note here to update you on Henry, Joe and Francie—which won't be much of an update since they hadn't really done anything except sit and listen intently to Grampa while he leafed through the pages of his father's notebook, letting each note, each inscription, each drawing or clipping, launch another part of the story. Shocking as it was that the Oidenoids turned out to be bad guys, Joe said he had suspected all along they were up to no good, what with all the whispering behind Warren's and Lily's backs. Henry, though, bravely admitted that he was surprised by the turn of events. And Francie, well, she had grown to like the little Oidenoids—as she had the Nuldoids, Morton and Kyle—only to find out now that they were actually "bad guys." So, her heart was broken. Again. Just like it had been broken when she realized that Morton and Kyle were bad guys. Only, now—with this information about the Oidenoids—it seemed that Morton and Kyle might have been good guys all along. It was all a little much for Francie and, frankly, she was miffed. So she sat quietly stewing, arms folded over her chest, feeling as though she'd been betrayed, twice, unsure whether to ever again give her heart to *any* of these ridiculous little creatures.

Nuldois

Part Three

Outer Naldoid

THE ANNOYED SLOIDELOBB picked up the receiver to an archaic black phone that sat next to his chair, unplugged and re-plugged several audio jacks, turned a hand crank and dialed forty or fifty numbers on the phone's rotary face. A moment later, a phone rang some twenty feet away on the other side of the turnstile, where another creature suddenly jumped up from a board game he was playing against himself and scrambled frantically for the phone, knocking over the game and all of its pieces in the process.

"Yeah yup! Hello, hello!" He spoke very fast, and in an agitated manner. "Pete is here! Here is Pete! Sure yeah!"

"Pete!" the Sloidelobb yelled into the phone loud enough that Pete could have put the phone down and heard him just fine.

"Sure yeah to dat. Who der is? Whoozit der?"

The Sloidelobb, now more perturbed than ever, held the phone to his chest and yelled over to him. "Ya droib! Is can only *be* we!"

"Ach!" said Pete. "Sure yeah."

The Sloidelobb put the receiver back to his ear. "Gots two toids. Plus we gots two an' a half..." he stopped and reconsidered Mishkin Hobble a moment before he finally said, "...nah, makes dat *three* noids! Harvesters is dey."

Once they had fed their tokens into the turnstile and passed through it, Lily and Warren and the Harvesters walked to the edge of the Blue Hole, where Pete was busy preparing the equipment. The hole was perhaps six or seven feet across and filled with a substance that gave off a vibrant blue light. The Nuldoid, Pete, was quite anxious to accommodate the travelers, though he had never seen humans before, much less prepared them for an entrance. He walked around both Lily and Warren several times, sizing them up and guesstimating their weight at 507 and 553 wads, respectively.

Pete took out a pair of heavy leather cuffs, attached to a long rubber cord, and began to strap them to Warren's ankles. As he cinched the cuffs tighter, Warren asked what exactly was involved in "an entrance." The Nuldoid explained that it depended on where you were entering from. This particular entrance, he went on, was over a daylight section of Outer Nuldoid, so the "entrancapators"—which wasn't actually a word, but he was trying to sound as technical as possible —had to be dropped through the Blue Hole. He attached a long chain to the leather cuffs, and said that the entrancapator would then fall exactly "a very way long down" before the rubber cord stopped him from "havin' big splatters."

Warren was about to ask what exactly Pete meant by "big splatters," when the little Nuldoid pulled a lever, and suddenly, violently, Warren was jerked upside down and hoisted into the air by the chain attached to his ankles. He was clearly not happy as he hung there over the Blue Hole. He yelled for Pete to put him back down, while the Harvesters seemed to enjoy all of this immensely, and even Lily had to suppress a smile. "Put me down! What the heck is this? Put me down!" Warren demanded, blood rushing to his head.

"Ya doesn't wanna wiggles so much, eh," advised Pete. "Wigglin' der is gonna makes ya miss dat hole, eh. An' 'at's not good."

"What? Miss what?" But Warren did not hear the answer, as the clamp at the end of the chain released, and he was dropped, headfirst, into the Blue Hole.

While, from above, the blue substance looked practically liquid—as Warren went screaming into it—he discovered that it was not liquid, but more like dense mist, so thick, in fact, it felt like... putty. Yet he could breathe. In all, it was perhaps ten feet, maybe twelve feet deep, and it seemed to grow brighter as he drifted farther into it. Oddly, he was no longer uncomfortable immersed in its radiant blue hue. He was even beginning to find the experience pleasant. Something about it felt euphoric. Relaxing.

A moment later, his head popped out the underside of the mist and he saw that he was upside down, high up in the air, very high, looking down on the outskirts of a small village. His shoulders soon emerged, and then his waist and then his legs, and suddenly he was gripped again by fear as he realized he was about to fall. He tried desperately to "swim" backwards, back up into the blue substance. But, of course, there was nothing he could do, except... well, scream again, vigorously. And when his feet finally emerged from the mist, he dropped like a rock out of the "sky."

He had forgotten about the rubber cord attached to his ankles, as he plunged toward the ground, where two small creatures in hardhats stood waiting for his arrival. But, he soon felt the cord's tug as his fall slowed and stopped altogether, a few inches from the ground. Then he was snapped back up into the air like the ball at the end of a child's toy, nearly to the blue sky again. And again he dropped back down, only to bounce back up again, and then down again, back up, and down, which he did several times, until finally he came to a stop, his head a mere four or five inches from the ground.

As the two little creatures approached Warren—he watched them upside down—they commented on his ridiculous size, each guessing at what must be his absurd weight. But they did not unfasten the cord at his ankles right away. *Could not,* in fact. Since Warren was as tall as he was, they could not reach the leather cuffs up around his ankles. Puzzled, they stood and assessed him like a hanging side of beef, cocking their heads this way and that, looking him up and down, one of them removing his hardhat to scratch his head. It was a definite conundrum. Finally, they decided that one of Nuldoids would just have to climb up Warren to unfasten him.

And, as the more agile of the two creatures began to scale Warren's body and detach the leather cuffs, the other rubbed his chin thoughtfully and mentioned another possible concern: that the resulting fall might break the toid's neck. But, since they didn't have a ladder, this method would have to do. Warren, understandably, began to protest about the broken neck aspect, insisting that he'd wait for a ladder. But, by then, his ankles had been freed and he was already dropping to the ground.

Well, he didn't break his neck, but he *did* land on his shoulder with a painful thud—a little extra painful, in fact, because of the additional weight of the Nuldoid who had been holding onto his ankle. At the same instant he hit the ground, the empty leather cuffs snapped back up into the air and into the bright blue mist. Warren sat up on the grass and rubbed his shoulder, yet one more pain to add to the many he was accumulating.

There was a village to one side of him, a rolling meadow to the other. He looked out across the meadow, saw that it spanned the horizon and curved with the crest of the sphere that was, he was told, Outer Nuldoid. Above him, the blue substance covered an expansive ceiling, extending beyond the rolling horizon in all directions and looking very much like clear blue sky.

"Ach," said one of the Nuldoids with his hands on his hips as he stood beside Warren studying him. "A toid is ya, huh? A 'huuuu-man,' eh?"

"Uh… yeah."

"So, does ya knows a guy name a Andy McCall?"

Warren shook his head. "Don't think so. Why would I know him?"

The Nuldoid shrugged. "Is a human."

"Oh, for crying out loud," Warren said as he held his shoulder, "there are six billion humans on Earth!"

The little creature sized Warren up for a moment. "An' is all dey so grumpy as ya?"

As you know, Warren had only slept a small amount in the days leading up to this—so that might have accounted for it—but, upon hearing the Nuldoid's question, he rolled back on the grass and, for the first time since all of this began, laughed heartily.

A moment later, Lily fell from the sky and nearly collided with him, then bounced back up into the air, and back down a few more times before she too was attended to by the Nuldoids.

The Harvesters' grocery carts—tarpaulins stretched taut over them—came next, though they did not land so gently. As the

Harvesters arrived, Mishkin Hobble presented the only real problem: He practically bounced back up into the Blue Hole. And he was still a problem after he stopped bouncing because he hadn't come down far enough for any of the others—even Warren or Lily—to reach. Orskin went to his cart and put together an extension pole with a hook on the end of it that Warren used to snag the little Harvester as he dangled above them, spitting out a litany of angry remarks.

() () ()

The village was called Dayville. It was one of several communities under the blue ceiling, where the creatures of Outer Nuldoid spent their time when they wanted to experience "day." And since it was always daytime there, when they were tired, they traveled over the next hill into another small hamlet called Duskville, where the blue mist was not so bright, and blended into something of an amber hue that looked like the end of a day. There, Nuldoids would often stop at one of the town's many pubs to enjoy a froote of beer, nacho-flavored dried froote peels or popcorn froote before taking a train into the nighttime communities. Most of the Outer Nuldoidians kept "partial homes" in Snorbleton or Snoozeville, where the ceiling overhead did not glow and was always dark—though one could see specks of light overhead from holes in the ceiling.

On the other side of Snorbleton and Snoozeville were the morning communities, where the blue mist started again. It was in these towns that some of the more affluent Nuldoids had partial homes of kitchens with breakfast nooks. Most Nuldoids, however, found the spry and buoyant tenor of the creatures in this area difficult to take. Morning Heights, for instance, was a bustling town of aggressive businesses and factories, a place where "ambitious noids" (a derogatory term) walked a little more briskly and talked a little faster than other Nuldoids. In fact, in Morning Heights and Earlyton, it was not uncommon for Nuldoids to greet each other on the street with cheerful and peppy salutations.

Most reasonable and argumentative Nuldoids found Morning Heights, Earlyton and Sunrise Villa entirely "annoysome," if not intolerable. If they stopped there at all, it was only to eat a quick breakfast before continuing on to Dayville or Noonish, while most Nuldoids avoided the morning towns altogether and simply stayed on the train or drove past.

According to Orskin, Nuldoids who lived and worked in Outer Nuldoid tended to be pretty "flakey in dat brains." That was because, as he explained, they experienced time at their own pace. They had no concept of *real* time, that is, time that passed in a standard, uniform way—though Mishkin Hobble was quick to point out that there was no such thing as a standard way for time to pass. So, it was understandable that these Outer Nuldoidians ticked a little differently than their counterparts in Downtown Nuldoid, whose days and nights were similar to those on the Crust.

() () ()

After Fiske argued with the two Nuldoids over how much was owed for their services, heesh paid them two-and-a-half grumpletts each, which was quite generous, and told them to be happy with that. But they were not at all happy with only two-and-a-half grumpletts, and said as much. When it was pointed out to them, however, that Fiske was a Delnoid and could easily cause their heads to burst into flames, two-and-a-half grumpletts sounded more than fair.

213

As the Harvesters gathered the froote that had fallen out of their carts, they explained to Lily and Warren that the nearest stairwell into Downtown Nuldoid was not far from where they were—only a few miles, following the curve of Outer Nuldoid. They would, of course, have to first cross to the other side of Dayville, the town they were beside, and then hike to Duskville, where the stairwell was. But, since the Harvesters had to take their froote into Downtown anyway, it wouldn't be a problem to bring the humans along.

Although, as Orskin pointed out, if they wanted to see the ceremony at the Wheel, they'd "better get onna pronto inna hurry." What Orskin did not say was that he suspected the ceremony had already begun, or that they had completely missed it—opting to keep those thoughts to himself since the humans were so "smooky" about getting to it on time.

DAYVILLE WAS A labyrinth of narrow brick and stone streets that wound through a hodgepodge of aging businesses and storefronts—none as serious as the businesses in Morning Heights or Earlyton, the humans were told. These were mostly mom 'n' pop operations: barber and beauty shops (with beard-ironing services), grocery froote stands, a stationery store, an automotive recuperation garage, a houseplant leash 'n' wagon store, a black eye and fat lip emergency services hospital, pubs where *non-abusive* language was "forbidden much," and, of course, many many coffee shops. The residential section of Dayville was several asymmetrical blocks of partial homes (houses without bedrooms)—mostly Tudor style with small round windows—where Nuldoids went during their "day" to have lunch or take afternoon naps on the sofas of their family rooms.

There were a number of churches, most fronted by signs with moveable letters that said things like, "Dumb is ya dat Trust," and, "Keeps Lloyd in yas Liver," each of them adding at the bottom in permanent letters, "Hib nobb del noid!" Frequently above the churches' modest spire-topped steeples were beautiful metal sculptures of Lloyd being crushed to death between two cogwheels. Fiske explained that most books published after Lloyd's tragic death claim that he was killed when he fell into the machinery of the Wheel, hence the double cogwheels with Lloyd's legs sticking out between them—often found at the end of Nuldoid jewelry. Some believed that Lloyd threw himself into the wheels' cogs because there was a shortage of grease froote during that time, and his blood was greasier than most. "Other noids is not in dat belief," Orskin explained. "Thinks dey he tripped on account of much big clumsy."

A small automobile zipped past with a tangle of vine-like pipes emerging from either side of its engine, its six or seven tires whistling loudly and then fading away as it passed. Another even smaller car pulled up behind a truck that was stopped at a light, and honked aggressively. Soon, both drivers were yelling at each other through their side-mounted bullhorns—standard equipment in most Nuldoid vehicles.

Nuldoids judged a vehicle's value mostly on its horn system. There were often between ten and twenty buttons for the horn— found on the floorboard, the doors, the dash, beside the seats, in the back seat and, of course, in the middle of the steering wheel.

At seeing so much activity, Orskin was convinced that they had missed the ceremony at the Wheel. He'd expected to see the streets of Outer Nuldoid deserted, or nearly deserted, because of it. His concern, of course, caused Warren even more concern because, if they missed the ceremony at the Wheel, it would be very difficult to find Leo. Warren worried even that he might not be able to find the boy at all. He prompted the others then to speed it up, to pick up the pace. And while Lily was certainly willing to put a little extra spring in her step, Warren's entreaties to the Harvesters fell on deaf ears since Nuldoids instinctively slowed down whenever they were told to hurry up.

() () ()

After leaving Dayville, it was a short hike through the Forest of Arching Trees—where trees grew up out of the ground, and then appeared to change their minds and grow back into the ground. Older Nuldoids loved the forest because the trees were perfect for attaching swings and then arguing over who would use them.

The forest opened up from there to a green meadow—rounded by the curve of Outer Nuldoid—that climbed a hillside and flowed down into Duskville. As you already know, the town was chockablock with pubs, which was why automobiles in Duskville were equipped with oversized bumpers that surrounded the vehicles and made them look bulkier than those in other parts of Nuldoid. The cars in Duskville were also designed to travel very slowly, which was not only safer, but was cause for a great deal of congestion, thereby offering Nuldoids even more opportunity to engage in open hostility.

There were a number of theatres, curio shops and restaurants. And, though there were not as many churches in Duskville as in Dayville, there were some. Duskville churches, however, were usually reserved for weddings, funerals and blopptisms, which were similar to baptisms on the Crust, but were not performed until the child's argumentative skills were fully developed (usually by one or two years of age). Then, the child was submerged in beer until he or she (or sheesh) became angry enough to complain about it.

There were partial homes, as well, in Duskville—having only kitchens and dining rooms—though these were usually older and often neglected since most Nuldoids, upon leaving one of the many pubs in town, opted to stagger on into Snoozeville or Snorbleton, where they could sleep it off.

As Lily and Warren and the Harvesters with their shopping carts made their way down Oyd-Figroid Boulevard, they saw that the sidewalk and part of the street in front of a church was blocked by a number of somber-looking Nuldoids gathered around a black automobile—not large enough to accommodate an average-sized human—with lots of twisting exhaust pipes streaming out of the engine. A Nuldoid in overalls was on a ladder beside it, tossing fuel froote into a funnel that rose up out of the back hood. Other Nuldoids were filing out of the church and lining up on either side of its front steps. The men wore dark top hats, black suits and very large floppy ties, while the women were in flowing black dresses and dark hats, many of which looked like tiny umbrellas (though in Nuldoid there was no such word). A moment later, a young couple emerged holding hands—they too were dressed in black—and walked down the front steps of the church, where the others offered heartfelt embraces and their deepest sympathy. Weddings in Nuldoid were mournful occasions, as couples were told that the lighthearted squabbling they earlier enjoyed would soon be fraught with misery and an overwhelming sense of responsibility, and that their lives would soon become a series of compromises. The newlyweds thanked their loved ones, and proceeded to the car, where they began to argue about who would open the door for whom.

Some of those in attendance, of course, were quite startled by the sudden appearance of the humans. When Warren and Lily came around the corner, in fact, several Nuldoids gaped in wonder at them, one of them even coming up to Lily and asking to see all the extra fingers on her hand.

It turned out that Mishkin Hobble knew some of them. Lily overhead them say they were surprised that he was "a small un' dis time 'round." Though it was said in a very casual and natural manner, Lily felt that it was a very odd thing for someone to say. Warren too overheard a strange conversation between two other Nuldoids, who were arguing about a debt not paid. "Ach," one of them said, "four hun'erd an' thirty years is gone now, an' still yas peeved out an' naggin' we! Ya lets it go, ya droib!" After they had passed the wedding, Warren asked Mishkin Hobble once and for all, "Okay… how *long* do Nuldoids live?"

The little Harvester thought about Warren's question earnestly for a moment and, apparently assuming it was something of a riddle, answered by asking another question: "Until we dies?"

It was starting to occur to Warren that he would never get a straight answer from these creatures, and he was on the verge of seriously confronting Mishkin Hobble, when Orskin suddenly appeared at his side and tugged at his pant leg. He had just asked one of the wedding guests—a Delnoid—about the Crystal ceremony. Sheesh told Orskin that the ceremony never took place. And certainly the Delnoid would have known about it, since the ceremony would have been *big* news in Outer Nuldoid.

Orskin thought then it might be a good idea to telephone the Emperor.

"You can just call him?" Lily asked. "He'll just talk to you?"

Orskin looked at her curiously. "He doesn't got no choice. Lowest job in Nuldoid. *Gotta* speaks to noids." He shook his head. "Ach, is a job ya doesn't want."

"So, we calls 'im, eh?" Mishkin Hobble said, having overheard.

"Sure yeah, we calls 'im."

Despite the import of the situation, though, none of the Harvesters wanted to impose on wedding-goers to use a phone in the church during such a somber occasion. As they turned off Oyd-Figroid Boulevard to Mindle Hobb Way, though, they heard glass breaking and raucous laughter, and the Harvesters realized they were nearing a funeral. They soon came upon a boisterous crowd of Nuldoids, all dressed in brightly colored clothes and singing discordant songs, while several of them stood around a small casket, bickering over who should have to "carries 'im, dat fat stinkin' fik stibble!"

Fiske made hish way up the steps of the church so that sheesh could use the telephone inside, but was first stopped by a group of funeral-goers who asked herm to snap a picture of them sitting on the casket.

While Warren and Lily waited for Fiske, another Nuldoid approached Warren and spoke to him in an almost respectful tone. "Dat big one ya is, eh! Dat Crust yas from, huh?" When Warren said he was indeed from the Crust, the little Nuldoid shoved a pen and paper at him and demanded that Warren give him his autograph. Lily smiled as the Nuldoid instructed Warren to make it out to "Duggo Homp." Warren did so, and handed the pen and paper back to the creature, who looked at the signature and was disappointed. "Ach, yas not Spielberg." He crumpled the paper, tossed it aside and walked off.

() () ()

Fiske's news, when heesh returned from using the phone, was not encouraging. Sheesh could not reach Emperor Ed, and the ceremony at the Wheel had been indefinitely postponed. In fact, Ed was not even in Downtown Nuldoid, where he would have been, if plans for the ceremony were underway. Instead, he was still at his regular job over in Morning Heights on the other side of the nighttime hamlets.

The news meant that Leo and the Nuldoids hadn't made it to Downtown Nuldoid.

It was grave news. *What happened to the Crystal? Where was Leo? Where were the other Nuldoids, Morton and Kyle? Had they been stopped by Oidenoids? Eaten by Fishing Worms? Were they trapped somewhere? And what was happening now on the surface of the earth?*

This was horrible. Terrible.

The Harvesters agreed it was a pretty bad deal. It was bad even for Nuldoid because Nuldoidians would begin to suspect other Nuldoids of having conspired to stop the Crystal, or of working for the Oidenoids—or worse, of *being* Oidenoids. After all, the Wheel itself was very closely tied to Nuldoids' beliefs about Lloyd and country. Mishkin Hobble speculated that there would be congressional hearings. Wild, unfounded accusations would begin flying. Many Nuldoids would be affected by it. It would be—as the little Harvester pointed out—just like the Great Bleak Listing of 954 all over again. The Emperor himself would certainly be taken to task and would, of course, bear the brunt of Nuldoid's furor. But there was at least a silver lining for Ed: He would not be reelected, which was something he had been trying to achieve for many years.

So, while Duskville provided an entrance to Downtown Nuldoid, there was no longer any point to going there if Leo and the Crystal had not even arrived. Now the questions were: *What were the Emperor and Nuldoid doing about it? Were they sending out search parties? Did they even know that Leo and the Nuldoids had made it as far as the Great Big Canyon?*

Warren told the Harvesters that he and Lily *must* talk to the Emperor. They had to tell him that the Crystal was near Nuldoid.

They had to convince him that finding the Crystal was vital, especially for the creatures on the Crust!

But—though Morning Heights was only a few miles on the other side of night—when Warren insisted that the Harvesters take them there, Orskin shifted uncomfortably. He explained that they felt great sympathy, of course, for the humans and the plight of humankind, et cetera, et cetera, but that they (Orskin, Fiske and Mishkin Hobble) *had* to get their froote into Downtown Nuldoid. After all, collecting froote was a serious and competitive business, and if they ran off to take care of someone else's problem every time something like this came up, well, they'd be "squitched" for sure.

"But, if we don't find the Crystal," Lily pleaded, "a lot of people will die!"

The Harvesters stood blank-faced for an uncomfortable moment. Finally, Mishkin Hobble looked up at the humans and meekly offered, "But... is only death."

Warren thought then of trying a different tack since he knew that these creatures held little regard for death. He suggested that those on the Crust who did not die would suffer tremendously. And, while the Nuldoids might be indifferent to death, he knew they were altogether uncomfortable with the idea of unnecessary suffering, Crustoid or otherwise.

"Ach," Fiske said, as heesh popped the silver ball out of hish eye socket to clean it, "hates we ta see dem big ouches."

So, it was decided that Orskin and Fiske would take the three carts into Downtown Nuldoid, while Mishkin Hobble escorted the humans through Snorbleton and Snoozeville and into Morning Heights, so that they could talk to Emperor Ed.

The Emperor

MISHKIN HOBBLE CHATTED briskly as they left Duskville and edged around Dorggob Bokk Lake—named after a hero of the Stinky War of Rotten Smells (723-728 C.C.)—which separated the early evening town from the nighttime communities. He seemed to be enjoying the authority he held without the other Harvesters around, while he struggled to keep up with Warren and Lily. In fact, before they reached Snoozeville, the only time he was quiet was when Lily offered to carry him on her back. He rejected the offer out of hand and grew quiet and sullen. Lily realized then that she'd hurt his feelings. Only when Warren asked about the Emperor's "other job" did Mishkin Hobble's injured ego begin to heal. And before long he was chattering away again.

Ed Pugg, the Emperor of Nuldoid, worked three days a week at the Morning Heights sewage treatment plant that serviced most of Outer Nuldoid and sections of Downtown. He was the plant's senior Flow Management Engineer, a job he was infinitely proud of, a job that he famously relished as the one thing in his life that brought him joy and kept him sane. He had worked there for nearly twenty-five years and insisted on keeping the job, even after he was forced to enter politics.

Though his was an elected position, Ed loathed being Emperor and wished with all his liver that he had not been saddled with the job. But, in each of the past four general elections—held every three years—he had been elected and reelected, despite his vehement and, at times, vituperative attempts to convince the citizens of Nuldoid that he was not right for the job. During the first election, in fact, he went so far as to say that he was without moral compass and would probably be a source of great incompetence and even corruption. But, try as he might, he could not convince the voting public that he was wrong for the job—the citizenry actually found his protestations entertaining, endearing even—and, consequently, he had been relegated to serve as Emperor for nearly thirteen years.

As Mishkin Hobble and the humans followed the curve of Outer Nuldoid and found themselves entering the dark city limits of Snoozeville, they passed a large sign, dimly lit by a flickering light bulb that said, "YA KEEPS IT SHUT UP FROM HERE ON!" Mishkin Hobble warned the humans that any noise made in the village was usually met by a swift and brutal vigilante response. It was, after all, a sleeping community. The little Harvester shook his head and said he had sure learned that lesson the hard way "nearly fifty an' a hundred years gone 'way."

"Nearly a hundred and fifty years?" Warren was angry before he even asked the question. "Okay, once and for all, how long do Nuldoids live?" But they had just entered the city, and he was met with a very sharp "Shhhhhh!" from Mishkin Hobble, who even stomped his little foot to make the point.

The journey through the dark streets of Snoozeville and Snorbleton was uneventful; aside from Mishkin Hobble's occasional and vehement shushes to Warren and Lily, even when they were not making any noise. Here and there, a few villagers were quietly slipping into or out of town, on their way to start or finish their days.

As they made their way quietly along the dark streets of Snoozeville, Lily realized she heard crickets chirping. Mishkin Hobble, of course, shushed her as soon as she mentioned the crickets, telling her later—as they walked the road in between the nighttime villages—that crickets were brought into Outer Nuldoid by a couple of practical jokers returning from an expedition to retrieve a Crystal from Hobbnibb Bibbler, the Nuldoidian name for ancient Mesopotamia. The jokers were summarily executed and then sentenced to solitary confinement in a chamber filled with the annoying varmints.

"You mean the other way around, right?" Lily said, naturally assuming Mishkin Hobble had accidentally reversed the order of their punishments.

"Nah to dat," he said. "Nuldoids was peeved pretty big. Them two got it tough an' rough *after* they was dead." Mishkin Hobble looked up at Warren, as though expecting the human now to ask another question about death or about how long Nuldoids lived. Warren, however, was growing all too frustrated with this bizarre game he knew that Mishkin Hobble was playing, and refused to ask anything else about death. He was certain that they, the creatures, Mishkin Hobble in particular, took great pleasure in not answering his questions.

After entering Snorbleton, it did not take long to get from one side of the village to the other. The amber running lights along the sidewalks were in excellent working order, having only been installed in the past ten years. Snoozeville, on the other hand, was an older community and, in many places, still relied on the tulip-style lights along its sidewalks that were either no longer functioning or were missing light bulbs. The loss of light bulbs was due mostly to Theevins (baseball-shaped birds with uneven wingspans and only one foot, known for stealing things), which were popular pets in Nuldoid.

There were several automobiles parked along the streets of Snorbleton, and, at one point, Warren stopped to look more closely at a couple of them. When he did, he had the peculiar feeling they were... breathing. He learned that the cars did indeed "breathe" through their many exhaust pipes. He learned also that the cars "slept," as the ones he was looking at were doing. And, he was most surprised to find out that, when a Nuldoid car had engine trouble, it was left alone in a "recuperation garage" until "it felts itself better." The cars did not, of course, have brains—they were just machines after all—but they were very nearly not *just machines*.

After they crossed out of Snorbleton and started to make their way up the steep incline of Roiden Buttle Highway, Mishkin Hobble flagged down a passing froote truck with a front flatbed large enough to hold the humans. He told the driver, a Nuldoid named Murddley, that they were on a very important quest. After Murddley demanded to know the details of this quest, and then argued its relative importance, she reluctantly agreed to take the trio as far as the Dorf Hibble turnoff, which was very near Morning Heights.

Mishkin Hobble climbed into the cab with Murddley. The humans sat on the flatbed in front. The truck pulled back onto the road and trudged along the dark highway for an hour or so before it began to climb the backside of the hills that flanked the morning communities. Not far up the incline, the truck heaved a strained, somewhat dramatic, sigh—obviously protesting the additional weight. Warren and Lily could see the ceiling light of Morning Heights as it appeared to edge over the crest of the hillside in front of them. They rounded the top of the hill and coasted toward the outskirts of the town—where Dorf Hibble Road intersected the highway. Murddley pulled the truck over and told Mishkin Hobble that she was not driving through Morning Heights because she, like many Nuldoids, found the morning communities, and their boisterous "do-can attitude," entirely too "annoysome."

Warren and Lily stepped off of the truck's flatbed and thanked her, while Mishkin Hobble jumped out of the cab and complained that the ride was bumpy. Murddley, in turn, called him a skag hasper, bunched her three fingers together and flicked them at him—an insulting gesture—before she drove off.

() () ()

As they walked toward the silhouette of Morning Heights' buildings and factories, Mishkin Hobble grew animated in anticipation of showing Lily and Warren the city's many points of interest. He told them about the monument to Nuldoids' Civil War—where the only casualties were the two opposing leaders, executed by their respective countrymen[*]—and the crater and charred remains of the building where the Nuldoid prohibition

---

[*] The reader might notice the similarity between this incident and the scene depicted within the ancient slide of the Droiden Frobble Dynasty, where Warren and Lily were sliding toward the Great Big Canyon. There were actually many such situations in the history of these creatures, where leaders were held accountable for their drastic decisions. Though very little was known about the Droiden Frobble incident, much was documented, recorded, written about, reenacted and celebrated after it happened during the Nuldoidian Civil War.

movement was conceived in the late 5th century. But Lily and Warren were in no mood for sightseeing and wanted only to be taken to the sewage treatment plant to meet with Ed. Mishkin Hobble was disappointed in their lack of curiosity, and told them as much. They were, however, quite tired and, frankly, by this time, entirely sick of Mishkin Hobble's incessant jabbering.

Compared to the other towns, Morning Heights was big and busy. Many of the businesses were manufacturers and distributors, like *Smuygle's Fine Household Nails, Lobbnik Stulb's Excellent Light Bulbs, Skeegs' Paper Bags for Occasional Occasions* and *Murk Hork's Fat Pants—Makers of Fat Pants*. Along the cobblestone streets of the city, there were many coffee shops—in some places three to a block—where Nuldoids in business suits and brightly colored work clothes hurried in or out as they finished or started their mornings. In fact, it struck Lily that these creatures were so busy hustling here and there that they didn't appear to spend much time squabbling or bickering or fighting with each other. As Nuldoids bustled past them, one offered, "Hey, toid! Careful ya doesn't skin dat forehead, eh!" Another chuckled at them. "What has ya gots yer own weather up der?"

After perhaps a dozen winding, confusing turns from one street to the next, they came at last upon the *Morning Heights Sewage Treatment Plant & Fertilizer Spreadin' Company*. The complex stood atop a small hill of its own, looking dark and foreboding like a medieval castle on a lightning-laced night. At the far end of the plant, a steel-plated burner building sat like a giant majestic kettle, round and narrowing at the top where it fed exhaust into three large ventilation pipes that sprouted out and snaked high up into the bright blue mist overhead like massive grapevines twisting into the sky. From there, the ventilation pipes fed into Niether Norr, where huge pockets of charcoal acted as filters. The fertilizer itself was shipped out to orchard Farmers who worked the areas in Neither Norr close to Nuldoid.

Visitors to the plant were required to enter through one of two large corrugated metal buildings, where they checked in with Security, a sleeping Sloidelobb who was not wearing pants. When finally Warren was able to wake him—never an easy task—the Sloidelobb did so with such a start that he soiled himself, his chair and the area around his chair. "Ach," he said and then plugged several phone jacks into the old black telephone beside him, dialed a long series of numbers and demanded that someone come to the visitors' entrance for a "nudda cleanups we is needed!"

The Sloidelobb then reached into a knapsack beside his chair and pulled out a number of rubber balls that he held up and asked the visitors to identify. After Warren, Lily and Mishkin Hobble each correctly identified the colors of the rubber balls—thus proving they were not Oidenoids—they were issued hardhats, the interior gate was opened, the Sloidelobb went back to sleep and two very disgruntled maintenance workers arrived to clean up the Sloidelobb's mess.

() () ()

Inside the plant, they stepped out onto a landing that overlooked three long canals of dark murky water, flanked on either side by wooden catwalks that fed into the bottom side of the huge burner building. Next to the middle canal, they saw a group of four or five workers leaning against, and sitting on, the railing of the catwalk. They were smoking cigars and arguing about whether pi repeated itself or not—one of them contending that, if the number is infinite, it can't help but repeat itself. They had not yet come to blows, when Mishkin Hobble approached and asked where the Emperor was. A worker jerked his thumb toward the end of the third canal, and went back to the argument.

Warren and Lily turned and saw Ed hunched over a large wrench, grunting feverishly and looking quite green in the face as he pulled and tugged, struggling in vain to loosen a rusted bolt on a seal valve at the foot of the burner building. His overalls were tight around his protruding belly and a thin gray and black ponytail popped out from under the back of his hardhat. When Mishkin Hobble yelled his name and they approached, Ed looked up, wiped the sweat from his brow and was only too happy to abandon the wrench and greet them. He had a warm smile beneath a large walrus mustache and brown eyes that glinted when the visitors introduced themselves. At first, he thought they had shown up for a tour of the plant—which he loved giving— and was disappointed to learn they were there for matters related to his *other* job.

He was, as you know, the sewage treatment plant's Senior Flow Management Engineer, a position he had long relished. When, however, he became Emperor of Nuldoid, he was presented with a unique problem that he was only just now learning to deal with. As Emperor, he held the lowest post in the land, and therefore technically worked for *every* citizen of Nuldoid. As a result, his subordinates at the sewage treatment plant became, in effect, his superiors. From that point on, nearly all of the requests he made of them were ignored, because they felt strongly that *he* was the one who worked for *them*. "Ya serves at dat pleasure a we!" they'd say to him and laugh or playfully punch him in the arm before they moved off to do whatever it was they wanted to do—like sit and argue about pi. Understandably, at the beginning of his first term, he found the situation altogether untenable. But, as time wore on, he grew used to the dichotomy and even began to enjoy it. That was because, like any Nuldoidian, he enjoyed arguing. So he began his day by asking his subordinates to do all sorts of menial tasks, knowing full well they would quarrel with him and refuse to do them. Then he would grab his toolbox, and pad off to do the work himself. Eventually he grew to enjoy this routine and his days passed quite pleasantly.

Compared to his other job as Emperor, his job at the sewage treatment plant pleased him immensely.

Ed Pugg
Emperor of Nuldoid

"Ach, dat Crystal," Ed said, after Mishkin Hobble and the humans had introduced themselves, and Lily explained how important it was that they find the boy and the Crystal. "Dat Crystal is givin' we some big pain inna clobbs." He shook his head and reached for a paper coffee cup on the catwalk next to his tool chest.

The humans were heartened to learn that Ed had already sent out a search team to find the Crystal. But the search team hadn't the foggiest idea where to begin looking, since no one in Nuldoid knew about the earthquake in San Francisco or the deaths of those on the original expedition team. Rumors had filtered back to Nuldoid—through Harvesters returning from Neither Norr—that some of the Nuldoids from the expedition were traveling with a human, but their whereabouts were never confirmed. So, as far as the search team knew, the Crystal could be just about anywhere between the "Southy Crust" (our Northern Hemisphere) and the inside portion of Neither Norr (near Nuldoid). As Ed all too sadly admitted, they were looking "for a noodle inna hatsack." Even when Warren pointed out that they had actually seen the Crystal in the Great Big Canyon, that it had to be somewhere between the Great Big Canyon and Nuldoid, Ed shook his head and told him that search parties had been all through the area and found nothing. In fact, so doubtful was the prospect of finding the Crystal that the search team had been instructed to do their best and then continue on to the "Northy Crust" (our Southern Hemisphere). There, they were to retrieve another Crystal that was "ripening" in Dobb Dibblenobb (Australia)—referred to by most Nuldoidians as "Uppen Over." The search team was eager to make the trip to Australia, since the Australian and Nuldoidian cultures had such similar attitudes about the importance of beer.

The problem—from the humans' perspective—was twofold: If the Nuldoids gave up on finding Leo and the other Nuldoids... well, Leo would be lost. This would, of course, affect everyone on Earth because retrieving the Crystal from Australia would take at least another week. And, as Lily and Warren learned from Ed, the

Wheel had already slowed by five seconds, and was expected to stop altogether within the next day or two. While an idle Wheel would present a momentary inconvenience to most Nuldoids, the repercussions on the Crust would be unfathomable.

The Doidell Void

THIS NEWS WAS as disheartening and depressing as any Warren and Lily had ever heard. There was nothing else to be done.

They thanked Ed and left with Mishkin Hobble. After they walked out of the sewage treatment plant and crossed the street to a small park, Warren sat down on a short bench and started to cry. Lily sat next to him and put a comforting arm around him. When Mishkin Hobble realized why they were so upset, he sat down on the other side of Warren, pushed aside the spotlight on his shoulder, and gently rested his head on Warren's leg.

Both Warren and Lily were utterly exhausted, neither having slept more than a couple of hours in the past few days, so it was not long before they were sound asleep. Mishkin Hobble, of course, was only too happy to doze off with them, and curled up at Warren's leg.

As you can imagine, they were quite a sight when Orskin and Fiske reappeared at the end of the street, pushing their empty grocery carts and towing Mishkin Hobble's smaller one on a tether behind them.

"Ach, sleeping in Morning Heights?" Fiske jabbed Warren's shoulder. "Ya doesn't s'posed ta do dat," the Harvester said with something of a twinkle in hish only eye. Orskin and Fiske had news to share. They had made quite a few grumpletts more than they expected at the froote market in Downtown Nuldoid. The price of shiitake and porcini frootes had nearly doubled since their last cash-out, and there were seven porcini frootes in the mix, as well as tobacco froote from just beneath the Crust's Fubb Hibble.* All in all, it was a profitable haul for the Harvesters and they were well pleased with themselves as they doled out Mishkin Hobble's share of the take.

Mishkin Hobble was pleased as well, until he noticed, in the bottom of *his* cart, three loose frootes rolling about. "Why doesn't ya sell dose der?"

Orskin put up a hand to calm his small companion. "Settle yas, Mr. Mishkin Hobble, settle," he said. "Traders was yer ones to say nah. Said yers was dat froote der dat wasn't weighted 'nuff. Said they doesn't not payin' for no empty frootes. So don't gets yer dander flyin' all over, huh. Was Traders 'at says it ta we. An', frankly, yoo-hoo is lucky ya wasn't got arrested for premature harvesting."

Well, of course, Mishkin Hobble *did* get his dander flying and expressed a great many offensive words, as he stomped both of his tiny feet and vowed to push his grocery cart back into Downtown Nuldoid, where he would slit the throats of the rotten Traders who refused to buy his froote. The froote was perfectly

---

* Cuba.

fine, he said, as he picked one up from the bottom of his shopping cart and dug into its skin to prove his point. When he did, however, he found that it was indeed empty... well, empty except for a purple mist that emerged from it and curled in the air in front of him. And then, without a moment's hesitation—before either of the two other Nuldoids could tell him not to—he put his nose into the mist and inhaled. His eyes suddenly bulged and turned a brilliant blue, and then he dropped to the ground, looking as dead as dead could look.

"Ach," said Orskin, "is stupid runs in dat family."

Fiske stepped over to the little Harvester and put a finger in his ear to check his pulse. After a moment the Delnoid looked up at the others and explained, "Isn't alive no more."

"Ach," said Orskin.

"But isn't dead not neither," Fiske added, standing up.

"What?" Lily bent down to look at the creature's supine body. "Which is it? Is he alive or dead?"

Fiske scratched hish ear and scrunched hersh face. "Well, is dead *now*, but, most likely, is wakin' later." Heesh shook hish head. "We doesn't really can say. Some frootes ya just doesn't not wanna suck up."

"But, he'll be okay?" Warren was still sitting on the park bench, hardly surprised by any of this.

Fiske shrugged. "Eh, 'cept it could be dat 'idiot froote.' Has hearda dat. Could be he up wakes without not much smartin'."

Orskin chortled. "He doesn't smarts with so much anyways."

"But, Fiske, you're a Delnoid. Can't you do something?" Lily protested.

"A Delnoid, yeah sure. But we isn't Lloyd."

Orskin then realized, in all the excitement, that he and Fiske had forgotten to share some other news they'd heard at the Trading Center. A couple of Farmers, who had passed the

Pockets of Roundlet on their way into Outer Nuldoid from Neither Norr, said they heard voices coming from within the Pockets. They said it sounded like someone was stuck in the endless looping wind of a doidell void. And one of the voices sounded human. But the Farmers decided to keep moving, since it was, at best, quite dangerous, if not impossible, to get victims out of a doidell void.

Warren suddenly stood and said it *had* to be Leo and the Nuldoids. They had to tell Ed right away so that he could send a crew to rescue them!

Both Orskin and Fiske, however, had a better idea: They thought it would be smarter, faster to go there themselves. After all, Ed was a bureaucrat through and through, and he would, of course, have to go into Downtown Nuldoid to petition Congress for a crew of "regular" Nuldoids (meaning not Harvesters and therefore not nearly as skilled as they), who would then embark from Downtown Nuldoid, travel through Outer Nuldoid and, finally, make their way out to the Pockets. Orskin reasoned that, since he and Fiske were already in Outer Nuldoid, the four of them should leave straightaway to rescue the toid and noids, and then return with the Crystal.

"But… what about Mishkin Hobble?" Lily asked, nodding at the partially dead Nuldoid on the grass beside the park bench. "You can't just leave him here."

"Eh, ya isn't worry none. He doesn't gonna hurt nobody," said Orskin, as he tilted his head to look his companion over, Fiske nodding along with him.

"That's not what I meant," Lily said, a little irritated with their callous regard for their companion. "Someone should stay with him until he… until he isn't dead."

Orskin and Fiske looked at each other, both feeling a tinge of guilt from Lily's remark, though why, they didn't know. "Sure yeah," Orskin finally said, looking up at Lily. "Fiske can stays with dat idiot."

"Bah! Nah to dat!" Fiske objected. "Orskin stays! Fiske don't stay ta watch no vegetable!" The disagreement, of course, turned into a quarrel, but before it escalated to mutual choking and kicking, it was agreed that, since Fiske was a Delnoid—more skilled at hovering, if need be—Orskin should be the one to stay with Mishkin Hobble.

() () ()

The Pockets of Roundlet were on the other end of the Great Big Canyon at the bottom of Neither Norr. The group would have to leave Outer Nuldoid through the midday community of Noonish to enter Neither Norr so that they would emerge near the Pockets. Fortunately—since they were already in Morning Heights—it was only a short trip to midday. Along the way, of course, they would pass through Dayville, where they had entered Outer Nuldoid, having made a complete circle. From there they would head slightly north (as Nuldoids called it) to cut across Stiggioden Floyden Goffle-off Course in order to reach Noonish.

Stiggioden Floyden Goffle-off Course was, like almost all goffle-off courses, beautiful. And as they made their way along the sweeping green slopes of the 37th hole, a tiny voice yelled, "Three!" just before Warren was nearly struck in the head by a small white ball. A moment later, a group of Delnoids, dressed in brightly colored clothes, approached and recognized Fiske. They insisted on learning what sheesh had been up to and asked when sheesh was going to give up the ridiculous life of adventure and harvesting so that heesh could enjoy the stagnancy of Delnoid life. One of them, named Tubbner Wass, glanced curiously several times at Warren and Lily, and asked finally why Fiske was keeping the company of toids. Fiske said that the humans were friends of hersh and that they were, all of them, on their way to rescue the Crystal from a doidell void in the Pockets of Roundlet. Tubbner Wass only shook hish head sympathetically, stymied still that hish friend would complicate hish life thus.

Before they moved on, though, another of them, Boggs Obb, insisted on seeing Warren and Lily's hands, close up. The humans held out their hands as the Delnoid counted and recounted their fingers, squealing with delight each time sheesh did. "Looks at 'em all! Dem is some whole lotta digits, eh! Ooo-wee, will ya looks at all dem pinkers!"

() () ()

Noonish sat at the foot of a craggy mountain that climbed into the blue mist and the ceiling of daylight. There were several mountains in Outer Nuldoid that were not only beautiful but actually served a purpose, since they held the Nuldoid sphere in place. Without the mountains, the entirety of Nuldoid would wobble and bounce hopelessly around the shell that encapsulated it.

The town of Noonish was a cozy cluster of gingerbread chalets with worn wooden balconies and thick round windows. Though Lily and Warren did not travel through, or into, the town, they could see it was considerably smaller than Dayville.

Fiske led them to a small park that bordered the lower side of Noonish. It rested at the incline of the mountain. Sheesh pushed the shopping cart along the grass, past the swing set and slide area, where some older Nuldoids were playing. A spattering of younger Nuldoids sat nearby on benches, reading newspapers and magazines. Where the grass ended at the edge of the park, several huge slate rocks leaned into the base of the mountain like bread sticks beside a ball of ice cream. Between them, an opening led to another elevator, where a Sloidelobb named Herbb was sleeping. When Fiske shook him awake, Warren and Lily were surprised to find that Herbb was rather pleasant compared to the other Sloidelobbs they'd encountered, even complimenting them on their height and fine posture. Only after they got out of the elevator in Neither Norr did Lily and Warren learn from Fiske that certain breeds of Sloidelobbs specialized in sarcasm, and that Herbb was making fun of them.

The elevator emptied out into a barren region at the far end of the Great Big Canyon. From there, Warren and Lily followed Fiske through a cavernous tunnel that opened to a vast area that was backed by the Pockets of Roundlet. As the humans stood and looked up at the massive structure, Warren shuddered at its size and what he perceived was the task ahead of them. It was several stories high and looked like the side of an inconceivably massive piece of Swiss cheese that someone had wedged into the earth. In fact, it looked so much like Swiss cheese that one had to get close to its cream-colored limestone to be sure it was not. Daunting as the sight of the mammoth structure was to the humans, it became even more so when they learned that they were looking at only a small portion of it.

As Fiske took some items from hish cart and then strapped the harpoon to hish back, heesh explained that the Swiss cheese effect was created thousands of years ago, when a group of less-than-intelligent Fishing Worms tunneled into the structure and got lost. Before they found their way out, some of the lesser intelligent of the less-than-intelligent worms panicked and began to tunnel in circles. And, though these stupid worms eventually did find their way out of the Pockets, they left behind a number of looping tunnels. Later, those tunnels became dangerous doidell voids when gusts of wind from the bottom of a nearby tunnel-hole became trapped in the circular loops.

Fiske approached the wall beside one of the wormholes, moved hish shoulder light aside and leaned against the wall to listen. Not only do Harvesters have extraordinary hearing, but Fiske was a Delnoid, so heesh could hear the *origin* of a sound. The Harvester listened intently for a moment, then stepped back and moved the shoulder light back up, turned it on and took out a small notepad and a pencil from one of hish many pockets. Sheesh began then to scribble some numbers.

Lily leaned in to look. "What are you doing?"

"Shhh! Is thinking." Fiske studied the numbers a moment. Then the Delnoid touched the page and moved the numbers around. Lily exchanged a look with Warren, which Fiske caught out of the corner of hish only eye. "Yoo-hoo doesn't wants to try this at home, folks," sheesh joked, and continued to move the numbers around until an answer appeared. "Ach, there dey is…" The humans leaned down to look at the pad. "Dey is in a doidell void, all right. Upper left, back quadrant is dey."

The numbers on the pad, of course, meant nothing to Warren and Lily. But they were intrigued by what Fiske had done with the images. Warren ran his finger down the page and felt nothing more than ordinary paper. "How did you do that?"

"Magic," Fiske said with a peculiar wink that caused the silver ball to roll up and reveal again its keyhole.

() () ()

Inside the first tunnel, there was ample room for the humans to crawl behind Fiske, and when it became level, there was nearly room enough for them to stand. When they turned into another tunnel and the climb grew steep or vertical, Fiske used a squeeze gun to shoot corkscrew hooks into the sides of the tunnel that they could step on to reach the next horizontal section. In other places, the tunnel narrowed so that Warren could put his back against one side, and push against the other with his legs, edge his way to the top, and then pull Lily and Fiske up after him.

The maze of tunnels twisted and turned in wild confusion like swirling strands of spaghetti in a bowl, as the Harvester and the humans made their way higher and higher into the Pockets of Roundlet.

Several levels up, when they had climbed through a tunnel that snaked left and then right a number of times, they heard the howl of fierce wind coming from somewhere above them. When the tunnel they were in finally leveled off, they made their way closer to the noise. Turning at the end of a long stretch, they saw, at last, the looping tunnel of a doidell void, intersecting the tunnel they were in. Fiske was quick to point out that it was not the doidell void they were looking for, but they'd have to deal with it. They'd have to get through it.

Warren stood and watched while some old froote and a chair swept past them at great speed, and then, a few moments later, did so again. And, though they stood only inches from the wind, they could not feel it, as all of the wind was contained in the loop and could not escape.

"They is two levels up," Fiske said, and then took the harpoon off hish back. Hesh adjusted the gauge at the end of the barrel, braced hermself and, after the chair passed, fired the hook low at the other side of the doidell void. The hook blasted into the wind, but suddenly whipped around and flew right back at them, its hook diving deep into the limestone wall a mere inch or two from Warren's left leg. Fiske looked at the hook in the wall, then sheepishly at Warren—who was looking back at Fiske with eyes like bulging poached eggs—and shrugged. "Maybe we aims again different, huh."

Fiske unclipped the hook from the wall of the tunnel, reloaded the harpoon gun and edged closer to the wind, so as to aim more directly into it. After the chair had passed again, the Harvester pulled the trigger. The hook shot out and bent quickly in a curve that sent it hurtling out the other side of the wind, at an even greater speed, into the back wall of the intersecting tunnel.

Fiske secured the other end of the wire to the wall next to them, strapped the gun to hish back, then turned and winked at the humans. "Big scary, huh." When the chair had passed again, Fiske took off running, was caught by the wind and was blown out the other side of it like a cannonball, blasting into the tunnel's far wall, where the Delnoid stumbled forward and fell over like a drunk.

Warren was next.

He clipped himself to the wire, waited as the chair bumped the wire and passed, then ran at the doidell void. He flew out the other side and landed near Fiske with a thud that knocked the wind out of him, but he was otherwise unhurt.

The circling chair, this time, missed the wire altogether and then Lily leapt across the wind tunnel without incident—even landing on her feet—prompting Warren to point out that he and Fiske had worked out all the kinks before she took her turn. She laughed and punched him in the arm.

After they collected the wire, and climbed up through another series of serpentine tunnels, Fiske stopped, shushed Warren and Lily, and then listened intently. Finally, the Harvester told them they were getting close. "Is a sound of a toid. An' noids is der too. Is arguin'."

And when finally they climbed to the tunnel that intersected the doidell void they were looking for, Warren approached the edge of the wind and saw Leo and the two little Nuldoids flash past him, followed by the bright streak of the Crystal. "It's them!" he yelled. "It's Leo! He's right there!" And when the boy and the creatures passed again, he shouted, "Leo! Leo!"

Soon Lily was yelling too, and a few moments later, when Leo and the Nuldoids flew past them again, Warren and Lily heard Leo shout, "Mr. Worrrrs..." before he disappeared again.

In pieces of passing dialogue, Leo and the Nuldoids let it be known that they were all healthy, but very hungry, and they were entirely sick of circling endlessly. Oh, and as each passed the opening, he let it be known that the other two were completely wrong about a number of things they'd been arguing about.

The problem now, as Fiske pointed out to Warren and Lily, was an obvious one: How would they get them out safely? After all, they could not simply shoot a wire across the doidell void and have them grab it—it could very well slice all three of them to pieces. Neither could they simply reach out a hand and grab them, as they themselves might also be pulled into the doidell void.

Fiske said heesh needed a moment to think, and then stood quietly, arms outstretched like a bird. Warren and Lily watched the little Delnoid as, a second or two later, hish feet lifted off the floor and sheesh began to hover an inch or so in the air. Apparently, this helped improve the Delnoid's thinking, as did passing gas. After another moment, Fiske dropped back to the floor of the tunnel. "Dat wind! We doesn't flies *against* it! We flies *with* it!"

The Harvester then took the harpoon gun and fired the hook directly into the wall beside them.

"What're you doing?" Lily asked.

But Fiske was too focused to answer just yet, too busy detaching the spool of wire from the gun and attaching it to the belt around hersh waist. The plan was quite brilliant, actually, though, in truth, heesh'd been considering what to do about the doidell void since they left Outer Nuldoid, only now letting the reality of the moment crystallize the plan. With one end of the wire hooked to the wall, Fiske would jump into the wind, and hold against it, waiting for the Crystal (or human or Nuldoid) to pass, then release enough wire from the spool so that heesh would be traveling beside it (or them), enabling the Harvester to grab it (or them). Then Fiske would slow the wire from unspooling until they were stopped near the opening, where they would swing out of the doidell void to safety.

And it almost worked, except Fiske did not take into account hish size. When sheesh jumped into the doidell void, the little Harvester was bounced back and forth like a tetherball, nearly colliding in the process with Leo and the Nuldoids as they passed.

After heesh managed to reel hermself back in, it was decided that Warren would have to carry out the plan since he weighed considerably more than Fiske and could remain in place.

After the spool was attached to the leather belt at Warren's waist, Fiske showed him how to operate the release. Warren smiled nervously at Lily, turned and then leapt into the wind— abruptly, so that he would not have time to think about it. Once inside the looping tunnel, the wind was deafening. He clung to the side, so that he would not be hit by the others, as he waited for them to come around again. When they did, he released the wire and was suddenly swept away with the wind and flying through the tunnel... next to Leo!

The wind was not nearly as loud once he was traveling *with* it. Quickly, he grabbed the boy and clung to him, then slowed the spool until they came to a stop—while the wind and the Nuldoids and the Crystal all whipped past them like pieces of shrapnel. Warren's heart was racing. He felt Leo's arms holding him tightly. They stayed close to the wall to avoid being hit by the Nuldoids or the Crystal. Slowly then he released more of the wire from the spool until they were again at the cross tunnel. He stopped and swung them both toward the edge of the wind where they flew out of the doidell void and fell at the feet of Lily and Fiske.

Fiske moved in quickly and detached the spool from Warren's waist as Lily was screaming and jumping for joy. Warren stood and helped Leo to his feet.

"Aw, man, I can't believe it!" Leo shouted and then, to Warren's surprise, hugged him. At that moment, Warren felt, perhaps for the first time in his life, like he'd done something truly significant. Though the hug lasted only a moment, in that moment, his feelings soared.

And when they released each other, neither was sure what next to do. "I, uh, I missed you," Warren finally said.

"Yeah. Uh… thanks, Mr. Worst," the boy said.

The awkward moment was broken by Fiske, who yelled, "Yas goin' again yas!" The Harvester had reset the spool and was reattaching it to Warren's belt.

Warren jumped back into the wind and disappeared again into the loop, to reappear a few moments later with the Crystal obelisk in his arms as he came rolling out of the doidell void. When Fiske helped him to his feet, Warren smiled at Lily and then handed Leo the Crystal like he was presenting a newborn.

Again he entered the doidell void and, a few moments later, came tumbling out with Kyle. The little Nuldoid sat up, rubbed his side and complained that Warren had kneed him in the process of saving him. Warren remembered now how disagreeable these creatures were, and pointed out to Kyle that he would have died in the looping tunnel if not for the efforts of his and Lily's and Fiske's. "Ach," the Nuldoid retorted. "Don't mean yas gotta gives we a pain inna side."

Warren decided to ignore the ungrateful Nuldoid as he prepared the spool for one more trip into the doidell void. Fiske fired the hook again into the wall of the tunnel, and Warren leapt into the wind, releasing the wire when he saw Morton come around the corner.

But, when he grabbed the Nuldoid and came to a stop, the spool slipped momentarily, jolting them hard and sending them nearly past the opening of the crossing tunnel. Though they couldn't swing out from where they were, they were close enough to the intersecting tunnel that Warren could reach one arm up around the corner where the two tunnels met. Lily quickly fell to the floor and grabbed his hand, while Leo and Kyle flew to Lily's side and took hold of Warren's arm to help pull him out of the wind. But as they struggled, Warren began to lose his grip on Morton and, though the Nuldoid clung desperately to Warren's free arm, by the time the human was dragged to safety, the wind proved too much for the little Nuldoid and he was swept away back into the loop of the tunnel.

What happened next was a bit of a blur and difficult to describe in terms of how quickly it all went down and how terrifying and confusing the sequence of events was.

It started with a small, barely audible *pop*. Fiske, of course, was the first to hear it. The Harvester turned to the hook, and saw that it was now surrounded by a squiggly black line. A crack. Warren, who was still lying on the floor of the tunnel, heard the second *pop* and looked up to see the crack around the hook widen. "Dat spool! Ya gets it off!" Fiske shouted, pointing to the spool at Warren's waist.

Warren struggled with the latch on the spool as the wall popped a third time, but the latch had been badly damaged and wouldn't detach from his belt. Suddenly a huge chunk of the wall tore out along the lines of the crack and flew past them into the doidell void, taking with it the hook and wire. Warren knew he had only a moment before the slack in the wire would catch up with him and he too would be swept into the wind tunnel. In the next instant, Fiske dove toward Warren with a small knife, scooped it under Warren's leather belt and sliced it in two, just as the wire snapped taut and yanked the spool, along with Warren's belt, from his pant loops with a *pop pop pop*, and hurtled them wildly into the endless rushing wind of the looping tunnel.

Where the chunk of wall had been torn away, wind now blasted through the gaping hole like confetti from a cannon.

Leo, still lying on the floor, reached into his pocket and fingered the old coin. As he did, he felt a surge of energy stab his hand. In a flash he knew he was in danger, that he must move quickly or be killed. He clutched the Crystal tightly and rolled toward Warren just as another piece of the wall, larger this time, cracked and ripped away, landing where Leo had just been and then hurtling into the looping tunnel.

Howling wind was all around them now.

Warren inched his way toward the torn edges of the new opening and used it to pull himself up. He saw then, in the darkness beyond the opening, a large brown eye, dead within, looking back at him as it slid past, followed by the endless oozing flow of a worm's slimy brown skin. A Fishing Worm. With the movement of the worm, the wall cracked again, and more pieces of limestone fell away, causing another gust of wind to blast into the tunnel over their heads.

As the humans and Nuldoids clung to each other and to the Crystal, the intersecting winds overhead continued to rush into the doidell void until, suddenly, the wind above them split in two, causing bursts of debris, chunks of limestone—and Morton—to hurtle past them into the newly made hole where the worm had disappeared. Now there was no hope of saving Morton.

Lily grabbed Leo's hand and pulled him toward her, while he held fast to the Crystal. Fiske grabbed Warren's leg in one hand and the collar of Kyle's shirt in the other to keep him from being swept away by the wind.

Then, as if they had not enough troubles, another chunk of the wall fell away and a crack suddenly jutted horizontally along the side of the tunnel. Warren saw it and had only a second to share a look with Lily before the crack split open and the floor of the tunnel dropped like a hanging door, hinging on its opposite wall, dumping all five of them and the Crystal into the slanting tunnel beneath them, where they crashed down—Kyle and Fiske landing on top of Warren in a series of thuds and "uooff"s— tumbling and sliding end over end down the twists and turns of the tunnel's unforgiving contours, until all of them, the Crystal included, came colliding into a heap where the tunnel finally leveled off.

() () ()

There they lay for a time, only breathing, listening to the howling wind far above them, the wind that took Morton, surely, into the belly of a worm. Finally, they began to untangle themselves and assess the damage and the extent of their injuries.

"Ach," said Fiske, as the Harvester picked up a broken shoulder light. "Worms! Worms inna Pockets! Hasn't been no worms inna Pockets since afore dat Droiden Frobbles. Ach, nah—afore dat!" heesh said, correcting hermself. "Hasn't been no worms inna Pockets since afore dat Time of Work! Is all mick fuddle!"

Warren moved his arm and winced in pain. He was certain he had broken a bone. Fiske moved to him and looked at it. "Holy Lloyd an' Floyd. Dat blood der is red." The Harvester shook hish head and whistled in amazement, adding that heesh'd never seen *red* blood before. Sheesh took out then a small key hanging from hish neck and popped the silver eyeball out of its socket and unlocked it. Heesh took a pinch of the dust from within and sprinkled it on Warren's elbow. "Hib nobb del noid," the Harvester said, and then lightly blew air at Warren's arm. The dust lifted slightly and coalesced like thin white swirling clouds, as the skin beneath it suddenly brightened in a vibrant blue with brown hue. The colors then merged and spun into something of a whirlpool before they vanished altogether with a small *pufff!*

Warren jerked his head back at the pop and then looked curiously at his arm. He moved it slightly and felt no pain. He moved it again. Same thing. Nor could he find a trace of blood. He smiled at Fiske, amazed yet again, as the Harvester locked the eyeball, and replaced it in its socket.

"Ach," said Kyle who stood watching the whole thing. "A Delnoid is yas, hah! An' a Harvester, eh? Never saw no two inna one afore!" He turned then to Warren. "An' you! You is dat toid! Dat toid inna basement onna Crust!"

Warren nodded. "We followed you."

"Ach! Yas were with dat Oidenoids, ya was!"

Warren and Lily both cringed. "Yeah," Lily said. "They lied to us. We didn't know."

As they all made their way back down—bypassing the other doidell void as a benefit of having dropped down to another level when the tunnel they were in cracked and fell—Warren told Leo that he was sorry they were unable to save Morton.

When they finally climbed out of the Pockets from the ground-level opening, Leo put the Crystal down and leaned against the wall while they waited for Kyle and Fiske to catch up. He shoved his hand in his pocket and felt the coin, glad that it was still there, knowing that it had saved his life.

As Warren moved to the Pockets' opening to listen for the Nuldoids, the boy jammed his foot into the dark sand and thought about his friend Morton, who had not been lucky. Tears began to well in his eyes. He quickly wiped them away, but knew that Warren and Lily had seen him do so. He looked at them and shrugged. "I liked Morton. Guess I'm gonna miss him," he said quietly, as Warren put a hand on his shoulder. "Eh," he finally said, "it's just death."

Warren was suddenly exasperated. "Okay, what does that mean? 'It's just death.' What is that?" he said, his frustration finally bubbling up like seltzer. "What's the deal with these guys and death?"

Leo shrugged. "He'll be back."

"He'll be back? Back where? What's *that* mean?" Warren really had had it.

"Leo…" Lily said, "do you mean like… reincarnation?"

Leo was stunned that neither of them knew any of this. For him it had all been obvious, evident, almost from the beginning. "Nah. Well, sorta. It's sorta reincarnation. But, see, they call it Roundabout. I guess 'cause they keep comin' back. An' they remember stuff. From other lives. They remember their other lives. So it's not like our reincarnation."

"Of course," Warren said, leaning back against the limestone wall. Now it all made sense. They lived for hundreds of years, *but not in the same bodies.* They reincarnated, or… *Roundabouted.*

251

That's why they were so casual about death. That's why death wasn't such a big deal. That's why they knew each other from hundreds of years ago. That's why they kept such close tabs on who owed money to whom.

"But here's the weird thing," Leo said, as if *everything* wasn't weird. "Some of them come through the Roundabout and they remember stuff, but others, they don't remember nothin'. They're like us, you know, when we were born." He smiled. "They call them *moronoids*—the ones like us. 'Cause they're stupid, an' they gotta learn everything again. Like us. An' the thing is, they don't know why some is stupid and others isn't."

"Some *are*, others *aren't*." Warren could not help correcting Leo. He was, after all, still Leo's teacher.

"What?"

"You said, 'They don't know why some *is* stupid...' It's *are*. 'Why they *are* stupid, and others *aren't*.' You're starting to talk like them. It's bad English."

Leo screwed up his face and smirked at Warren. "Ah, fik dibble."

Downtown Nuldoid

WHEN THEY RETURNED to the park across from the sewage treatment plant in Morning Heights, they were disappointed to see not only that Mishkin Hobble had, apparently, still not "returned to life," but that Orskin too was unconscious beside him, snoring like a sputtering motorboat. When Fiske stepped over to rouse Orskin, Mishkin Hobble's eyes popped open and he sat up, having only dozed off after returning to life.

"Ach," he said lazily. "Yas back ta joins we inna big bubble a Lloyd's love." Which was a peculiar thing for anyone to say, let alone Mishkin Hobble. And, as the others would discover, though he appeared to be as healthy as ever, he was not quite the same. He had a dazed and placid look on his face that was, at first, chalked up to the residual, and hopefully short-term, effects of the froote's mist. But Orskin and Fiske would later find that the effects were not wearing off and, in fact, the "flakey" look on Mishkin Hobble's face would be there for some time to come. And worse, the two Harvesters would see, in the days that followed, their friend was no longer combative, frequently agreeable and often perfectly content to sit quietly and observe his surroundings. In fact, at times, his personality would border on downright pleasant. While other Nuldoids would be bickering about this or that, he would sit nearby, reeking of loftiness, smiling smugly with half his mouth, as though watching a performance by inferiors.

() () ()

When they went back to the sewage treatment plant to show Ed the Crystal, they were told that he was not there, that he was at the Emperor's Palace in Downtown trying to deal with the problem of the Wheel's slowing rotation. Things were so serious, in fact, that the Emperor had cut short his three-day work schedule at the plant to do so.

The nearest stairwell into Downtown Nuldoid was between Duskville and Sunset Mountain in the early evening region. Since they were in Morning Heights, they figured the quickest way to the stairwell would be through nighttime, rather than dealing with the daylight communities.

Both Snorbleton and Snoozeville were quiet as usual with only a few Nuldoids here and there going home to bed or waking and heading off to daylight. The group trudged through the cities using the sidewalks' running lights, where they existed, and the Harvesters' shoulder lights where they did not. They were yelled at thrice for the squeaky wheel that was developing on Mishkin Hobble's grocery cart. Each time, Mishkin Hobble merely smiled and said, "Boy, is dey crabby blabbs." And, each time, Kyle yelled back at the complainers, calling them yuddle stubs and stinkin' droibs, and that he and the others were on "genuine, official, fida-boned business of dat Crystal!" adding, "Ya stinkin' drobbs horkels!" At one point, an annoyed party shouted from a dark window that Kyle and the others should use the Crystal in a very unpleasant, and, frankly, improbable way.

When they'd passed through Duskville and could see Sunset Mountain in the distance, they came upon another small park— there were many parks in Nuldoid—with a small brick building that looked something like a public restroom. A sign was posted on the grass in front of it that said:

CITY OF NULDOID

DOWN IS UPSTAIRWELL

YOU IS WELCOME!

Before they entered the building, the Harvesters pushed their shopping carts to the side of it, where there was a large opening in the lawn, surrounded by a concrete lip and a small gate. Another sign, suspended from an arch above it said, "HARVESTERS YAS CARTS." After Orskin, Fiske and Mishkin Hobble strapped thin canopies over the tops of their shopping carts, Orskin opened the gate and pushed his into the hole, where it dropped straight down. There was no crash, though. It did not hit anything. And Orskin seemed not in the least concerned or worried that anything bad would happen to his precious shopping cart. Fiske next pushed hish cart into the hole, and then Mishkin Hobble did the same with his. Warren stepped over then to look down into the opening and saw, perhaps fifteen or twenty feet beneath him, the underside of Mishkin Hobble's cart, it having flipped completely over, as it floated at the bottom of the hole. The other two carts, having flipped upside down as well, were floating below it.

"Hey, toids!" Kyle yelled from the opening of the building. "Goes we here!"

The humans followed Kyle into the little brick building that housed the stairwell and, while Warren had had his share of unusual experiences since this whole adventure began, he experienced nothing more unusual than he did in the few moments it took to walk down the stairwell from Outer Nuldoid, up into Downtown Nuldoid.

When he looked down at the first of three flights of stairs, he did not find it particularly unusual, didn't think it looked any different than the countless stairwells he'd seen in, say, parking garages all over San Francisco. The second flight of stairs, however, twisted away from the landing and *appeared* to continue downward to the next landing. But the peculiar thing was this: As Warren descended the second flight of stairs, at some point, he found that he was no longer walking *down*stairs, but *up*. He felt only a brief moment of weightlessness, an odd sensation like his weight had shifted slightly, but he felt nothing profound—it was not a significant sensation. And though he never stopped moving from one step to the next, his *downward* steps, away from Outer Nuldoid, became *upward* steps, toward Downtown Nuldoid. But he couldn't tell how, or when exactly, this had happened. He realized then, as he stepped onto the second landing, that he was looking *up* at the third flight of stairs. He felt as though he had walked into an Escher drawing, where one absolute perception had shifted seamlessly into its exact opposite.

(M. C. Escher made the trip to Nuldoid in 1923 and was greatly influenced by the stairwells into downtown.)

A moment later, he found himself emerging from a similar brick building *inside* Downtown Nuldoid. And though he was now upside down, relative to where he'd just been, he was, in fact, right side up and standing in one of the city's small and rather pleasant parks. As the others stepped out of the brick building, the Harvesters quickly scuttled over to retrieve their shopping carts from the opening in the lawn beside the building. They, the carts, were floating right side up now and waiting for the Harvesters—Orskin's cart on top, since his was the first to have been dropped through from the other side.

And there they were.

In Downtown Nuldoid.

Warren, Lily and Leo were flabbergasted as they stood and looked up and around themselves and saw the magnificent city that surrounded them… because that's exactly what it did—*it surrounded them.*

While Outer Nuldoid rested on the *outside* of an enormous sphere, Downtown Nuldoid rested *inside* the sphere on its concave wall—like a colony of ants blanketing the inner skin of a basketball. And while gravity pulled Outer Nuldoid *down* onto the outside of the "basketball," inside the basketball, gravity pushed *out* in all directions, so that one could look right straight up overhead and see—perhaps a couple of miles away—the exact opposite side of the city. From where they stood, they could see an "aerial view" of Downtown Nuldoid's opposite side: its streets weaving throughout business and residential areas in a circuitous and often circular route, connecting to nearly every other street and forever ending back at their own beginnings.

It was absolutely stunning.

And most odd was the city's source of light. Though quite pleasant, the light seemed to come from nowhere in particular. The entire city, Lily and Warren learned from Kyle, was lit from its very center, where there was a great luminescent ball called, appropriately, the Source. It was perhaps 200 feet in diameter and remained suspended over the city throughout the "day," emitting a great deal of light and, at times, heat, but paradoxically seeming not to have a source. That is, if you looked directly at it, you'd see nothing but the other side of the city. And yet it provided all of the light and heat the city needed.

And, since Nuldoids so enjoyed routine, and so eschewed discomfort, the Source was made to rise to the center of the city, and descend into a large hole each day by the magnetic pull of the Wheel itself. So, by the turning of the Wheel and the subsequent rise and fall of the Source, Downtown Nuldoidians were able to mark time and experience "day" and "night" much like it was done on the Crust—though without, of course, the inconvenience or discomfort of weather, which, in their opinion, would render life unbearable.

From the stairwell, it was perhaps a twenty-minute walk to the Emperor's Palace. Though the Crystal was considerably heavy, Leo insisted on carrying it this last leg of the journey, despite Warren's offer to do so for him, and Orskin's offer to carry it in his shopping cart. The boy felt that, since he had carried it from the Crust, he wanted to carry it the rest of the way to the Wheel.

And carry it he did, proudly through the streets of Nuldoid, where one creature after the next saw it on his shoulder and let out a Nuldoid cheer—a disagreeable and disrespectful sound, similar to a Bronx cheer. But still, to the entourage with the Crystal, it was entirely welcome because—as the humans were learning—a show of disrespect in Nuldoid was how the

Nuldoids showed their appreciation for things that deserved respect.

After a few blocks, Warren noticed that several Nuldoids were following them. A short time later, more Nuldoids had joined the others, and soon the little creatures were singing songs, as still others joined them with beer froote and froote that opened up to corn chips, cheese and various dips. They were in a celebratory mood over the arrival of the Crystal—not so much because it meant that the rotation of the earth would continue, but because, with the Crystal's arrival, there would be a celebration.

Their singing, unfortunately, was very unpleasant to listen to, as Nuldoids did not believe in harmony. And it only got worse, as even more Nuldoids joined in the parade until there were well over a hundred of the little creatures all singing discordant songs and arguing over their lyrics. The resounding favorite, certainly, was *Dat Crystal of Ours*, which went mostly like this:

> *We're off to see dat Wheel!*
> *Dat wonderful Wheel of ours!*
> *We're here we is with Crystal biz*
> *If ever a biz der was!*
> *If ever, oh ever, a biz der was*
> *Dat Crystal of ours is one because…*
> *Because, because, because, because, because…*
> *Because of dat wonderful stuff it does!*
> *We're off to see dat Wheel!*
> *Dat wonderful Wheel of ours!*[*]

---

[*] The observant reader will notice the similarities between this song *(Dat Crystal of Ours)* and *The Wizard of Oz*. L. Frank Baum visited Nuldoid in the summer of 1889 during a Crystal ceremony where he heard the song and wrote it down in his journal. Years later, songwriters Harold Arlen and E.Y. "Yip" Harburg found the journal and used a variation of it for their song. No plagiarism charges were filed by Nuldoid because the attention would have brought the possibility of human migration, which Nuldoids were very much averse to.

There were, of course, many *full* homes in Downtown Nuldoid—since night and day, morning and dusk were all experienced in the same place—none resembling the other though, as conformity was very much frowned upon by these creatures. A number of homes and buildings were made of stone, some of brick, many of them in something of an old Tudor style. It was apparent, as well, that Nuldoids were fond of spires atop the corners of their homes, as there were quite a few of them, even though most of the homes looked like they should not have spires. And, since there was no weather in Nuldoid, the roofs of these homes and buildings—those that had roofs—were not weatherproofed, but built only to block light from the Source. This was mostly so that Nuldoids could nap during daylight. Most windows were round because Nuldoids very much disliked square windows—which, understandably, prompted some homeowners to install square windows in order to annoy those who loved and insisted on round windows.

As you might expect, there were many coffee shops and pubs along the way. The market area and business sections throve with one shop after the next boasting a variety of products and services from *Funeral Party Planning* to the *Argumentation Center for Singles*. There was a *Respiratory Machine Shop* for older cars that was next to *Mibbler's Smoke and Bicker Shop,* which bragged of "Fine Cigars and Quarrelsome People." *Findler Lobb's Stereo Store* sold stereo systems that played Nuldoid music (quite horrific) through speakers that could be set up to face a neighbor's house. It was next to a novelty shop that featured actual "Crust Rocks." Still farther down the same street, there was a *Less Hearing Aid Center,* where Nuldoids could buy devices that were programmed to cut out voices—the store's sign claiming to have saved 867 marriages.

Bookshops featured best sellers in their front windows like *Ed—Lousy Emperor* (by Edward Pugg), *Raising Dat Stupid Baby* and *Thirty Days to a Bigger Belly*. Of course, there were also the classics: *To Kill a Gloib, One Hundred Years of Noise, The Frootes of Wrath* and *Children of a Lesser Lloyd*.

When finally they turned the corner from Droggs Moiden Street to Dibblenord Nubbledorf Drive, they looked up and saw in front of them the Emperor's Palace. It was imposing and majestic with its monolithic white columns and arched windows that flanked an expansive entry. Sprawling marble stairs spilled out to a lawn that surrounded a gurgling fountain with a plaque paying tribute to the memory of Lloyd's accountant, Carl Dutt. (Dutt did nothing significant beyond keeping Lloyd's financial records. In fact, he was nearly forgotten in Nuldoid lore until he reemerged 350 years after Lloyd's last death as a Delnoid architect, and lobbied to build the fountain at a very low rate.)

When they entered the front of the building and started down its spacious corridor, they found themselves stepping around shabbily dressed Nuldoids loitering and lounging about. Small groups of them were curled up together in klumpanoids, sleeping in the alcoves and corners of the hallway, others sat in folding chairs across the doorways to the palace's various offices, like the *Ministry of Crustoid Disinformation,* the *Bureau of Sloidelobb Oversleeping* and the *Department of Internal Squabbling*. A large klumpanoid of creatures were sleeping beneath the statue of Ebbott Schmupp (author of the largest-selling insult book in Nuldoid's history, for which he became a national hero and was awarded the *Congressional Medal of Conflict).* Others were sharing froote or smoking cigars, and all were annoyed by the infusion of the Crustoids and Nuldoids, despite that they were carrying the Crystal.

Warren made his way past a woman wearing a tattered caftan, who spit out a stream of tobacco that landed on his foot. He shot the little woman a look and stopped to wipe off his shoe, grabbing Kyle as he passed. "Who are these people?"

Kyle looked around and shrugged. "How does we supposed ta know?"

"Well, do they work here or something?"

"*Work* here? Nah to dat. They doesn't work nowheres. They doesn't has no jobs. Doesn't even has no homes!"

"They're homeless?"

"Sure yeah," Kyle said, as if it should have been obvious. "Is Hoboggs. Luckless droibs is dey. Bums is dey. So lives dey here."

"In the Emperor's Palace?" Warren said, incredulously.

Kyle thought about it and shrugged again. "Where else?"

As Kyle explained, the Hoboggs thought of the palace as their home, reasoning that it was a public building and therefore belonged to everyone, of which they considered themselves a significant part. For the Emperor, the Hoboggs were yet another source of irritation, since, whenever he entered or left the building, they peppered him with annoying questions and demands. It was, of course, the job of every citizen to do just that, but the Hoboggs did more of it than anyone else because, well, they were living right there in the corridor, and they had nothing but free time.

At the end of the hallway, Orskin stepped to a door with a sign over it that read, "Janitorial Services." "Here we is," he said as he rapped on the door.

Lily, who had been walking beside Leo, shared a look with the boy, and then leaned down to Orskin. "I don't understand. 'Janitorial Services'? That's the Emperor's office?"

They heard shuffling behind the door as Warren, Fiske and Mishkin Hobble joined them. Orskin explained that it wasn't *technically* the Emperor's office. It was the janitorial supply closet, and the Emperor was only permitted to use a portion of it while his offices were being remodeled, the remodel having begun nearly eleven years earlier. The arrangement was inconvenient, to say the least, and while Ed was growing impatient with the *Department of Palace Inhabitation* (responsible for the remodel), the palace janitors were, it's safe to say, entirely fed up with having to share their space with "Nuldoid's Lowest Person."

When, at last, the door opened, Ed stood on the other side, surprised to see the Crustoids and quite happy to see the Crystal. But he did not want to take the time to invite them into the supply closet, as he would have to move aside mops and mop buckets and various other cleaning supplies to do so—though the idea certainly appealed to him, since it would have greatly annoyed Elmo Ek, Vice President of Janitorial Services, who was snoozing quietly near the back of the room, his large feet propped up lazily on his desk.

Ed quickly stepped outside and slammed the door loudly enough to wake the sleeping janitor. He explained to the humans that there was no time to waste, that the Crystal preparation team had to be notified at once. He crossed then to a small red phone on the wall beside a vending machine that sold ready-made protest placards and rotten throwing froote. And, after he unplugged and plugged several of the phone's jacks, he spoke to an operator.

"Is Ed here," he said. Then, frustrated, added, "Ed Pugg! Dat Emperor!" He listened another moment and grew more agitated. "Aw, croib an' drobble, ya stinkin' drobbs horkel! We doesn't owes ya bupp cups! Was six an' sixty years gone now! Ya thinks we—"

"Ed!" Warren blurted, and then caught himself. "I mean, uh, your… majesty? Your emperor-ness?"

"Ach nah," said Kyle, as he stepped up to Warren. "Is here how yas talks to dat Emperor!" He then turned to Ed. "Ed, ya dim bulb! Ya tells 'em 'bout dat Crystal der!"

"Bah, sure yeah," said Ed, turning back to the phone. "Doesn't ya matters 'bout dat grumpletts! Dat Crystal we has! Ya sends we dat Crystal Team onna big pronto, eh!" He hung up the phone and shook his head. "Noids is gonna melt we brains, sure as up's down."

As the humans learned, it would still be many hours still before the Crystal was actually installed. There would have to be a thorough inspection of it for nicks and chips, and then it would need to be cleaned with emollients from a specially grown froote before it was sprayed with a coating of Crystaloid Glopp,® a clear liquid glass that would then have to dry and harden.

"Hours?" Warren was exasperated. "But what if the earth stops moving? You said yourself it could just stop!"

Ed was trying his best to be sympathetic to the humans, since the stoppage of the earth meant something altogether different to Nuldoids. "Eh, is probably don't gonna stop," he offered.

"Probably?"

"Look," Leo said, stepping forward, "isn't there any way to speed up the process?"

Ed cringed slightly as he looked up at the boy and shook his head.

A moment later, there was a great deal of commotion in the corridors of the palace as shrill sirens wailed outside, followed by a series of screeching brakes.

There was more commotion then as several officious and purposeful Nuldoids made their way through the throngs of milling celebrants and Hoboggs. They were beefy-looking creatures, one of them with significant tufts of hair protruding from her ears. They wore large, white fluffy gloves, three-fingered of course, and coveralls with stark black letters printed across their backs: C.R.A.P., which stood for Crystal Retrieval and Preparation team. Each—there were five of them—had strapped to his or her head a yellow hardhat with a flashing yellow or red light on top of it. A couple of them pushed a gurney, as though they were paramedics rescuing an accident victim.

The leader of the team, a woman named Guthry, stepped loftily over to Ed and beside Leo, placed both of her large fluffy hands on her hips, and, with great authority, said, "Crystal Retrieval and Preparation Team, here by official empirical order of Ed!" She paused to let that sink in, looking this way and that, before she continued. "Now, where is we Crystal?"

Well, no one, humans or Nuldoids, knew quite how to answer the question, the Crystal being up a little, but right smack in front of her. Finally, Leo wiggled the Crystal and said, "Uh, it's here."

The little Nuldoid looked up and saw that the boy was indeed holding the Crystal. Leo was told to lay it on the gurney, where it was securely strapped down by the other members of the team. The leader then produced a small clipboard and pen that she shoved at Leo. "Ya signs der for dat Crystal."

After Leo signed the paperwork, the team's leader blew a whistle to clear the crowd, and the gurney was rushed down the corridor, where the swift-moving team turned right instead of left and, a moment later, reappeared and turned right again, instead of continuing straight, which would have taken them to the palace's entrance. Another moment later, they returned to the intersection of the corridors and turned right again, so that they were finally headed out of the building.

Ed put his hand on his forehead, clearly troubled by this. "Ach. Is a grumplett short of a stubb."

The team proceeded with all haste to the front of the palace and out to the phalanx of emergency vehicles parked in front. There were eight or ten of them waiting, each with flashing red and blue and yellow and green lights that, apparently, were causing several bystanders to fall asleep and float in the air. The vehicles were a hodgepodge of shabby and mismatched secondhand ambulances, garbage trucks and hearses, repainted white, with bold red letters along the sides of each that spelled the team's unfortunate acronym.

After the Crystal was loaded safely in the lead vehicle, the entourage of vehicles took off (except for one that would not restart), sirens wailing, only to return a moment later, pass through the area, and head off in the correct direction for the Crystal Preparation Lab.

The humans were told that when the preparation was completed and the Crystaloid Glopp had dried and hardened, the Horn of the Great Wheel would sound throughout Nuldoid. So, it was agreed that the humans, Ed, Kyle, Orskin, Fiske and Mishkin Hobble, would meet back at the palace and then hurry over to the Cathedral of the Wheel for the installation. "Acause," Ed said with uncharacteristic pride, "dey doesn't can do nothin' 'til ol' Ed says so ta go."

The humans had plenty still to worry about—with the delay of the Crystal's installation—but they had no choice but to accept that the situation was most definitely, and quite literally, out of their hands. They would simply have to find a way get their minds off everything, and hope now for the best.

As most of the Nuldoids scurried off to prepare for the celebration, Ed turned to Warren and Lily. "Doesn't yas worry. Is all gonna turn out sporky."

It was an unusual act of empathy for a Nuldoid, and perhaps, Warren thought, that was what the Nuldoidians saw in their emperor. He then provided the humans with tickets to the symphony—performing, as luck would have it, that afternoon—and a street map of Downtown Nuldoid. The map was a hollow rubber ball that opened into two halves. The streets, parks and communities were recreated in miniature on the inside of the halves that could also be turned inside out, in order to see the tiny streets better.

Before they left, however, Ed insisted the humans sign the palace guest book near the entrance, where, unfortunately, a cluster of Hoboggs were sleeping. Ed had to jab and jostle them awake to get them to move, so that the humans could sign in. The Hoboggs, of course, were none too happy with the inconvenience and were sure to let Ed know about it. All of which, he quite expected and responded by reminding them to remember their anger when the next election rolled around.

Orskin announced then that he and the other Harvesters were heading over to the Exchange to buy a new harpoon gun, since theirs was lost in the doidell void. While Fiske turned hish shopping cart around to leave, Mishkin Hobble said he was just going over to the park, maybe stretch out on the grass and enjoy the Sourcelight. It was, after all, he said, such a beautiful day.

"Beautiful day?" Orskin was beside himself. "Is Nuldoid. We doesn't happens any nuthers, ya droib!"

"Exactly," Mishkin Hobble said, and smiled.

And as he ambled out of the palace with his shopping cart, Orskin exchanged a look with Fiske and subtly mouthed the words, "Is flakey."

Warren opened the guest book as the other two Harvesters pushed their squeaking shopping carts out and down the ramps beside the stairs. Ed moved off to the janitorial supply closet to get some work done. The immense book had bold raised letters declaring, "Book Dat Guests Signs In." Warren and Lily were stunned to find pages and pages of signatures and comments that went back hundreds of years. They could not believe their eyes, as Warren turned one fragile yellow page after the next. And though Leo and Kyle were bored by it and anxious to leave, Warren and Lily insisted on staying long enough to look through the book. Warren tried twice to engage the boy—pointing out the wonder of what they were seeing—but was met only by the contemptuous look of a bored pre-teen and his friend.

The guests in the book had been in Nuldoid either as a result of having followed a Crystal expedition back to Nuldoid from the Crust—as was the case with L. Frank Baum—or from happening upon a Crust entrance, as J.R.R. Tolkien had. Steven Spielberg had signed the book in the winter of 1964, after traveling to Nuldoid from an access tunnel near Phoenix, Arizona. Most of the names, of course, were unfamiliar to the humans, but in and amongst the many signatures and comments, several names stood out. Copernicus, for instance. John Lennon. Samuel Adams. Rosa Parks. W.C. Fields.[*] At first, it seemed to Warren that those he recognized had little in common with each other. Though later he would realize there was a thread of similarity amongst them: Each visitor, in one way or another, had come away from Nuldoid willing to—if it was called for, and sometimes when it wasn't—go against the grain. Each challenged tradition. Most challenged authority. Whether this was because of who they were *before* they visited Nuldoid, or who they became *after* they were in Nuldoid, was cause for much speculation.

When Warren and Lily had finished looking through the guest book, they stepped out onto the stairs in front of the palace with Kyle and Leo. The emergency Crystal recovery truck that would not restart was still there; the side hood was open,

---

[*] See Various Nuldoid Visitors at the back of the book.

exposing a sick and wheezing engine. Two workers stood beside it, shoving each other's chests and blaming each other for the illness of the vehicle. Beyond the statue, they could see the reflecting pond that stretched the length of Dibblenord Nubbledorf Drive. The street and reflecting pond were neatly cradled by froote trees and colorful flowers, all of which, Kyle explained to the humans, were tended to by angry groundskeepers who had strong opinions about how the grounds were to be kept. Their horticultural opinions were so strong, in fact, that no two gardeners could be simultaneously issued gardening tools—shears, hoes, rakes or any other potential weapons—in order to prevent casualties and even fatalities. The gardening, therefore, could only be done by one gardener at a time and was painstakingly slow.

Though there were plenty of sights to see, as you can well imagine, Warren had a difficult time not worrying about the Crystal and, well, the future of the world. But, with several hours to kill, he and Lily agreed it would still be better to fill the time sightseeing and staying busy.

When Warren suggested they might as well attend the symphony, both Leo and Kyle made faces like someone had proposed lobbing their heads off, opting instead to wander over to Dougg's Famous Arcade, a spot that Kyle frequented in the lifetime he was a Delnoid. Before Warren or Lily could insist the four of them stick together, the boy and the little Nuldoid had bounded down the steps of the palace and were gone.

After Lily found the symphony hall inside the ball map, they headed back down Droggs Moiden Street, turned onto Ruddle Pogg Boulevard and passed the park where they'd earlier entered downtown. Only once did they make a wrong turn and have to ask directions from a group of Nuldoids who were gathering noisemakers from a tree in preparation for the Crystal celebration.

"A toid, is ya?"

"Yeah. We're trying to find the symphony hall."

"Careful ya doesn't bumps yas head on dat Source, eh!" one of the creatures said and then laughed hard enough that he fell over.

"You know," Warren said, his temper finally starting to flare, "I've only heard that joke maybe fifty times since I've been here!" But he saw that the little Nuldoids were only smiling and looking up at him after he'd said it, delighted to see that they'd gotten under his skin. "Which way to the symphony hall?" he asked.

"Ach, turns yas left at Doiden Hoidell, an' cross Boiggen Stiggen Parkway, an' yas doesn't miss it." He suggested that, along the way, they visit "Wogg Stobbler Oggber Fibble Toogleduff Hibbler-Gobb Murdle-Hoid Lane." "Is a hoot, dat lane!"

"Why? What's so great about it?" Lily asked.

"Nots ta says why. Is a hoot, is all."

As they turned left at Doiden Hoidell Road and walked toward Boiggen Stiggen Parkway, they were told several more times by several other Nuldoids that they absolutely, positively, *must* visit Wogg Stobbler Oggber Fibble Toogleduff Hibbler-Gobb Murdle-Hoid Lane. When, finally, the humans came upon the entrance to the lane, they saw it was a tiny cul-de-sac, not twenty feet long, with room only for one small house on either side. Lily and Warren stood there somewhat confused, while nearby Nuldoids could hardly contain themselves. Apparently, it was riotously funny to these creatures that such a small street had so large a name, and funnier still when they saw the confused expressions of Warren and Lily.

Farther down the street, they saw the Great Symphony Hall of Nuldoid. It was an impressive, monolithic stone building that dominated the area and housed the magnificent and elaborate works of Nuldoid's greatest composers: Halfin Hibble, Dorr Stibble and Fenger Stogg.

Unfortunately, Warren and Lily wrongly made the assumption that a professional group of musicians—in Nuldoid or anywhere else—would produce pleasant, reasonably mellifluous, music. The "magnificent and elaborate works," it turned out, were performed off-key by violins, basses, flutes, et cetera, all kept finely out of tune with great care, and brought to life by accomplished musicians, who spent years perfecting their ability to make the most discordant of sounds.

The symphony was, mercifully, half over by the time they arrived, it having begun earlier than usual in anticipation of the Crystal installation and celebration. So, while rows of Nuldoids sat blissfully listening to the cacophonous "music," Warren and Lily managed only to suffer through it, snugly wedged in their tiny lounge seats, until it was thankfully over. They left with ringing ears and splitting headaches—oblivious to the various jibs and jabs of passing Nuldoids about their height—Lily vowing never again to sit through anything so agonizing.

When they stepped back onto the street, they tried in vain to find an open pharmacy, hoping Nuldoids sold such things as painkillers. But nearly all shops were closing down—except restaurants and pubs, which were not allowed to close—while Nuldoids rushed here and there, collecting beer froote and snacks for the various Crystal celebrations throughout the city.

As they ventured farther down Doiden Hoidell Road, they passed a courthouse and were surprised to come across several Nuldoidians locked in wooden stockades, having been convicted of Non-Dissidence, Conspiracy to Support the Government and

Religious Myopathy. The shackled creatures greeted Lily and Warren cheerfully and wished them well.

As celebratory car horns blared sporadically and bounced echoes through the concave streets of Downtown Nuldoid, Warren and Lily decided it best to head back toward the palace, lest they get too far away. They saw on the ball map that Drobbs Tubble Boulevard emptied out near Dibblenord Nubbledorf Drive and the Emperor's Palace. So they turned onto Drobbs Tubble and started to make their way back.

Along the boulevard, they passed a small pet shop that was still open, and, since the Horn of the Great Wheel had not yet sounded, Lily insisted they go in. Over the pet shop door, a neon sign boasted "Gurd's Pets—Better Much than Skibb Dibble's Pets!" Though Warren was now feeling quite anxious about the Crystal and the rotation of the earth—Lily was as well—he agreed that it would be good way to kill some more time.

The store was run by an elderly Delnoid named Hargis Gobb, who had long white hair that swept into several ponytails, and Coke-bottle glasses with a number of different-colored filters that were flipped up to hish forehead.

"Ach, is closin' we down for dat Crystal, so yas doesn't stay! Big toids or no!" sheesh barked when Lily and Warren ducked down and entered the store.

"We'll just stay for a minute, if that's okay," Lily said, and then smiled warmly.

Lily's smile was not to be trifled with, and the crusty old Delnoid was no more immune to it than any other Nuldoid or Crustoid. "Sure yeah, yas stay, stay, sure."

As they meandered into the shop, Warren whispered to Lily, "Not too long."

There were a few Theevins in cages along the wall near the register. A group of noisy Wett Woggs were on another aisle, and, in the store's front window, several Blobalobbs chewed contentedly on pellets or snored away—their only significant activities besides growling and eliminating the pellets. The Blobalobbs ranged in size from a couple of feet in diameter to the younger ones, called "slabbs," that were about the size of a hamburger patty.

"So… what is it you do with a Blobalobb?" Warren asked Hargis, nodding to them.

"Do with it? Is a pet. Yas pet it." Hargis dug a finger into hish ear to relieve an itch.

Lily reached into the pen of Blobalobbs to pet one. It, of course, began to growl.

"Okay, but… it just lays there," Warren said. "It doesn't do anything."

Hargis shrugged. "It growls."

"Look… where I come from, we have dogs for pets. They have four legs and a tail and you can do stuff with 'em."

"Doooogs ya has, huh?" Hargis squinted up at Warren. "So, what was ya does with a dogs?"

"Well, you take it to the park and throw a stick for it," Warren explained.

"Yuh-huh-yuh-huh. An' what den happens?"

"Well, the dog chases it, and brings it back to you."

"Yuh-huh. An' den what?"

"Uh… and then you throw the stick again."

"Yuh-huh-yuh-huh. Den what?"

"…Well, you… throw it again."

"Humph…" Hargis scratched hish head. "So, why doesn't yas just keep dat stick?"

"Because, if you keep the stick, the dog can't chase it and bring it back to you."

"Uh-huh-uh-huh," Hargis said, nodding, considering all this. "So… ya likes dis stick, but ya doesn't wanna keeps it?"

"Okay, the stick really isn't important."

"Yuh-huh-yuh-huh. It doesn't important, eh? An' ya keeps throwin' it 'way?"

"No, you're missing the point. The stick doesn't matter."

"But ya wants dat dog to brings yas it back?"

"Well, yes. But only because the dog likes to chase it."

"So… dat's because of it's fun?"

"Right, yes!" Warren said, encouraged that the Delnoid was finally getting it.

"So…" Hargis was thinking very hard about all of this, "…on dat Crust, if you has a dog…"

"Right, right…"

"…ya doesn't never able to gets ridda sticks."

Warren deflated like a punctured balloon, and Lily laughed.

Then the Horn of the Great Wheel blared and warbled throughout the city.

The Wheel of Nuldoid

A
S WARREN AND Lily made their way back to the palace, tiny revelers were everywhere, blowing noisemakers and shoving each other in what promised to be a lighthearted evening of bitter arguments and impromptu fistfights.

They met Orskin and Fiske at the foot of the palace's front steps. Mishkin Hobble was not with them. "Is off him, Lloyd knows where," Fiske explained. Leo and Kyle soon joined them, as Emperor Ed hurried out of the palace and down the steps, followed by several complaining Hoboggs.

He led them past the fountain and the broken emergency vehicle—where a few Nuldoids were still asleep, floating in the air—down Dibblenord Nubbledorf Drive, and along the reflecting pond. In the middle of the block, Noidel Frobb Lane opened wide to their right, where they could see the Capitol building at the end of it. Congress had adjourned earlier in the day, Ed explained, for the ceremony. Above the entrance to the majestic domed building, words were chiseled into the marble archway: "DIVIDED WE STANDS!" and beneath that, in smaller lettering, "E Pluribus Bicker."

Lily noticed there were large metal bins on either side of the Capitol steps and more of the bins along the front of the great building. A Nuldoid stood beside one of them and hoisted the contents of a garbage can into it. A garbage truck attached itself to another and slung it overhead to unload trash into its back end. "You dump your garbage at the Capitol?" Lily asked.

Ed looked over at the building, then back up at Lily. "Ya doesn't?"

At the end of Dibblenord Nubbledorf Drive, they entered the Park of the Wheel. And when the humans walked onto its cool grass, they looked up and there, at last, they saw the magnificent Wheel of Nuldoid.

But they were only seeing a small portion of it, as it emerged from an elongated opening in the middle of the park—the length perhaps of two football fields. A huge lawn, dotted with trees and small ponds, surrounded it. The colossal cogs along the outer ridge of the massive Wheel were the size of school busses, as they emerged from the ground at one end of the park and lolled high into the air like lumps on the back of a majestic gray whale. The top of the Wheel rose perhaps 300 feet above the park's floor, where it lumbered slowly to the other side and then disappeared back into the ground. Nearer the Wheel, the grinding gears of its machinery could be heard churning away beneath the park. Immense round openings in the body of the Wheel appeared and grew to full size, as they climbed and then slowly sunk like an endless series of setting suns. It was machinery the likes of which the humans had never seen.

On a typical day in the park, Nuldoids could be seen out dragging their pet Blobalobbs behind them, unless they carried the disagreeable creatures under one arm, or pulled them in small wagons the way many Nuldoids did their favorite potted plants. On a typical day, one would find Delnoids sitting in lawn chairs, enjoying newspapers or magazines, while their tethered kites bobbed in the air above them, kept aloft by personal industrial fans. On a typical day in the park, younger Nuldoids could be found playing bocce ball on the grass, reminiscing about past lives and better times when Nuldoids cared more about "Lloyd an' Country." On a typical day, Nuldoid youngsters could be seen sitting in small groups around chessboards dotted with playing pieces, all the same color. They preferred to play board games—especially chess—with all black or all white pieces, so that it was difficult to tell who was winning, and, therefore, prompted a great many more arguments.

But this was no typical day.

Followed by the humans and the swelling throngs of Nuldoids, Ed walked the length of the park and around the great Wheel to the cathedral's elevator. Surrounded by even more Nuldoids, all arguing and vying to get in, the elevator was housed in a small white marble building that looked more like a family mausoleum than the entrance to a cathedral. Ed made his way through the crowd, shouting that he was the Emperor, that it was imperative he and the humans be allowed immediate access to the elevator. At the same time, however, another group of Nuldoids was making its way through the crowd from another direction. There were five of them, dressed in green jumpsuits and hardhats, carrying buckets and large plastic bags.

"Ach," Ed said when he saw the group approaching.

"Who are they?" Leo asked.

"Department a Sloidelobb Clean-Up," the Emperor explained, shaking his head. "Is dat Sloidel has kah-blammed."

The enormous head of the elevator's Sloidelobb, Gordon, had exploded, and now the elite crew of cleaning specialists was there to clean up. They were highly regarded, this crew, because an exploded Sloidelobb had to be dealt with in an effective and timely manner. If not, machinery throughout Nuldoid and Neither Norr would bog down and simply cease to be of use.

No doubt, when Gordon looked outside and saw hundreds of Nuldoids waiting to use the elevator, it was much too much for him. It was an enormous goof to expose the Sloidelobb to that much stress and—after Gordon declared, "Is too many! Too many! Too many noids is dey!"—his shaking head blew up.

As they waited for the crew to drag Gordon's massive body out, and pick the pieces of his brain and skull off the walls, Ed explained to Lily and Warren that the celebration promised to be a "doosey hoosey," since it would now be two-fold: the Crystal's installation, of course, being the main thrust of the revelry, but also there would be a lively and well-attended funeral for Gordon. The funeral was expected to be large and especially raucous since a significant number of Nuldoids, if not all, knew and greatly disliked Gordon.

As Ed moved to the elevator and prompted the humans to do so as well, there were a good many objections from the other Nuldoids waiting. "Nah, ya doesn't, ya horks dobble." "Thinks yas holier than Lloyd, eh?" And while those waiting felt that Nuldoid's Last Person should go last, the case was made, yet again, that time was of the essence, and that the installation of the Crystal could not officially begin without the Emperor being present.

Once Ed ushered Lily, Warren and Leo inside—to more objections—Ed pushed the down button, which was still slightly green from Gordon's blood. The elevator chugged a few times and then slowly descended toward the cathedral.

A moment later, it jolted to a stop, and the doors crawled apart. When the humans stepped into the Cathedral of the Wheel, they could do no more than stand and stare in awe at the wonder of what they were seeing.

The Cathedral of the Wheel

ED EMERGED FROM the elevator and punched a button to send it back up to the park. He joined the humans who were still dumbstruck, staring down the nave of the cathedral— its burgundy carpet sweeping past rows of small wooden pews, filled here and there with celebrating Nuldoids—as it billowed up to an elaborately adorned altar that rested at the very center of a huge and magnificent cogwheel. From the altar, the Wheel soared to the ceiling, towered overhead and swept out away to either side, the tremendous force of it at once obvious and resplendent in its monolithic and breathtaking grandeur.

In the middle of the altar, a gold-plated ring stood on its side like a huge propped-up pineapple slice. At the hole in its middle, the old Crystal—installed a hundred years earlier—was held snugly in place. This magnificent gold ring was called the Holey

The
Cathedral of the Wheel

Cylinder, and, while it measured perhaps ten or twelve feet across, it was dwarfed by the massive metal lug nut just behind it that looked like it weighed many tons and held the Wheel in place.

Before Ed moved off to let the engineers know they could begin the installation—there would not be the usual pomp and ceremony beforehand, in order to speed up the process—he invited the humans to have a look around, to wander wherever they wanted.

As more Nuldoids—including now Kyle, Orskin, Fiske and even Mishkin Hobble—entered the cathedral, the humans made their way down the burgundy carpet, gaping at the expansive and sweeping ceiling overhead and the leaded glass windows that lined the side walls, depicting the thirteen lives of Lloyd. They moved cautiously up the steps of the altar, between the wooden railings and padded balustrades that ran from the center out to either edge of the giant Wheel's tremendous cogs. The railing faced the body of the Wheel itself, so that Nuldoids could kneel down and spit on the massive machinery.

"They spit on it?" Warren asked. "Why?"

"Is disrespectin' for dat Wheel," Ed explained, "on accounta was deservin' big lotta respect."

Since Nuldoids so disliked showing respect for anything (or anyone) that deserved respect, they showed great disrespect for those things that deserved great respect. In so doing, by the way, the creatures helped the machinery, since their saliva was considerably more viscous than that of humans, oily even, and actually helped grease the machinery.

Lily, Warren and Leo stepped carefully up to the Holey Cylinder, where they saw it was made up of thirteen chambers, each containing the ashes of one of Lloyd's bodies.

From the front of the Holey Cylinder, only the backside of the old Crystal—the flat bottom—could be seen. When Lily walked to the back of the cylinder, she saw the quadrilateral top of the old Crystal protruding through it. From its tip, a beam of intense red laser light shot out into the dark center of the gigantic lug nut at the Wheel's hub directly behind it.

She craned her neck to follow the contours of the Wheel as it towered overhead and disappeared into the elongated hole in the ceiling, where it rolled through the Park of the Wheel far above them. The bottom half of the great Wheel could not be seen from where they were, since the altar and the floor of the cathedral rested just at the Wheel's center. There were stairwells on either far side, leading down to the gargantuan jumble of interlocking cog and pinion wheels of the machinery, all slowly churning away.

There was a great deal of chatter and much hubbub as the cathedral filled with more Nuldoids. They became immediately silent, however, when an ominous moan emanated from beneath the floor. *Hmmmgggrrrr.* Then, as quickly as it appeared, it vanished. The Nuldoids remained stock-still for another moment, processing what they'd heard.

"I think it's the machinery," Leo said quietly to Lily. "It's slowing down. It's under a lot of stress."

After the moment had passed, the creatures grew animated again as a siren sounded and yellow lights began to whirl and flash at the side of the altar. A large metal door clanked to life and rolled open. From within, Ed emerged, urging several engineers behind him to move quickly. A small forklift truck beeped repeatedly and rolled out, flanked by several engineers in hardhats. The Crystal was resting comfortably on the padded arms of the forklift, shining with the luster of a polished diamond.

Several of the engineers moved quickly then to the Holey Cylinder, where they snapped on pristine white gloves and positioned themselves. The truck rolled up to them and stopped, proffering the Crystal. They looked then to Ed, assuming that he would have a few words to say, as Emperors usually do in situations like this. But Ed was clearly in no mood for the trivialities of tradition. "Uh, Lloyd is great, an' off we goes," he said hurriedly.

"Ach!" complained a young Nuldoid in the crowd. "The National Pledge we does! Is always how is we does it, Ed!" Younger Nuldoids, as you know, were sticklers for tradition.

"Nah to dat, ya droib! We doesn't has time!" Ed retorted.

"Demandin' yer lowness' attention," another youngster in a pointed felt hat, stepped up and said, "is doesn't count, least we does the pledge!"

Ed was clearly frustrated, his cheeks flushing green with anger. "Fine! Does dat pledge, does it! But ya hurries it up, huh!"

With that the Nuldoids in attendance launched into the National Pledge:

> We pledge us to bicker for dat Wheel,
> Dat turns we all our Noidelloyd.
> An' to dat Crystal
> Stuck inna core,
> Dat gives it juice an' turns we circle,
> We squabble much to brings we'round…
> With argy-bargy an' beer froote for all.

Because of the hurried nature of the situation and the many fuzzy memories, the pledge sounded more like a jumble of non-sequiturs than a pledge. But still it satisfied the younger "mud-in-a-stuck" Nuldoids.

When they were finished, the engineers gently lifted the Crystal from the arms of the forklift and, with two on either side, they moved toward the Holey Cylinder, where another engineer placed a stepladder and quickly climbed up to the old Crystal. With one quick heave, the engineer shoved the backside of the old Crystal through the center opening. It popped out the other side of the cylinder and fell onto the floor in front of the giant lug nut, where it shattered into hundreds of tiny pieces. The engineer scooted back down the ladder and moved it aside. The others then stepped in front of the Holey Cylinder with the new Crystal on their shoulders, all of them moving like pallbearers, until they stood directly in front of the Holey Cylinder.

But the creatures were obviously much too short to reach the opening, and Warren exchanged a look with Lily and Leo. The little Nuldoids appeared to be concentrating very hard as they stood in front of the Cylinder. In unison then, they chanted, "Hib nobb del noid!" and slowly they began to hover and, like rising dough, they floated to the level of the Cylinder's opening. The two engineers at the Crystal's point guided the tip of it, as the other two pushed the back end of it into the opening. Finally they gave one last shove and it clicked into place.

On the other side of the Holey Cylinder, the point of the Crystal began to glow red, and blink a couple of times. Then, from its tip, a steady bright red beam streaked into the dark center of the lug nut. Gradually, the whirring sound of living machinery, of energy moving metal, the sound of pure full force, could be heard returning, coming back to life. As it did, a Nuldoid cheer arose from the creatures in the cathedral. There was even some regular applause, but it was quickly squelched, as its perpetrators were shot scornful looks to discourage open adulation. Whoops and yelps, however, were apparently quite apropos, and they rose up abundantly as more Nuldoids entered the cathedral and saw that the new Crystal had been put in place.

The lighthearted mood quickly evaporated though as many of the Nuldoids realized that they were ill-prepared for the evening of celebration that was to follow, and began to bicker over the small amount of beer froote that was on hand in the cathedral. That the world had just been saved—or rather, the Crustoids on it—was a trifling matter to them and certainly not the focus of their celebratory efforts.

Warren, Lily and Leo, on the other hand, were quite happy and altogether relieved now that the new Crystal had finally been installed and the machinery was working. And they were exhausted, Lily and Warren having slept very little in the last several days. Leo, as you recall, had slept during his trip through warped time, but still he was duly tired.

As more Nuldoids filed in to see the new Crystal, and others filed out to get beer froote, Ed told the humans to go get some rest. He told them that they had been invited to stay at Downtown Nuldoid's finest hotel, The Boggs Tuddle Inn, at a "significantly reduced rate." A number of beds at the inn had been shoved together for the oversized guests. Ed was even kind enough to spot Lily and Warren twenty grumpletts so that they would not run into any problems with hotel management, a disagreeable woman named Wadda Spigg.

Lily, Warren and Leo found Kyle arguing at the side of the cathedral, thanked him and said they were going to the hotel to get some sleep. After they'd informed the Harvesters of the same, they said good-bye and headed for the elevator.

As the doors of the elevator opened, and more Nuldoids entered the cathedral, another slow-rolling and eerie howl emerged from the bowels of the machinery beneath the cathedral.

Hmmmgggrrrr.

The Crust Recovers

WHAT WARREN, LEO and Lily had done obviously benefited those living on Earth's crust more than the mildly grateful Nuldoids—who were only really spared from having to reset their clocks. But no one on the Crust was aware of what had been done on their behalf.

With the installation of the new Crystal and the resumption of the earth's regular rotation, overt tensions around the globe and the lethargy felt in the preceding days began to lessen. As people began to feel more like themselves, they experienced a surge of energy.

Television executives in Los Angeles and New York were flummoxed by national ratings on shows which, only a week earlier, had drawn record audiences, that were suddenly being ignored. Apparently, viewers were getting off their couches, turning off their television sets and doing things again.

(Television watching in the late twentieth century and early twenty-first was a primary activity of humans, especially in the Northern American continent. Most experts agree, it was largely responsible for the Era of Wide Loads, as it was later called, and the Age of Ignorant Acceptance, when countries like the United States were taken over by oil companies and extreme religious groups.)

One of the more tangible effects of the earth's varied rotation was seen at the Tower of Pisa, where there was already something of a "leaning" problem. After October 1989, when the earth's rotation had slowed and then sped up again, Italian officials noticed a bit *more* leaning, and by January 1990, decided to close the building to the public, once and for all.

Some Rest, Some Relaxation

LILY, WARREN AND Leo headed for the hotel. Along the way, they saw that nearly all of the businesses in Downtown Nuldoid were shutting down or had shut down, except, of course, for the pubs and restaurants.

When they reached the Boggs Tuddle Inn, they were much too tired to appreciate the asymmetrical stonework of the hotel's many cottages, or the winding walkways beside the Nuldoid River, a huge industrial pipe that wove through the city. After a brief argument with Wadda Spigg, the hotel's owner, over Warren's lack of "proper" identification—he had only a very suspect driver's license from a place Mrs. Spigg had never heard of called "California"—the humans retired to their respective rooms, crawled into their respective beds and slept.

And sleep they did.

They slept soundly from well before Sourcedown, until nearly midSource the following day, when Warren was awakened by Mrs. Spigg, who knocked on his door to let him know that he had slept past checkout, which was eleven o'clock. Warren nearly apologized to the little woman, and then remembered that he had paid for a couple of days, so it shouldn't have mattered. When he mentioned as much to Mrs. Spigg, she huffed and harrumphed and said curtly that it was the principle of the thing. To which Warren said she was "loopy in the beanbag," which confused her because there was no such expression in Nuldoid. He added that, if she didn't watch herself, he'd badmouth the hotel all over Outer Nuldoid.

Pleased with himself after the argument, Warren went back to his beds and slept another two hours, until he was awakened by an ominous rumbling that momentarily shook the walls of the hotel room. He tried to go back to sleep, but couldn't. So he got up, took a hot shower, having to huddle low in the tiny shower stall to do so. When he was dressed, he ducked out the door of his room and saw the owner carrying a stack of folded sheets along the stone path.

"Mrs. Spigg, what was that noise? A little while ago."

"Wasn't no noise," Wadda Spigg said, and quickly turned to continue on.

"No, there was a noise all right. The walls shook. Like an earthquake."

She stopped and whirled back. "Ach, ya doesn't gets no moneys back! Dat noise was nonna we fault!"

"I'm not saying it was your fault. I just wanna know what it was!"

"How does we know? Is never a sound 'at comes afore," she said, and moved off down the stone path.

After Lily and Leo awoke, the three of them left the hotel for the day to catch up with Kyle and the Harvesters. But none had any notion of what had caused the disturbing rumble. Only that it felt like, and sounded vaguely like, the noise they'd heard in the cathedral the day before.

They ate lunch together at a restaurant Kyle suggested, where the humans had to squat on tiny Nuldoid chairs to eat. Afterward, Kyle nearly came to blows with the waitress and manager over the bill. They settled finally on a total of eight-and-a-half grumpletts.

Though Kyle was enjoying his return to Nuldoid—after the long ordeal he'd suffered bringing the Crystal back from the Crust—the truth was he missed Morton. Certainly, he enjoyed his arguments with young Leo, but they were not as satisfying as those with his old partner. Which was why he would privately brighten at any mention of a year or two or three down the road, when he knew Morton would be returning to life.

Orskin and Fiske were naturally uncomfortable in the city and anxious to get back to the wilderness of Neither Norr. They agreed though to stay a little longer, since the humans were still there and because they were worried about Mishkin Hobble, who seemed to have no intention of leaving. It appeared that the littlest Harvester—who, by the way, no longer insisted on being called Mishkin Hobble—was happy to be wherever he was, no matter *where* he was, and his companions were growing more and more concerned about his mental health.

Most disturbing were his vague references to Lloyd, and how he had come to know Lloyd personally. That, apparently, was the crux of the problem—if you viewed his condition as such—because he sincerely believed that the froote he inhaled had allowed him to see things that no other living Nuldoid had ever seen.

All of which was chalked up by Orskin Wobb as evidence that his "brain was gone flakey." Orskin's greater fear though was that the little Harvester's brain might grow so flakey that he'd become an Oidenoid. In fact, Orskin had taken to carrying different-colored rubber balls so that he could occasionally test his friend.

For a time, Harlo Fiske was on the fence about Mishkin Hobble's mental state. The Delnoid, in hish many years of life, had heard tales of froote with special powers that did indeed allow one to see things others could not. But, most of those tales had been proven false. And after the little Harvester stood one day and loudly declared, "Lloyd needs hisself a good barber, but pronto!" Fiske, as well, concluded that Mishkin Hobble's brain had gone flakey.

What concerned them most was the remaining froote in Mishkin Hobble's grocery cart. Of the two that remained, Mishkin Hobble had sold one of them for the handsome sum of seventy-six grumpletts to a musician at the market—who was exactly the type of Nuldoid, Orskin and Fiske felt, the little Harvester should *not* have been involved with. The other froote, the one remaining, he'd left at the bottom of his grocery cart, where it rolled from side to side. That was the froote that Orskin and Fiske were worried about. After all, if one froote had caused him to become as stupid as he appeared, they couldn't imagine what a second froote might do to him.

() () ()

The next few days for the humans were languorous and restful. There was not much for Warren, Lily and Leo to do but wander the streets of Nuldoid and get to know one another. They had long and short conversations, a good deal of laughter, and, of course, spirited arguments. They saw Kyle and the Harvesters a number of times, and traveled once to Outer Nuldoid to visit Ed at the sewage treatment plant, where they were treated to a full-blown tour.

Around town, Warren made an effort to remain unruffled by the Nuldoids' snide remarks and their jokes about his height. Not just because he was beginning to appreciate the Nuldoidian culture and their peculiar behavior, but because, when he didn't respond with anger, it confounded and bothered the little creatures immensely.

After a few days, though, they were weary from seeing so many new sights, from meeting so many Nuldoids, from hearing so much bickering. So Lily suggested they do something by themselves, without any Nuldoids. Something like a picnic. Warren liked the idea, and it was decided that they would stop by the open market, buy some picnic froote, and take it to one of the smaller parks, where they could spread out a blanket, sit quietly beneath the warm afternoon Source, and enjoy their own company.

The idea did not at all appeal to Leo, who had been invited by Kyle to attend a Thankless Dead concert over in the Park of the Wheel, where a number of older Nuldoids would be speaking out against the government and the Emperor's incompetent leadership. (Ed himself was expected to attend and speak out against himself.)

Warren—who was starting to feel like he had some providence over the boy—said no, that he couldn't go. He said that Leo should spend a quiet afternoon with Lily and him. Leo balked at the idea, said Warren wasn't the boss of him, and that he was going to the concert anyway.

But, as the boy collected his things to leave, Lilly stopped him. "Leo? Listen… I'd really like it if you came with us," she said in a most sincere tone. "Then tonight, you can go out with your friend."

"Aw, Lily..." He was entirely prepared to argue and defy Warren, but for this, for Lily, he had no defense. There was no way to combat her gentle smile, her soft hand on his forearm, the earnestness in her eyes. He agreed to go to the park with them, but chided Warren when Warren came up three grumpletts short at the open market and needed to borrow money. Reluctantly, the boy dug into his pocket and handed him the three grumpletts.

A short while later, they were sitting on a blanket spread over the cool grass of Arlo Muttle Park, sharing warm hamburger froote and breaking open crunchy corn chip froote. Arlo Muttle, they learned from a brass plaque, was a third century Emperor (245-267 C.C.), who enacted a series of laws requiring all citizens to question and oppose newly enacted laws. The citizens of Nuldoid thought the new laws were ridiculous and unnecessary and argued against them, thereby supporting the new laws. The Arlo Muttle laws, the plaque explained, came to be considered the "most perfectist of dat Nuldoid laws."

As adults often do, Warren started telling stories about how much trouble he used to get in when he was a kid, which both Leo and Lily were encouraging him to do. But what Warren *didn't* know was that they were making fun of him. His "crimes" weren't very criminal (he hid his teacher's blackboard eraser, for instance), compared to Lily in her youth (she'd run away from home) and certainly compared to what Leo had done just a few days earlier when he stole a car.

To his surprise, Leo found himself enjoying the company of Lily and Warren, even though they were adults. Then, as he peeled open a cola froote and laughed at something Lily said, it occurred to the boy that these two people actually *cared* about him. They certainly cared more about him than either of his parents ever had.

And while it was clear that Lily too was enjoying herself, there was a moment for Warren—he had just leaned back on the blanket, bit into his potato salad froote and watched the two of them—that he was struck by an overwhelming thought: *They were a family*. The three of them. No, he and Lily weren't married, and Leo was not their son, but still they had the soul of a family, didn't they? And, in that instant, he sat up and blurted out, "Why don't we all live together?"

Well, that sure stopped the laughter. Lily and Leo stared back at him. "You mean, all three of us?" Lily asked.

"Sure," Warren said, and shrugged, now feeling like he'd blurted too much, too fast.

Lily hardly thought about it before she smiled and said, "I'd like that."

Warren was, of course, pleasantly surprised, and then they turned to Leo. The boy looked from Lily to Warren, considering the proposal. After a moment, he put forth his conditions: "First, I want my *own* room. I want twenty dollars a week allowance. Midnight curfew. I don't do chores. And you'd better pay me back those three grumpletts!"

Warren weighed the demands for a moment. "We'll see about the room. Ten o'clock is *bedtime,* not *curfew! Five* dollars a week allowance. And you'll take out the trash and do the dishes."

"What about the three grumpletts?"

"I'll borrow it from Ed."

"He's tired of loaning you money."

"Fine. I'll get it from the Harvesters."

"Didn't they just loan you, like, fifteen?"

"Look, I'll get the money!"

"You have no intention of paying me back, do you?"

"What do you need grumpletts for anyway?" Warren asked. "We're going back to San Francisco!"

"See, ya got no intention."

"I *said* I'll pay you back, so I'll pay you back, ya stinkin' droib!"

Warren's unintentional use of the Nuldoid profanity caught everyone by surprise, even himself. Leo and Lily stared at him for a moment, and then all three burst out laughing.

As they walked back to the hotel, it was decided that they would live in Warren's house, that Lily would keep her loft down the street to work out of, and they'd see about building a spare room for Leo.

Grampa's Done?

THE CHILDREN WERE all glad that the story had worked out so well. That the Crystal made it to the Wheel, that Warren and Lily had fallen in love. Francie especially was pleased to learn that, when they returned to Crust, they and Leo would all live together.

"So it all worked out, right, Grampa?" Joe asked. "They all lived happily ever after, right?"

"Happily ever after?" Grampa said, seeming more irritable than usual. "Nonsense! Who lives happily ever after? Happily ever after only happens if you stop telling the story in the right place!" He had a sour look on his face as he began to rub his chest. "*Everything* exists in a circle! Everything! Hib nobb del noid! How many times have I told you? Happy, unhappy, life, death—it's all next to each other, all in the same place. All on a circle!"

Francie looked up at him. "You've never told us that."

"Well, I told someone. But you should know it!"

"So what happened?" Henry asked, again becoming irritated with his grandfather. "They saved everyone on Earth, and then they came back to San Francisco, right?"

"Not exactly... but... let's just say that's it. 'Cause I don't think I got the time... to tell ya the rest..." He grimaced sharply. "Ach, I feel pain. This is it... the end... kaput. No doctors... don't need no doctors. Good-bye, you kids. Henry?" he said to Joe. "Take care of... your brother and sister."

"I'm Joe," Joe said.

"Ach, always with the argument." He winced and added, "Good." The children exchanged a look, each not knowing if they were more concerned about their grandfather's dying, or about not hearing the end of the story. Henry, in particular, was concerned because he'd looked ahead at Warren's notebook and saw the sequence of events. But it was not clear at all what happened when the humans returned to the Crust.

And there was no mention of Leo's return.

"Ach, this is it!" Grampa leaned back on the pillow, his face in anguish. "I'm done." He winced again, but then, instead of dying, he suddenly released a horrific storm of flatulence that shook even the mahogany posts at the corners of the bed. After a moment, his face relaxed and he looked comfortable again. "Nah..." he said, "was just gas."

The children, having grown accustomed to keeping a distance at such times, patiently got up and crossed the room to wait until they knew it was again safe to return. When they did, Grampa leaned back and told them the rest of the story...

...as unhappy as it was.

A Problem at the Wheel

THE NEXT MORNING, Lily woke early and decided to walk to the small coffee shop on the corner.

She enjoyed the early morning Source on her face as she ambled down the sidewalk and ducked beneath a street lamp. The fresh scent of spearmint from the chewing gum flowers that lined the uneven squares of the walkway filled the air. She had seen much since their adventure began and she knew, when she returned home, that it would engender a great many ideas for new sculptures and paintings. She would no doubt always remember Nuldoid—but she knew, as well, it was time to leave.

Stubbux Coffee did a brisk business. Baristas behind the counter picked fresh coffee froote from a variety of coffee trees at the side of the shop, and then squeezed out piping hot coffee into paper or white porcelain cups. There was warm apricot muffin froote and slices of brownie froote that had to be heated up, since they could not be picked fresh, like the coffee. A rich aroma permeated the place, as one Nuldoid after the next stepped up to the counter to argue with a barista over a complicated litany of coffee particulars. Cacophonous music rattled out of the speaker system inside, so Lily chose, after she got her coffee and muffin froote, to sit outside, where she could watch the comings and goings of Nuldoids, and not have to listen to the music.

She moved aside an abandoned copy of *Noidsweek* and sat at a small table, when she heard the squeaking wheels of shopping carts. On the other side of the street, she saw Orskin and Fiske pushing their carts toward the hotel.

It turned out they were on their way to say good-bye to her and Warren. That they were still even in the city was a bit of a surprise, but they had stayed longer than expected trying to talk some sense into Mishkin Hobble.

"Ever since dat misty froote..." Orskin said, and shook his head.

"Ach," Fiske added. "Dat drobbs horkel doesn't does nothin' but sits 'round in dat park. Gots dat big idiot grin onna face."

Both Nuldoids grew quiet for a moment. Clearly they were heartbroken over the virtual loss of their friend. But ever since he inhaled the froote in the bottom of his cart, he had changed. And they had given up hope that it was a temporary affliction, since he was still so content, happy even. He was no longer the Mishkin Hobble they knew or cared to be with.

This good-bye business was all rather awkward for the Harvesters. They knew they would probably not see Lily or Warren again, once the humans returned to the Crust. The concept was difficult for them to grasp—Nuldoids were not accustomed to saying *permanent* good-byes to anyone. So, when Lily knelt down to kiss them, Orskin welled up and could only offer a weak criticism of the way she wore her hair. She smiled and thanked him for the slight, as Fiske stepped over and took her hand, then lifted off of the ground until heesh could kiss her on the cheek.

But just as the two Harvesters pushed their shopping carts back onto the road and headed toward the hotel to say good-bye to Warren, they were stopped by a another slow, ominous moan that rose up from somewhere beneath them. It was like the earlier sounds, like the plaintive groan of a dying elephant.

And then it faded away.

In the next moment, the Horn of the Great Wheel blasted out from the cathedral and rattled through the streets of Nuldoid.

Back at the hotel, Warren was jolted out of bed by the noise. He threw on his clothes and ducked down to exit his room, where he saw that Leo had done the same, as had a number of other hotel guests.

Something had gone wrong at the Wheel.

A Good Idea and Some Bad Luck

WARREN AND LEO found Lily and the Harvesters midway between Stubbux and the hotel. From there, the five of them made their way over to the Park of the Wheel, where they learned that Ed and the engineers were already in the cathedral trying to figure out what to do.

A Sloidelobb named Milt had replaced Gordon in the elevator. Milt was huge, leaving only a small amount of room for the humans to squeeze in. "Is big troubles inna grindy thing," he informed them on the way down.

"Do they know what it is?" Warren asked.

"Nah to dat. Ed's near 'bout to bust a gurd."

When they entered the cathedral, they saw the Emperor near the Holey Cylinder, surrounded by several animated engineers, his hand on his head, his eyes steeped with concern as he studied the blueprint laid out in front of him.

Lily and Warren moved past a number of concerned Nuldoids, closer to the altar, where one engineer after the next was explaining the problem to Ed, and pointing to a particular spot on the blueprint. Ed tugged at his ear and shook his head as though he had been presented with a question there was no answer to.

A small fracture had developed in one of the lower-level pinion wheels, due to the added stress when the machinery had slowed. If nothing was done about it, the wheel would surely crack, split apart and the broken pieces might very well destroy the entire 3rd Level. In that case, the machinery would have to be shut down until the appropriate repairs were made.

So, it seemed the only reasonable alternative was to stop the machine right away—get a welder down to Level 3 and into the 12th Sector to fuse the crack in the pinion wheel before it got any worse. That, anyway, was the opinion of the engineers.

As Ed stepped away from them to mull things over, Lily and Warren exchanged looks, and Leo moved up to look at the blueprints himself. The Emperor rubbed his nearly bald head, and looked up at the great Wheel, deep in thought. Warren approached him cautiously and leaned down to speak quietly. "Ed, listen, I don't mean to interfere, but, if, say, you *stop* the machinery, you *stop* the Wheel, right?"

"Huh? Sure yeah," Ed said, hardly paying attention to him.

Warren moved closer. "Okay, but that means the earth... uh, Hoidenall, will stop too? Right?"

"Sure yeah. Is a big fat pain inna cobbs for alla everybodies. Alla noids, alla toids! Dat Source up der, middle a downtown, it doesn't gonna go up an' down for a time. Stays stuck." He shook his head. "All we clocks is gotta be fixed."

"But, Ed..." Lily said, stepping up now beside Warren, "if you stop the rotation... If you stop the earth suddenly, the oceans will keep moving. Right?"

Ed looked sheepishly at Warren and Lily and shrugged. "S'pose, yuh. But doesn't we got no choice."

It was the worst scenario Warren or Lily could imagine. Cities, forests, deserts, all would be swept over by a rolling mountain of water. It would mean millions, no, billions of deaths.

"But you can't do that," Warren said. "You have to—"

"Ed, there's another way!" It was Leo. They turned and saw the boy standing behind them. He moved beside one of the engineers and knelt in front of the blueprints as Lily, Warren and Ed joined him. "Now just hear me out," he said. "The cracked pinion wheel is three levels down in the 12th Sector..." He pointed to it. "It's in a cluster of wheels here, held in place by stabilizing bars across here, here and here," he said, pointing to each. "So... if we loosen the bracket here... the one that holds the stabilizer here, okay... and then we apply pressure here, like with a crowbar or something, we can disengage the cluster, while everything else coasts. Sorta like the transmission in a car..." Then he thought to add, "...the transmission in a car on the *Crust*. Anyway, if we get a welder up in here, see, while the cluster's disengaged, stabilize the pinion wheel and fuse the crack, then we can re-engage the whole thing. See? An' the big Wheel never has to stop."

Ed rubbed his chin and thought about it for a moment. Then, finally he shook his head. "Eh, it doesn't gonna works."

Warren looked at him. "What? Why not?"

Ed shrugged. "We doesn't has no crows-bar."

Warren was apoplectic. "It doesn't have to be a crowbar, Ed! It could be anything!"

"Ach," said one of the engineers, "is right, dat toid. Needs we just somethin' for dat leverage!"

"Nah to dat," piped in still another engineer. "Even as we gets leverage, we doesn't has torque! Needs yas dat torque!"

"Torque? Torque?" Ed said, trying to stay in the discussion. "Torque is what?"

"Ya stays outta this, ya rod-nim!" another of the engineers snipped to Ed.

"Ach, yas all got rotted brains," the other engineer barked. "We has toids for torque. Toids is plenty nuf strong for torque."

"Sure yeah, dat toids is got strong for torque," said an engineer named Hewitt. "But is a toid can get inna Twelf Sector? An', hoooey, is big trouble getting' outta dat. Toid'll be lucky for spit as ta not gettin' hisself squished dead."

As the engineers argued and hammered out the practical application of Leo's idea, Warren could see that the boy was getting ready to go into the machinery himself. But Warren knew that he couldn't let him do it. It was too dangerous for an eleven-year-old boy. He'd have to go in himself.

"It's a brilliant idea, Leo," he said, trying to soften the blow. "It's the only hope we have. I'm really proud of you."

"Right. So we'll need a steel bar, something, to give me leverage."

"But I can't let you do this."

"What? Nah to that," Leo said defiantly. "I'm doin' it! It was my idea! I know what to do!"

Warren shook his head. "I can't let you. It's too dangerous." He saw the disappointment in Leo's face, but persisted. "Between the two of us, I have to be the one to take this chance."

The boy thought about it. "Nah, I'm doin' it."

"No, you're not!"

"Yes, I am."

"No, you're not."

"Yes, I am."

"No."

"Yes."

"No!"

"Yes!"

"Leo!" Warren yelled, fully exasperated. He stopped to regain his composure. Then, figuring he might appeal to the boy's ego, he said, "Look, if this works, your idea, you'll have done something really important. You'll have saved a lot of lives. And I think you should be around for that. You should see that. You should get the credit."

Leo hadn't considered that, and had no answer.

Satisfied he had, more or less, put the matter to rest, Warren touched the boy's shoulder and moved off with some other Nuldoids to look for a steel bar that could be used for leverage.

Leo shoved his hands in his pockets. So that was that. Lily moved to him and rubbed his shoulder sympathetically, as Kyle wandered over to join them. "Big toid is goin' inna hole, eh?" Kyle asked, nodding to where Warren had disappeared.

"Yes," Lily said, and furrowed her brow at Kyle to say that he should be quiet.

Leo sighed and then felt the ancient coin in his pocket. Wait a minute, he thought, he had a lucky coin. It had kept him alive in the doidell void. He took it out and looked at it, flipped it in the air and then held it up for Lily. "You see this? It's a lucky coin. I'm goin' in the machinery!

"Leo, you can't."

"No, don't you get it? If I have this, I'll make it out alive! Warren won't. I will. Because of this!"

"Is right dat," Kyle offered. "Is froma Droiden Frobble Dynasty, der," he said, nodding to Leo's coin. "Is an Uky coin. Kid doesn't gonna has nuthin' but good."

She turned back to Leo and studied the coin. Was he right? Would he be protected by this coin? If Warren went, would he not return? It was in that moment, that she realized she was in love with Warren. It would be terrible to lose him. And, she thought, if Leo could do this and return safely...

But he was only eleven.

The two thoughts tore at her.

Their attention was drawn then to a welder named Daphne who stepped over to tell Ed that workers down in the machinery had found a piece of metal large enough to use for leverage. It was in the 11th Sector of Level 4, so it was relatively close to the problem area. She said some engineers were moving it now, and that she and the welding team were ready to go. All they needed was a human to enter the machinery and get into place.

Leo turned back to Lily and looked her squarely in the eyes. "I'm doing this, Lily. I have to."

She hesitated, wanting to say no, knowing that she should say no. But she could not bring herself to do it. Leo watched her a moment, then shoved the coin into his pocket and turned to the Nuldoids. "Let's go."

The little welder nodded and padded off to the staircase at the side of the altar with Leo close behind. As they descended, the boy saw that the stairs spiraled down a few hundred feet beneath the floor of the cathedral to Level 3, continuing on from there to Levels 4 and 5. All of it was built for small creatures, of course, not for a gangly young human like himself. So, he was forced to stay hunched over as he made his way behind the welder and engineers, barely squeezing through a number of narrow openings in the process.

() () ()

Back on the floor of the cathedral, where many more Nuldoids had gathered, Kyle found himself standing beside Orskin and Fiske. He had not meant to stand anywhere near them—since most regular Nuldoids were quite uncomfortable around Harvesters—but he hadn't noticed Orskin, who had bent down to adjust a back wheel on his cart.

The Harvester stood and recognized Kyle. "Carl der, is it?"

"Ah! Kyle," Kyle said, surprised at his proximity, trying to affect casual. "Sure yup, is Kyle we is! Kyle Glukk. Kyle Glukk is we." Orskin and Fiske looked at him. They did not particularly like interacting with regular Nuldoids whose strange and uncomfortable behavior annoyed them. Kyle shifted awkwardly under their gaze, and then, for want of anything better to say, said, "Yup, sure hopes we dat kid der comes out good an' not dead."

"Uh-huh," both Orskin and Fiske said together.

"Sure yeah," continued Kyle, blabbering now, "is lucky dat kid has 'im dat coin. Is finded he inna Cavern a Warped Time. Is an Uky coin der."

Fiske had been about to push hish cart elsewhere, but Kyle's reference to the coin drew hish attention. "Is an Uky coin, says ya? How is ya knowin' dis?"

"Ach, is Droiden Frobble Dynasty. Sure as spit. Says 'uky' onna backside."

"An' yas founded dis coin inna Warped Time says yas?" Orskin asked, having become himself interested. The Harvesters had spent a great deal of time in the Region of Neither Norr, so they knew quite a bit about the Droiden Frobble Dynasty. Subjects of the dynasty, at one time, crisscrossed Neither Norr in great numbers, often stopping or congregating in certain areas.

308

One of those areas was the Caverns of Warped Time, where they could spend weeks or months and then return a few minutes later. (This was long before their descendents, the Nuldoids, developed the Roundabout system, so, naturally, the Droiden Frobbles feared death. It was this fear then that led many of them to spend large chunks of time in the caverns, so as to stretch out their lives—unlike the Nuldoids, who realized it was pointless to prolong any particular life.)

"Yup," said Kyle. "Dat kid finds dat Uky coin, an' smack offa bag, he has hisself good luck! Was causa dat we got us outta dat doidell void." Then, remembering Morton. "Well, *almost* alla wees."

The two Harvesters exchanged a look, and Kyle caught it.

"Huh what?"

"Droiden Frobble coins is fulla luck, sure yeah," said Fiske. "But is halfa time good, halfa time bad. Is three sides to dat coin."

"Nah to dat," Kyle sneered. "Is founded side right up. Fulla good luck, an' not kaplooey."

It hardly seemed like a fair argument to either of the Harvesters, because they had seen many Droiden Frobble coins and were nearly experts on them. So they simply looked at the Nuldoid and shook their heads. And though Kyle continued to argue, a sinking feeling in his liver told him the boy was due some very bad luck.

() () ()

When Leo and the others reached Level 3, they stepped out of the staircase onto a steel catwalk that ran out into and amongst the machinery. The boy could see that ladders descended from the catwalk to the various sectors. He followed one of the other engineers out along the tiny walkway, beneath and through the massive complex of whirling machinery, surrounded by a dizzying array of huge interlocking cog and pinion wheels, where flywheels spun overhead and below, many of them millimeters from his head. Near the ladder at the 12th Sector, they were met by another engineer, who said he'd just finished loosening the bolts around two of the support beams near the cluster of wheels.

Daphne, the welder, double-checked her lighter and torch, hooked her helmet to the clip on her belt and slid the water pouch into her overalls. The welder's assistant loosened the hose from the oxygen cylinder and pulled out enough of it to reach the site.

When Leo looked down the ladder to the 12th Sector, he saw that the opening amidst the machinery was narrow. He took his shirt off so that it would not get caught on anything, and then greased his arms with oil.

() () ()

After his argument with the Harvesters fizzled out, Kyle felt terrible. He knew they were right, that Leo was destined for bad luck.

He had to find Lily.

The cathedral was getting crowded with Nuldoids now who had come to argue about the problem and Leo's proposed solution. Most were content to simply squabble, but a few fistfights were breaking out here and there. A significant number of creatures, as well, had preemptively worked themselves into a fierce and indignant anger—anticipating that Leo's plan wouldn't work and that they would *still* have to readjust all of their clocks.

When Kyle found Lily at the side of the cathedral, he grabbed her pant leg and tugged. "Hey, big lady!" She looked down, and he grinned apologetically. "Is a piddle a information should be knowed by yas."

Lily was aghast when he told her that he was mistaken about the coin's luck, that Leo was in grave danger. Actually she was more than aghast. She was terrified. She had to find Warren, though he had not yet returned from his now pointless excursion to retrieve a steel bar. She had to tell him that they must stop the boy, that they must force him to return to safety and, yes, that Warren would have to do this dangerous task himself.

() () ()

When the little welder was set, Daphne nodded to Leo, and he descended the ladder. As he climbed down through the machinery, many of the flywheels were so close that they rolled against his pants and the skin of his back. They were mostly rolling downward, though, in the direction he was moving, which made the going easier. But he could see that it was going to be very difficult to return back up the ladder.

() () ()

Lily tried pleading with Emperor Ed to send someone down into the machinery to bring Leo back. She explained that Warren was older, that he should be the one to do this. Her argument, though, that the boy's death would be tragic, seemed only to confuse Ed and the other Nuldoids. To their mind, there was no point in stopping Leo, since he seemed perfectly capable of exerting the necessary "torque." And, if, in the process, the boy was killed, well, *it was only death.*

() () ()

311

At the bottom of the ladder, Leo made his way along the steel girder of the 12th Sector within the massive grinding machinery, then out to the cluster of wheels where the cracked pinion was still rolling precariously. Two dwarfy Nuldoids were already there, holding the steel bar from Level 4 between them. They carefully handed it to Leo, and crawled out.

() () ()

Lily was about to enter the staircase herself, when she saw Warren emerge at the other end of the altar. He and several Nuldoids had found a steel bar on the other side of the Wheel, down in the 2nd Level.

() () ()

The boy slowly, cautiously, lowered himself onto the girders that supported the cluster of wheels, and then waited for Daphne to catch up. When she did, he braced his back against a vertical beam, wedged his foot beneath the bracket next to the steel girder that he was balancing on, and jammed the steel bar into position over a support beam and under a steel truss.

() () ()

Warren looked at Lily as if she had betrayed him. "You told him he could do this?" he said, when he learned that Leo had left to take on this dangerous task.

Lily felt terrible and explained that she hadn't told him he *could* do it—but she hadn't told him he *couldn't* either, which, in both of their minds, was about the same thing as saying he *could*. The point being this: She hadn't stopped him. And, now, with the news that the coin in his pocket would probably bring him bad luck, Warren was beside himself. He was angry with Lily, but he didn't say so. He only turned and hurried to the staircase, hoping to reach the boy in time.

() () ()

Warren didn't know it, of course, but he was much too late for anything.

Leo was in place and ready to start lifting the machinery. He nodded to Daphne, and she dropped the helmet over her face, lit the blowpipe of the torch, and signaled that she too was ready. As Leo gripped the steel bar and pushed on it, the Nuldoid moved closer to the cluster of wheels. When it did not lift, Leo took a deep breath and heaved again, this time, with everything he had.

Slowly, the wheels began to rise, and the welder wedged herself in a little closer. But still the cracked pinion wheel was not disengaging from the one above it. "Yas go more! More!" the welder yelled to him over the churning of the machinery. "More!"

Leo could feel the veins in his neck and head bulging, the blood pumping against his skin, his arms straining. Beads of sweat were popping up along his slick shoulders. The wheel's cogs, he could see, were still in sync with the adjoining cogwheel. Its teeth, though barely touching, continued to roll with the rest of the machinery. He breathed in, closed his eyes, gritted his teeth and envisioned strength firing into his arms like the cavalry arriving. He heaved again. And finally the cogs parted.

Instantly there was a flurry of movement as the little welder scooted in and stopped the cracked wheel from spinning, found the wound, and began welding. Leo forced his mind to lock his muscles, to hold the weight. To stay steady. And, as sparks bounced out and fell away from the pinion wheel, he closed his eyes and absorbed the pain coursing through his arms, his back, his legs. The weight of the cluster felt like it was compounding, and the burdened steel bar started to wobble under the pressure. He knew, though, if his arms gave out, the cluster would drop, the welder would be crushed, and the cracked pinion wheel would break apart, its pieces falling into, and mangling, the machinery. The system would have to be shut down. All would be lost.

And as the pain grew worse, as the steel bar wobbled even more and the wheels above the welder edged down slowly, he prayed to endure.

He prayed for help.

() () ()

If the staircase had been a tight squeeze for Leo, for Warren it was practically a straightjacket. Several times, his body was so snugly wedged between the stairs he was on and the bottom of the stairs over him, that he considered crawling through the railing and climbing down the outside of the staircase. But he soon found, when he was wedged tightly, if he took a moment, relaxed the muscles of his chest and breathed, he could push past.

() () ()

Leo, in his mind, was resigning himself to the calamity that would follow if he could not continue to hold the cluster of wheels up. The breaking machinery, he began to realize, could very well start a massive chain reaction that would, most likely, swallow him as well.

Then something happened.

Something welled from within him. He didn't know what it was, or where it came from—his soul maybe—but he heard words being repeated in his head. Four words that quietly spilled out from his mouth. "Hib nobb del noid." And though it was he who said the words, he didn't feel like he'd been the one saying them.

Suddenly, his body surged with strength. And, as if he was only a spectator, he saw the wheels of the cluster lift again.

() () ()

When Warren finally reached the opening to the catwalk of Level 3, he squeezed out of the staircase and crawled along the walkway toward the 12th Sector, where he could see in the distance, between the massive pieces of machinery, two dwarfy Nuldoids, an engineer and the welder's assistant. They were leaning over the catwalk's railing, watching Leo and the welder at work.

() () ()

Finally, the sparks stopped flying as the welder lifted the torch. She double-checked her work, the metal of the repaired pinion wheel now glowing red. She tightened the gas control on the welding torch and killed the flame, took the pouch from her coveralls and squeezed out a stream of water over the glowing wheel, where a burst of steam billowed up into the machinery above and vanished.

She nodded then to Leo to say he could lower the cluster.

His arms shaking, but careful not to let it move too fast, he eased the tension on the steel bar.

In the next instant, the cogs of the repaired wheel were caught by the wheel in the cluster above it, and all of the wheels began again to turn in unison.

Leo and the welder waited. Watching.

Finally, they saw, it had worked.

The machinery was engaged. The giant Wheel was rolling as usual. The little pinion wheel was repaired and pulling its weight.

() () ()

Engineers in the meter room at the side of the altar reported to the crowd of Nuldoids that all systems appeared to be engaged and running normally. A Nuldoid cheer rose from the floor of the cathedral along with a number of whoops and hollers.

() () ()

Leo wiped the sweat from his brow and smiled at Daphne, who flipped up the welding helmet and gave a cheerful thumbs down. "Is yas hoo-ah on dat one!" she said. "Good luck, yas, gettin' outta here." And as she scuttled away on the steel girder and up the ladder to the catwalk, Leo looked around himself and knew that it would not be easy to return. Indeed, trying to go back the way he'd come might be impossible, since he would have to climb through small areas where the wheels were spinning in the opposite direction.

() () ()

When the two dwarfy Nuldoids and the welder's assistant had helped Daphne up onto the catwalk from the ladder, they turned and saw Warren, at times crawling on all fours, making his way toward them. They assumed that he was just impatient and couldn't wait to find out if the plan had been successful.

"Ach, is alla kaput," Daphne said with a glint in her eye, as Warren approached. "Gotta wheel's all busted flat!"

"What?"

The little Nuldoid tried to keep a straight face, but couldn't, and burst out laughing. "Ach, is just pullin' yas hooey. All is kay-oh-ay. Dat kid does a pretty good plan."

While Warren was relieved to hear it, he pushed past them to the ladder at the 12th Sector. Cautiously, he leaned out to look down the narrow throat of the ladder's passageway and saw that it was even narrower than the staircase.

The engineer, who had earlier loosened the bolts to the support beam, stepped up beside Warren. "Hey, toid! Is inna way!"

Warren turned to him.

"Needa gets yas ta movin'! Gotta tighten dem bolts!" the little engineer said, waving a large box wrench in Warren's face.

"Sorry," Warren said, as he moved aside, and the Nuldoid moved past him to climb down the ladder.

When Warren moved farther down the catwalk he was finally able to see Leo, who was standing below on the girder of Sector 12.

"Hey, Warren," the boy yelled up when he saw his teacher. "It worked! I did it!"

"I know! "Warren hollered back. "I'm proud of you! Now get back up here!"

"I don't think I can use the ladder! The wheels are turning the wrong way!" he called out.

"Try!" Warren shouted.

Leo shook his head. "Too tight!"

"No! Not if you go slowly!"

"Nah. I'm gonna jump for that crossbeam up there," he said, pointing to a thick beam that ran overhead between the 12th and 13th Sectors, "an' swing over there. The opening 'round that ladder's bigger."

"No! Don't! You have to come this way!"

"I can do it!" he yelled back.

Warren could see the boy wasn't going to change his mind. He figured then, he had to, at least, tell him about the coin. "Leo!" he shouted, his voice sounding desperate. "Listen to me! You have to throw the coin away!"

The words made little sense to Leo. "What?"

"The coin! Throw it away!"

The boy screwed up his face, wondering why in the world Warren would say such a thing. He reached into his pocket, and pulled it out to look at. "Why?"

"Because it's not good luck! It's bad luck!"

Leo already knew that the coin was good luck. It was very good luck. "No it's not!" he shouted.

"Yes, it is!"

"No, it's not!"

"Yes!"

"No!"

Warren could not hope to win this argument. There were too many things working against him. The first and most obvious being that Leo thought Warren was dead wrong. Another was Leo's age. At eleven, he was not quite a teenager, but he was certainly thinking like one, a human one, that is. And teenagers, human ones, are notorious for believing their knowledge of everything is superior to just about anyone's.

Another thing working against Warren was that human teenagers pretty much consider themselves indestructible. And

Leo was clearly thinking that too. In fact, after all of the dangerous things he'd already been through, he was feeling downright invincible. It's peculiar, this invincibility thing in human youngsters. Nuldoids have a difficult time comprehending it, since young Nuldoids are extremely cautious—they know they have the bulk of their current lives ahead of them. Conversely, older Nuldoids are inclined to take chances, to live a little, to leap into the unknown, since they have already lived the bulk of their present lives.

Another factor was that Leo had just finished doing something pretty brilliant and significant—if you consider saving most of humanity brilliant and significant, and why wouldn't you?—so he was feeling quite proud of himself. And this pride— along with the coin in his pocket—filled him with a great deal of confidence. But here's the thing about confidence:

Sometimes it assures success.

Sometimes it assures failure.

Much the way an Uky coin brings good luck *and* bad.

Well, it was all of these unfortunate components that played into the circumstances of the next few moments. The strongest of them being the *bad* luck that was coming due from the Droiden Frobble coin.

Anyway, Leo wasn't about to throw the coin away. And he was determined to jump for the crossbeam between the two sectors, to swing onto the girder of the 13th.

And there was nothing Warren could do about any of it.

All he could do was watch.

And hope.

But, just as Leo bent his knees to make the leap, Warren saw something that the boy did not—an untied sneaker. More specifically, he saw the frayed shoelace that gently dropped down from the top of the boy's shoe into the meshing cogs of two small wheels just beneath his feet.

"Don't jump!" is what Warren shouted. But his shouting, like the steel bar he found earlier, was pointless. Leo was already leaping into the air, flying toward the support beam that he would never reach.

Naturally, when the shoelace became taut, it stopped the boy in midair, jolting his left leg. And there he hung for a fraction of a second, wondering what in the world was going on. Then he swung back the other direction, beneath the girder he'd been standing on, and back up again into the air, where he hung yet another fraction of a second. That's when the two cogwheels that had gripped his shoelace released him, set him free, and allowed him to freefall.

And fall he did.

Down, down, down.

Into the large wheels of the machinery far below.

There are two ways to describe what became of Leo Fickett that day. One is that he became a "part of the great Wheel," much like, it is said, Lloyd did at the end of his thirteenth life. That's the nice way of saying it. The other is that he was squished like a bug in the machine's grinding wheels.

Whichever way you say it, Leo Fickett was gone.

() () ()

Several of the Nuldoids, including Daphne the welder, had witnessed all of this from the catwalk, along with Warren. The little welder just shook her head. "Ach, is a skull-num move 'at one der, eh!"

Her assistant, though, was concerned and tugged at her sleeve. He nodded at Warren, who had simply sat down on the catwalk and was crying. The Nuldoids exchanged confused looks. It was, after all, odd behavior. Why was he so upset? It was understandable to be disappointed when a loved one died, but this was extreme. Finally, the little welder stepped over to him. "Why is yas all hooky, eh? Dat kid's only dead."

Warren shook his head. Leo wasn't just dead, he was gone—forever. But Warren didn't have it in him to explain. He only wiped his eyes and put his head down. The Nuldoids weren't sure what was going on, but felt it was better to move off, to leave the Crustoid alone.

The engineer, the dwarfy Nuldoids, the welder and her assistant returned to the Cathedral of the Wheel to join in the celebration.

Lily approached them to ask where Warren and Leo were. If they were on their way up. The Nuldoids were hesitant to tell her about the boy, after they'd seen the other human react so peculiarly. They stood a moment, looking up at her. Finally, the welder's assistant shifted awkwardly. "Dat kid," he said, trying to be as delicate as possible, "got hisself squished dead."

The Nuldoids all took a step back, afraid of what the human might do. For all they knew, humans might explode like Sloidelobbs. At first, Lily just looked confused, but soon tears welled from her eyes and rolled down her cheeks as she shook her head—she was devastated. The little creatures stood awkwardly another moment until, finally, the welder, hoping to lighten the situation, offered, "Dat big toid, though, isn't got hisself squished at all."

It didn't seem to do much good. The human was still a mess. A few more Nuldoids joined them to look at her, curious about the human's strange behavior. One leaned toward the welder's assistant and quietly asked, "Why all dat hooky tears der, eh?"

The assistant whispered back, "Dat kid is squished dead."

"Ach, sure," said the other Nuldoid. "But why is all dat works-water?"

The dwarfy, standing nearby, shrugged. "We doesn't know. *Botha* dem toids is all hooky."

"Hmm," said another, with an incredulous look. "Just a'cause dat kid goes kaplooey?"

When Warren returned to the floor of the cathedral, Lily went to him, her eyes crimson beneath a stream of tears. She fell into his arms and hugged him.

He hugged her back, but not tightly. He did not, in that moment, feel like hugging her. Earlier he'd been angry with her for not stopping the boy.

Now all of his feelings were awash in the sorrow that was flooding him.

Two Broken Hearts

ED SIDLED UP to Lily and Warren as they made their way through the crowd to the cathedral's elevator. He was elated that the boy's plan had worked out, and said he always figured it would. Then he remembered to mention that it was too bad the boy got squished, adding, though, that the funeral was gonna be a "polla-lugooza."

Warren and Lily were not in the mood to talk. They wanted only to leave, to go back to the hotel. At the elevator, Orskin, Fiske and Kyle caught up with them. When they saw how upset the humans were, Orskin asked why.

Warren finally told them that humans had no such thing as Roundabout, that Leo was not going to return. Ever. Orskin's jaw fell open. Fiske staggered back to lean against the Wheel Oil stoup beside the elevator doors. Ed too heard it. They were thunderstruck. And Kyle looked liked he'd been slugged in the gut. He, after all, had traveled a great distance with Leo, shared a great many arguments with him. They had become close. And now, for the first time in the little Nuldoid's several lives, he was feeling grief.

As Warren and Lily stepped into the elevator, word of this rippled through the cathedral like fire sweeping over a dry field. The notion that death was the end of life so befuddled the Nuldoids that most were left speechless. (Certainly, Nuldoids did not reincarnate forever, and some, like Lloyd, had not returned, or else stayed hidden, incognito, while others returned with limited Roundabout—that is, a fresh memory. The thought, however, that one would never again see someone they had grown to care about was unfamiliar to most Nuldoids.)

When the elevator's doors closed and, as news of the toids' inefficient system sunk in, the revelry wilted like stick candles on a summer day.

There would be no party to celebrate the machinery's repair.

And a funeral sounded like no fun at all.

Time to Go

WARREN AND LILY returned to the hotel where they sat on the beds together. Lily reached out and took hold of Warren's hand. He tried to offer her solace, to say appropriate things, but he felt empty doing so. And she felt his distance. The truth was, he hurt too much to comfort her.

Lily was starting to feel sick, and excused herself to go into the bathroom. Warren got up and decided to go for a walk. News had spread throughout Nuldoid about the young boy's *permanent* death. Warren was stopped twice by Nuldoids who'd found it hard to believe, one of them commenting that, without Roundabout, humans should stay indoors and seated, not take any chances.

While he walked, his mind kept going back to Lily. He didn't blame her for Leo's death. He knew how headstrong the boy was—he probably wouldn't have listened to her anyway. And

Warren tried not to think the other thought—that she should have *tried* to stop him. And, when he made an effort not to think it, he couldn't help but think it.

All of this left him confused about his feelings for her. And though he didn't know exactly what he *should* feel, he knew he didn't feel the same. Which is not to say he didn't want to. He did. He wanted very much to feel about her the way he had. But when he looked at her, when he thought about her, he was reminded of how much he had grown to care for, maybe even love, the boy.

And that hurt.

Maybe his grief would pass. Maybe he would feel differently later. But what he knew—as he walked the curving streets of Nuldoid and nodded to the little Nuldoidians who'd heard the news and offered, believe it or not, sincere condolences—was that being with her made him feel worse.

The next morning, he told her he was going to return to the Crust and, if she was ready to go, she could travel with him. He owed her that much. But he also asked in such a way as to make it clear that he was going with or without her. Lily forced a smile and quietly thanked him for the offer, but she still did not feel well, and said she would stay in Nuldoid for another day or two, until she felt better. She, too, knew that things were different between them. And, while she yearned to tell him that she loved him, wanted to put her arms around him, she didn't. She knew, could see in his eyes, that it wouldn't feel the same.

He looked at her a moment and then kissed her good-bye, feeling, with that kiss, that he *did* love her, but it was now too painful a love.

() () ()

After he left, Lily wept the rest of that afternoon until she could weep no more, and then, exhausted, fell into a deep sleep. She was awakened a few hours later by a brisk knock on the door.

It was Mishkin Hobble, whose cheeks were glowing green from a Sourceburn, having spent the late morning and afternoon sitting in the park. He'd seen Warren, who was on his way out of Nuldoid with Orskin and Fiske. The Harvester had heard the news about the boy. All of it was very sad, he said, adding that human death "don't make yas basket a sense."

Lily thanked him for his concern, expecting then that the little Nuldoid would be on his way. But he did not leave. He seemed genuinely worried about her. She mentioned that, earlier, she felt sick and had thrown up, but she assured him that all she needed now was some rest before she too left Nuldoid.

Mishkin Hobble, though, was not convinced that rest was all she needed, and told her that she should eat something to help her regain her strength. She thanked him for the suggestion, and promised she would eat later. He took a lunch bag from his grocery cart. "Here ya is," he said, taking a froote from it. "Is ice cream froote. Yoo-hoos ta has some. Makes yas all much gooder."

She was surprised by the Nuldoid's compassion. She had not seen that side of him before. And he certainly didn't seem detached or, as Orskin and Fiske described him, "of dat flakey."

And though she was not really in the mood for ice cream, he'd already peeled part of the skin away, and held the froote up for her to taste. But, as the purple mist entered her nostrils, she realized that it was not ice cream at all. Then she slipped from consciousness.

She fell back onto the beds, where she lie not dead, but not alive.

Mishkin Hobble then held the peculiar froote to his own nose, breathed in the mist and fell back onto the floor beside the beds.

A Little Nap

THE CHILDREN SAT speechless beside Grampa's bed.

Leo had died.

Warren left Nuldoid *without* Lily.

And Mishkin Hobble had tricked Lily into breathing the froote that made him stupid.

"Well, I'm tired," Grampa said. "Gu-night. Let yourselves out."

"No!" all three of them yelled at once.

"Grampa, ya gotta tell us what happened!" Joe said. "You can't go to sleep now!"

"Oh yeah? Watch me." The old man rolled over to face away from them, while the children sat there a moment, annoyed that he would just ignore them like this and go to sleep. Now!

Then Francie's voice broke the silence. "Grampa..." she said calmly, firmly, "if you go to sleep, I'll kick your rotten head in!"

Neither Henry nor Joe had ever heard their little sister utter a threat, and especially one so convincing. And whether she meant what she said or she was just trying to make a point, they weren't altogether sure.

Whichever it was, Grampa was not about to take a chance on the former. So he rolled back over and, with a wary eye to his young granddaughter, resumed the story.

The Return

Part Four

Is circles all
  Dat Roundabout.
With some noids in
  An' some dat's out.
                    The Book of Nuldoid
                    Schisms 2:15

The Council of Elders

AFTER HAVING DELAYED their departure for Neither Norr once already, Orskin and Fiske were now overly ready to leave Nuldoid. And when they offered to escort Warren to the access tunnel near Fresno, he accepted. The trip was without incident. Well, except for a confrontation just outside the Borffs of Confusing Mud, where they came across a group of Oidenoids led by the notorious Worgus Wogg. The Oidenoids were collecting donations for their new ministry—The Ministry of Lloyd's Love. Worgus Wogg had somehow determined from Lloyd's writing in *The Book of Nuldoid* that it was essential for the ministry to build a nuclear arsenal. Unlike other Oidenoids, Worgus Wogg was not the least bit intimidated by the Harvesters, and he was determined that they and Warren not pass.

When, finally, they demanded that Orskin and Fiske "donate" their shopping carts to the ministry, Fiske lost his temper and set one of the Oidenoid's heads on fire. It wasn't fear though that caused Worgus Wogg to release the travelers; it was intolerance. Because Worgus Wogg believed that Lloyd's plan did not include Delnoid Harvesters, he said he was "ooked out," and no longer wanted the travelers in his presence. Which was just fine with the Harvesters and Warren.

When, at last, they arrived at the giant rock—where Warren and Lily had entered a week earlier—Warren thanked the Harvesters and shared a tearful good-bye. Orskin and Fiske became quite emotional when they realized they would probably never see Warren again.

Lily's truck was still parked in the dirt beside the big rock wall where they'd left it. It was covered by a thick layer of dust, as was everything inside the cab, since they'd left the windows open. Surprisingly, it had not been touched by anyone. In fact, the key was still in the ignition. Warren rolled up the windows and put the key under the front seat. From there he walked to the freeway and hitched a ride back to San Francisco.

When he returned home, he saw no sign of Howard, his cat. He sat down on the couch in the living room—the couch where Leo had slept—and ran his hand over its smooth worn leather. He was tired and dirty and depressed and he realized that he no longer felt comfortable in his own house. When he went to work the following day, he learned that he had been replaced by Mr. Richardson, the basketball coach—*until a permanent replacement could be found*. Warren was going to protest, to speak his mind, started to, but realized then that he didn't have much of an excuse for missing work, at least an excuse that anyone would believe. Besides, the truth was, he just didn't feel like fighting it. When he admitted as much to himself, he was surprised by what he felt—relief. And once he realized that he felt relief, he had to admit that he just didn't want the job any longer.

When he returned home again, his phone was ringing. It was an old friend from college who was living in Chicago. The friend just wanted to chat and catch up, since he'd not spoken with Warren in some time. The friend didn't have much to say really. Warren listened, not adding much.

After they hung up, Warren stood to get something to eat, but turned back to the phone and sat down again. He decided—right then—that he'd call a Realtor and sell his house. In that very moment, he decided that he was going to leave San Francisco and make a new start. A new career. A new life. In Chicago. Why not? Chicago sounded like as good a place as any.

It was an altogether impulsive move—one that he might regret—but right then, it felt like the only thing to do. He knew he was not happy about staying in San Francisco. He wasn't happy about a profession he felt he'd failed at. But mostly, he didn't want to stay in a house that reminded him of the boy he failed.

() () ()

And Lily?

After she'd been tricked by Mishkin Hobble into inhaling the vapor from the peculiar froote and had then passed out, she became not alive, but not dead. But, she did not lose consciousness. As a matter of fact, she was more conscious of everything around her than she'd ever been before.

As soon as Mishkin Hobble's body fell onto the floor beside her, she shook her head and sat up. But here's the thing: She did so *without* her body... though she didn't realize it until she stood up. When she looked down at the beds, and saw that her body was still lying there, she knew something peculiar was going on.

A moment later, a blurry image of Mishkin Hobble emerged from his body and stood up as well. He looked up at her and smiled broadly, and though she'd seen him do this out of the corner of her eye, when she looked directly at him, she could see through him, like an apparition, like a bashful hologram. He apologized, cringing a little as he did, for having to trick her. But he said he didn't think she'd go along with him if he hadn't.

"What is it? What is this froote?" she asked, holding her hands up to examine them, only to see them disappear when she looked at them.

Mishkin Hobble shrugged. "Dunno. Musician says ta we is called 'side door froote.' Rare. Illegal, says he."

"Illegal? Why? Is it dangerous?"

"Nah to dat. Is a cut-short."

"Cut-short? A shortcut?" she asked.

He nodded.

"A shortcut to where?"

"Cut-short to every bit. Allswhere." He reached up to take her hand. When he did, she felt it, felt the pressure of his hand, but did not feel skin touching skin. Only energy. He took her outside of the room and led her down the street, and, as they passed the coffee shop, Lily saw that no one noticed them. They had to be careful, Mishkin Hobble explained, that no one walked into them, or drove a car through them, because it hurt like a "yuddle stub"—which was another lesson he said he'd learned the hard way.

When she asked where they were going, he suppressed a grin and said only, "Is gonna see."

They soon passed the Emperor's Palace and entered the Park of the Wheel, where they approached the entrance to the cathedral. There they had to wait a few moments for some Nuldoids to come along and ring the bell to wake Milt, the

Sloidelobb that had replaced Gordon. When the door to the elevator was cranked open, Mishkin Hobble and Lily snuck in beside the Nuldoids and pressed themselves into the corner.

Inside the cathedral, he led her around a group of Nuldoids, shuffling down the nave toward the balustrades. She and Mishkin Hobble stepped onto the altar and up to the Holey Cylinder, where the Crystal had been placed a few days earlier. As they stood in front of it, the little Harvester told Lily to pay close attention, to watch, to listen, because she'd have to do the same. Then he told her to be quiet so that he could concentrate. He closed his eyes tightly and, after a moment, his feet began to rise from the carpet until his eyes were level with the backside of the Crystal. He reached out then and pressed his hands into it and—though Lily had not yet seen either of their "bodies" sift through anything, certainly not through anything solid—his hands sunk into the Crystal like it was butter.

With his hands submersed, the little Nuldoid took a deep breath and whispered, "Hib nobb del noid." In the next instant, his arms slid farther into the Crystal as the features of his body began to fade from view and shimmer like a glimmering dust. This "dust" then was suddenly, and somewhat startlingly, sucked into the Crystal like smoke into a powerful vacuum cleaner… *pffft!*

And he was gone.

Lily bent down and looked into the Crystal, but saw no sign of Mishkin Hobble. No remnant. She walked around the Holey Cylinder and saw only a small lump of green light that shot along the red laser beam from the Crystal into the dark hole at the center of the huge lug nut behind it.

She moved back to the front of the Holey Cylinder, took a deep breath and put her hands into the backside of the Crystal, as she'd seen Mishkin Hobble do, and they too sunk easily into it.

She felt warmth in her fingertips. She whispered slowly, "Hib nobb... del noid," and... nothing. At first. Then a tingling sensation that washed over her like a wave of warm syrup. She felt a little light-headed, a little dizzy. Then... a slight tug on her arms as the vapor of her body's image was suddenly and vigorously sucked into the Crystal... *pffft!*

And as her "vapor" sped into the Crystal, she was still conscious. She knew that she had nothing now even similar to a body, that she was no more than energy bouncing at light speed from one side of the Crystal's labyrinthine prism to the other, to the other, to the other, perhaps a million times in that fraction of a second. And, when she was finally shot like a bullet down the beam of red light—though her clump of light remained red—into the void of the lug nut at the center of the Wheel, she felt something close to exhilaration.

She was *only* light now, blasting into a whirling vortex of energy, where she sensed that she was falling end-over-end, and then blasting in all directions and scattering like a thousand fireflies shot out the barrel of a shotgun. And again there was the tingle of energy that burst through her core, as the electrical particles that made up her soul collided into each other and came back together again in mutual and familiar attraction like stars falling into a black hole. Quickly, the charged image of her being began to reassemble.

After another brief feeling of vertigo, she realized that she had come back together, that her body, or the image of her body, had regrouped. She looked down and saw that Mishkin Hobble was standing beside her—that is, until she looked directly at him and he faded from her view.

But they were not in a place that she was familiar with.

They were standing inside of a huge ball that looked something like an enormous soap bubble. And there with them, inside the soap bubble, were perhaps fifteen or twenty creatures, Nuldoids, just sitting around, each as translucent as she and Mishkin Hobble. Most of them were reading magazines or newspapers as though waiting in a doctor's lobby, none of them paying any particular attention to her or Mishkin Hobble's arrival. And though they were inside of a large bubble, because gravity seemed to pull outward in all directions—the way it did in Downtown Nuldoid—the other creatures sat at a number of places on the wall of the sphere, some of them to the side and some upside down (relative to where she was).

She looked at the bubble's skin beside her feet as it stretched and swirled slowly in a kaleidoscope of abalone shell colors. She was able to faintly make out that there were objects *outside* of the bubble, but they were far away and hard to define. "Where are we?" she whispered to Mishkin Hobble.

"Is dat Source," he said, stepping over to a red dispenser beneath a sign that said, "YA TAKES ONE." He tore off a protruding piece of paper with a number printed on it.

"The Source?" Lily was incredulous. "That thing in the sky, in the middle of Nuldoid? Up in the air? We're inside of that? No way!" She looked again at the sphere's elastic wall and squinted to see through it. The objects outside, she realized, were the distant streets and buildings of Downtown Nuldoid, all of them now far, far beneath them. And when she looked above and to the sides, past the waiting Nuldoids, she saw the other parts of the city. And to the left side, she saw the cogs of the giant Wheel churning away down in the park. "Oh, my," she said at last, "we *are* inside the Source."

"Hey!" said a small voice beside them. "You is a toid, eh?" Lily and Mishkin Hobble turned and saw an older Nuldoid standing nearby, a newspaper folded and tucked under his arm. "Does yoo-hoos know of a toid is goes by Leo Fickett?"

Suddenly Lily realized who this was. "Morton?"

The little creature squinted at Lily and Mishkin Hobble suspiciously. "Who is ya dat's wantin' ta know?"

"I'm a friend of Leo's! We tried to rescue you!"

"Ach!" he said with a sarcastic sneer. "Tootin' rootin' job yas did, too, eh? Gots we squished like smashed potato froote."

"Wait a minute. You're dead?" she asked.

The little Nuldoid nodded. "Yeah sure ta dat."

Mishkin Hobble stepped over to Lily and indicated to the other creatures waiting. "Is all dey dead. 'Cept for we. Is why dat froote we takes is flookey."

"So..." her mind was reeling, "Leo is *here*?" She looked at Morton.

Morton shook his head. "Hasn't seen 'im. But is *never* no toid inna here." He turned to Mishkin Hobble. "'Cept fer she der, dat big lady der," he said nodding toward Lily. "Didn't thinks no toid is could be inna here. Thought is can only be noids." He shrugged and chuckled slightly. "Eh, die an' learn, huh?"

When Morton went back to his newspaper, Lily turned to Mishkin Hobble. She realized that he'd taken her there, hoping to find Leo. She smiled... but it was a sad smile. "This was very sweet of you."

Mishkin Hobble blushed green. "Nah to dat. We keeps goin'."

"Keep going? Where?"

Suddenly a small orb of amber light appeared above them and seemed to hang in midair at the very center of the bubble. After a moment, it began to strobe and then grew larger, until it was several feet in diameter. An opening began to appear at its center, where a rope ladder rolled out and unfurled to the floor of the bubble. It landed perhaps ten feet from where Lily was standing.

A bell chimed, and the waiting Nuldoids all looked to the amber orb where the number "83" was flashing. A few of the creatures pulled the paper stubs from their pockets and checked their numbers, then went back to reading or whatnot. A small woman put down her magazine, and struggled to her feet. She moved to the rope ladder and began climbing. At the top of the ladder, she wiggled through the opening and disappeared like a rabbit down a rabbit hole.

When the ladder began to ascend, Mishkin Hobble suddenly moved for it, sliding across the floor of the bubble and leaping for the ladder's bottom rung. The rope swung with his weight as he moved up it. "Come on! Come on!" he whispered vehemently to Lily as he was being pulled into the air. Lily started for the ladder, but found that she could not move so easily, the wall of the Source sinking like a thin trampoline beneath her feet. She managed to grab the ladder just above Mishkin Hobble, and then she too was being pulled into the air. The little Harvester quickly climbed past her until he was at the opening, where he crawled through and turned to help her do the same. When the last of the ladder slipped in, the opening closed like the aperture of a camera, and the amber orb shrunk again into nothingness... *tssfffft.*

Once inside, Lily found that she could stand and, once she stood, she saw that the space they were in was not at all small. They were in a rounded, sweeping corridor where a large sign pointed to the left and said "MAIN ENTRANCE, YA GOES DER!" But the "Main Entrance" was around the bend and could not be seen from where they were, though they could see "Number 83" walking in that direction beside a plodding security guard. To the right was a door with a sign warning that, "YA STAYS OUTTA HERE!" Mishkin Hobble stepped over to the door, turned back to Lily and put a finger to his lips. Then he quietly opened it and tiptoed in.

She followed him and saw that she had entered an immense round room that looked like it was made of translucent marble, all beneath an expansive gold-domed ceiling. They were standing beside several rows of wooden file cabinets that Mishkin Hobble made sure Lily crouched behind. She could hear courtroom proceedings in progress as she watched the little Nuldoid crawl to the end of the cabinets and signal for her to follow. She moved up beside him and then cautiously peered around the corner of the last filing cabinet, where she looked out and up to an imposing magisterial bench. Behind it, six robed jurists sat—each an apparition of sorts, like she, on either side of a large, empty, upholstered chair. On the floor before the bench, a small translucent Nuldoid with close-set eyes and a large flat nose stood nervously clutching a tattered fedora as he made his case.

"What is this?" Lily whispered to Mishkin Hobble.

"Council a Elders," he whispered back, with self-importance.

Lily took the information in, but found it hard to believe. She'd heard of the Council of Elders, but she was told it didn't actually exist. After all, the Council was referred to only once in the *Book of Nuldoid* (Contentions 7:6), and most Nuldoids assumed it was nothing more than a pipe dream of Lloyd's when he wrote, "a council woold [sic] be super smooper *if der was one to be.*"

When Mishkin Hobble saw that Lily fully understood the significance of where they were, he could hardly contain a smug smile, told her they'd wait for the right moment and then approach the Council.

"We can do that?" Lily asked.

"Sure yeah," Mishkin Hobble whispered. "We does it afore."

"So, you came here before?"

"Sure yeah. Wit dat other misty froote," he said with a wobble of his head. "A 'side door' froote is dat. Even when we doesn't s'posed ta be here, we is." The Elders, Mishkin Hobble explained, now beaming with pride, would help them find Leo.

The tentative Nuldoid making his case before the great bench was named Durbin Tuggs. He'd died accidentally when he drove his car into a large mural of a sunset that was painted on the side of a building. It was admittedly a stupid death, and he was quite embarrassed about it, so he was understandably annoyed when the Council of Elders found it as humorous as they did—a couple of them erupting into laughter every time they tried to ask a question. But Durbin Tuggs had lived a good Nuldoid life: disagreed with his parents when he was young, demonstrated against the government when he was older, argued his bills with utility companies, hardly ever treated his superiors with respect and spat on the Wheel during major Nuldoid holidays. So, the Council deliberated briefly and then informed him that they would recommend he be granted *full* Roundabout.

Tuggs was pleased, of course, though the final official decision had not yet been made. The fact was, however, that only in extreme cases did the Council ever recommend *limited* Roundabout—which was Roundabout with no memory of past lives. Even Oidenoids were usually granted full Roundabout, despite their off-putting agreeable nature.

Those unfortunate Nuldoids condemned to limited Roundabout were forced to begin life anew as "moronoids." These idiot babies, sometimes called "leakers," had to learn again to speak, to walk and to control their bladders and bowels. It was a horrific scenario by any standard, but it had two purposes: It wiped the slate clean with "problem" Nuldoids, and leakers were sent to parents who had committed unpunished crimes in current or past lives, and therefore paid a price for their crimes.

Finally, one of the judges stood, reached for a thick rope that hung from the dome overhead and yanked on it twice. A moment later, a door behind the bench opened and an ancient-looking man appeared, wearing a sweeping red robe and a baseball cap that was too large for him. He had long white hair that he tied off with a shoelace, and an extraordinary beard that extended well beyond his feet. He stood for a moment in the doorway, his thick-knuckled hands on his hips, as he surveyed the room with an air of authority.

Lily turned and whispered to Mishkin Hobble, "Who's that?"

Mishkin Hobble smiled, clearly savoring the moment. "Is Lloyd."

Her eyes grew wide. "Lloyd? *The* Lloyd... Lloyd?"

The little Harvester nodded.

Lily turned back to look again at the famous Nuldoid, as he started down the stairs toward his seat at the center of the judges' bench. She felt as though she was witnessing something significant, something magnificent, something like... history? She was a smidgeon less impressed, however, when, halfway down the stairs, Lloyd tripped on his beard and tumbled to the floor behind the other judges.

He was enormously clumsy it turns out—hence his last death between the cogs of the wheels—though few people knew this because little was ever written about it. To be fair to Lloyd, however, his clumsiness in the between life was frequently due to a beard that he could not figure out how to cut in a nonphysical world.

He pulled himself up with an air of dignity—something he'd cultivated over the centuries—brushed himself off and took his place in the chair at the middle of the judges' bench.

Mishkin Hobble, now the authority, explained to Lily that the Council of Elders was sharply divided into two distinct branches, each diametrically opposed to the other on one particular, but important, issue: Lloyd. While most living Nuldoids saw Lloyd as something of a spiritual prophet, their views were colored by a great span of time. After all, Lloyd had not appeared in Nuldoid for nearly a thousand years.

The Elders, however—who saw him on a day-to-day basis— were divided in their opinion of him. The three Elders to his right believed that he was indeed a spiritual prophet, an omniscient oracle, a divinity—while the three Elders to his left thought he was a nincompoop. As a result, virtually everything Lloyd said was viewed by half as sage and profound, while the other half saw it as moronic.

This nasty division amongst the Elders created so much personal anxiety for Lloyd that, over the years, he began to speak more and more cryptically to avoid being so harshly judged and so greatly admired. So much so, in fact, that eventually nobody in the between-life had any idea what he was talking about. And, while his often-indecipherable musings served to solidify the views of those who judged him harshly, those who followed him blindly managed to find great meaning in every word he spoke, cryptic or not. This phenomenon added greatly to the animosity of one side and the zealotry of the other, and, consequently, to Lloyd's overall mystique.

After the Elders presented Durbin Tuggs' case to Lloyd, the old man leaned back and struggled to find his chin beneath his beard so that he could rub it contemplatively. "Ach," he said after a moment. "Life! Is happens in plenty of time!" Which Lily and Mishkin Hobble certainly did not understand, nor did Durbin Tuggs, but the Elders to Lloyd's right nodded their heads in sincere and appreciative agreement, while the Elders to his left smirked as though his words confirmed that he was a buffoon.

Tuggs was granted *full* Roundabout, of course, and was delighted, though he would remember none of it when he returned to life. Apparently, living Nuldoids had "flimsy memory" of all things that happened inside the Source. Their memory of interactions with the Council disappeared as soon as they were drawn (by birth) into their next body. Though this was obviously not true of those who entered the Source by way of a "side door," as Mishkin Hobble and Lily had.

Lily was pleased for the little Nuldoid, and watched as he was led, whistling happily, out of the courtroom by a squat and officious guard into a back room, where he was summarily shot by a firing squad.

As inured as Lily had become to the many idiosyncrasies of this world, she was shocked to learn that this was how the dead returned to life. She supposed it made sense. After all, if *leaving life for death* required the death of life, it followed that *leaving death for life* would seem to require the death of death. But it was all still a little disturbing. Then something else occurred to her—something even more disturbing. "Wait a minute. Is that how we get back? They *shoot* us?"

Mishkin Hobble shook his head. "Nah to dat. We isn't dead."

"So, how do we get back?"

He shrugged. "We gets sucked back up is all." They would begin to feel dizzy, he explained, then there'd be a slight tug, and *zap*, they'd vaporize and wake up back in their bodies. (Since neither he nor Lily was actually dead, their bodies still had strong links to their souls, and tremendous magnetic pull.)

When Mishkin Hobble saw that Lloyd was about to leave the Chamber—he was never present for opening arguments—he licked the palm of his hand, pressed it across the top of his head to flatten his hair, and said, "Here goes we." He stepped out then from behind the file cabinets. "Hey der!"

The Elders turned, as did Lloyd, who was suddenly angry. "Ach!" he yelled. "Is you again! How is ya keeps gettin' inna here, huh? Ya isn't scheduled, ya rotten droib! Outta here ya gets! An' pronto!"

"Demandin' your pardon, dat Lloydness! But we has official fida-boned business!"

A jurist named Wuddle Moss eyeballed the Harvester. "Official business, ya says, huh? Is what?"

"Is lookin' for a Crustoid."

The judges laughed. "A Crustoid? Toids doesn't do no business with the Council."

"But is a dead one, dat toid!"

"Dead or doesn't, der isn't no toids here! Toids is a whole lotta dif'rent stuff. Now out goes ya, and spickity-lit!"

"Ach! Why doesn't ya checks dat books?"

"Out! Out, ya droib!"

Mishkin Hobble did not like being told what to do, even by such an esteemed Council. Or rather, *especially* by such an esteemed Council. It was clear to Lily, however, that this was not going to end well, especially when she saw two more security guards enter the courtroom, intent on "escorting" Mishkin Hobble out. "Excuse me," she said as she stood up from behind the filing cabinets.

A collective gasp emerged from the Council, and even from Lloyd, who had seen humans before, but not in many, many years, and certainly never in the between life. "You is a toid!" Lloyd declared, pointing a knobby finger from within his robe.

"Yes." Lily stepped farther out into the open. "Mishkin Hobble brought me here because someone I knew died. A human. A boy named Leo." She saw the curious looks on a couple of the judges' faces. "I know death isn't such a terrible thing in Nuldoid, but we humans, when someone dies, someone we care about, it hurts us very much. And it hurts even more, for me... because I should've stopped this boy from doing what he did." She was quiet for a moment, trying to keep herself from crying. "Anyway, Mishkin Hobble here thought that we might be able to find him here. But... I think we've just been wasting your time... and I'm sorry."

She started to cry.

The judges watched her, fighting the urge to cry as well, as one of them—a fuzzyheaded woman named Bickly—took a tissue from a box, walked around the bench and stepped down to the floor, where she approached Lily and offered her the tissue.

"Thank you," Lily said as she took it and wiped her nose.

"Only we gets Nuldoids here," Bickly said when Lily sat down on the floor beside the little woman. "Dat boy... is goes back uppa dat Crust. Is der dey gives 'im Roundabout, huh?"

Lily dabbed the tears in her eyes and shook her head. "We don't have Roundabout."

Though none of the Nuldoids gasped out loud, a few of them exchanged looks that were not quite, but very nearly, looks of horror. Two of the judges made their way around the bench and cautiously approached Lily so that they could gently pat her on the back—and to get a closer look at a Crustoid. Soon even Lloyd had joined them, after holding his beard with one hand and walking carefully along the side of the bench.

"Toids an' kaput," Bickly said, "is a sad business, dat."

Lily nodded and began to cry again.

"Yeah to dat," said Lloyd, who was trying to be sympathetic. "Dey has dat whole nuther systems."

One of the other judges sat down next to them and shook his head. "Ach! No Roundabout, eh? So what's dey does up der wif all dem dead toids?"

Mishkin Hobble sat off to the side, dumbfounded and perhaps even a little annoyed by Lloyd and the Elders' overly kind treatment of Lily, especially in light of the shabby way they'd treated *him*. Clearly these ethereal Nuldoids were enamored not only with Lily's size, but, he suspected, with her beauty.

When she had regained her composure, the judges peppered her with questions about her height and about the Crust and about all of the horrific types of weather she'd seen in her lifetime. And, naturally, they wanted to see her hands. She smiled and held them out as the judges squinted and turned their heads slightly to the side, so they could get a clear view.

But it was clear to both she and Mishkin Hobble that they were not going to find Leo. Not here. Not ever. And when Mishkin Hobble said he was starting to feel dizzy, Lily told the judges that she would soon be leaving. Lloyd took her hand and told her he was sorry about "dat dead kid 'at's gone kaputs fur good."

And, as Mishkin Hobble disappeared, and Lily began to feel dizzy, each of the Nuldoids wished her well and thanked her for stopping by.

life on the Crust

AFTER SEVERAL PROSPECTIVE buyers and lookie-loos had been to see the house—had meandered through it, poked at this, snooped behind that, flipped this light switch and that, asked about the neighbors and what sort of people lived here and there—a Realtor phoned Warren to say that a young couple had made an offer to buy it. But their offer was for much less than Warren had asked.

He told the Realtor to take the offer.

And then he booked a flight to Chicago.

() () ()

Lily, meanwhile, had woken up from the effects of Mishkin Hobble's froote mist to find Mishkin Hobble waiting there in the hotel room. He said he was sorry they did not find her young friend Leo, but he hoped it was somewhat comforting to know that the boy was *somewhere*. And, though she still felt a little unsteady, he offered to accompany her on her trip back to the Crust.

She accepted his offer.

Later, the two of them went over to the marketplace, where they hooked up with some Harvesters, who were on their way out of Nuldoid. As luck would have it, they were headed for the outskirts of Neither Norr, near Stimp Dibble (Chihuahua, Mexico), because they'd heard that a froote with "apple" in it (a rare commodity) was growing there in abundance.

Lily's return trip, like Warren's, was mostly uneventful— aside from a brief encounter with twin Sloidelobbs named Roland and Fowland, who operated the suspended gondola that climbed a treacherous hillside near the outskirts of Neither Norr. Unfortunately the Sloidelobbs had converted to Oidenoidism, and refused to allow Lily and the Nuldoids access to the gondola.

Finally Mishkin Hobble stepped forward to speak privately with them. He confessed that he knew Lloyd personally and that he even had a handwritten note from Lloyd that he was willing to show the Sloidelobbs as proof. Before he took it from his pocket, however, he explained that the note was visible only to the dead. He then held it out for them to examine. They, of course, couldn't see it because they weren't currently dead, but they stared at Mishkin Hobble's empty hand in speechless wonder, astonished to be looking at a note they couldn't see that was actually written by Lloyd himself.

They agreed then to take the travelers up the hillside in the gondola.

When their route finally forked between Stimp Dibble and Drobbs Mubble (Fresno), they parted ways with the other

Harvesters, and Mishkin Hobble escorted Lily the rest of the way to the access tunnel near Fresno.

Before they said good-bye at the rock wall, Lily thanked the little Harvester again for his efforts to find Leo. "I'll miss you," she said, and bent down to embrace him.

Mishkin Hobble had never said a final good-bye to anyone before, did not know how to express what he was feeling. "Yas'll be kay-oh-ay den. An' so, ya does dat..." He looked at her, his words failing him, his lower lip quivering. "Ach! Is got dat liver's all horked up."

Lily put a hand on his cheek, and told him that saying good-bye on the Crust was often bittersweet. After they parted, Lily walked to her dust-covered truck and heard Mishkin Hobble burst into heaving sobs. She turned back and saw him just as the rock walls slammed shut between them.

She found the key that Warren had stashed, brushed away a layer of dust on the steering wheel and dash, and drove back to San Francisco. Around noon, she pulled up to her warehouse, exhausted and sleepy and just feeling plain lousy. She slid open the steel door and stepped over the mail that had spilled out onto the floor of the entry, found her bed and climbed into it, intent on sleeping well into the next day.

She woke, though, a couple of hours later with a pain in her stomach that she thought would go away, but didn't.

She put some clothes on and drove to see her doctor.

() () ()

Warren was sitting in the terminal of the San Francisco Airport reading a newspaper article about the widespread unrest in Europe, when the announcer announced that the plane to Chicago was boarding. He put the newspaper down, picked up his bag and approached the gate, where he gave the attendant his boarding pass.

But, as he entered the breezeway to his plane, he heard a woman's voice yelling his name. He looked back and saw Lily making her way down the walkway toward him, pushing past a number of disgruntled passengers. A flight attendant appeared just behind her, clearly not happy about this, telling her she was not allowed to go where she was going.

"Lily? What are you doing here?" Warren asked when she reached him.

"I had to find you," she said, and fell into his arms. "I had to see you. I went to your house. A woman, a Realtor... she told me where you were, where you were going. I got here as fast as I could."

Warren held her with mixed emotions as the flight attendant approached and two security guards, having been alerted to the problem, entered the walkway from the terminal.

The attendant put a hand on Lily's shoulder. "Ma'am, I'm sorry, you're not allowed to be here." Two security guards had also entered the breezeway and asked what the trouble was.

Lily held tight to Warren, looked up at him. "I'm pregnant."

"What?"

"I just saw my doctor," she said, as she felt the flight attendant's hand squeeze her shoulder more tightly. She started to talk faster. "He did a blood test. He said everything was normal, then he said it wasn't normal—"

"Ma'am, you're going to have to come with us." It was one of the security guards.

Lily, though, would not let go of Warren, and talked even faster. "—and then he told me, the doctor told me, that something was wrong with the blood, that there were platelets in the blood that weren't right, that weren't the right color! And I thought it was bad, at first, but the doctor said they were *green,* the platelets were green! He said they were behaving differently. And I realized—"

"Ma'am, come with us, please, or we'll have to use force…"

"Hey, hold on a minute," one of the other passengers said, "she's gonna have a baby."

"—and then I realized," she held on to Warren like he was a rubber raft in the middle of an ocean, her eyes locked on his, "I realized what was happening!"

The attendant stepped back as the guards now moved to either side of Lily, and took her arms. When they began to pull her away from Warren, he held her more firmly. "Wait, hold on, wait!" he shouted.

"It's Leo!" Lily said. "It's Leo! I'm going to have a baby! And it's Leo! He's going to be *our* baby!"

() () ()

It was an assumption on her part, a big one, but she had seen enough in the previous week to know it was possible. Or even probable. And, the fact of the matter was, she was right.

What she *didn't* know was this: Paperwork regarding Leo had arrived at the Source (this was, of course, *after* she and Mishkin Hobble had returned to their bodies). There'd been a bureaucratic mix-up and more than a little confusion at the Office of Souls (the Crust's version of the Council of Elders). Apparently, since Leo died in Nuldoid, and, since no human had ever done so, all sorts of problems arose. His soul, for instance, could not be categorized as a "deceased human," since he died outside of human jurisdiction. (A similar situation was narrowly averted years earlier when the astronauts of Apollo 13 were nearly sent hurtling into space.) As a result, officials at the Office of Souls had no way to process him or send him on to a spiritual status, without verification from Nuldoid. So, the boy's soul had been routed to the Council of Elders so that they could provide the necessary verification to clear up the matter. He was then to be rerouted back to the Crust for final processing.

But when he arrived in the Source, the Council of Elders and Lloyd were so delighted to meet the youngster—were still so enamored with, okay, gah-gah over, having met Lily—that they decided to process him through their *own* system, and route him to Lily. As a gift, of sorts. Besides, they were wholly unimpressed with the system used on the Crust.

Officials at the Office of Souls were, of course, upset and eventually outraged—which only delighted the Nuldoids even more—and tried their best to undo the maneuver. But it was all too late. By then Leo had already been routed to, and safely ensconced in, Lily's womb.

() () ()

At the airport, Warren refused to let go of Lily, as the security guards tried to pry her away from him. The more they pried, however, the more tightly Warren held on to her. And when he held on to her so tightly that she could not be pried away, they were *both* arrested.

After explaining and re-explaining to the security personnel that Lily was only trying to tell Warren that she was pregnant—having decided to leave out various other details—they were released with a stern warning not to engage in such nonsense ever again in any future pregnancies.

() () ()

Warren married Lily straightaway—they were, after all, in a bit of a hurry. At the wedding, many of the guests were confused, some even a little upset, by the black gown Lily chose to wear at the ceremony.

Warren backed out of the deal he'd made to sell his house, and he and Lily started building a spare room a few weeks later. He also decided to fight for his job, which didn't do any good because the school had permanently replaced him with a teacher named Bosman Osgood, who was even less interested in what he was teaching than Warren had been. But Warren was determined now to teach, and to teach well, because he didn't want another kid like Leo to hate school the way Leo had.

Soon, he was hired at another school, a better one, and eventually he became the teacher he'd always wanted to become—though, to do so, he had to occasionally break the rules. His classes became popular, in part, because he often told his students silly stories about a "fictitious" society where north was south and great was mediocre, where conflict and dissent and bickering were good and welcome things and where spit was greasy. His students were openly encouraged to argue their points with him, which they got better and better at, which, in turn, made them *care more* about the things they were learning— and, by the way, got them into a bit of hot water with a number of other teachers.

Warren did run across a few other Leos in the course of his teaching career, and he became very important to them. Two of the more prominent names were Darlene Pringle, who led citizens in the American Revolution II, and Mary Mohammed Xiang McCall, the forty-ninth president of the United States.

But, perhaps more significantly, he was a great help to a lot of kids who were just average kids. And, of all the things he taught them, of all the gifts he gave them, none was more valuable than learning to tell important people true things. Even when those things were unpleasant—no, *especially* when they were unpleasant.

When baby Leo was a few weeks old, he lay on the bed of his crib, looking up at his adoring parents while they leaned over the railing and cooed at him. Then his father picked up a small rattle from inside the crib, and gently waved it in front of the boy—who looked at it, batted it away and said, "Three grumpletts ya owes me, ya droib!"

Warren's eyes grew wide, Lily's too, as they looked at each other and then back at the baby.

Neither could have been more proud.

Hello, Good-bye, Hello

LIKE WARREN, THE children were wide-eyed as they sat beside their grandfather's bed. "So then... *you're* Leo?" Henry finally said. "That was *you*?"

But Grampa did not answer.

When he'd finished the story, he simply closed his eyes and died.

It was not dramatic, certainly not like the times the children only *thought* he was dead. But this time, he really *was* dead, and they knew it. Still, they sat for a while longer, just to be sure. And to look at him. They were sad, naturally, to see their grandfather die, but they were also awed by how he was, a moment earlier, alive and inside of his body, and then he simply was not. It was not something they'd ever seen before. It was odd, death.

Finally, Henry took one of the plastic pill bottles off Grampa's nightstand and read it. "'L. Worst TAKE 3 PER DAY'." Another bottle of medicine said, "Leonrd Wurst [sic]." Like many grandchildren, they'd probably been told their grandfather's first name, but none had ever used it or remembered it.

They sat quietly for another moment.

Francie began to cry.

"What're ya cryin' about?" Joe asked.

She shrugged. "Grampa's dead."

Joe thought for another moment. "Yeah... but it's just death."

"Besides..." Henry added, trying to make her feel better, "he wasn't very nice."

"He wasn't nice *at all*," Joe said.

Francie nodded. "I know." She ran a finger under her damp nose. "That's what I liked about him."

For some reason, Francie's words struck all three of them as funny, and they began to laugh, each certain that Grampa would've been just fine with that.

() () ()

Several days later, the children sat in the back seat of their parents' car on the way to Grampa's funeral. Their mother asked what they'd talked about with Grampa in the days before his death, and Francie jumped in, enthusiastically explaining what she could remember about Nuldoid and Grampa's journey there, which, frankly, was not at all easy to follow, since she mixed up quite a few of the details and—at least in Henry's opinion— pretty much mangled the story. And as the car pulled into the parking lot of the cemetery, their mother told Francie that Grampa sure had a wild imagination. Their father mentioned then that sometimes old people, near the ends of their lives, weren't in charge of "their mental facilities." All in all, their parents didn't take the story seriously and seemed mostly concerned that the children not be too upset by Grampa's death. Their mother reminded them that Grampa lived a long life, and that death was a natural part of life.

"Yeah, we know," said Henry.

() () ()

A cool zephyr whipped up from the ocean through the branches of the pine and cypress trees that lined the dark green grass of Seaview Cemetery's hillside. Besides the children and their parents, there were only a handful of other people standing next to the hole in the ground and Grampa's waiting casket. They were mostly employees of his—his gardener, his housekeeper, his nurse, his accountant—but they were not particularly upset or sad; they having mostly thought of him as a grumpy old man. He had always tried to pick arguments with them, a concept that none of them was ever able to get used to—the idea of quarreling with their own boss.

As the stone-faced priest said some final words about Leonard Worst—words that didn't really sound like they were about Grampa—Henry, Joe and Francie watched the casket sink slowly into the ground like a pad of butter melting on a griddle. When a few handfuls of dirt were tossed onto the casket and all was said and done, those in attendance stood quietly for a moment and then turned to leave. The children followed their parents down the grassy slope of the cemetery as the breeze from the ocean turned away and flitted instead along the sand of the beach below them.

"Psssst!"

Henry heard it first, as they passed one of the larger pines. He turned and saw, beside the tree, a small man poking his head out.

"Psssst!"

The little man had a large nose and dark curly hair that sprouted from his head like fingers. And he was short. Very short. Henry stepped toward the tree as Joe and Francie saw that he'd stopped, and then they too saw the little man behind the tree. "Yeah?" Henry said quietly, cautiously, as he approached and saw another little man standing just behind him. The second man had fat blowfish cheeks and a thick lower lip that he pumped out pugnaciously.

"Leo is dat der?" the first one said, pointing to Grampa's grave, where two men in blue work shirts were now vigorously shoveling dirt.

Henry looked over at the grave, then back at the little men. "Yeah. Leo Worst."

"Ach," said first the little man. "Hears we he was sick."

"Who are you?" This was Joe, who'd come to stand beside his brother.

The two little men looked at each other, before the second of them pointed to himself. "Is here Morton," he said, and then pointed to the other, "Der's Kyle der. We was s'posed ta has gots here sooner, 'cept for Kyle is a rod-nim 'at don't knows which way ta up! So here we gots late!"

They were young, these two small men, too young to be the exact same Morton and Kyle their grandfather knew. "Nah to dat, ya frump dobbler!" said the one named Kyle, as he shoved the other one. "Yas dat murk fuddle 'at takes we a wrong way!"

"Ach! Is who dat zigs we left, steada right, inna Valley a Weather?"

"Who says we goes left at Puddin' River?"

"Eh, ya lost dem marblets!"

And as one lunged at the other and each clutched the other's throat, Francie looked up at her brothers. "Are they..."

Henry nodded to his little sister.

361

() () ()

The children got back into the car, and Francie happily told their parents about the encounter with the little people. Henry and Joe smiled while their little sister prattled on about how she and her brothers met two little men from Nuldoid, and how they were friends of Grampa's when they were alive in different bodies, and how they came to visit Grampa, but got here too late, which made them mad at each other, so they got in a fight, which was okay because those two always fought, and on and on she went, while her parents half listened and occasionally said things like "Uh-huh" and "Isn't that interesting" and "Well, I'll be."

() () ()

It wasn't until several weeks later that the children learned about the baby.

They were all in the car again. Only this time, they were on their way out to dinner. The children knew something was up when their mother put the car in driverless mode, and both she and their father swiveled the front seats to face them.

"Children..." she said, "Daddy and I have some news for you." She smiled and exchanged a look with their father before she turned back to them. "We're going to have a baby."

Francie's mouth fell open. Henry's brown eyes grew wide as he looked to his brother and sister. Joe suddenly clutched Henry's knee. Each was oddly aware of a peculiar feeling. An instinct maybe that said this was more than just a baby.

"I knew it," Francie said.

Their mother was surprised. "You did?"

Cautiously, Joe asked, "Can we name him after Grampa?"

Their father scrunched up his face disdainfully, as the car pulled into the restaurant's automatic parking lot. "Grampa? Aw, gee..."

"Sweetheart," their mother turned to Joe, "Grampa's name was Leonard. And, well," she cringed, "I don't know if I really like that name." But, as she finished saying the last, she winced suddenly in pain and then moved her hand to her stomach. "Ow!" she said and looked at her husband. "He kicked me."

"That's great." Her husband smiled.

"No," said their mother, "he kicked me *hard*. Or he punched me."

Francie beamed and assured her parents that Leonard, "Leo," was a fine name for a baby, an excellent name in fact, and that she was looking very much forward to seeing and playing with baby Leo. Henry and Joe, too, were pleased with the news—although they were fairly certain that their new little brother would be a grumpy kid, prone to bickering.

As their parents swiveled back to the front of the car and got out—their mother complaining still about the severity of the baby's kick or punch—Joe leaned to his brother and sister and whispered, "Hib nobb del noid."

Various

Nuldoid Visitors

(In alphabetical order)

Samuel Adams (1722–1803) Considered, by many, to be the real father of the American Revolution, *this* Adams was one of the first Colonists to complain about the British government. As a young man, however, he was not particularly combative or argumentative until the fall of 1745, when he was approached by a group of Nuldoids. He was lugging malt (used for making beer) through the streets of Boston, when the Nuldoids caught scent of it and followed him. He ended up traveling to Nuldoid and spent seven months there, returning to the Crust with a chip on his shoulder and a thirst for politics. By 1775, the British were so annoyed with his constant rabble-rousing—especially after his Tea Party idea—that they sent troops to Lexington to arrest him. He escaped capture, but the ensuing battle was the beginning of the Revolutionary War.

L. Frank Baum (1856–1919) Author of *The Wizard of Oz*, Baum was greatly influenced by what he saw in Nuldoid. He was there in the summer of 1889 during a Crystal ceremony, which is where he first heard the song *Dat Crystal of Ours,* and wrote it down in his journal. Years later, when music for the movie was being written, songwriters Harold Arlen and E.Y. "Yip" Harburg used a variation of it for their song *The Wizard of Oz.* (No plagiarism charges were ever filed by the Nuldoids because, to do so, would have brought great attention to

Nuldoid and the possibility of human migration, which Nuldoidians were very much averse to.) Another of Baum's journals was discovered in 2053 outside of Aberdeen, South Dakota, where a full description of the emotional trees in the dell of Neither Norr explain where Baum got the idea for the angry apple trees of Oz. There was also a description of the strange orange flowers that lay beyond the dell, as well as the "moribund fate of the proud Gloibs."

John Cage (1912–1992) The atonal composer spent much of his youth in and around the Los Angeles area where, as an only child, he would often wander off and spend time by himself. In the summer and fall of 1921, he met up with a group of Nuldoids on the beach near Santa Monica and traveled with them into Neither Norr and Nuldoid. It was there that he began his appreciation—some would say obsession with— atonal sounds, leading him to later brag that his major contribution to music was "the elimination of harmony."

Jesus Christ (0000–0033) It has been rumored that Jesus spent his "missing years" in Nuldoid, which was then the Droiden Frobble Dynasty. For the record, this theory has been mostly discredited. Nuldoid Historian Thurlow Gern, in his book *Wasn't Not No Jesus Wid We*, dispelled many of these claims, especially that Jesus learned to levitate from a Droiden Frobble named Bobb (supposedly explaining how Jesus perfected his ability to walk on liquid surfaces). Other notions that Jesus plagiarized Nuldoidian ideas, most notably that those with power must serve the needs of those without, were found to be baseless. One story that Jesus spent a weekend in the Emperor's Palace, where he was so impressed with Emperor Asgar Weed's treatment of the sick and homeless that he adopted the idea himself, was easily disproved, since the Emperor's Palace was not constructed until our own 10th century. Asgar Weed ruled Nuldoid in our 13th and 14th centuries.

Stephen Colbert (1964-2072) After brutally satirizing the George W. Bush Administration (in front of President Bush) at the White House Correspondents' Association Dinner, April 2006, a secret investigation was launched by government officials into Colbert's past. Although the investigation turned up no untoward association with terrorists or communists, it was discovered that Colbert had a deep and lasting relationship with several groups of Nuldoids, dating back to his senior year at Northwestern University. The school was located near an access tunnel beside Lake Michigan (referred to by Nuloids as Dooblehoid Nubbledorff Water). Colbert's quarrelsome nature and lack of respect for authority was largely attributed to his association with these contentious creatures. Later in life, Colbert was greatly involved in ousting the Oidenoids from Downtown Nuldoid after the Croibish Stigg Oiden Invasion of 1046 C.C. The following year, when the Nuldoidian creatures threatened to elect him Emperor of Nuldoid, he left and never returned.

Nicolaus Copernicus (1473–1543) Copernicus visited Nuldoid in 1530, after a Crystal placement team accidentally tunneled into his cellar. He helped the confused creatures return to Nuldoid, and then spent seventeen months there. After he returned to the Crust in 1532, he managed to cause a great stir in Rome with his theory that the earth revolved around the sun. What most astronomers don't realize, or refuse to believe, is that he was not serious. He was, in fact, as convinced as his contemporaries that the opposite was true—that the sun revolved around the earth—but he'd apparently grown so fond of arguments while he was in Nuldoid that he presented the "absurd claim" just to rile the Catholic Church.

M.C. Escher (1898–1972) Escher made the journey to Nuldoid in the fall of 1923 while he was visiting Spain. Though the young man was impressed with the stairwell into Downtown Nuldoid—it having influenced a great deal of his artwork— the trip itself affected him more in his ability to recognize and reject tyranny, hence his early distain and brave resistance to the growing Nazism of the 1930s.

W.C. Fields (1880–1946) Fields spent several years in Nuldoid during his early twenties, where he developed much of his disagreeable attitude. He was stranded near the Lake of Rubber Balls and consequently passed the time learning to juggle, a skill that he incorporated into his early Vaudevillian act. That he had a great love of peculiar-sounding names and words (used in his movies)—Otis Cibblecoblis, Egbert Souse, Baby Elwood Dunk, Cuthbert J. Twillie, J. Pinkerton Snoopington, Mr. Muckle—was due to his time in Nuldoid, where he would often repeat creatures' names and make rhyming stories out of them, which annoyed a great many of the Nuldoids and almost got him killed.

Theodor Seuss Geisel (Dr. Seuss) (1904–1991) Though Geisel never saw the inside of Nuldoid itself, he did travel through the Region of Neither Norr, and spent time in the Plains of Low Weather. There he befriended a "circle" of Globb Trobbers and actually traveled with them for a time, learning their language, and even teaching them to recite poems. He, of course, came across a great many other creatures in Neither Norr (Gloibs, Theevins, Blobalobbs, etc.) many of which influenced his work.

Joseph Heller (1923–1999) Heller visited Nuldoid in the winter of 1944, while he was stationed in Italy during World War II. After falling through a large opening near the outskirts of Palermo, he ventured into Neither Norr and then Nuldoid. It was there he grew to appreciate a lack of respect for authoritative figures. He was quite taken by the Nuldoids' system of government, especially their standards for choosing officials—that is, those Nuldoids who had no interest in politics and self-aggrandizement were considered most suited for politics and aggrandizement. He later incorporated the idea (some say stole) in his classic novel *Catch-22*.

John Lennon (1940-1980) While on tour in Germany with the Beatles in the summer of 1966, Lennon was involved in a minor motorcycle accident just outside of Munich where he lost his glasses. After the Beatle and road manager's assistant, Tony Teesdale, searched the roadside for nearly twenty minutes, Lennon was approached by two small creatures who offered to sell him the chipped glasses for an outrageous sum. When Lennon refused to do so, he was called a number of names by them. A lover of peculiar words, Lennon became intrigued with the language of the creatures and accepted an offer to journey with them to Nuldoid where he spent the remainder of the summer. He returned to the Crust a changed man. In August, 1966, he began to experiment with his music and speak out about the Vietnam War. While his attitude pushed the Beatles to new creative levels, his love of squabbling led to problems within the group.

George Lucas (1935–2050) In the summer of 1967, filmmaker, George Lucas, traveled through the Region of Neither Norr, where he encountered an enormous Fishing Worm. He was so impressed with the giant worm that he later incorporated a similar creature in *Star Wars: The Empire Strikes Back.*

Rosa Parks (1913–2005) To those who knew Rosa Parks personally, it was a conundrum that the soft-spoken African-American woman so boldly refused to give up her seat on a bus in Mongomery, Alabama, and consequently launched the civil rights movement. In 1955, however, she took a job as a housekeeper in Monteagle, Tennessee, where, in the summer, she ran into a group of creatures and ended up traveling with them into Nuldoid. In Nuldoid, Parks found that *everyone* was treated like a second-class citizen, and *everyone* complained bitterly and vehemently about it. While in Nuldoid, she was not allowed to ride the busses, not because of her race, but because of her size. And, though she was never granted access to a Nuldoid bus, she grew quite fond of standing at the bus's open door, and arguing with the driver. Her act of defiance in December of 1955 was merely an extension of the arguments she'd grown to love in Nuldoid.

Darlene Pringle (1995-2026) A student of Warren Worst's, she was greatly influenced by him and his teachings about Nuldoid. In May of 2026, she famously led citizens to revolt against the religious and corporate takeover of the United States (from 2021 until 2027 the United States had been officially called the United States of Petroleum and God— where all dissent was forbidden). Though executed for her heretical and subversive role against the government, her legacy lived on and motivated the masses, eventually bringing about the American Revolution II, reestablishing the United States of America.

Andrei Sakharov (1921–1989) Pages from the physicist's private journal were discovered in the fall of 2022 at a small library outside Scherbinki, where Sakharov was exiled by the Soviet government from 1980-85. The journal's pages described, in detail, Sakharov's journey into Nuldoid during the early part of 1964, where he claimed to have gotten "an incredible taste for beer" as well as his "first black eye." Though he never spoke of the trip when he returned to the Crust, it was obvious that he had been greatly influenced by the Nuldoid culture, as he became a great irritant to the Soviet government and a hindrance to their plans for expanding their nuclear arsenal.

Steven Spielberg (1946–2055) During his senior year of high school in Saratoga, California, Spielberg went back to visit his mother and sisters in Phoenix, Arizona. While there, he accidentally fell into a Nuldoid access tunnel and spent nearly a month lost in Neither Norr. He eventually stumbled upon Nuldoid, where he spent another week before returning to the Crust. The trip would become a significant influence on much of his future work, most notably *E.T.* Though he had often characterized *E.T.* as a story "about the divorce of my parents," many film historians believe it had more to do with his memories of feeling like an alien lost in the unfamiliar world of Neither Norr.

Jay Tarses (1939–2056) Though his name was not a household word until the end of the 21st century, Tarses was fairly well known in his own time for television programs he'd written. After spending several months in Nuldoid during the early 1980s, where he acclimated well to the Nuldoidian culture, he returned to the Crust with a brisk attitude toward the television industry that got him in a lot of hot water. In 1992, he and playwright Richard Dresser produced a television show called *The Black Tie Affair*. Though the show garnered little attention at the time, it became immensely popular on Cerebral ChipCasts of the late 2070s, and a favorite of Iceland's emotionally unstable prime minister, Ólafur Björnsson—one of the most powerful men in the world. It was Björnsson's obsession with the show in 2081 that delayed his use of the world's first chain link mega-nuclear bomb, ultimately saving the world from nuclear annihilation.

J.R.R. Tolkien (1882–1973) While it is well known that Tolkien spent a good deal of his time as a child playing and exploring Moseley Bog near Birmingham, England, it is generally not known that he disappeared for nearly three weeks in the summer of 1899 when he was seven. After search parties had given the boy up for dead, young J.R.R. came striding into his mother's kitchen with a band of "diminutive and objectionable culprits who demanded quite rudely that they be supplied with crackers and a good deal of ale." Mrs. Tolkien kicked the "culprits" out and marched the boy to his room, where he proceeded to tell fanciful stories about little people at the center of the earth until, finally, he was severely beaten for it. He, thereafter, confined his "fanciful stories" about little people to his writing.

Glossary of
Nuldoid Terms

᠙

Blobalobbs – Nuldoid house pets resembling throw pillows, sometimes found in the wild, and hunted by Oidenoids. Blobalobbs are furry creatures with no appendages of any sort. They are generally quite unpleasant and, though they cannot actually do any harm, they can growl when they're annoyed. Nuldoids enjoy the creatures' unpleasant personalities, and—with the use of a small round diaper—they are practically maintenance free.

Dorggob Bokk – Hero of the Stinky War of Rotten Smells (723–728 C.C.). Bokk famously argued with the commander of a firing squad that he *could not be shot* because his "last meal" was "much not cooked." In fact, Bokk lived another eleven days, eating mediocre meals until, finally, he was served a perfectly prepared flank steak froote, medium-rare, smothered in a cilantro-almond pesto, that he thoroughly enjoyed and eagerly gobbled up before he was executed. Hence the Nuldoid expression, "Food dat's fit for Bokk."

The Croibish Stigg Oiden Invasion (1046 C.C.) – After nearly 250 years of relegation to the wilderness of Neither Norr, the Oidenoids retook Nuldoid. Though the invasion is not referred to in this text, it was the subject of a book by Russ Woody, published in 2015.

Crustoids – Although, technically, this term refers to *any* creature that lives on the Crust of Hoidenall, it is generally used in Nuldoid to refer to humans.

Cylindrical Calendar – Developed near the end of Lloyd's thirteenth life, the Cylindrical Calendar is based on the Holey Cylinder in the Cathedral of the Wheel. Since the Cylinder is divided into thirteen sections (depicting each of Lloyd's lives), the Nuldoid year is, unfortunately, divided into thirteen months, which, after nearly a thousand years has rendered its correlation to our calendar as virtually impossible.

Delnoids – Nuldoid's third sex. The Delnoid lifestyle is highly coveted by Nuldoids, since it's leisurely and devoid of relationships with an opposite sex. Delnoids spend most of their time pursuing hobbies (a favorite is Goffle-off). Their powers are greater than regular Nuldoids because they are not subject to the distractions associated with sexual relationships, allowing them greater focus.

Disinformation – Out of a deep concern that humans might one day wise up and move "inland," Nuldoids began—in the early 19th century—to disseminate as much misinformation as possible about the earth's core. The following excerpt, for example, is supposedly from the "Nevada Seismological Laboratory," and is quoted freely in school textbooks:

> The core is composed mostly of iron (Fe) and is so hot that the outer core is **molten**, with about 10% sulphur (S). The inner core is under such extreme **pressure** that it remains solid. Most of the earth's mass is in the mantle, which is composed of iron (Fe), magnesium (Mg), aluminum (Al), silicon (Si), and oxygen (O) **silicate** compounds.

As anyone who's been to Nuldoid knows, this is all gibberish.

Doidell voids – Large circular tunnels formed thousands of years ago by confused and less-than-intelligent Fishing Worms within the Pockets of Roundlet, where wind has been trapped indefinitely. As a result, anything or anyone caught in one is usually doomed to circle forever.

Draggirds – Small creatures with bodies like lizards and wings like bats. They are considered a nuisance and a safety hazard because, when startled or frightened, fire bursts from their backside. The Draggird, by the way, is the origin of medieval dragon legends here on the Crust. An expedition of Nuldoids (sent to retrieve a Crystal from the countryside of England in our 11th century) accidentally left behind a pet Draggird just outside of Ipswich, Suffolk. When a group of surveyors came across the little creature, the Draggird was quite frightened, of course, and let out a number of small bursts of fire. The surveyors easily killed the helpless creature and ate it. Then, as they passed through one village to the next, the story of their encounter became more and more exaggerated. By the time they reached their home in Great Baddow, the Draggird had grown to nearly thirty feet, was fierce in nature, and breathed huge, billowing bursts of fire from its mouth. Stories of these "dreaded" creatures grew throughout Europe until the little Draggirds became the terrifying dragons we know of today.

Droiden Frobble Dynasty – The Droiden Frobbles preceded the Nuldoids, and date back several thousand years. Though their exact origin is unclear, most Nuldoid scholars agree, its founder was a woman named Lois.

Fishing Worms – Large worms that live and tunnel in the walls and structures of Neither Norr. They are so named for their uncanny ability to place themselves at the opening of a tunnel and align their massive lips to the contours of the tunnel's opening, so that the casual observer (usually a Nuldoid) sees only the entrance to a tunnel and steps in unawares. The Fishing Worm's mouth then slams shut and the little Nuldoid is crushed and swallowed. Future filmmaker George Lucas nearly became a victim of a Fishing Worm in the summer of 1967 when he was traveling through Neither Norr. The experience became the basis for the horrific creatures in *Star Wars: The Empire Strikes Back.*

Froote (pronounced fruit) – All food in Nuldoid and the Region of Neither Norr comes from froote. Froote also provides a great many other things like motor oil, detergent, hand lotion, medicine, plastic and (as Mishkin Hobble and Lily learned) certain things that cannot be easily explained. The more tasty and exotic froote grows near the underside of the Crust.

Globb Trobbers – Large wooly animals that roam The Plains of Low Weather. When these creatures have to travel great distances, they gather in small groups to form large "wheels," enabling them to roll from place to place. Unfortunately, this method of travel precludes them from seeing exactly where they're going, and so they often run into things, and occasionally off cliffs.

Gloibs – Extinct breed of Draggird. They died out perhaps a hundred years before this story began, when the older males became competitive with each other and forced their offspring out of their respective nests before the little ones were capable of flying. Even though the older males hadn't realized the consequences of their actions, the females did and would no longer have anything to do with the males, which also helped doom the breed.

Goffle-off – Leisurely sport similar to "golf." It is enjoyed by Delnoids and regular Nuldoids alike (though Delnoids have more leisure time). Goffle-off differs from golf only in that there is not a hole in the green. Instead a convicted public official is confined to the green by a secured tether. Nuldoids score by beaning the official in the least amount of shots.

Good Riddance Day – The kicking out of Oidenoids from Nuldoid in 813 of the Cylindrical Calendar (C.C.), referred to by Oidenoids as The Unjust Purge of Nuldoid. For nearly fifty years beforehand, the Oidenoids of Nuldoid insisted that theirs was the *only and true* interpretation of Lloyd's word (*see* War of Decaying Values). It was a source of irritation and argumentation for most Nuldoids, so the movement went pretty much unnoticed until 812 C.C. The Oidenoids then refused to argue the point any further, opting to push for legislation enforcing their interpretation of *The Book of Nuldoid*. Nuldoids then decided to banish all Oidenoids to The Region of Neither Norr.

Gorkken Stobbles – Extinct animals with long snouts and bulbous bodies, depicted on the coins of the Droiden Frobble Dynasty. They were frequently used by the ancestors of Nuldoidians to siphon liquids and clean up spilled substances. Unfortunately, a young Droiden Frobble named Budd discovered that stomping on a Gorkken Stobble created a prolonged and humorous farting sound that many of his friends found humorous. After the practice became a common, the creatures died out.

Grumplett – Nuldoid unit of currency, the fronts of which depict thinkers and philosophers who have caused a great many arguments in Nuldoid. The face of the one-grumplett bill shows a Nuldoid street sweeper, Lute Hoggle, who reportedly engaged in over 87,000 individual arguments before his sixth death in 924 C.C. The front of the three-and-a-half grumplett bill displays Her Lowness, Eunice Tukk, who invented a faulty blender that caused most of the domestic squabbles of the early 960s. The backs of all Nuldoid currency depict the end of Lloyd's 13th life when he was crushed to death between two cogwheels in the Cathedral of the Wheel.

Harvesters – The frontiersmen of Nuldoid, a motley group of Nuldoids who care not so much for city life or cleanliness.

Harvesters roam the outer regions of Neither Norr collecting exotic froote to bring back to Nuldoid in their shopping carts. They usually have spotlights mounted on their shoulders, and wear long dark coats with many pockets. And, while it is true they do not like Oidenoids, they do not actually enjoy killing them and collect their skins.

"Hib nobb del noid" – The essence of Nuldoid. The term is used when Nuldoids are performing acts of magic, but its significance runs much deeper. It refers to the Nuldoidian belief that everything exists in a circle. Therefore happiness is next to unhappiness, evil is next to good, fat to thin, wrong to right, etc. The literal translation is: "Within dat circular circle, circles all dat is ta be moved in dat circle." An often-overlooked aspect of the concept is movement, which Nuldoids believe is essential within any circle. This movement, they believe, is brought about by conflict and dissent.

Hoboggs – Nuldoid's homeless. Many of them reside in the corridors of the Emperor's Palace. While most Nuldoids find Hoboggs greatly annoying, the same can be said for how Hoboggs feel about most Nuldoids. After all, Hoboggs consider public property to be their personal property because, to their way of thinking, no one is more the public than they.

Hoidenall – Nuldoid word for Earth.

King Hal – One of the last of the Droiden Frobble rulers, before the establishment of Nuldoid. Droiden Frobble coins of the era depicted his beheading—"Kingg Hal's Beann Choppin'." While little is known about Hal himself, it is known that he believed the "peeeple serves at dat pleeesure a Kingg Hal," which, most historians assume, is what prompted the "peeeple" to take pleasure in the beheading of Hal.

Klumpanoids – Groups of sleeping Nuldoids. All Nuldoids enjoy napping, and do so usually in groups of three, four or five. Males, females and Delnoids intermingle, curl and wrap around each other until the group looks something like a "clump" of Nuldoids.

Lloyd – Founder of Nuldoid. Though he has not been seen—or perhaps has not identified himself—in a thousand years, his influence on Nuldoid is indisputable. Having written *The Book of Nuldoid* shortly before his 13th death (when he was crushed between two pinion wheels), he has become somewhat iconic, if not sacrosanct, to a great many Nuldoids. The Oidenoids of Neither Norr, however, seem to have gone too far with their belief in the literal word of Lloyd—they having mangled its meaning in their interpretation. Lloyd, unfortunately, became something of a victim of his own teaching however, as his writings strongly discouraged respect and worship—while greatly emphasizing disrespect and iconoclasm. And, since many Nuldoids respected Lloyd, even worshiped him, they began to show him great disrespect and even ridicule. Which may explain why he didn't return for a 14th life.

Moronoids – Nuldoid babies born with *limited* Roundabout—that is reincarnation without memory. The Nuldoid that comes back to life with limited Roundabout does so as a "blithering idiot" or a "stupid baby." As newborns, they must learn to walk and talk and control their bladders and bowels all over again, hence they are often called "leakers." It is always a sad occasion when Nuldoid parents learn that their baby is a moronoid. As a result, however, Nuldoids have great sympathy for Crustoids, who *only* have moronoids.

Music – Music in Nuldoid is quite unpleasant to humans. Nuldoids, however, are fond of disharmony in any form. And, since the discordant and irritating sounds so closely reflect their social and spiritual beliefs, they quite enjoy a cacophony of strident and off-key tunes. The Oidenoids, on the other hand, insist on harmony in all aspects of life, and their music, as a result, is actually quite pleasant.

Noids – Casual, often derogatory, term for Nuldoids.

Nuldoid Powers – By most standards, Nuldoid powers are not terribly impressive or significant. That they can hover a few inches above the ground for a limited time—until someone breaks their concentration—is not an especially practical power. Their ability to cause minor aches and pains—such as headaches or temporary pain in someone's pancreas—is somewhat useful, but has its obvious limitations.

Oidenoids – "Wandering Conformists" as Nuldoids jokingly refer to them. Since they were kicked out of Nuldoid on Good Riddance Day, 813 C.C. (referred to by Oidenoids as "The Unjust Purge of Nuldoid"), Oidenoids have roamed the Region of Neither Norr in small bands, hoping to one day return to Nuldoid.

Region of Neither Norr – The region extends a couple of thousand miles from the underside of the Crust to the shell that contains Nuldoid. It is a vast, untamed wilderness that Nuldoids must journey through to retrieve, or plant, Crystals on the Crust. Because a great many frootes exist in Neither Norr, it is constantly traversed by Harvesters, who often travel to the far reaches (the underside of the Crust), where the froote is more exotic and richer. Usually, the only others in Neither Norr are the outcast Oidenoids and the Sloidelobbs who have been assigned to work there. Within the region there are a great many sights, only a few of which were included in this story.

Roundabout – Nuldoid reincarnation. Though vaguely referred to in *The Book of Nuldoid*, Lloyd and the Council of Elders (supposedly) review the lives of Nuldoids who have died, in order to decide which form of Roundabout—full or limited—is to be granted. Most Nuldoids are granted full Roundabout and continue on to their next life with their memory fully intact. Those who have committed heinous crimes, however, are reincarnated without their memory and must begin life again as a baby without any skills whatsoever (*see* Moronoids). Jurisdiction matters—like those referred to in this book—would not be tested again until the first manned flight to Mars in 2047, when astronaut Jon Rootness was outside of the module repairing a satellite receiver, and the crew, forgetting he was out there, took off without him

Sloidelobbs (sometimes called Slobbles) – Hibernating Nuldoids, grossly overweight (often weighing between 250-350 pounds, they usually become unable to walk by adulthood), Sloidelobbs operate much of the machinery in Nuldoid and the Region of Neither Norr. Especially the machinery that requires mundane repetition and much downtime. They are notoriously sloppy, unkempt and extraordinarily disagreeable whenever they're asked to actually do the jobs they have agreed to do. As well, they are highly sensitive to stress.

The Source – Surrounded by Downtown Nuldoid, the Source is located at the very center of the open air above the city, providing it with light and warmth. It is magnetically connected to the Wheel, so it rises and descends once a day, similar to our sun. And though it cannot be seen by looking directly at it, it is quite substantive.

Theevins – Baseball-shaped creatures with wings of unequal size and one foot. These creatures fly at night around various Nuldoid neighborhoods, stealing ashtrays, light bulbs, wallets, anything that they can loosen, lift or unscrew. Then—because they fly only in circles—they return to their owners' homes and hide or bury the items in the backyard. Nuldoids consider them excellent pets because the owner can look forward to finding a great many "treasures" in his backyard, and because the creatures are so "annoysome" to neighbors.

Time of Workin' – Little is known about this era—preceding the Droiden Frobble Dynasty—except that a great many things were built, and that these ancient workers had not yet discovered beer (believed to be related factors).

Toids – Short for "Crustoids." This is a derogatory term, used freely by Nuldoids because derogatory terms are quite acceptable. Oidenoids, however, use the term only when Crustoids are out of earshot.

Tunnel-holes – extending several thousand miles through the Region of Neither Norr into the Crust. They are great chambers of gravity-induced winds.

Unjust Purge of Nuldoid – (*See* Good Riddance Day)

Wad – Nuldoid system, or unit, of measuring weight.

War of Decaying Values – Touted amongst Oidenoids as their battle to reform and save Nuldoid, the War of Decaying Values was a fifty-year period leading up to Good Riddance Day in 813 C.C., when the Oidenoids were kicked out of Nuldoid. The War of Decaying Values was the Oidenoids' push to convince other Nuldoids that there was only one way to interpret the writing of Lloyd: their way. They, however, ran into trouble when they decided to no longer argue the point, and insisted on legislating their beliefs.

The Weary Forest – This area in Neither Norr was quite dense and dangerous. Apparently, a couple of times a day, the trees grew tired of standing and would simply fall over.

Wett Wobbs – Small beetle-like creatures that stand on their hind feet and congregate in dry creek beds where they imitate water.

ACKNOWLEDGMENTS

໐

First and foremost, I must thank Norm Felchle, who believed in this project early on and sent me incredible sketches before I even knew what a Nuldoid looked like. His renderings breathed life into this book. That he was willing to extend himself, to put so much work in on spec, to trust me, is something I will forever be indebted to him for.

To my family, thanks. Catherine, my wife, for repeating things to me while my mind was off in the haze of Nuldoid. Henry, my son, for offering to read the manuscript and then almost nearly doing so. But thanks, Henry, for listening to me read it. And to Joe Woody, who read it, cover-to-cover. I often joked to my writer friends that they haven't lived until they've sat across from their ten-year-old son and taken notes. The truth was, Joe's notes were terrific, and more remarkable, he pitched out an incredible idea that will be the sequel to this book.

Joe Dungan, my editor, scoured this book with a fine-toothed comb (fine-toothed is hyphenated, right?), and I thank him. Many thanks, as well, to the imagination and artistic eye of Margaret Griffin-Ross—and her company, Design Just 4 Me—who designed the cover.

All of Nuldoid would probably still be smoldering in a file on my computer and at the bottom of CAA's stack of scripts if not for a discussion with Chris Moore, who was generous enough to lead me through the publishing process. His insight, encouragement and pioneering spirit have been a serendipitous blessing to me. As was the advice of Dr. Camille Caiozzo, my therapist, who told me to get off my ass and peddle myself... well, nicer words.

Then there's Aroma Café, a small coffee shop/restaurant in Studio City, that I frequent and often work. That its owner, Mark Gunsky, and extraordinary manager, Moira Shevlin, were kind enough to let me do so, I am eternally grateful. As well, I must thank the many great people who work behind the counter, and usually know what I'm going to order before I do. Each is headed for a big and starry-eyed future. The denizens who inhabit the place on a regular basis have become much like real friends to me. They have been my community.

I must, as well, extend my gratitude to Rick Dresser, who has been an inspiration to me. His writing sheds insight into the lighter and darker shades of the human psyche, where a proclamation of undying love masks deep-rooted hatred, where success means failure, where kindness is the ultimate expression of cruelty. It is brilliant, limitless writing that should very well emanate from the mind of a lunatic, yet he is resoundingly sane. And, damn, is he funny.

Though I don't know him, I must thank William Goldman. His masterpiece *The Princess Bride* was a huge influence in my day-to-day process. Goldman's style, the flow of his words, his humor, all of it left me awed. I read some of his book every day before I began my own work, hoping a little of it would rub off.

A number of people read early and late drafts, and helped me tremendously with their thoughts and catches: Caroline Ambros, the McCall kids (Francie, Mary, Carly and Andy), Samantha Plotkin, Emily Waterhouse, Stephanie Harper, Juliette Diggs, John De Soto and especially B.J. Hegedus—who went above and beyond the call with her enthusiasm and insightful notes. As did Rebecca Lawson, who is sharp as a tack. Whitney Anderson was instrumental, early on, with her brilliant and thoughtful perspective. She will, I'm sure, become a force to be reckoned with in Hollywood. I also owe huge dollops of thanks to Gary Dontzig, Norm Gunzenhauser, Georgia McCreery, Jim Peronto and Adri Trigiani for their encouragement and dear friendship.

READING GROUP GUIDE

༃

1. As Warren and Lily traveled through the Region of Neither Norr, Lily began to notice strange behavior amongst the Oidenoids. What were they doing that was peculiar? And why were they doing it?

2. Outside the tunnel with the drooping magma, one of the Oidenoids, Ebnetter, hunted down and killed a wild animal. What was the animal, and what does Ebnetter's action say about him? What does it say about the Oidenoids in general?

3. The Harvesters used which test to figure out if a creature was an Oidenoid? Later, after Orskin, Fiske and Mishkin Hobble killed the Oidenoid Obbman, what did they do with the body, and what had the humans been told they would do? How did this make you feel about the Harvesters?

4. The residents of Outer Nuldoid were said to tick a little differently. What was unusual about their world that made them experience life in a different way, and why?

5. As the humans entered Downtown Nuldoid, they looked up and saw the opposite side of the city. Why was that? And what *didn't* they see when they looked there?

6. What are Sloidelobbs? What jobs did they perform and why? What caused the Sloidelobb's head to explode in the elevator to the Cathedral of the Wheel? Why did some Sloidelobbs appear to be nice?

7. The Crystal Recovery and Preparation team seemed not to be particularly good at their job, nor were their vehicles in

very good running order. Why was that? (It has to do with how often they're called upon to work.)

8. Why was it difficult for Emperor Ed to get his subordinates at the sewage treatment plant to do anything? How did he come to terms with this dichotomy?

9. What was a Delnoid, and why were they so much better at performing magic than regular Nuldoids? How did most Delnoids spend their lives? Why was Fiske so different from other Delnoids?

10. Why did Leo believe that he should go into the machinery to fix the cracked pinion wheel?

11. Where did the Council of Elders meet? What type of cases did they hear? Who headed the Council? What did the Council disagree about, or, rather, *whom* did they disagree about? And what did that disagreement cause him to do?

12. What was the difference between *limited* Roundabout and *full* Roundabout? What were "leakers," and why did Nuldoidians look down on them?

13. What made the children realize that they'd see their grandfather again in a few months?

14. What is the common thread between the famous visitors to Nuldoid?

15. How would our relationships, our society, change if we retained our memories from lifetime to lifetime?

16. Which characteristics of Nuldoid society would be helpful in our own?

Regarding
The Wheel of Nuldoid

The author and publisher would be most grateful to hear of
any mistakes made in this, the First Edition, of
The Wheel of Nuldoid.

Please go to the "Author/Artist" page at
www.Nuldoid.com,
and include them in the comment box.

Thanks.
Charles M. Campbell
Managing Editor
Pointless Ink Publishers, LLC

PUBLISHERS
LOS ANGELES

QUICK ORDER FORM

To Order Online:
www.Nuldoid.com

To Order by Email:
PointlessInk@aol.com

-- ✂ -------

To Order by Snail Mail:

Name:_____

Address:_____

City: _____ State: _____ Zip: _____

Phone: _____

Email: _____

☐ *The Wheel of Nuldoid*—$15.95 each.   _____

Sales Tax: (Add 7.25% for book[s] shipped within California)   _____
Postage/Handling: $2.50   _____
Total: _____

Make Check Payable to: *Pointless Ink Publishers, LLC*

Send check or money order to:
Pointless Ink Publishers, LLC
11684 Ventura Blvd., Suite 479
Studio City, CA 91604